At the Table of Want

Larry Kimport

Foremost Press
Cedarburg, Wisconsin

Also by Larry Kimport

In the Kingdom of the Wilderness
A Small Harvest of Pretty Days

Larry Kimport
Lumberton, New Jersey

Published by Foremost Press

ISBN-10: 1-936154-02-1
ISBN-13: 978-1-936154-02-9

For Sam and Libby.
Thanks for all the fun.

At the Table of Want is a coming-of-age story that
is so much more than one young man's journey
into adulthood. Truman's experiences, thoughts,
feelings, and struggles become the reader's own.

We are more than merely ourselves; we belong to
the world and those who live on it, making us who
we are. I feel not only that I better know this "kid
from New Jersey" at the end of this novel, but I
better know myself.

Laura Wurtzel
Allentown High School
Allentown, New Jersey

CHAPTER 1

Young Truman shifted in his seat, rehearsing bullying and clubbing his way through the family occupying the seats before his own, should the need arise. They were too happy, carrying on carelessly between Truman's seat and the starboard rear emergency door, which, of course, served little good at 35,000 feet.

A blue, three-ringed binder lay open on his lap. Truman bought it obediently at an airport gift shop in Seattle. "July 10, 1980" was entered upon the top left-hand side of the lined paper. Two spaces below, Truman had written: "I guess I'm having trouble with this thing—I feel talked into it—" in ink, in a cursive hand still groping in a hard-held, childish development. Truman was eighteen years old. Forgiving his handwriting, he was also handsome, excepting a scar that haunted the left side of his otherwise boyish good looks.

The fleshy splash, thick and wide, corralled his left, untouched eye, clinging to his cheekbone as a weeping crescent moon, like clown's makeup gone forever wrong.

About him, within the cabin of the wide-bodied 747, passengers carried on to the steady whine of the engines. Some read, others listened to headphones amongst scattered napping between movies and meals. Somewhere trays clattered.

Truman looked fast, something else to think about. This was his second time flying. The first frightened him worse, days before, delivering him to his group's staging in Seattle. Truman, with twenty-two other Americans, having joined the United States Peace Corps, was headed for the tropical heat of Malaysia, with oodles of more fun in the sky to come. This flight for Tokyo, then on to Hong Kong, to rest to rise to fly again, bound for bustling Kuala Lumpur, Malaysia's much discussed, sweltering capital city.

The pretty flight attendant smiled above the mishandled trays. A passenger, a man, helped her.

Truman looked back to his notebook. The aircraft's laboring Rolls-Royce engines whined steadily as he wondered why he was even doing what he was doing. He peeked out his small window. Clouds spread out far below. He marveled again at his promised two years of service. He'd be twenty years old, a sentence self-imposed.

By the time he and his party of twenty-two others touched down in the dark heat of a Kuala Lumpur night, Truman's three-ring binder was tucked into his carry-on luggage. Its first entry read:

July 10, 1980

I guess I'm having trouble with this thing—I feel talked into it—July (I'm not sure—dateline thing?)

I'm writing this from my 18th floor room in Hong Kong. It's dark & raining out, and also very hot (cool in here).

One of the bosses or leaders (or whatever) back in Seattle urged us to keep a diary or a journal of our P.C. experience. He said everyone starts one, no one finishes & everyone wishes they had. So here I go! Several of the others are starting one, too. I don't know how to do this so I'll just ramble.

I'm pretty sure it's Saturday & I'm almost a week gone from New Egypt.

My last days home were strange ones. They went by like I was doomed or something. I messed up saying good-bye to Mr. & Mrs. Van Heflin. The nicest times were just sitting out in the yard with Aunt Mabel, especially after I cut the grass & it smelled so good & all (makes me think of good old barking-away Buddy—dead now).

There are 23 of us going over. I think all of them went to college. Even the Youth Ext. people like me. Jesus, I barely got out of high school. I've been rooming with a guy named Ben. He's real nice. Another guy was asking him about his degrees. He must have gone to college a couple of times.

Tonight I'll be in Malaysia. Last night I dreamed I was in downtown New Egypt, saying good-bye again to Aunt Mabel, Chet & Jimmy & even Scotty W. (old B. Archer also sort of slid by—sitting in a chair) as one of McGuire's Air Force tankers circled overhead. Then suddenly I was alone at the RR track bed & I didn't know which way to go. Then poor old Mabel rose up from the weeds behind me. She was crying, & she wouldn't talk to me as she slowly waved her one hand back & forth, like she was stuck that way or something. (She should have cried. This whole trip was her f—king idea.)

Oh yeah. Another thing. This flying's scaring the shit out of me, but I don't think anyone can tell.

(Huh—I guess this is how you write in a journal!!)

CHAPTER 2

Young Truman was a bit of a Piney.

This didn't hurt him as he smiled easily, within the hot night air of Kuala Lumpur's surprisingly modern Subang International Airport. He even laughed, swearing quietly, scurrying for his accidentally opened luggage sliding sideways down the stainless steel baggage claim.

Things could have been worse. He could have been in the air.

If asked, Truman could tell something of his parents, who he had little of, yet wondered much over. He could name his grandparents, but without first-person memories. His tier of great grand-parentage remained the dark wall that separated his life from the nameless ghosts that led to his being, a lineage snaking clean back to the American Revolution, an ancestry lost, resting in scattered graveyards deep in the Jersey Pines.

Truman's line, his particular Kramer, hopped in when four hundred Hessians invaded Burlington, New Jersey, in the winter of 1776.

Amongst these mercenaries was a reluctant youth named Hermann Kramer. More unloyal than disloyal, and in debt, Hermann, with no one waiting across the Atlantic, fled east one early morning, alone, into the colony's heavy central forests. By the mid 1780s, he was married to his employer's lone daughter, Estella, and settled into a small cabin outside the village of Kimmon's Mills, a meeting of rough wagon-cut roads, defiantly referred to as New Egypt by its sparse citizenry, after the Genesis tale of the world having to travel to Egypt for its grain.

Hermann and Estella were happy. Their six children lived their lives in and around this secluded village. Four married, two didn't, seeing themselves through the depression of 1817, aging through the next of 1837. Estella's youngest left their wooded, sandy plain, never heard from again, for the Erie Canal, lured by fireside stories of the great route west. Hermann Kramer himself died before seeing grandchildren.

These children of Kramers' children sprinkled themselves about the forests between the pull of the Delaware and the lapping of the sea. Steady farmers and woodsmen, they married neighbors and ran off with passing through risks as their surrounding forests were razed for shipbuilding and charcoal, fueling the scattered forges of a brief pineland iron industry. As their forests fell, pitch pines, hardy forty-foot starlings of photosynthesis, swept their forests like weeds.

By 1850 several of these children of Kramers' children, still about New Egypt, reared children of their own as fallen Quakers from the swelling of westward Philadelphia began sowing themselves into their forest, some with hearts differing from brethren, others from deeds hard to forgive. Truman's own mother would ascend from one of these lines as their young nation trembled into civil war.

Mr. Lincoln lost New Jersey in his re-election bid of 1864, to favored son, General McClellan of Trenton, a day's wooded travel northeast, where the Delaware River shallowed, blurring New Jersey from Pennsylvania. Their distant, sad President, his brutal war over, won the nation in spite of this, then died as he did, a sorrow to all the states. Several seasons later, in quiet New Egypt, brick roads were laid, courtesy of the Oakford Land Company, in exchange for changing the town's name to Oakford, a municipal sleight-of-hand enticing the railroad.

And due track was laid, in the form of the Pemberton-Heightstown spur. But by the spring of 1870 their town leaders honored their own fathers, officially changing their town's name back to New Egypt, as their iron works faded into stilled forges, as long dead mercenary Kramer faded into the folklore of his great-grandchildren who cared to remember. Sustenance farming, blueberries and cranberries settled into their sandy pineland clearings as the population of their plain declined for fifty years. Of those who stayed was mercenary Hermann's one great-grandson, Truman's great-grandfather, born in 1899 in a farmhouse outside of New Egypt, the son of a farmer-tinker.

A year later the town's dam broke, without detriment to the local economy. The pooled cedar water poured like tea from behind the retired mill, long overdue to the curious who watched from on horseback, amongst marveling children and unruly dogs. Seventy years later, the remains of the compromised stone-blocked structure, overgrown with encroaching trees, would be trod upon by a roaming, friendless boy named Truman Kramer.

* * *

Two years into Wilson's presidency, the cranberry industry lured Truman's great-grandfather, at fifteen, deeper into the Pines, where a local squire married him to another child laborer of the bogs. His young bride died three months after their child-like wedding, birthing in a warehouse made comfortable.

Still a boy, the young widower moved on, giving his baby to New Egypt, to his grandparents, for far off Europe breathed world war, prompting the construction of nearby Camp Dix, where money was to be made as a stretching of their sandy forest was changing forever.

This baby, Truman's grandfather, grew up snuggled in the ease of rural New Egypt, a boyhood of chores, a bit of schooling and play amongst Jersey's meandering streams. As distant cities roared through the twenties, Truman's grandfather saw occasional motorcars, while hearing the distant guns of Camp Dix as he marveled, with scattered neighbors, over the occasional hum of the floating dirigibles that anchored in Lakehurst, a town he'd never see, east through the Pines. He'd be married when the big one from Germany exploded and burned, cleansing the pineland sky of the slow floating ships.

Then New Egypt rebuilt her dam, becoming a temporary tourist attraction to summer cottage people in those '30s. There was swimming, fishing and boating. Carnival rides even emerged as their town went rough with soldiers and outsiders, bringing alcohol, strangers and fighting. Then something changed. These New Egyptians believed they willed it themselves as their small town relaxed back into its sleepy self. By then Truman's grandparents had produced two children of their own, a daughter, Mabel, and a son, George.

* * *

George Kramer, born in the winter of 1932, was given to daydreaming, and often caught at it. He grew up good-willed, handsome and clever, but shiftless and impatient. What he possessed in physical stature, he lacked in virtue. His sister, Mabel, three years older, was industrious and thoughtful, and gangly and plain.

Older sister and kid brother were children when the world convulsed into its second world war. George was a young teen when it justly ended. Mabel was eighteen, working on the base as a civilian employee. She had also fallen in love with a soldier, but told no one, as Camp Dix, rebuilt into Fort Dix, was quartered off for the Army Air Corps. The prosperity wouldn't grace nearby New Egypt. In the 1950s, Route 195, Trenton to Belmar, at the shore, was measured and dug out and poured, slipping miles north of the town. Smaller Route 70, a state highway, from Camden to the shore, showed hope, but arched out east of New Egypt for Point Pleasant Beach, leaving the New Egyptians to their porches, their gardens and fields, pondering losses and blessings.

None of this mattered to young George Kramer. Bustle and growth never sang to him anyway. At nineteen he wandered south for work in Chatsworth, in the blue-skied, deep-green heart of the Pines.

In this hamlet of several hundred, according to the post office, George labored as a mechanic, learning light automotive work at a family-owned Gulf station.

Chatsworth suited him, for he stayed, living in an oddly constructed addition to an older man's home. This older man, Barlow Archer, lived in the original framing of the same house. His own children were grown and gone. His faithless wife ran off so long before that it didn't matter to anyone. At times even Barlow Archer couldn't picture her, which gave him peace, as did the pines and the sand and the distance that made up his property of several acres. His neighbors felt likewise.

Well-behaved dogs weren't tied in this town where George gained several friends but saved no money. He drank often, but never heavily at a local watering hole as he remained quietly loyal to his employer. One girl once, and another a few years later, gained his affection, but neither made him more than he was, until the late spring of 1961, when in a sudden whirlwind of desire, at twenty-nine years old, George met, and married a month later, a seventeen year old who appeared in Chatsworth without notice, claiming in a whisper to be somehow related to the family who owned the crossroads general store.

Her name was April Applegate. No one argued her claim. She was soft of flesh, small breasted before a rounded ribcage, weak in her walk and a bit pimply about her mouth. Her eyes were large and her hair was thin and straight. She wasn't very pretty.

The following February, in a dark and windless cold, young April gave birth to a baby boy in George's rented addition to Barlow Archer's home. She sweated and cried and ached. Old man Archer sat with her at her bedside, tending to her as best he could, for two months before, a week before Christmas, was the last either of them had seen of husband George, hunched over in the cold, walking off to work with gloveless hands in his pockets, never turning back for swelling April who watched him off.

At eighteen, stranded in an old man's home, April named her suckling baby, Truman. Truman Kramer.

* * *

Eighteen years later, without blush, Truman gathered scattered underwear, socks, shirts and jeans at Kuala Lumpur's Subang International Airport.

He'd have to write Aunt Mabel. This sort of public stumble would charm her, for she was something of a Piney, too.

CHAPTER 3

July 16, 1980

It's 9:15 in the morning & already hot as hell & muggy as shit. I'm on my way to Malacca in a cab driven by an old man who can't speak English. There're 3 other P.C. volunteers in the back seat. Two of them won't shut up & one's pretty quiet. I think the driver's scaring her. He's scaring the piss out of me! One of the blabbermouths keeps trying to talk to him. He mumbles the same thing again & again, tossing his hands in the air. (I thought the flying was bad.)

Kuala Lumpur was pretty neat. I hope I can learn the language. I roomed with Ben again & he said I could room with him in training. We stayed 3 days in Kuala Lumpur while they ran us through a bunch of meetings. Everyone had tons of questions. I felt kind of stupid. Couldn't make up a good one.

I wish Jimmy & the farm help could have seen me. No drinking age!! Well, I have plenty to look at & the people in the back seat have quieted down, so I'll quit here. Besides, I feel like I have to watch the road for this guy.

* * *

That night Truman dreamed of rats at their training site outside of Malacca. Friendly ones, wanting to be petted, brushing his ankles like cats. They wouldn't appear in his journal though, nor would Kuala Lumpur's hot heavy air, its modern skyscrapers and so many smells. He didn't write of the opposite lane traffic, rendering the simple crossing of a city street a curious new task, and, of course, he had no idea that several of the others had already discreetly discussed him as a likely failure. Too young. Misplaced.

In Malacca, Truman's group's first task was to be trained across two and one-half months of intensive language instruction, learning Bahasa Malaysia, the national language, while being exposed to and instructed in becoming respectfully mindful and appreciative of the cultures that shared the Malay peninsula, primarily the Malays, the sons of the soil, some with the Chinese, and a sprinkling regarding the Indians, a people oddly divided between rubber plantations and law firms. British colonization, they'd learn, brought these others to this land of tropical contrasts.

Meanwhile they'd also be introduced to their specific assignments, ensuing at the break of training. They were Group 97, twenty-three strong, with several engineers, a small number of English and Special Education teachers, four social workers and a handful of agricultural Youth Extension people, who were to imagine and promote some sort of Future Farmers of Malaysia amongst the rural youth of the kampongs. Truman, having spent his teen years on an American dairy farm, was among this last group, expected to work the sleepy villages.

And Truman worked hard at his Bahasa, priding himself, staying close to Ben, an intelligent and thoughtful civil engineer in his late twenties, whose voice went to a whisper the few times he spoke of his failed marriage.

In their time off, Truman swam in the Straits of Malacca with the others. They also played pickup games of basketball and touch football. Truman seldom complained of the heat which descended heavily, every midmorning, thickening the air until an hour or two after dark.

To the more articulate complaints of the others, Truman claimed that the Islamic call to prayer didn't bother him. The cryptic song, sung out at 5:30 a.m., from unseen PA systems, was repeated five times across every day.

"I think it's kind of pretty, and spooky," Truman said.

"You think so?" asked Dave, a burly farmer from Iowa. "It's a pain in my ass at 5:00 a.m."

"Is it in Bahasa, or Arabic or what?" asked a teacher.

"It's in 'freaks-me-the-hell-out'," said the Iowan, laughing.

Truman listened, for the others were older and better educated. He didn't dare share the public prayer's somehow prompting thoughts of the midnight guns of Fort Dix, the track bed, and once, a pineland cemetery.

For when alone, Truman's thoughts returned easily to New Egypt, the farm, his loving Aunt Mabel, gangling Jimmy McCleary, and Angela, when quietly wishful. His returned laundry, done by a local Chinese woman, provided a sweet deja vu of its own upon its bundled return, as Ben's friendship acquainted him with the nation's daily newspaper, the *New Straits Times*, with its daily reflection of culture, crime, human interest, and always the creeping, sinister menace of westernization.

After their group toured a Buddhist temple and an Islamic mosque, Truman thought Buddha less demanding of His followers, perhaps willing to listen to troubles and wishes, yet reticent to act. Islam seemed to forbid human folly altogether, to the right of the double yellow line, or nothing at all. However, churches of any kind made Truman uneasy. The last time he prayed hard was as a younger boy, asking Jesus to be of the same mind as Mabel's, regarding the guilt and innocence of his childhood's single, defining act.

Then news came to Truman and his Youth Extension peers. Three Youth Extension volunteers from the field were brought in to share their own ongoing assignments. One was a tall, homely girl, dressed in the colorful splash adorned by Malay women. Their trainers noted this; in spite of Islam, Malays liked colors. The other two were young men. One heavy and happy. The other determined to be informative. All three were candid.

"Only one in ten do anything meaningful," explained the homely girl.

"Easiest job you'll ever love!" said the happy man, mocking the TV ad back home. "Just show up at your office, whenever you're not on your next vacation."

All three stayed the night, and with Truman included, went out drinking with a handful of trainees.

After their departures the next morning, it was emphasized that some volunteers have to create their jobs to be rewarded. The response of the six Youth Extension volunteers varied. One quit within the week, his roommate relieved. Another gritted his teeth with determination, as two more rejoiced. Truman was undecided. He did, though, enjoy Ben's sharing an article Ben found in the *New Straits Times*, of a man roaming the villages of the northeast, laying for school children, to suck their toes in exchange for trinkets. Local *bomohs*—"Lay doctors, to be kind," explained Ben—along with the police, converged on the scene. Hysteria was feared.

Mail came, a first letter from Aunt Mabel, in graceful blue ink. Truman opened it, proud of receiving mail, imagining her old-lady knuckles working her pen. She mixed local news and gossip, and passed along several "hellos" from her own friends about New Egypt, sprinkled amongst the things she thought about while eating alone, or while brewing coffee in her home without Truman.

* * *

August 8, 1980

It's after supper. I had some slop at a local shop with some of the others. I've been in a bad mood. Maybe it's this cold I caught. Can you believe that in this heat? I also know the others are older & smarter than me, but I do get sick of hearing them going on and on about this & that & how the food's so goddamed grand & all. Mabel's letter cheered me up, though. I wish I could eat some of her food!

Some volunteers (already out there) came to tell us about Youth Ext. work (what there is of it). It's hard to tell what I'll be doing. Afterwards we went out drinking & it was fun but the one guy (the fat fuck) had to ask me about my scar, saying real loud, "Hey, kid. How'd you damn near whack out your eye?"

I lied, sort of. Everyone was listening (all of sudden) so I told him it happened in a bicycle accident. Not far from the truth. (It was a bicycle & I didn't want it to happen.)

In a few days I have to go & stay with a Malay family for a week. We all have to do it. It may be a drag but I'll save some $. I'm nearly broke, & payday's a week away!

CHAPTER 4

April Kramer, Truman's mother, kept her Kramer name in spite of being abandoned. Applegate didn't bring her much luck either. Besides, along with her baby, it made her someone else, if not better, at least different.

At eighteen, she remained fleshy, covered with a layer of her pale soft self as a stinging of acne resurfaced about her small mouth. The sharp angles of baby Truman's face were George's. So was the wave in his baby hair. Beneath the few blouses and T-shirts she owned, April remained small breasted in spite of her nursing, atop small hips and shapeless legs. She also feared too many things, thus baby Truman spent much of his infancy lovingly guarded from contagions real and otherwise.

Old man Archer asked April to stay on, within the small addition to his tired house in the Pines that she already occupied. Barlow was a quiet, gravelly-voiced man somewhere in his sixties. His potbelly heaved when he laughed, and sweated in concert with his face and neck when he toiled. A single man, he ate when hungry, regardless of the time of day or night. To support himself he worked without schedule, for modest wages in a local cranberry bog, when not serving a part-time arrangement at a local Sunoco station. His home was a mess, and he owed no one a dime. Tools and sawhorses had long since worked their way indoors, into a chaos he didn't know very well, aside from the room where he'd last seen a particular tool or resource, which was where the clamor began.

Across that first spring, Barlow assured April of George's eventual return, which he never believed. To lessen her despair, he shared his own loss of a woman while serving in the army, in Texas, leaving him with both small children, since grown and gone. He guessed his wife somewhere in one of the Dakotas, the last he and the kids had heard from her. April's eyes widened.

Across that summer and into the autumn, their friendship grew into something between foster parentage and respectful, denied affection as their duties and chores crept into the assigned rooms of each other's lives.

Baby Truman, in time, toddled freely between. Blessed with April's love and Barlow's pleasant sensibilities, utensils and tools became his toys amongst their togetherness that would stir in his mind of later years as distant snapshots, elongated, blurred, walkways through occupied messes of hallways and rooms. Carrots laid out for Santa's reindeer, which real ones ate. Barlow, shirtless and sweaty. The anvil kept, for some reason, in Barlow's kitchen. A heavy vice bolted to a table that wasn't a dining room table in old man Archer's dining room. Then haunting ones, products of his mother vanishing for a time, to return to him, and their clutter, without her right leg, forever sadder than she already was. For in the summer of 1967, April was struck by a car while collecting the mail. Truman was five. Barlow, back in the house, heard the bang. Out front, on the shoulder of the road, little boy Truman stood helplessly by, his little mind forever stained with his mother flying and spinning, arms and hair outstretched.

A man was driving the car. And nothing more.

* * *

The following autumn, Barlow knocked out the wall between the adjoined sections of his home. He built strong, unhandsome ramps over his few stairs, and he cleared domestic pathways, allowing April's crutches and wheelchair as April gained social security for her handicap, finding her own way back to her duties about their little Pineland family. Their Pineland neighbors never talked.

That fall the Woodland's Township Board of Education added Barlow's sandy driveway to one of its stops.

Little Truman liked first grade, making memories that could now move, events watched in silence, yet far away, as though through the opposite ends of binoculars. There was Chatworth's elementary school playground, and its lunchroom, crowded with children's noises, waxed paper, sandwiches and milk. A water fountain hummed chilled water. Desks were bolted to the floor. Decorated shoeboxes, coarsely slotted by children, wrought sentimental riches on Valentine's Day. Somewhere a substitute teacher, or some kid's mother, explained that if one never sinned they'd live forever. Truman felt cheated, never having been told this divine bargain until sinned beyond repair at six or seven.

Laced into those years was the excitement of men on the moon, Americans, of course. The event made everyone childlike, even quiet Barlow, who thought the event a respite from that summer's distant war heating up in a distant land.

Truman learned of rabies in the lethargic aimlessness of certain wild animals. Barlow, because he cared, explained it as best he could. The possibilities were horrifying as Truman sawed and banged at scraps of wood alongside some project of Barlow's.

Once, while walking somewhere, through trees, Barlow answered little Truman's concern for bedtime, awing him. "Sometimes, Truddy, I don't go to bed at all!"

Another time, as Barlow worked at bathroom plumbing, breathing hard and lying on his side, little Truman, amongst the clutter of tools and living, pulled a box of sanitary napkins from within a curtained closet, extracting two of the soft white pads.

Old man Archer's big belly heaved as he answered from his back upon the floor. "Mouse mattresses, Truddy. Your mother's so kind and decent she even puts out beds for the mice I try to catch. What'd ya think of that?"

Little Truman, with a mallet across his lap, compared two lengths of pads. "I thought people didn't want mice in their houses."

"Whelp, your mother figures they got to sleep somewhere. She's like that." Breathing hard, he added, "Now, Truddy, hand me that white tape. And put them little beds where you found 'em. That's a good boy now."

Several months later April feared a staying pain, something unlike her seasonal concerns. Truman was told nothing. Barlow, in hushed tones, got her off to a doctor. At twenty-seven years old, and already disfigured, April learned she was indeed terribly ill. It started cervical, before it spread.

* * *

Midway through third grade, Truman learned that certain kids were bused in from Birch Creek Village. Awed by the word "village," he also soon learned that Birch Creek had neither teepees, nor the perpetual campfires he imagined. Meanwhile, his mother's change was slow as she stayed in her chair more, her crutches leaning against the side of their refrigerator for days that turned into weeks. She hadn't hopped since between Thanksgiving and Christmas, as she hugged at him more, as he and Barlow quietly helped her about.

Late that spring, April had bouts of crying that Truman seldom saw. When he did notice, Barlow was already there. Little Truman also noticed that she began coming down from Barlow's room in the mornings. She answered his single inquiry. "My dreams are bad, honey. Barlow helps me rest, and I need my rest."

"Can I help, too?" Truman asked.

"Yes. Be a good boy. And you're already that."

* * *

That summer April told little Truman that she was sick. They sat alone out on their perpetually-shaded Pineland porch. "I hope to get better, honey, but I probably won't."

She cried, then clung to him. Little Truman cried, too, because she cried.

When Barlow got home, he found Truman out in their larger shed, scribbling numbers and lines on a rafter with a stubby pencil. He was playing carpenter. His eyes were swollen, and his little chest heaved as old man Archer hugged him down from the stepladder.

That summer of 1971, Barlow Archer became April's constant companion as dressed-up people began coming around.

One time they brought a woman who claimed to be Truman's aunt. April confirmed her as her errant husband's elder sister from the northern Pines of New Egypt. Best of all, Truman got a brand new bicycle, for no reason at all. It was his first, a lime green Roll Fast 20-inch Monkey Bike, with a banana seat and high handlebars. The bike's front sprocket was small, allowing quick acceleration, enabling him to plow, in a standing peddling, through the sandy surroundings of their home.

The treads of his bike's front knobby tire fascinated little Truman, appearing to spin backwards at certain speeds. His new bike's chain guard and fenders were of shiny chrome. Sharp to the eye, sharp to the touch.

* * *

The new school year, Truman's fourth, rolled in with the autumn as his mother weakened. Barlow assumed nearly all of the household duties, arranging their parlor into a downstairs bedroom for his fading friend. Truman slept with her at times, as did Barlow. She seldom left her new room. Little Truman feared her bad dreams, for he, too, feared November's winds that swayed the Pines.

Into the winter, the dressed-up people returned. They were from New Jersey's Division of Youth and Family Services. Their interest was Truman. Twice they brought back the woman he was asked to address as Aunt Mabel. Her surname was Ludwig. Truman overheard that her husband, Fritz, was dead, yet left her provided. He had been a soldier.

Little Truman saw her as older, and tall for a woman, much taller than his inclined mother, and even taller than Barlow, whom she nervously leaned toward in conversation. In her midlife, she had a tendency to lean toward whomever she was speaking with, making Truman think of her as a big bird, as he watched her, within the front room of Barlow's cluttered home. It didn't help that she kept her arms up close in front of her, like a praying mantis, as though supporting two of her large purses, one on each elbow, instead of the one that swayed and jerked from her left arm. Years later, pondering a photograph, a friend of Truman's likened her to Margaret Thatcher.

With a nervous shake, Mabel spoke deliberately to little Truman. "Would you like to come visit with me, up in New Egypt, sometime soon?"

Minding his manners, little Truman said, "Yes. For a little bit."

Then much of that winter became lost to Truman. Photographs could have captured the swelling of his little boy pain, but neither Barlow nor April owned a camera. In time, Mabel would try an album.

Truman then saw his frail mother naked, in confusing glimpses, for Barlow began bathing her after Christmas, having to carry her, blanketed, into the bathroom.

Somewhere in there, his teacher, with wet eyes of her own, kissed him hard on both cheeks, right in front of the other children, for no reason at all.

Then came one winter night, remembered by Truman as dark and cold with only a single light on, when, in fact, their house was well lit. Old man Barlow appeared leaning in their kitchen archway, hardly able to speak.

"Your mother's gone, Truddy," Barlow Archer choked.

Truman was at their stove, a good boy, stirring supper. He answered, "I thought this was going to happen."

His young shoulders heaved. It was his tenth birthday.

CHAPTER 5

August 12, 1980

I'm in my 2nd day of staying with this Malay family out here in the sticks. It's raining like hell & there's nothing to do. My "host friend" is 16. His name's Mohamed. (It's like 'Steve' around here.) He's nice but I can't understand a word he says. His friends bother the shit out of me & all they want to do is hang out here or there & do more of nothing.

The other night I dreamed I was home & Angela was telling everyone that she hated me & that I screwed everything up. Then I was shooting an ugly deer in the recreation field, & I followed it to the track bed where I took over driving Mabel's car, & wrecked it. So much for my dreams.

I've been in Malaysia for a month now & I'm not sure where I fit into this group of trainees, who I'll tell you about. (I can't believe this journal or diary or whatever is becoming my friend.)

There's the in-bed-by-10:00 gang. They study their Bahasa (so do I though). They're very courteous, take care of their bicycles (we all got one) & they receive & send lots of mail.

Then there's (who Ben calls) the wheat germ crowd. They're like hippies, I guess. They rave on & on about the food, believe in ghosts (like the Malaysians) & often cut up we Americans & our ways. With them everything's either real cool, or all fucked up.

Lastly, there're sprinkles (like me, I think) who don't fit into any group. Some are old people & a couple are assholes (others think so, too). I won't mention any names, in case anyone sniffs around my stuff. (You never know.) But I do like these sprinkles & I hope they like me, too.

I could go on. Everyone in this family's fast asleep. (It's about 1:00 p.m.—nap time.) But I don't know what else to say, except that I don't know how I'm going to stand 3 or 4 more days here with Mohamed, & his folks & friends & his little brothers & sisters. I am proud of my Bahasa, though. (Just think—me knowing another language!!) But I can't understand much of what these people are

saying. There's a guy down the trail who thinks I'm a riot. Him &
his big fucking monkey teeth, laughing away. He should get a job.
It's also still raining like a prick out there.

* * *

Mohamed seldom let Truman out of his sight, unable to understand his guest's desire to walk off alone. But he relished teaching him soccer.

Mohamed's home, a *kumpang* property of single-sheathed, wooden planks, stood atop strong stilts. Truman had seen the likes for over a month. The hard rains played metallic havoc, in rhythmic sheets upon its corrugated tin roof. By week's end Truman found these commotions a soothing residue of the swirling skies above.

Truman's journal also reflected the long ditch of brown water that paralleled the dirt road out front. One morning he watched a slow-moving wake slide by, from some creature below. He also wrote of sharing simple gifts, a Frisbee to the kids, a T-shirt to Mohamed, who innocently preferred another. He wrote of finding Malays more handsome than the Chinese and the Indians. Thicker, with better postures, reminding him of a girl at Allentown High School, the daughter of a black man and his oriental wife. She was popular, so Truman never spoke to her.

This same entry also chronicled Truman's shock over Mohamed's family's toilet arrangement, a single deep hole some thirty yards from the house, enclosed by a roofless clapboard wall, maybe four feet high. Truman didn't like his own head showing. Mohamed instructed that one carried water with him, squatted over the hole, then cleaned himself with the water cupped in his left hand. Truman learned this in training, but thinking it foreign, believed little of it. He didn't chronicle his efforts to go the week without a bowel movement, for this venture failed. With two days remaining, when Mohamed's surveillance erred, Truman slipped off into the thick green and relieved himself. He returned sockless, and mosquito-bitten.

He was also able to convince Mohamed that he wouldn't get lonely if he walked off alone, for Malays truly cared. Truman wished to stroll to a shop, some two miles off, for a *New Straits Times* in English, a good habit he had picked up.

The little *kedai* was a relief, its coffee strong and hot. A goat peered around a wall as he read. Carter's presidency, hostage-ridden, struggled on. Reagan, on the campaign trail, was growing formidable. A Malaysian soldier and his girlfriend were fined for kissing in public. Truman wondered of Ben. A governing body drafted a resolution calling for a law forbidding Malays from calling one another "infidel," the F-you argument-ender around here. Four pages later, "Acid Attack," titled a story regarding a disgruntled Chinese man accused of disfiguring his doubtful fiancée. The article came up a week later in training.

"You'll see it again." Andy exhaled through smoke. "It's one of these things over here. They just do it. It's fuckin' nuts, I know."

Perhaps reasonable, who knows, to Truman's host, Mohamed, and his brothers and sisters who learned more English than Truman learned Bahasa by the time Truman hitchhiked out, to the soft touching of Mohamed's Malay handshake. The Malay teen spoke softly, and smiled broadly. "*Salamet jalan.* Good bye, Mr. Truman."

Truman smiled back. "Salamet jalan, Mohamed."

Truman turned, with his denim laundry bag slung over his shoulder, to head down the dusty road in the heat of midmorning.

* * *

Upon returning to their training site, Truman learned that only a third of his group stayed their appointed week with their host families. He was proud of himself.

The following week the trainees marched through their language training around geography and political orientations. Two weekends later they hosted a party of gratitude for their host families. Most tried mingling through the carefully staged agenda, but in the idle time between scripted activities, Malaysians and

Americans quickly polarized. Truman, thinking he missed Mohamed, learned that he didn't, and felt bad about it.

Days later the four Special Education teachers stirred with news. A sixth site opened as another possibility. Andy described it as, "quaint, and needy, in a small town deep in the center of the peninsula." One teacher mooned. They'd all visit. Learning of an extra seat in the van, Truman asked if he could make the day trip, too, for the engineers were off on visits of their own as the social workers were occupied with some sort of seminar. Andy smiled, lighting his smoke. "Sure. Why not."

The three-and-a-half-hour drive excluded Truman from the teacher banter of individualized educational plans, adaptive curricula and particularly troublesome disabilities. Keeping to his wind-whipping window, Truman sniffed professional one-upmanship. Their driver, Andy, did, too. Somewhere in his mid-thirties, Andy was a quiet, chain-smoking happy man who drove like the locals. He kept his black hair slicked back. Thin, and always in baggy pants, he was soft spoken when speaking to Truman.

Their van weaved through jungled hills, sporadic small villages and the blinking even rolls of tapped trees of numerous rubber plantations, finally emerging upon Kuala Harap, having skirted the muddy Pahang River for the past twenty miles, bursting forth from their shaded drive, into the heavy heat of the early afternoon.

Excitement picked up in the van, in spite of the slowness of the little town, shaped by two streets into a T, sitting off the East-West Highway that crossed the peninsula. Steering with his elbows while lighting a cigarette, Andy suggested lunch. "What'll it be? Malay, Chinese or Indian?"

Truman dreaded the impending chorus of decision-making. Concurring, Andy's voice rose above the others, "Malay it'll be. If any of you chose this assignment, you'll have to get used to it."

So they parked and filed into a little Malay shop, stirring a commotion as they ordered, working their individual degrees of infant Bahasa. After sliding two tables together, they chatted again regarding the five other sites for Special Education; two in Johor Bahru. "Oh, so close to dazzling Singapore," one woman agreed with another, before turning to the school in Kuala Lumpur, the nation's booming capital. There was another in Ipoh, a Chinese city south of Penang, bustling and forward. "A branch campus of Singapore," offered the smaller man of the teachers, Danny, who brought up the last, on the beautiful island of Penang, a site so appealing that three of these four teachers agreed to interview for it.

Andy sort of laughed, affecting cheer. "We're in Kuala Harap now, in the middle of nowhere," he said, regarding this dusty community serving as a hub to the nation's lumbering and central plantation industries, a midpoint once reined to the harness of British colonialism.

After their lunch, the six strolled back out into the heat for the short ride up into town to find this Home.

"It's supposed to be down over a hill," Andy said, "off the top end of the two streets that make this town."

* * *

Andy worked the van down and around the narrow river-skirting road, to a pitted dead-end drive that separated chest-high weeds. It was a homely little place, nestled into the bank of the Pahang River, above the reaches of her rainy season marks. A rotting, leaning wooden fence topped the growth strangling the grounds.

The building, in need of painting, came quick to Truman as a converted six-bay garage. Andy thought it a former motor pool of long gone Brits, turned refuge for some eight children who could walk, and a number of others who couldn't. Five of the bays were cinder-blocked closed. The last, on the far right, was fitted with a full-sized sliding gate. Their van quieted when the gate slid open. A well-dressed Malay man emerged as their van lurched up the pitted driveway amongst weeds and debris. Rising from out back on the far left, arched a tremendous tree. Truman thought of the festive finish of the children's classic, *Go Dog Go!*

The Malay man identified himself as Encik Azman, the Social Welfare worker who oversaw the home, which meant seeing that food was delivered, and that the two women who lived there with the children were paid to prepare it, while being trusted to not wander too far off, for too long a time.

The six Americans were politely led into the building. Two of the children were naked. Five or six partially clad. Several more ran off in panicky hobbles as others remained in their beds. None ventured outside.

The air inside was acrid of urine and feces. A back storage room, from the motor pool days, served as a bedroom for the two Malay women. A smaller attachment to the side of the building, the office of the earlier era, served as the kitchen.

Encik Azman waved off Andy's smooth Malay. "My English is most fine," he said, surmising the history of the place, describing the children as wards of the state of Pahang.

"Visitors come, but this event not often," Azman said. "I fear because the children are quite behind, and stupid, some more worse than others. One quite dangerous." He nodded to a boy of about fifteen, nude below his soiled T-shirt, off to the far end of the dark building.

The teachers, having stolen glances, could professionally observe. The boy didn't disappoint. He shrieked, slapped at his head, spun about, then moaned before repeating the cycle.

Another boy, an Indian, maybe ten or eleven, cautiously sidled in from the kitchen. He looked down, then up again, toward the guests who were speaking politely with Mr. Azman. He was dirty and shirtless, and concerned with the contents of a lumpy bag he held up and pointed to as he spoke the garbled sounds of Tamil.

Truman tried to listen to the teachers' conversation, knowing nothing of their concerns for previous evaluations, the apparent lack of basic custodial care for the children, not to mention the building and grounds, nor of where Encik Azman's local Social

Welfare office envisioned this project in a year or two. Mr. Azman smiled and nodded, conceding nothing.

Andy hiked his trousers. "Maybe that's where we come in," he answered for Azman, to calm his teachers' emboldened chorus. Meanwhile, Truman roamed off from the middle of the dark bay, for the kitchen. The mumbling Indian boy hopped in pursuit, his lumpy bag at a dangle in this darkness and stench.

The youngsters who fled for the kitchen divided themselves over Truman's curious entry. Three into a corner, crying. Two cowered in broken wheelchairs as two more bolted. One dragged herself across the smooth concrete floor. Truman, listening for the teachers, heard Mr. Azman, then made his way outside, through a closed back door. The Indian boy followed closely.

Out in the heat of the midday, Truman surveyed chest-high growth amongst aged mounds of trash. The dark boy's garbling became urgent. He shook his head, pointing to the growth, then back toward the door Truman left ajar. Truman turned and followed him back into the darkness. A multitude of scars splayed across the boy's bare back and legs.

Inside, the four teachers and Andy moved tactfully for the refuge of the van out front, amongst the high weeds. Smiling and expressing gratitude in cheerful Bahasa, they piled into the van, waving to Mr. Azman, and to the little faces that began peering through the grid of the sliding gate. As Andy backed out over the pitted driveway, Mr. Azman shooed off the Indian boy with his wavering bag. To all's surprise, the boy's brown face smiled wide.

"Good-bye!" he called out in an English parroted from somewhere.

* * *

Weaving south through the rain forest, the teachers reviewed and criticized their visit, the Home and the small town of Kuala Harap.

Windswept within the opened windows, they offered collective and separate opinions, comforting one another's intentions of never returning. Specific issues developed as fast favorites: the lack of cleanliness while expecting guests, no apparent support from anywhere. The loudest of the teachers, a woman from Virginia, led their protests with pretty sweat upon her upper lip.

"I'm concerned about the calamity of no case histories," said Danny, the short fellow, who talked a good deal of Chicago's tough white sections, but never lived there.

A quieter female teacher revisited the vision question. "How could I, or any of us, commit to a project the local district government has obviously abandoned?"

"Crippled from the start," Danny agreed.

"In Kuala Lumpur," sang out the Virginian in the wind, "if a kid has lice they—"

"All right, all right!" Andy took over. "You're all safe now. No one's talking anyone into anything. It's just, Jesus, we have to show you guys what's out there."

He pulled from his cigarette. "What'd you expect? Happy little Easter Seal kids? Those other sites, those schools and institutions, they've got their problems, too. We just didn't see 'em."

Acknowledgement and stifled dissent swept the rocking van.

Truman, uncomfortable, but trying, said, "The place could use a handyman."

Andy waited, then answered over his shoulder, "He'd have to roll up his sleeves, and he or she would have to be as much handyman as teacher." He flicked his butt out the window, and slicked back his hair, his fingers his comb.

Shortly, their conversation turned to lesser demands. Then sleep crept into their long ride home. Just after nightfall they arrived to the familiarity of their training site in Malacca, far from the little home amongst the weeds of the banks of the River Pahang.

Safe and sound from those filthy, crippled children.

* * *

August 29, 1980

I haven't written in a while because not much has happened. We swim most days & classes are dragging along. Ben's been fun, but I think something's bugging him. I hope not me. One afternoon we were in this kedai (Malay word for their little open air shops) drinking & talking & some beggar grabbed Travis J. by his nuts!! The Chinese guy who runs the place ran him off. Boy, Travis was pissed. Ben & I laughed like bastards.

Last week half the group went to seminars & meetings so I asked if I could go with the teachers up to this town (Kuala something) to visit with them. They all thought it was a waste of time (the little home, that is—not me—I hope!). To be honest, I still think of the place. In fact I dreamed the other night that Barlow was still alive & for some damned reason lived there. Then he got killed in a car wreck & all those dirty kids were crying over it. He wasn't bloody or anything—just lying there like he was asleep out in those weeds, with a crumpled-up blue car nearby & those kids all inside bawling about it. That's the first I thought of Barlow in quite a while.

Oh well, enough craziness. As I said, I'm still a little bored & Ben got me to workout with him. Just running & doing sets of push-ups & sit-ups while counting for each other. It does make you feel good.

CHAPTER 6

Early in the summer of 1972, little Truman was moved into his Aunt Mabel's home up in New Egypt. "It's best, Truddy. Trust me," Barlow Archer explained. "She's your family and she's a kind woman, who can care proper for you." Rubbing at Truman's hair, he added, "I'll be coming to visit you, up there in that nice big town."

Barlow Archer, figuring himself unable to prevail over Mabel Ludwig and New Jersey's Division of Youth and Family Services, also measured the middle-aged widow. He thought her kind. She visited every weekend prior to April's death and through her quiet burial, up until the June morning when she took little Truman away. Her visits brought little gifts, surprises of curious warmth. Twice she took Truman north through the Pines, to New Egypt to see his home-to-be.

Truman finished fourth grade in Chatsworth. He had friends, but none of the sort, at ten years old, to see him off with his shopping bags of possessions, and his brand new suitcase for the vacations Mabel anticipated. His monkey bike was tied to the top of her brand new American Motors Hornet station wagon. The dealer's temporary tag was pasted to her rear window. With Fritz somehow watching on, she believed she could finish what her aimless brother had started.

That morning, Mabel's bravest, old man Barlow stood at the mouth of his sandy driveway until they were out of sight, weaving north. Truman only cried once. Mabel, birdlike while driving as well, moved quickly, suggesting ice cream and his favorite foods all summer long.

"Mr. Archer will be fine, honey. Really, he will," she insisted, never noticing the Pineland graveyard they passed several miles before.

* * *

Mabel's home was a cottage turned rancher, nestled amongst others on the south bank of New Egypt's narrow Oakford Lake. Years before, her neighborhood overlooked the hoopla of long-gone summertime recreation.

The forty years that passed was how long it took Mabel's neighborhood to come to its various states of upkeep, disrepair, adornment and decay. On a map New Egypt was shaped like a run-over hand. Newer homes and the older, along with businesses lined the six roads that met downtown. New Egypt's neighborhoods webbed the fingers of the unfortunate hand with bi-levels and split-levels, amongst aged saltboxes and colonials, nearly all adulterated with additions, some tasteful, others hasty. New Egypt was quaint and pretty, and cluttered and ugly, with no section all bad, nor none all good.

Mabel's home, clean and tidy, was something out of a magazine compared to the place Barlow kept. Although echoing another time, everything seemed new to little Truman. Fritz Ludwig, married to Mabel in 1948, lost in Korea in 1951, stared out twenty-one years later from two lookouts in the living room. In Mabel's bedroom his memory clung to three more posts. Truman feared him, five photographs, one expression, two in uniform, one trying to smile, as though Fritz the soldier knew his own fate back in those days of yellowed black and white. The balloons and streamers Mabel scotch-taped up for Truman's arrival didn't cheer Fritz's gaze from his other time, excepting the one, in Mabel's living room, where he's trying to smile. Years later, Truman learned that a younger Mabel took that picture, the very photograph she dusted and spoke to that June morning, before leaving for Chatsworth, reminding herself to settle down over finally fetching 'their' little Truman.

Mabel's community, New Egypt, was immense to Truman. The distant pounding of the guns of nearby Fort Dix, and the mammoth military transports circling overhead from McGuire, in time gave him a sense of nation, and something of living purpose to Fritz's frozen expressions.

That first summer, Truman grew used to Mabel's back screen door slapping shut with a single clap of wood on wood. At first coaxed, then alone, he tried to befriend their aged neighbors' German Shepherd, a dog that lived a wired pace within its chain-linked fence. His name was Buddy. Mabel guessed his animal irritability due to the elderly couple's mutual deafness. "That dog must live with a lot of yelling going on in that house, honey," she comforted his efforts.

Truman also noticed Mabel's hands and long fingers as she worked about her kitchen, sinewy tendons working beneath thick blue veins, far from his mother's chubby fingers that changed hues with the weather. He leafed through her *National Geographics*, stacked neatly within the order of her tidy living room. Mabel, quietly pleased, never read the things herself. Her subscription went back to Fritz. To little boy Truman, the yellow periodicals were pictorial wonders, unlike anything he ever saw about Barlow's home of clutter and love. He paged slowly through the magazines' jungles and ice packs, its tremendous animals, living and dead, and always people, hardened and rough, dark skinned and strange. Some colorful, some naked. Some staring back at his little boy wonder.

On his monkey bike, Truman pedaled about New Egypt's early summer neighborhoods, discovering the recreation fields, east of the heart of town, the place to be. He took several passes a day. In patches of surrounding trees, he also discovered forts, constructed from stolen and scrounged wood, tacked together before dead campfires, the work of other boys, places a boy had to be invited into.

Meanwhile, working at getting Truman out, Mabel dressed him up to take him to Burlington Center Mall, where he enjoyed the cycles of the fountains as he sipped cool sodas. She walked him through Sears, her store for everything. Truman preferred the pet store and the hobby shop. The darkened arcade Mabel coaxed him into, disturbed his quiet nature. The people within, their attentions bent to machines, appeared menacing amongst the metallic sounds.

The money they spent was Mabel's own. By midsummer she sat little Truman down in her kitchen, explaining social security.

"Due to your mother's passing," she said, looking down, then back up, "we are, honey, entitled to money on a monthly basis. State money. Food and clothing allowances, Truddy, for a proper upbringing."

She rose, abandoning her coffee, pacing birdlike. "We'll save this money for your adulthood. I make enough at my office."

"At State Farm?" he asked.

"Yes, at State Farm, Truddy."

"But you haven't been there," Truman said.

"They've given me time off, the whole summer, until you go to school. They're good to me, and I have a small pension. Your Uncle Fritz's," she dared. "And prudent living, honey, will provide us comfort enough."

Her rehearsed speech was truthful, and beyond little Truman. Nonetheless, proud of herself, she twice stole glances to one of Fritz's frozen expressions out in the living room.

Later that summer Mabel telephoned her friend, Kathleen Van Heflin, securing Truman a job at the Van Heflins' dairy farm across Route 537, in Cream Ridge. Kathleen, a sweet-natured woman, once worked with Mabel in Heightstown. Her husband, Chet, was a large man, of awkward build. His barreling torso atop spindly legs made a migrant hand, who was studying for citizenship, liken him one time to George Washington, from a picture adorning the cover of the text he studied from at night.

To Mabel, all work was blessed. To little Truman, at ten going-on-eleven, his sole duty of mowing the property was a benchmark of aging making him happy to pedal the four miles of country road. The Van Heflins also had a daughter Truman's age, but her movements about the farm were of little interest to Truman, unless, of course, she, or anyone, happened to see him commanding his John Deere riding mower along the fences and around the trees, and so carefully about the farm's pole sheds, twin silos and scattered outbuildings.

When resting quietly, Truman also liked the pigeons.

* * *

That autumn Truman entered fifth grade at New Egypt's Elementary School. He thought it huge, fitting of the town, Mabel's mall and the air force transports and tankers that circled above. In the school's library, he found Mabel's *National Geographics* amongst the magazines. The changing of classes was new as well, but most of all, he gained his first true friend.

Scotty Winslow and Truman Kramer were drawn to one another. What one had, the other desired. Scotty, a thin, freckled boy, with close-cropped red hair was sneaky and harmless. An only child of a preoccupied-with-who-knows-what single mother, Scotty found great comfort in Truman, his audience of one, who marveled at Scotty's exciting little world.

Truman thought his new friend full of knowledge, big plans and daring. Scotty's clothes were unkempt, unlike Truman's, under Mabel's eye. One time Scotty even pitched a stolen tomato at a slow-passing Mr. Softie Ice Cream truck, spattering its windshield. A week later, standing foolishly in line with his mother's spare change in hand, Scotty was recognized. The driver, reaching through the service window, jerked Scotty close, and slapped him good. New Egypt was like that.

Scotty also demonstrated to Truman his ability to say, "Fuck you," and "Suck my dick," through a harmonica a brief boyfriend of his mother's bought him. He floated these insults to teachers, other kids' parents and any other adult within range. Truman couldn't believe the clarity of Scotty's obscenities, perceived as playful tunes that didn't work.

Scotty also warned Truman of Dale Rowland, the schoolyard bully who managed to rough up some hapless kid every now and again, while maintaining a remarkable popularity from his seventh-grade throne. To Truman's horror, Scotty once told Dale, through his harmonica, "Blow a dead dog, Dale. Fuck it good while you're at it." Dale Rowland sneered. "What the hell's that thing? Why don't you learn how to play it."

Scotty taught Truman the facts of life. Someone had to. He had a couple of the mechanics, but offered nothing of fertilization. When pressed, he offered curious Truman, "It's just knocking something loose in there, starting the new baby. Like winging a stick into an apple tree for apples, or into a beehive for fun."

Scotty erred worse at the birth sequence, holding Truman spellbound. "The baby tears its way out anywhere down there between her legs, favoring whichever hole it works closest to."

This explained the urgency, the screaming and yelling, all the blood and the subsequent hospital stay. Truman was glad he was a boy.

As Scotty sweated out periodic report cards, the two fifth graders enjoyed the movies Mabel happily drove them to, silently wishing Truman had endeared himself to a better boy. She and Scotty's mother remained distant. In the theaters Truman insisted they sit down front, as far as Scotty allowed. Scotty's mother, vaguely vigilant, noticed Truman liked his television loud, ketchup on everything, his car windows down and peanut butter by the spoon, chokingly straight.

One day per week Truman continued to work at the Van Heflin dairy farm. Chet managed the charity of always having something for the boy to do, as late that winter Truman discovered the retired railroad tracks as a route home. The level bed of buried crushed rock, ties and rail was all that remained of the Heightstown-Pemberton spur that served New Egypt a century before. Truman hustled the walk, picking up the bed behind the Van Heflins' lower fields, to follow the ghostly cutting across a wooden bridge, still strong in Hornerstown, then across Route 537 and on into New Egypt.

The walk, often foggy in the morning, appealed to Truman. Skirting other people's backyards, it was quiet through the woods and over the fields, overgrown, yet solid and straight, whispering to Truman's lonesomeness. Its own past dying into the present. For young Truman, walking alone beneath trees, a comforting reminder of things swept away, yet never lost for good.

* * *

The following spring awakened New Egypt's trees and flushed her streams as the skies moaned with military transports, and roared with the fast might of occasional fighters.

Scotty and Truman discovered Elvis Presley and Bobby Vinton through Mrs. Winslow's old 45s. Mabel's other neighbor, opposite Buddy the dog's family, had extensive work done to their problematic septic system, making for exciting days of heavy equipment, holes, trenches, and erupting fecal smells, and the discovery of a damaging clot of condoms. Kids spied and jeered. Buddy, two yards away, barked and gasped, reaching new heights of dog hysteria behind his chain-link fence.

Truman also signed up for Little League baseball, at Scotty's urging. Mabel, overjoyed, rummaged her low attic, retrieving Fritz's childhood glove, a leathery thing with fat stubby fingers and a corncob-sized thumb. Reading Truman's forced receptiveness to the fossilized mitt, she dashed him off to Burlington Center for a new one, along with a bat, both signed illegibly by men neither had ever heard of.

That spring, Truman, growing into a graceful boy, sat the bench with Scotty, who cared only for being seen in his uniform, taking strategic pains to dirty it after the games he didn't play in, figuring unsuspecting passersby to take him for a little hero of sorts.

There were laughs as well. Little Mike Laychur peed out in right field to the angst of his coach, the fury of his mother, and the joy of everyone else as Truman and Scotty staged hole-digging competitions in their dugout with their little used cleats. Meanwhile, Mabel made it to every game, to watch Truman occasionally sub in for a final inning or two, up until two weeks into that lazy summer.

One Wednesday evening, just after suppertime, Truman's team, the Wawa Blue Jays, beat the Agway Pirates 5-4 in the bottom of the sixth. The Blue Jays, thrilled, checked their celebration within their dugout. Unspoken, but understood, was Dale Rowland, the visibly pissed-off Pirates' pitcher, pulled from third base in the bottom of the fifth to rescue the game. Dispersing parents mistook the subdued joy of the Blue Jays for maturity. But Scotty Winslow, clean as a whistle, couldn't resist, and executed a uniform-dirtying slide over by the bike racks while waiting for Truman.

After the game Truman and Scotty headed downtown where Scotty bought himself Tootsie Rolls and Truman a Snickers bar. Eating, they crossed the rec field, with Scotty nestled between Truman's monkey bike handlebars. Five boys were crossing the far end, two in Pirates' uniforms.

Dale Rowland called out, "You faggots were lucky!"

Scotty, gummed up with Tootsie Roll, told Truman, "Let's get out of here."

"Just don't say anything," said Truman. "We'll head back to the school."

The five boys, angled toward them, like unruly dogs, needing only sudden movement to excite them.

"What's that? What are you saying?" Dale hollered, as the five broke into a trot.

"Let's run," cried Scotty.

"No. We'll never get away."

"We're gonna get it, Truman."

"We didn't do anything," said Truman as they stopped, waiting.

Scotty climbed down from Truman's handlebars.

"What the fuck ya sayin' about us?" Dale asked, panting, his hands businesslike at the hips of his Pirates' uniform.

"Nothing. Honest," Scotty answered all five.

"Don't give us that shit, ya fuckin' weasel. You and your dirty uniform. You didn't even play. What a fuckhead."

Dale's friends laughed. Truman vaguely knew two of them. Scotty glanced down at his grass-stained smear.

"We're just mindin' our own business—Dale," said Truman, venturing the bully's name.

"Don't talk to me, peckerhead!" said Dale. He stepped fast, pushing Truman from his bicycle, then again, unto the ground.

"Stay there if you know what's good for you, ya sis." He kicked his cleated heel repeatedly into the spokes of Truman's back wheel, bending several as the tire stopped and changed direction.

"Leave my bike alone!" spoke Truman from the ground.

"Shut the fuck up," Dale answered him. "I'll do whatever I want."

His friends laughed.

Truman sat up as Dale moved to the front of his bike, kicking at the front spokes, missing once, bending the top of the chrome fender. Scotty backed up. Truman noticed he was crying.

"Please, I want my bike," Truman tried. "It's from my mom."

"You want it, sissy-boy? I'll give it to ya!" Dale answered as he picked the bike up, chest high, with a grunt.

Scotty yelped.

Truman saw pale blue sky above the towering boy in uniform, holding the weight of his monkey bike.

Then he closed his eyes to the shock of sudden heaviness, upon his head, face and shoulders.

He rolled from beneath his bike that seemed to cling to him. He grasped at a fleshy wetness about his left eye. One of the boys spoke.

"Jesus, Dale, he's bleeding."

Then another. "Holy shit!"

"You guys saw it. He made me do it!"

"Let's get outta' here!" Their voices floated about Truman's awareness of pain and loose flesh. Drops of crimson appeared upon grass beneath him. Truman let go of his face, his hands matted with red.

Scotty pulled the bicycle away, the boys fleeing behind him. Truman sat up, blood soaked to his elbows, appearing new upon his Blue Jays' uniform.

"We have to get your aunt," said Scotty. "We have to." He looked to his own bloodied hands.

Truman's eyes swelled into tears. "She can't find out. We can't tell her. I have to get cleaned up. Look, I can see," he said as he demonstrated between heaves. "Go home, and don't tell your mom. I'll call you tonight."

Scotty whimpered. A fresh stream of blood dripped from Truman's jaw.

"I'm going home, too, Scotty. I just have to get cleaned up."

Scotty nodded, and turned into a run. Once home, he told his mother everything. Busy Mrs. Winslow telephoned Mrs. Ludwig, after finding her name in the phone book.

* * *

Alone upon the bloodied grass, Truman climbed one-handed upon his bicycle. He cycled hard, across the grassy field, northbound, out of town. Once upon the open fields of Highbridge Road, he worked his bike into knee-high soybeans, then pushed it, one-handed, for the stream he knew of, to clean himself up.

The cold water burned. Truman cried. Holding at his fleshy wound, he made his way through a lower field of youthful corn, for the track bed. The sun was setting behind him when he came upon Route 537.

Upon the shoulder of smooth road, he noticed a sliver of eyebrow matted to the twisted chrome of his front fender. His left eye had swollen shut. He pedaled north, for the Ford dealership at the intersection of Routes 537 and 539.

He sought cover within the dealership's shrubbery at the meeting of roads as darkness fell. The lights of the car lot streaked into his hiding. His clotted wound seeped fresh when he removed his hand too quickly. Behind distant glass, salespeople milled unaware. Above and nearer to him, the set clicking of the traffic light's control box mechanically directed the evening traffic.

Hiding alone, Truman thought of Barlow Archer, relieved the old man wouldn't learn of this. He thought of his mother, of her sandy grave, finding himself weepy. He whispered that he was all right as the box clicked yellow. At red, he told his bicycle the same.

When the darkness above deepened into stars, Truman rose into bicycling, one-handed, southbound on Route 537, for Highbridge, into New Egypt, for his aunt's home. Fainter behind him, from its box the traffic light worked its perfect fairness.

A half mile upon Highbridge, parallel to the track bed, the lights of Mabel's Hornet dipped into slowing, then hard into stopping. Mabel hopped out, leaving her driver's door open, illuminating the interior of her new car.

She hurried, birdlike, across her headlights, hugging and kissing at Truman, atop his head, hushing away his pleas for forgiveness.

Taking charge, she inspected his wound in her low beams. She loaded his bicycle into her hatch, before buckling Truman into her front seat, to drive him to Freehold Hospital's emergency room.

It took the young doctor fifty-seven stitches to close the arc of separated flesh. Truman remained quiet, determined to not make matters worse. Then he raised the eyebrows of the attending nurse, asking her, "Is there a room here for people with rabies?"

On the ride home, Mabel feigned cheer, stopping for pizza and ice cream to take home. Once home, after aspirins and a hot bath, they stayed up late. At her kitchen table, Mabel asked Truman, "Now tell me the whole thing, honey, once and only once."

Stitched and swollen and stained with pizza sauce, Truman told her everything, his relief complete. Excepting the throb in his face, and until late that night, when he awakened to soft sounds from out in Mabel's lit kitchen.

He slid from his bed from Sears, his face aching. He crept to his bedroom door, ajar, Mabel's doing. Her weeping was muffled through his thin line of sight. She sat tightly robed at their table. Before her at their table sat a propped picture of Fritz, the one where he was ready to smile back to her.

* * *

That summer Truman's scar pinked over thick. He remained on his Little League baseball team, but seldom played. Excepting Scotty, most kids shied from him. Mabel worried. Truman thought it little to overcome compared to the mailbox years before, or that night at the stove, not yet two winters before.

His social worker from the Division Of Youth and Family Services showed up, but spoke more with Mabel. At one point, Mabel excused Truman from the room, asking earnestly, "Are they planning to take him from me?"

Truman's case manager, Cecile, a thin unkempt woman in her forties, quietly enjoyed this erroneous assignment of authority.

"Oh no. Of course not, Mrs. Ludwig. Kids get hurt. They hurt one another. Nothing could have been done to prevent this."

Mabel leaned toward her. "Thank you," she whispered.

Cecile leaned back. "Rest assured, D.Y.F.S. will continue to support your custody," she said, never mentioning the beleaguered system's dire need for foster placements half as wonderful as Mabel.

The next day, Mabel drove out to the Rowland home, outside of New Egypt's downtown, in a recent development of larger colonials of four types, interspaced to avoid monotony.

Dale's parents were cordial, expressing sorrow for Truman.

"That is his name, isn't it?" asked Dale's father, peering above his reading glasses.

"We just wish he hadn't picked a shoving match with a bigger boy," Dale's mother added.

Mabel flustered. Her challenge uncertain.

"Other boys were present," Mrs. Rowland continued. "Again we're very sorry. We hope the two youngsters can manage to get along, or avoid one another."

Seeing Mabel to her front door, Mrs. Rowland furthered, "We've asked this of Dale. You might wish to give the same advice to your nephew. That is the relationship, isn't it?"

Meanwhile, Chet Van Heflin kept Truman busy at the farm. Only Angela, his daughter, ventured curiosity.

"Does it hurt anymore?" she asked him one afternoon, over cheese sandwiches and iced tea. They were sitting at the Van Heflins' backyard picnic table. Angela's crossed legs dangled beneath her.

"Not anymore," Truman answered.

"It doesn't look too bad either," she assured him. "You can't even see it from this side."

* * *

That summer Chet granted Truman new responsibilities at the farm, as something of a friendship germinated between Truman and the farm's lone, permanent migrant, Juan Santana, the Mexican who quietly saw the father of his new nation within his employer.

Juan liked this boy who seemed to share his immigrant status in spite of being native. Having spent a brief season in the minors years before, Juan was excited by Truman's tentative interest in baseball. When time allowed, he coaxed young Truman out into the Van Heflins' massive side yard to shag flyballs, and knock down grounders.

Truman, courteous and compliant, by August looked forward to the impromptu lessons in Juan's tight English, for the small man's praise was sincere.

Truman's innate balance and growing strength served Juan's love for the basics. Juan taught Truman to not fear the ball, but to anticipate its path, to intercept it. Unruly grounders had to be caught, or knocked down, from a sensible position of readiness. Batting came easier, as Truman learned form, engaging his entire body as Juan taught him again anticipation, swinging smooth with weight, stepping into the pitch to drive the ball hard.

With fielding, Juan was more earnest, instructing Truman the critical throw to first, and with care, the long one from third. Juan laid out measured pieces of scrap wood as bases, demonstrating the art of relaxing, doing one thing at a time. The hit ball had to be brought under control with sound fielding, before squaring off, giving speed to the long throw to first.

With Scotty Winslow, Truman also fished the area ponds and streams. They talked of the likelihood of a Jersey Devil, and, of course, of sex, and of what the area teens may be up to. Then September summoned them back to school, the duty of childhood.

* * *

In sixth grade, Truman liked the long stretch of his morning teacher, before rotating through three others after lunch. His scar didn't draw the attention he feared, as late that winter he turned twelve, a week after eighth-grader Dale Rowland beat up some high school kid upon the ice of New Egypt's Oakford Lake. The story moved fast. After all, the kid was in high school, never minding that he was known to be timid, while managing the work of fighting Dale while wearing ice skates.

Across that winter, things slowed at the farm. Juan anticipated Little League in the spring as Angela shared stories of her own smaller grade school over in Imlaystown. Truman was unaware as that spring brought a special health class—for sixth-graders only, separating the boys from the girls—rolling over a good deal of Scotty's notions regarding human reproduction. Truman's classmates, boys and girls alike, reunited amid snickering, silliness and awe. Truman braved up, and took these revelations to Mabel. She confirmed them over a fresh pot of coffee in a nervous kitchen sitting. Fritz's frozen expression watched on. Truman silently marveled over the dead man's probably having tried such stunts on Mabel.

By late May, Truman and Scotty were again Wawa Blue Jays, beneath McGuire's fighters and transports that tore and floated across the skies. To Juan's delight, to Mabel's joy and to the Blue Jays' manager's surprise, Truman was a star, a lone talent on a team poisoned with a clustering of Scotty-Winslow-like ten-to-twelve-year-olds.

The Blue Jays shied from the plate in fear. They longed for candy, and they cried too long after hit by errant pitches. They displayed grief after striking out, but stuck gum to one another's bats and hair in the same innings. Their fielders celebrated relief not having to field, and when not at bat, it usually took the play of Truman and two other capable boys to get the Jays back to the plate several runs later. By late May, nearly halfway through their season, Truman led the league with a smoking .613 batting average, trailing one other boy in home runs. But the other boy's midseason slump wouldn't matter. Truman's own season would end on the hot asphalt of his sponsor's Wawa parking lot after one of the three games the Blue Jays won.

With eight school days remaining, on an unseasonably warm Wednesday evening, the Wawa Blue Jays clipped the Agway Mets 6-5. The second place Mets lacked their three-way infield brother team to an outbreak of poison ivy. They also spooned out oodles of luck with wild pitches, walking seven around hitting three more Jays before Truman smacked a three-run, go-ahead homer in the top of the sixth. Mabel stood amongst the parents, bird-like, clapping and cheering. After running an errand twenty minutes later, she'd drive past a milling crowd at the Wawa, wondering what a certain commotion was all about.

* * *

After winning the game, the Blue Jays' manager rounded up his boys and enthusiastically lied about determination and perseverance, pausing once, telling Scotty, "Cut the shit, Winslow!"

Scotty straightened. His grass stains could wait.

After promising the boys great victories ahead, he dismissed them with a clap and a cheer.

Truman left on his monkey bike, with Scotty seated between the handlebars.

It was still early and hot. Truman peddled his pal into the side streets. Scotty cussed about his "old lady" not being home, before hopping off to walk the rest of his way. With his glove laced through the left handlebar, and with his bat rested across the tops of his working grasps, Truman pedaled back through shady streets, toward downtown, for the Wawa, a block beyond the turn for his and Mabel's home. He coasted, patting his pocket for money, thinking a Pepsi and a Three Musketeers.

Crossing light traffic, Truman bumped up over the lip of curb, into the parking lot, hearing his name called from beyond parked cars.

"Hey, Kramer! Gimme some change," Dale Rowland called to him. Another kid hurried to catch up. His name was Wayne.

"A buck or two will do. Don't you think, Wayne?"

Wayne grinned. Truman thought Wayne's teeth inordinately large, a trait he noticed in the boy's kid sister at school.

Still on his bike, Truman answered, "Sorry. Less than two dollars is all I got."

Dale stepped in front of him. "That's all I said I needed. You deaf?"

Truman braked hard.

"I'm not giving it to you. I don't owe it to you. Now excuse me," his voice cracked as he straddled his bike, edging it forward.

"Don't hit me with this piece of shit bike," Dale smiled wide.

Truman looked about. He couldn't imagine why the people behind the plate glass of the Wawa couldn't see what was happening.

"Come on, Kramer, give me your change," he said as he grabbed the base of Truman's handlebars.

Truman brought his ball bat down to his side, not wanting it near Rowland.

Dale's eyes followed.

"You fixin' on using that, hero boy?"

"No. It's mine, that's all." Truman's voice shook.

"Your change. Come on."

"No. I'm going home," Truman replied, trying to back his bike upon the hot asphalt.

Toothy Wayne stepped behind him. "Then give us the bat instead. Maybe we can sell it."

Truman turned to Wayne, then back to Dale, who slapped his Jays' hat off.

"Bullshit. I'll take the fucking thing home and ram it up his ugly aunt's asshole next time she comes to my house."

Wayne laughed.

The hot asphalt beneath them frightened Truman. Its hardness wouldn't give way as the cool grass did a year before.

Dale's dirty knuckles leapt to his attention.

"Just leave me alone!" Truman said, drawing the attention of an adult passerby.

"Don't yell at me, pussy," Dale hissed, jerking Truman's bike to the pavement as Truman stepped from it, his bat in hand.

"Start something, so I can fuck up the other side of your face."

Wayne stepped back, smiling.

Dale looked to him, pleased, as Truman, in his Jays' uniform, squared, planting his feet, choking down on his bat.

Dale turned back to Truman, his smile freezing, an unknown farewell. Truman swung his bat, picture perfect, against the left side of Dale's skull, just above his ear.

The smack was sharp, wood against flesh and bone.

Dale half turned, then fell forward, like a small tree.

Then stillness. Then convulsing, sluglike upon the pavement.

Truman looked to Wayne, who was backing up.

"Jesus Christ!" sounded out from the passerby.

Bat in hand, Truman looked back down to Dale. He lay strangely arranged, as though he had fallen from above. Then he started flexing, with his eyes and mouth open, but motionless. Blood pooled about his head, appearing to affix him to the asphalt.

"The baseball kid did it!" rang out from the front of the Wawa.

"Grab the little cocksucker!" leapt into Truman's awareness as he picked up his bicycle and climbed on, still holding his bat.

Truman stood hard upon his peddles, working his bike past dumbstruck Wayne. Then faster, out into the light traffic, onto the single street of downtown.

* * *

Truman pedaled hard through New Egypt's downtown, rocking his bike side to side, following the route he took the year before.

Emerging north of town, into early evening farmland, a siren sounded out into the warm sky behind him.

On Highbridge Road he slowed, breathing hard. He needed to hide, to sit and to think. The landscaping of the car lot wouldn't do. He turned left, pedaling toward Allentown.

Miles from New Egypt, he passed the empty track bed, and pedaled on to Cream Ridge Golf Course, where he turned right upon a quiet country road.

Two hundred yards later he came upon a gentle, tree-lined rise, his track bed on its way to Heightstown, separating fields of young corn. Sweating, he looked about, then to his bat. Being called cocksucker came back to him. He thought it only a children's term. Maybe the guy heard it at the ballpark. He peddled on, to a T in the road where he turned left, toward the village of Imlaystown, where he came upon a small, red brick country schoolhouse, perched atop a gentle rise. He turned in, thinking of Chatsworth. Mother. Old man Barlow.

He placed his bike in the empty steel rack, leaned his bat against it, and walked out back for the swings.

Sitting and rocking gently, he kicked at the dirt beneath him. Mabel washed Chatsworth away. He thought of Juan and of Mr. and Mrs. Van Heflin, then he stood and walked to his bike, all alone, save his leaning bat. Climbing on, he noticed the breeze. The ride would be cooler.

Behind him, the sunset reflected yellow off the classrooms' large windows. One was adorned with artwork. One picture portrayed a yard with trees, a dog and a smiling boy riding a lawn mower cartoonishly close to a robin pulling a worm from the grass.

The picture was signed: Angela Van Heflin.

* * *

The New Egypt police were at Mabel's when Truman pedaled up after dark.

Voices crackled over their cruiser radio as Truman eased past it in their small driveway. He hoped they weren't talking about him.

Inside, Truman was told to sit, and asked a series of questions. Mabel wasn't crying, but had been. Truman was told that the Rowland boy's injury was very serious. That's all they knew, that, and that charges would follow. They also advised Mabel to keep Truman home from school for a few days.

Truman tried not to cry, but did. Mabel wouldn't cry again for a month.

After nearly an hour, the two officers packed and left, after stating that Mabel would be advised of the Rowland boy's condition as soon as possible. Everyone concerned would need to know.

* * *

That summer of 1974, President Nixon, mired in lies and deceit, resigned his office to Gerald Ford. This news quieted Mabel nightly before her TV set. Truman pitied the beleaguered man as something parallel to his own summer of tragedy, for Nixon resigned two days after Dale Rowland was medicinally awakened in a Philadelphia hospital, four days after shaking down Truman for some change.

There were new words and new grownups: aggravated battery, neurological damage, lengthy rehabilitation. Court dates and uncertainty punctuated Truman's farm work, his lone liberty. Through coincidence, he was appointed a new caseworker from the Division Of Youth and Family Services, Miss Constance Embley. Truman and Mabel met her the week before their hour of decision in a juvenile court in Toms River, in late July.

The judge seemed too young to Mabel, who went to great pains to dress Truman in a brand new suit from Sears. Truman mistook the judge's quiet attentiveness for anger, but was relieved when the man took the time to speak to him thoughtfully.

In the end, and it wasn't long, the judge apologized to Truman for the judgment he had to render, ". . . for one child was nearly killed." Then more of the words: fractures of the left temporal and parietal plates, apparent and predicted neuro damage, and anticipated learning problems. The nice man went on, "True, the victim of the battery was probably, in part, an antagonist, and Truman Kramer's school records reflect a good boy, but this attack does appear . . ."

The young judge reminded the boy's standing aunt that it was not this court's duty to punish, but to see to the rehabilitation of children. Then his voice went more deliberate, addressing Constance Embley. "I assign you, Miss Embley, with finding a suitable therapeutic community, as this boy's D.Y.F.S. case manager, for this boy to reside within, for a length of time deemed fitting and of service, by that facility's appropriate professionals."

From behind his bench, the quiet young man wished all well, especially extending that sentiment to the boy before him, that handsome boy with that wretched scar.

"Thank you," Truman replied, stilling the young judge for a moment, before turning to his aunt, offering her a tissue he pulled from the pocket of his new suit.

She was weeping again.

CHAPTER 7

Sept. 21, 1980

Earlier today I hitched in from Singapore (damn near broke with 9 days until we get paid). I'll have to bum $ from somewhere. Singapore was fun though. Probably more fun for those still there. I hung out with Dave (the one agricultural ext. guy). (They gave us a 5-day weekend to go down.)

Dave was fun. (I might have mentioned him before.) He's a real farmer from Iowa & he went to college, too. He & I drank too much— he went wild for the Newports he found & we took in some good & some shitty movies. I only saw Ben once & felt sort of funny. He hung out with the touristy gang. A lot of the others were buying up tape players & stuff. Anyway, Dave & I had to hitchhike back early— about 200 miles. Like I said, everyone else is still down there, but it was nice to hang out with someone who doesn't think McDonald's is poison & that Americans are wrong about everything. Dave also said he wanted to fuck Anne, the one social worker & Jamali, our one Bahasa language teacher. Both are pretty, I have to admit.

I tried to talk to Dave about this Ag. Ext. stuff we're both in, but he doesn't care. He says he'll worry later—as long as Uncle Sam keeps making the payroll.

We made it back in 4 rides—2 long ones. One long one was some Chinese guy who spoke good English & he told me about his friend who used to live in Kuala Harap. He said the place is dead— "mostly lazy Malays—the less said the better." It's funny though—it did make me think about those crummy kids up there sitting around in shit & piss.

* * *

Two months into their three months of training, two more of their group bowed out to go home. Their commitment was moral, not legal. The Peace Corps welcomed this, not needing unhappy volunteers at large in host countries.

Reactionary, and discreet group speculation guessed young Truman might survive the training, but hardly the two-year tour of duty ahead.

Interrupting one of these discussions, Ben pulled himself from his daily *New Straits Times.* "The kid survived his visit into the villages. An assignment most of us couldn't pull off. Me included."

Dave, the Iowa farmer who hoped to inseminate at least one of the women sharing their porch, concurred. "He can drink and hitchhike. Does it take more?"

* * *

Two days later their group traveled south, to the rural town of Batu Pahat to witness a Javanese ritual featuring Malay men in self-induced trances, riding about in a corral upon homemade horses, not unlike children's toys.

In the cooler night air, the shirtless men started slowly, then began romping about, crashing into and falling over one another as they galloped and sweated for some twenty minutes. The American guests remained quieter than their villager hosts, also watching. When it was over, several trainees searched for meaning.

"How does this expression serve these people?" asked a social worker.

"Oh, the concentration!" chimed a teacher.

Others likened the trances to flights of fancy. "Perhaps escapes from the rigidity of rural Islamic life?" offered another social worker.

Ben, not as cerebral, resigned himself to the sad, apparent disco within all of us.

In the tropical darkness, Dave whispered to Truman, "How many chances did we have to trip one of the flaked-out bastards?" referring to their closer passes that brought rises from the locals about the spindly corral.

Truman wondered quietly if they did this sort of shit in Kuala Harap. Later, as they boarded their van, he asked Andy, "Could I speak to you, in private, sometime tomorrow?"

Andy paused, working at his cigarettes. "Sure. First thing. How about breakfast somewhere?"

"I'm trying to stretch my money," Truman whispered.

Andy smiled, striking a match that illuminated his face. "It'll be on me. I look forward to it," he said as he thought of the group's opinion.

* * *

The next morning the man and the boy settled into their wooden seats in the open-air kedai.

Andy expected a termination. Truman was uncertain how to couch his request. A ceiling fan creaked above them at 8:00 a.m. Diesel fumes and equatorial heat were already at work.

Andy ordered in fluent Malay. Truman struggled. Andy drank deep from a glass of water. Then he asked, "So, how can I help you, Truman?"

Truman fidgeted. No silverware to straighten. "I was wondering, if we trainees, if we're allowed to switch jobs. I don't mean with each other, but to different jobs."

Andy smiled. "Anything can be discussed."

"Well, you know, with everything those visiting volunteers said about this agricultural stuff. You know, how it's a crapshoot if you even have a job or not."

"Those stories can be true," Andy replied. "A good deal of Peace Corps work is what one makes of their particular assignment. Some work hard. Some don't. But that's been discussed." He tapped a cigarette from his new pack for the day.

Truman was silent.

"What do you have in mind?" Andy asked.

"Well, I don't want to be a quitter or anything, but I was wondering if I could be placed at that home, with those kids up there in Kuala Harap? The one we visited with the teachers. By the river."

Andy smiled. "I know the one. What brought this about?"

"I want to help, however I can. I'm a good worker. I'm not a teacher, but I could clean the place up, make repairs, paint. Maybe, you know, build the kids a playground, take 'em for walks, things like that." He paused, fearful of the leap he took. "I'd leave or stay whenever a real teacher came."

"Just don't hold your breath." Andy smiled, exhaling smoke.

Truman, missing the sarcasm, leaned forward. "I've been thinking of the place. I once lived in a home myself, a place for boys, and I guess that's what led me to think of that Kuala Harap place, after seeing it and all."

"You lived in a 'home'?"

"Well, it wasn't a dump like that one. Mine was much nicer, with a bunch of buildings and all," Truman quickened, not wanting Andy to imagine such a place in New Jersey. "And no one was retarded or crippled, at least not real noticeable."

Andy leaned back, their food being set before them.

"Oh, I'm sure it was nice enough. I'm just surprised to learn that you lived in a home. It's not a common experience. In fact, you may be the first person I've known having done so."

Andy hoped for the reason why. Truman started into his breakfast.

"Yeah. I guess it's not an everyday thing. My mom died when I was little, and I never knew my father, so my aunt took me in, and then I got myself into a world of trouble," he said, as he worked at his egg-dipped bread. "A juvenile judge, a pretty nice guy, sent me to this boys' home for a school year. It could'a been worse."

Andy listened, his own breakfast before him. "That's it?"

"That's it." Truman perked up. "I never got in any more trouble after that. And like I said, it wasn't anything like that place in Kuala Harap."

Andy wondered over the "trouble."

"Anyway," Truman added, "do you think it's a possibility? I'd work hard."

"Oh, I believe that. Let me talk to Kuala Lumpur," Andy answered. "I'll be honest. I have no idea how they'll respond, but it makes sense. It could work out for everyone."

Truman relaxed. Andy sensed it.

"Come on," Andy said, "eat up so we can get some more," as the ceiling fan creaked above. He wouldn't venture into the "trouble" until their van ride home. Truman wouldn't mind.

Turning back from his rolled-down window, Truman told Andy, "The kid who gave me this scar, about a year later he came after me again. I clubbed him with a baseball bat. It was after a Little League game."

Andy nodded acknowledgment. Truman went on, "He was in the hospital for a while. I was real sorry about it. Still am. I didn't mean to hurt him like I did. I was just real scared of him. All us kids were."

"Few things are fair in this world," said Andy. "But we keep trying to make 'em that way. It's probably hardest for kids," he added, as a blue stretch of the Malacca Straits came into view.

* * *

Back at their training site, a discreet corner of the concerned were surprised Truman hadn't begged Andy for tickets home. Two of the teachers expressed admiration for his interest in the Kuala Harap site. One was genuine.

Two days later, Truman, with two others swam into jellyfish. They retreated to the beachy shade, where Iowa football was passing by big Dave Hayden, as a social worker was missing Wisconsin's autumn nights. Truman, listened, missing Mr. and Mrs. Van Heflin, their daughter Angela, and both McClearys as Ben shared an article from the *New Straits Times* concerning censoring western kissing across the nation's cinemas and television programming.

Then good news came. Sandaled and smiling, Andy approached their gathering beneath palms, and slapped young Truman's back.

"They want you, Truman! Kuala Harap says, 'Send us the kid!' You happy?"

Truman straightened and smiled back, tightening his scar. "Yes. What next?"

"You join the teachers for their final two weeks of technical training, swear-in in K.L., hop a bus for Kuala Harap, and head out there and save those kids."

"Congratulations," said Ben.

Dave drank deep from his Carlsberg beer, then smiled wide. "I know it's remote, but there's pussy everywhere."

Across the following days several of the teachers offered ideas as Truman wondered if he blundered, passing up living with other Americans in towns or cities that didn't snuff out at sundown. Andy sensed this, as a group relaxed over music and beers in the men's small wing. "If you can clean the place up," he said, slicking back his hair, "help out, and see to it that everyone's having some fun, you'll be moving their earth. That's all there is to it."

After Andy left, a bat fluttered in through their gated door, circled their room and escaped as quickly. Their stilled conversation had turned to women. Ben went shy. Dave stayed foul as two others remembered aloud. Truman admitted none in his past.

Clouded with beer, he wanted to lie, but Angela Van Heflin didn't count.

* * *

Several nights later their training group had their close-of-training party, a ritual of sorts, marking their separating into occupational disciplines, a party of many to come.

The following morning young Truman and the Special Education teachers traveled south, by any means, to reconvene at a potential site in Johor Baru before traveling north, visiting other possible postings, to ask and answer questions with potential soon-to-be superiors.

These final days would also determine outstanding placements. Penang, the Pearl of the Orient, remained unmanned.

Truman hitched the 180 miles in three rides. The first, a brief skirting of villages for thirty miles, the second from a handsome

Indian family who spoke fluent English, and the last with a car-load of young Malay men. Their only English that Truman could make out was "morphine," "marijuana," and "army." Ben would later cherish the irony.

Truman arrived first at the main bus station. Hungover from the party, he found a bench in shade amongst twin lines of rickety food vendor carts. A breeze sliced through, thinning the diesel exhaust that billowed about the terminal's traffic.

He bought a newspaper, then went into his bag for his journal. A tailless cat slipped by. He paused, breathing deep into his bag, seeking his neatly wrapped laundry and the sweet deja vu it provided, materializing into the Puerto Rican sisters who did the laundry years before at the boys' home.

Upon his lap he wrote in his journal, recording the jesting he took from big Dave and Ben, for having to travel with the four teachers. Truman never heard teachers take it so bad. Dave claimed he wanted to shove Sandy's head up Danny's ass, but couldn't decide whose head deserved to be up whose ass due to their similar, endless complaining.

By late afternoon the five were together again, with an administrator from Kuala Lumpur named Bruce Statton. Truman had hoped for Andy. They saw less of Bruce, who was much more businesslike; however, by the next afternoon he'd lose his articulate demeanor, snapping at Danny after visiting the second site.

"Good God, Danny! Of course the kids in these places are going to be dirty and lice-ridden. Where in God's name do you think you are? Student-teaching in Illinois?"

An hour later, in their van heading north for Kuala Lumpur, Bruce lost it again. "And that's another thing exhausting me," he spoke to a reoccurring theme of Sandy's. "Do you think sexual misconduct doesn't exist for the institutionalized back in the States? You should have nosed around a few dark corners while doing your training, schooling or whatever. I don't mean to be short, but good God, you guys!"

After visiting a scheduled site in Kuala Lumpur, and staying the night, their orientation ventured north for Ipoh, a smaller

Chinese city nestled beautifully against hills with hot springs and all. Then farther north, for the island of Penang, The Pearl Of The Orient, with graceful Georgetown as its city. Renewed hope and professionalism leapt from the teachers at Georgetown's Sunshine Manor—clean, behaved and orderly.

Ideas and questions abounded, until they retired their tour for the night.

* * *

That evening the four teachers took off upon the gaiety of two bicycle-powered rickshaws, leaving Truman to roam on his own, where in a nearby kedai he stumbled upon Bruce Statton.

"Hey there. Have a seat. Not bad grub here," Bruce said.

"Sure. Thanks," Truman answered.

"Where are your esteemed colleagues, Mr. Kramer?"

Truman smiled. "Probably bangin' at the door of that Sunshine Manor."

Bruce laughed. "You want a beer?"

"Sure. An Anchor, please." He noticed that older Bruce had already had several. Three empties were lined up before him, the tally of his bill. Malaysian men kept theirs on the floor under the table, not wanting passersby to see how much they were drinking.

Like everywhere, a ceiling fan above them cut away at the heat.

Bruce complimented Truman's collecting checklists and curriculums and whatever else he could scrape up at the sites they visited. This pleased Truman. Over more beers the older man figured Iraq to soon topple Iran's infant revolutionary government. The two nations had been hard at their border war for two days. Malaysian Muslims were pained. Everyone thought it would be quick.

Closer to the mark, Bruce figured Larry Holmes to batter the aging Ali in their fight a week away. The same Malaysian Muslims, Ali fans and keen with anticipation, and not pained at all, felt otherwise.

"I don't know, Bruce. I think he can do anything," replied Truman, reflecting the talk of the migrant help of Van Heflins' farm, from two months before. "The other trainees think so, too," he added for credibility. "He's got that magic."

"They're full of shit," said Bruce. "He had it, but Holmes is young. He can fight or box, with both hands, and if pressed, all night long. Holmes by a knockout, late in the fight."

Truman noticed Bruce's heavy sweating. "Well, I hope Ali does well. He's done a lot of good things."

"It's not about that, Truman. It's about money and pride, and Marciano's 49-0 haunting the hell out of Holmes. He's sick of being a nigger to a ghost, and to an Ali who won't go away. Wait and see."

On a roll, Bruce picked Carter to beat Reagan in November by a handful of electoral votes, figuring Texas and New York to silence the California democrats crazy enough to go with their buffoon of a former governor.

Truman, though, yearned for the hot showers of their hotel, something missed these past two months. Before they retired, he also spoke of Kuala Harap, before sharing his discovering the word fuck spelled "fack," surrounded by Chinese characters on the bathroom wall of their corner kedai. Drunk Bruce, having already seen it, pondered aloud Holden Caulfield's similar dilemma. Truman didn't get it.

In the morning, their happier crew headed south, for Kuala Lumpur and the others, for their final week of paperwork, details, reassurances and finally swearing-in, becoming eager personifications of John Kennedy's dream. Out of nowhere, somewhere on the ride, Bruce advised Truman of another volunteer posted near Kuala Harap.

"There for a year or so by now," Bruce claimed as he drove. "Maybe longer. Don't rely on the guy for friendship or support."

Truman stayed silent, and he didn't know why.

"His name's Singer. John Singer, an accountant for the forest and game department. He's a loner. Never attends the parties and get-togethers we host to ease the strains of placement."

Their final week of training went fast. Big Dave didn't have to talk Truman into beer and hamburgers, nice and spicy, the way the Malaysians liked them. And movies, too, the shittier and more carved up by the national censors, the better.

Midweek, Truman asked Andy if he could hop a cab or bus, out over the peninsula's spine of mountains, for Kuala Harap, overnight, to poke around. Andy was surprised. The teachers again expressed admiration. Andy meant his.

Then final days came. Days of tears and laughter, partying, unexpected sex, promises and arrangements to get together soon, and, of course, hushed speculation over who amongst them wouldn't make the two years, and why.

Broadcast live on a special 11:00 a.m. telecasting, Larry Holmes beat the shit out of a diet-pilled, trimmed-down Mohammed Ali. Far away, the young war in the gulf waged strong into its second week.

Then suddenly, they were volunteers, going their separate ways.

* * *

Truman worked at his thoughts on his own lone ride.

Sept. 20 something

I'm in a cab, again for Kuala Harap. Haven't written since the bus station back in J.B.—2 weeks ago. Much has happened & now we're all volunteers & all split up. I'll miss Dave & Ben. Hope Dave doesn't get machetted (sp?) for messing around with some big bastard's wife.

Hanging out with the teachers wasn't too bad, except for Sandy crying in the restaurant about having to be around such dirty kids & the perverts who care for them. Danny's psyched & hellbent on rooting out all the evil in sp. ed. here. The institutions were pretty grungy though, so he's got a point. I also managed to collect a bunch of stuff for if I ever try to teach the kids (my bunch) to learn anything. I'll have to read the stuff first—that'd help, huh?

Back in K.L., we all had fun. The hot showers & baths were great—so was the western food & booze. Dave was a blast! He claims he finally fucked Linda. (I was a bit surprised about who wound up liking who—& what they did about it.)

I got another letter from Mabel, & one from Mrs. Van Heflin, who said Angela said, "Hello." I wish she'd write to me (Angela—not her mom).

Dave & I also saw a lot of movies & guzzled a lot of beer. The worst of the movies was Empire Of The Ants. *It was so stupid that Dave began to SCREAM at the spots that were supposed to be scary. (Of course, everyone looked at us.) (Dave was funnier than the movie.)*

I did get to visit K.H. once more in our final week. The Indian boy was glad to see me. I think his name's Ramasami. The 2 women who live there were as shy as before. I tried to be nice. I stayed at the Rest House & ate at this line of food stalls that opens at sundown. When I was leaving (on foot) I saw a white guy on a motorcycle. I waved for some damned reason & he waved back! Not bad. I won't pester him.

CHAPTER 8

Dale Rowland, bully in a stupor, convalescing at home, was stringing together sentences by mid-July, several weeks after being struck with a baseball bat while extorting a dollar and some change. He spoke of bees.

Two weeks later, in the rain, in a less affluent section of New Egypt, young Truman and his Aunt Mabel loaded Truman's belongings into social worker Constance Embley's state car, D.Y.F.S. insignia and all.

Driving through the rain, Miss Embley reassured Mabel and Truman that The Children's Home of Burlington County was the best in the state. "Spread across lovely grounds at the edge of Mount Holly."

Asking to be called Connie, Miss Embley spoke of new friends, caring staff, home visits every weekend and of all the exciting trips the boys took. To the steady swipe of her wipers, she promised his school year, his probable stay, would snap right by.

Mabel, perched tall in the back with Truman, tried hard to agree. Truman, beside her, dressed in new clothes from Sears at Burlington Center, thought of the promised home visits to Barlow Archer's that never happened. Two seasons before, Mabel had claimed that the old man's health was failing, leaving him to move in with a sister somewhere deeper in the Pines.

* * *

The Children's Home of Burlington County was indeed pretty. Stately oaks and sycamores adorned the grounds that made up a triangular acreage at the southeast corner of Mount Holly, the seat of Burlington County. The home boasted roots as a Civil War orphanage.

The central building, a 19th-century structure, claimed the corner of a 1940's strategic approach to Memorial Hospital. The administrative office, a 19th-century home converted into offices, sat on Pine Street proper. A brand new gymnasium graced the back of the property at an angle to three sturdy brick cottages, housing the youngsters.

Truman was sent here to heal amongst forty other underdeveloped, needy young boys expressing behavioral anomalies from thievery to compulsive lying and fighting. Constant fighting. They lived with belligerence, homosexuality, the malice of stormy young hearts, and, of course, despair and loneliness. Constant god-awful childhood loneliness.

Truman wasn't permitted a home visit for a month. Policy favored a thoughtful look without interference as he acclimated himself to his program. Mabel was dubious, sitting in one of the smaller conference rooms, her big purse knocking about from her elbow. Truman, beside her, saw his placement simply, as a duty with an end. He even liked the food that nearly everyone apologized for. And he could eat all he wanted.

The other boys seemed foreigners to Truman in his first weeks. He wondered if the staying-smell of his returned laundry was due to the blending of races he now lived with. The art therapist, who he took to, assured him it was just a matter of detergent.

Three-fourths of the kids were inner-city blacks from Trenton, Newark, Camden, Atlantic City and the Oranges—a name he thought pretty. Within his first month a third of these kids liked him, a white kid scarred as nasty as themselves. The older kids ignored him. The remaining, one at a time, challenged him amongst the perverse minuets of their pecking order that was fought over, tightened and adjusted every bitter, cussing day.

Truman consequently learned to fistfight after a perfect shiner preceded two bloody noses in five days. It didn't fit his nature, but came nonetheless with his father's balance and skeleton alive inside him at nearing thirteen. He worried these altercations might lengthen his stay. A night-staff cottage parent, laughing, answered his concern. "Fuckin'-A, Kramer, you know how many kids are tied up in this system? You'd have to repeat your ball bat trick, or get caught butt-fuckin' before they'd keep the likes of you around.

Your ass'll be gone in the spring. Go to sleep now. And keep your pecker out of your hands."

Like everywhere, if one wasn't in medicine, or higher education, the human services didn't pay.

So Truman learned to not talk, but to strike first, and always in the center of the face, following with more, in brutal pursuit. His fighting ended by November. His place secure amongst the risings and tumblings of the others.

To some of the staff, Truman's model behavior, aside from defense, was an unusually long honeymoon. Molly, his art therapist, objected. She thought his placement an error. Unlike most of the residents, Truman was loved as a baby, as a child, and again by his aunt. He carried an understandable heartache, but never having learned the world as wicked and cruel, he lacked the hungering angry hopelessness of the other boys, welded into their hearts since infancy.

Molly saw it in his artwork, where he favored drawing over clay. Molly, dark-eyed and shapely, pointed to little truths in his art at a weekly staffing. Handsome pine trees bookended a little house. Sometimes crutches showed up, or an empty wheelchair.

"A faceless man, watching Little League baseball from afar, appears early in his pictures," she added. "Truman works hard at him, trying to get him right."

"Hocus pocus," commented the lead teacher. "It's all about want and reward. Behaviorism. What does the kid want right now? That's all we need." He and Molly had dated briefly. Molly ended it.

"Authority or approbation of some sort. Maybe lost father. Who knows? But he is someone," Molly leveled. "Truman called him 'scary.' A mailbox, worth mentioning, sometimes materializes as well."

* * *

And thus Truman's school year ensued, amid therapies, schooling, fighting, cussing and crying. The weekend home visits came, but Scotty had a new best friend, leaving Truman to wander New Egypt alone beneath the floating of the military transports, to the roll of the distant guns. Truman didn't seem to mind, for at The Children's Home the flip side of instant enemies was instant commitment.

Back at The Children's Home, Truman's on-grounds school was an odd little thing, called The Mary Dobbins School after some 19th-century do-gooder who loved children of another age. A child's grade, society's great benchmarks of childhood, was virtually ignored here. The teachers, fresh out of college, or otherwise unemployable, avoided the boys' questions and quarrels concerning their own true grade. Who knew? Unlike half the others, Truman took his lessons seriously, amongst the daily classroom ejections. He also learned, in near disbelief, that farts could be lit—ignited into fast flames of blues and greens.

And winter came, with trips to local movie theaters, where Truman coaxed friends way down front, to peer up at the vast action, filling his vision. Other trips took the boys to see the Philadelphia 76ers, and the Phillies across the great bridges that spanned the Delaware. Vanloads of fighting and swearing, they'd go to the Spectrum and Veterans Stadium; huge structures, sounds, smells and distant skyscrapers flooding Truman's senses.

By spring, Truman had also fallen in love with art therapist Molly. Quietly, he fancied her his mother, with her fleshiness and big eyes as she talked with him, as he worked at his art. Away from her, he daydreamed they'd meet years later, and that she'd wish to marry him. She'd kiss him with her perfect mouth, excusing his youth that he retained in these flights of need, unable to envision himself a physical adult.

By early June, Truman had his ten months in. He was bigger and stronger, his straight-backed childhood posture staying with him. The strong smell of his returned laundry now meant clean to him as he packed to return to Mabel's, taking a quiet satisfaction in his squirreled-up possessions, stowing them neatly, not hearing his cottage parents manhandling fighting kids in a room down the hall.

* * *

After the racket of The Children's Home, the slam of Mabel's back screen door seemed the loudest thing in New Egypt. Next door, barking Buddy had aged another seven years, yet gathered enough fit for Truman's comings and goings as the rest of New Egypt had apparently gotten along well without him.

Loving Mabel was tactful, although Fritz's postings about her home had heard a good deal concerning Truman's impending return. Scotty, however, stayed distant. His overworked mother didn't need her goofy-enough son hanging around with a truly bad boy. She had seen Truman's sort featured on her investigative television shows. However, the Van Heflins, as though nothing had happened, welcomed Truman back to their sprawling farm, simply expecting him to be there. Angela had grown, too. Her hair was longer, and her breasts now pushed out at her shirts, getting her set for her freshman year over in Allentown in September.

That summer, Truman's quiet walk home from the farm along the abandoned track bed came easy. He dreamed well there, of entering eighth grade, and of Molly, who hadn't answered the single letter he wrote late in July.

That fall he settled easily into school, after that whatever-it-was year of puking and fighting, chalk throwing and wrestling kids to the floor at the Mary Dobbins School. It was an autumn of new hope. Truman felt it everywhere. On Mabel's nightly news, a beaming southern governor gained The White House from Gerald Ford on the single promise that he'd never tell a lie, and Ford wasn't even a liar. Even Dale Rowland was up and about, hobbling around fine at Allentown High School, in Angela's grade.

And Truman schooled well. Mabel flushed with joy over his report cards. The other kids were pleasant, but no friends emerged from the curious that circled. To be certain, Truman was never picked on. The more nervous of his classmates deemed him something of a mild-mannered short fuse, lurking in the lunch lines, or quietly studying the pages of their little library's *National Geographics* he enjoyed.

To Mabel's relief, Truman also didn't go out for any of the sports his earnest Phys. Ed. teacher tried to talk him into. Maybe he should have, for Truman felt outside of things, somehow older, having lost his mother, then assigned another. His beating at the hands of Dale Rowland, then his own great crime, and subsequent penance.

All went smooth in his lone boy's world, until late that spring.

* * *

While mowing the Van Heflins' majestic lawn, Truman came upon a snapped clothesline. Wet laundry lay on the grass as it had fallen, in a quiet drag. Truman shut off his John Deere rider, and unfastened the fallen clothes, draping them over the remaining parallel lines that held until he could retie the fallen lines. But while rehanging the wet laundry, shaking each free of clinging grass, a volcanic Angela stormed out from within the screened-in porch. She was beside herself, her wet hair wrapped in a towel. Spots of wet shower showed through her clothes.

"What are you doing?" she demanded, marching across the freshly cut lawn. Tiny green clippings leapt up about her.

"Hangin' clothes," Truman replied, with Angela's and her mother's wet underwear draped over his left forearm.

"I can't believe this! I just cannot believe this!" she hissed, jerking the laundry from Truman's arm.

Truman offered no resistance.

High schooler Angela glared. "Do you have to be touching my things? For God's sake, my mother's things, too?"

Truman waited for a directive.

Angela turned, then spun back. "Just do whatever you were supposed to be doing!" she said as she fumbled for clothespins.

"The line fell, I thought—"

"I don't care!" she fired, pretty moments before as she worked the surviving lines with feverish intent. She turned. "Oh no. You're not going to just stand there and watch me do this, are you?"

Truman backed a step. "You want help?"

"The mowing, right? You're supposed to be mowing?" Her toweled head jerked as she furiously snapped clippings from the fallen whites.

Truman backed another step. "Yes."

"Then just get on the stupid mower, and do it. Get away from me!"

Across the lawn, the Van Heflin back screen door opened again. It was Mrs. Van Heflin. "What's all the fuss out here?"

Truman's fear heightened. If Angela had cause for anger, her mother had enough to report to Mabel.

"It's Truman, Mom! He's out here handlin' all our things." Angela shouted, spearing a glance at Truman.

"You're pitching a fit because he's hanging wet clothes?" asked her mother.

"It's not just that . . ." Angela's voice trailed off.

"Come in the house, honey," her mother said. "I'll hang the rest."

As Angela marched off, Truman tried to speak. Kathleen Van Heflin cut him off.

"She took offense to your touching her underthings. Girls can be funny. I'll get the rest. Go on, honey, and mow." She smiled.

Truman looked to the house. "Will she get better?"

"In a couple of minutes. Go on and mow."

The school year closed weeks later. In Truman's eighth grade class photograph, taken in the lunchroom/gymnasium, Truman sat high, and to the left. Truman was more moved, though, by the portrait Mabel had him sit for at Sears, at Burlington Center. She presented Truman, with coupons, in a suit she purchased upstairs. When the glossy eight-by-ten came back, Mabel framed it and lovingly worked it next to her favorite of Fritz in their living room. The one where he was just beginning to smile, years before to a younger Mabel.

* * *

That summer, another of farm work, big guns in the distant night, and walks alone on the abandoned track bed, bridged Truman's ascent into high school.

Angela, long calmed and friendly again, chatted casually with Truman about her new friends at Allentown High School. They were pretty girls, coming and going about the Van Heflin farmhouse, often laughing, or talking intensely. High school mattered to Mabel, too, for she brought it up several times that summer. It was bigger. Three grade schools, New Egypt, Millstone and Upper Freehold, fed the sprawling building.

That fall Truman got lost acclimating himself within the grid of the high school's intersecting hallways. Mabel thought his freshman year a howling success, all A's and B's, as Truman experienced it as a year of quiet loneliness.

He saw little of Scotty Winslow, as popular Angela made the cheerleading squad. Discreetly, Angela acknowledged Truman's passing between classes. He wondered over how much he liked her, doing nothing about it. One weekend, just after Christmas and bundled warm, she followed him about his feeding of the heifers in her father's barn.

"You know, Truman, you showed up in Allentown with something of a reputation."

Truman turned to this, both arms wrapped around feed.

"It makes sense. Most everyone knows of, or once feared, Dale Rowland."

Truman noticed her hands in mittens. Angela continued, "Dale's a junior now, shuffling between those special ed. classes down in first hall. Kids are intrigued with the story." Then she shied. "The teachers talk, too. I have friends who've heard them."

"Like what?" Truman asked.

Angela loved having scoop. "Oh, you know, 'Such a loss to two families,' and, 'Both seem to be such nice boys,' and the old, 'It's New Egypt, you know. It's in the water out there.' Stuff like that."

But Truman's freshman year passed uneventful, as his father's skeleton broadened his shoulders. He favored geography and history, while enjoying Mabel's *National Geographics* at home. He had to work harder in math and English, around working at the Van Heflins' farm, the dairy cows, their feed, the milking parlor, the outbuildings, the machines and the earthy fields that spread out from the big house and central barn, giving him a sense of purpose and belonging.

* * *

A new hand was hired. A middle-aged man, Bob McCleary. A farmhand of fifteen years, he could do it all. And he had a son in tow, just Truman's age, named Jimmy. The McClearys, womanless, from somewhere in northern Pennsylvania, moved into one of the trailer parks that surrounded New Egypt like a scattered army bivouacked in a tired siege.

Jimmy McCleary was wiry and tall, with spread teeth and a big nose. He hung around the farm, but not on the payroll. He carried a lighter, claiming he'd done so since he was eleven or twelve, for whatever cigarettes he could bum or steal. He asked Truman about the school he'd have to attend in September, curious about the "fucked-up teachers and the dick-headed kids," he'd have to deal with. "After all," Jimmy bemoaned, "I'm only fifteen. I can't quit, by law, until I'm sixteen. What a fucking law."

Truman asked Jimmy about the schools he attended in Pennsylvania, in the meaningless names of Lock Haven and Jersey Shore, what a curious name. Truman also answered Jimmy's questions regarding his scar. At least Jimmy asked. But he shied from Jimmy's remarks one afternoon, concerning a sunbathing Angela.

"Jesus H. Christ," Jimmy smirked, "what'd I give to poke the shit out of that little bitch."

* * *

That August of 1977, Elvis Presley turned up dead on a Graceland bathroom floor. Truman thought of Mrs. Winslow and her 45s. A week later Mabel casually brought up the Peace Corps, as a television commercial aired a sunset panorama of tired adults leaving a partially erected structure on some African-looking savannah.

Mabel leaned forward. "That sounds so exciting, Truddy. Fritz would have enjoyed something like that if they had it back then."

"Is it the army or something?" Truman asked.

"Oh no. Not at all. It's a job where young people go to poor countries to help out." She sipped at her coffee, her attention fixed to the voice-over testimonial. A bearded man played guitar for partially clad children.

"Do they do farm work?" Truman asked. The same man was then giving advice to two black men in khakis.

"Oh, I imagine." Mabel perked to the bite. "I guess they do all sorts of work. It's something to think about. You'd see the world, help people out. Something you'd never forget. My Fritz used to go on and on about the Korean villages with their food and their different customs and all. Oh, Truddy, you should think about it."

And Truman did, to occasional television commercials, and while nosing about in Mabel's *National Geographic*s. Then stretches came when it never occurred to him at all, as tenth grade rolled in with the autumn. He liked school more, in spite of Algebra I, as he enjoyed a double period of Ag. Shop. He was also humored to discover a surly, silent Jimmy McCleary in his second period Phys. Ed., big nose and all.

"Just doing my fuckin' time, Kramer," Jimmy told Truman as they dressed in the locker room in the first week of September.

But trouble followed motherless Jimmy. After a P.E. class toward the end of October, about the time when the chores changed about the farm, Truman overheard an altercation back between the lockers while awaiting the bell. No teachers were around. A happy crowd assembled. Something fun could happen.

"Who pissed in my fucking sneakers?" Jimmy demanded.

Truman thought his nose unusually red.

"You never wash 'em anyway," remarked one of four boys who could have been as guilty as any of the others. All were happy, their weirdo cornered.

"Jesus Christ!" howled one. "He's puttin' 'em on!"

"I got to, you cocksuckers. They're all I have."

"Who are you callin' cocksuckers?" asked one boy, an offensive guard on Allentown's hapless football team.

Jimmy went quiet. The assembled crowd shouldered in between the lockers as Jimmy worked his right foot into a urine-soaked sneaker.

"Who you calling names?" the boy pressed. "I should pitch the rest of your shit in the fuckin' toilet."

Truman shouldered his own way through the crowd.

"Jimmy, it's me. I got a clean pair. I'm wearing my work boots."

"Oh, a butt-buddy? Come to save your day?" The football player straightened.

The crowd snickered and quieted. Some wondering, having heard.

"Just put 'em on, Jim. The bell's gonna ring," Truman said.

"You guys butt-buddies or what?" the big kid asked, giving Truman a light elbow, between the lockers.

Truman dropped his sneakers at Jimmy's feet. Jimmy's socks were filthy.

Truman turned to the offensive guard. "Fuck you," he whispered.

"You're gonna take that one back, asshole, or—"

SMACK!

The boy's head snapped to Truman's straight punch, tight-fisted in the middle of his face. He snorted fast blood.

The crowd lurched and flexed.

Jimmy grabbed at Truman's sneakers, then rolled away as Truman stepped squarely, angling his controlled hard punches, following his stunned quarry along the length of the lockers, an earnestness learned at The Children's Home. No rules. Prevail.

The big boy covered, then opened, groping with swinging misses as Truman stayed in front of him, squaring again with straight punches to his head, shoulders and arms that caught the blows.

The big boy lurched forward, toward tackling. Truman stepped aside as the boy fell to his hands and knees. The crowd flexed back, as did Truman, to kick his foe, three full times in his face, as he tried to rise.

The big boy doubled upon the littered floor.

The crowd quieted.

Truman backed off, and looked about. Then he collected his things, breathing hard, keeping an eye on the football player.

The bell rang. "I don't know your last name," Truman said between breaths, "but I'm going to the office. You should, too."

Someone laughed from the dispersing crowd. "The nurse's office is more like it."

That did it for friendless Jimmy, who ranted in the principal's office, ". . . those constant pains in my ass . . ." and later to his disinterested father, "Just pretty goddamned lucky I didn't hop in on it. That's all I got to say." That day Truman became Jimmy's fast friend indeed.

For Truman, and the offensive guard, their fight meant a three-day suspension from school, an excuse-ridden fall for one, and a furthering of the mystery that shadowed the quiet other.

Mabel telephoned Truman's caseworker at New Jersey's Division Of Youth And Family Services, thinking she'd beat Allentown High School to it. Overworked Connie Embley dismissed the affair as, "isolated and episodic, just growing up." Mabel was relieved. Allentown's Vice Principal chuckled over the well-deserved beating.

So Jimmy learned Truman's simple routine of school and work, presenting himself, always on foot, at Truman's one or the other. Truman accepted. A questionable friend was better than none.

* * *

Into the winter, Mabel's back screen door slammed more often with Jimmy's friendship. Jimmy teased Truman about Truman's still riding his monkey bike. Its seat, split down the middle long before, was adjusted to its highest height. His once-prized chrome fenders and handlebars long since rusted over. The chain guard was simply gone. Truman was also wary of Jimmy's hitchhiking, but he went along with its cautious nature of mutual once-overs, constructed conversations and peripheral vision. Of course, Mabel never knew.

That spring Truman worked all over the farm, particularly enjoying the planting. He shared his track bed walk with Jimmy, who was unable to feel whatever it was that called to Truman. In return, Jimmy shared his own, mildly criminal, window-peeking route. Its ten or eleven stops meandered in and around New Egypt's barking dogs, chain-linked fences and scattered streets. The two boys watched families watching TV and doing dishes around lights turning off and on. Only one stop ever panned out.

In the back of Jimmy's own trailer park, where it began, lived two older woman, perhaps a mother and daughter, who apparently bathed around TV shows. From a strategic branch in a flimsy white pine, the two boys watched the heavy younger woman descend down and away into her tub, catching glimpses of her fleeting nakedness. Her breasts hung long and narrow. Jimmy hushed disgust for her large dark nipples. "Like chocolate chip cookies, Truman." Both boys marveled over flashes of pubic hair as she eventually stood to towel off in their sliver of vision.

Jimmy reasoned if the moment was right, she'd "fuck" him. "Maybe both of us, at the same time! She's got to be lonely, living in there with that other old bag."

The thought of Jimmy's nakedness so close to his own repulsed young Truman.

The woman, somebody "Ferguson," Truman learned from a mailbox, became a quiet fantasy of his own. It was Molly, the art therapist, for the longest time, but she faded away. He tried Angela, but she was too real.

Late that spring, Dale Rowland went to Allentown's prom, capping his senior year. Some girl's boyfriend dumped her two weeks out, sticking her with tickets and a dress. Dale filled in.

He was handsomely harmless and everyone understood, according to Angela. That same week, Mabel brought up college, the Peace Corps, or the military.

"You're getting to be a young man, honey. You'll need a plan," she advised. "Anything. Just move forward when the time comes. Think about it, will you, Truddy?" She stroked at his head in passing, clearing their dishes.

That summer Truman and Jimmy discovered parties in the near pines. Truman liked beer, but seldom drank too much. Jimmy boasted great capacity, yet fell often and early. He even shit himself once, bent and puking at the same time out along Long Swamp Road. Truman, with one of the farmhands, laughed at the sight of Jimmy doubled over in the car headlights, slinging strings of vomit from his mouth and big nose as he worked his pants down, slurring, "The fuckin' potato chips did me in."

They hitchhiked to nearby Cookstown and Browns Mills, tough military towns, strip joints intermingled with fast food. Then once over into Millstone, daunting with wealth, after a girl that wanted nothing to do with Jimmy. Then school rolled around, eleventh grade, promising to parole Jimmy October 17th, his sixteenth birthday.

* * *

Truman's junior year, with no sports or extracurricular activities, had a double Ag. Shop, learning little he didn't already know, as Angela, a senior, began a long steady with some kid named Kyle. October 18th, Jimmy quit school, with a sneer and a swagger. He returned a month later, humbled, after getting beat up by his father. Jimmy didn't realize that a steady job was the next idea. Guidance promptly enrolled him in an at-risk program called the Alternative School. "It figures," Angela told Truman at the farm. "It's out in Imlaystown, my old school. For the losers and the druggies. Just ask Kyle."

That spring, Truman bought his first car from friends of the Van Heflins, a snow-tired Dodge Dart that cost him $300. The light green body was on its way, but the slant-six engine, one of Dodge's better ideas, ran tight at 85,000 miles. Jimmy was critical of the unique push-button automatic transmission gearshift on the dashboard. "You couldn't find something with a real man's stick on the floor, could you, Kramer?" he said, never reckoning his own walking and hitchhiking.

That May Truman also learned of the passing of good old Barlow Archer. Mabel told him one night after supper. She learned of it, having snooped around, via Connie Embley, hoping for a visit of some sort. Apparently, Barlow's health failed him back in November, and he never survived the winter at his sister's.

Taking Jimmy with him, Truman visited anyway, driving south in his Dodge Dart, catching Route 206, skirting the Pines, and Mt. Holly, his home for the length of a school year, then east, into the Pines.

At the sandy graveyard, the two boys easily found Barlow's grave. At five months, the scar upon the lawn of monuments stood out amongst two others, both adorned with flowers. Where the earth was once opened for his mother was harder. Truman remembered which corner of the graveyard, but from there they had to read. Jimmy found it first, pointing a bony finger toward the small stone that Barlow paid for. Jimmy softly offered to leave his friend alone. Truman declined. Again, goofy friends were better than none.

The stone, struck simply, April Kramer, about two dates, both new to Truman, didn't hit him as he worried it might. He also tried to think about God, but thought instead of the blue sky above, and of the Pines surrounding them, and, for some reason, a lone light bulb dangling from a ceiling.

* * *

Then summer was upon them, farm work for Truman, and washing dishes and some painting for Jimmy. Truman, at seventeen, now drove by the track bed where Route 537 crossed it. At times he slowed, looking down the quiet stretches, pleased with his own aging.

Angela and Kyle graduated, and spent their evenings together. Jimmy wanted to spy on them. "Like the old days," he urged. "He's got to be fucking her. Remember the tub lady with the nipples? It'd be that easy."

Truman was firm. Jimmy couldn't understand his touchiness that summer of 1979, as raving Iranians clung to American hostages on nightly television, as gas lines formed around odd and even license plates. On Mabel's nightly news, Jimmy Carter, smiling seldom, fired most of his cabinet in a try-anything week, seeming forever far away from his lone triumph at Camp David.

While out cruising in his Dodge Dart, Truman prodded his lanky friend to ponder a future, mentioning the Peace Corps. Jimmy thought it crazy, after learning what it was.

"We have to do something beyond this, Jim."

With no time horizon of his own, Jimmy lit a cigarette, rolled his window down, and bitched to the passing air, "You, too? Jesus Christ. Everyone's up my ass. All the fucking time."

* * *

Then came school, September, their senior year. Jimmy returned to the Alternative School, as Angela, still going with Kyle, attended nearby Mercer County Community College, unsure of what to major in.

That fall, a campaigning Ronald Reagan never mentioned the hostages as America experienced rage and despair over Carter's fiery, failed rescue. That winter, good old Buddy next door, went cloudy eyed, and too old to bark, only lifting his head to Jimmy and Truman's comings and goings.

Then just after Christmas, Truman received a telephone call. "It's a girl," Mabel happily whispered, hiking her eyebrows twice.

It certainly was, and to Truman's delight, but she wouldn't give her name, and he didn't know her voice. And another listened in, at her side, or on an extension. Pauses and giggles shadowed the phantom speaker.

"I don't know who she was," Truman reported to an anxious Mabel.

* * *

In February, while helping Jimmy's father and Chet Van Heflin build a secondary corncrib, Truman asked his boss what he thought of the U.S. Peace Corps.

"What do you wish to wind up as?" the large man asked, breathing heavily.

"A farmer. Kind of like you," Truman answered, suddenly sheepish, not wanting it to sound as it had.

Jim's dad laughed. "You'll need a farm first. A hard thing to get."

"Eventually, is what I meant."

Chet Van Heflin stayed to his slatted planking. "I know what you meant. Now Bob here's a farmer without a farm," curbing the senior McCleary. "And there's plenty of others, too. You've been around here long enough. Some are laborers, some are farmers without farms. I was lucky. Born into mine," he answered the boy, while apologizing to the man.

"I just need to make up my mind. I do like the pigeons, though."

"The pigeons?" asked Chet.

"Flying rats," snarled Bob McCleary.

"I like their sounds," answered Truman, steadying a cross brace for Bob McCleary.

"By all means, Truman," answered Chet. "If you can get out and see the world, you should," he breathed. "There'll always be this farm, or another. And the pigeons ain't too bad neither."

* * *

In March Truman drove alone to Philadelphia, to the regional Peace Corps' office, a small corner in the Federal Building, and quietly enlisted. After a good deal of questioning, and with a detailed letter from Chet Van Heflin, proprietor of Van Heflin Dairy Farms, and a copy of his Allentown High School transcript, testifying to three years of Agricultural Mechanics, the assignment of Agricultural Youth Extension became Truman's, reaching out to the rural youth of Honduras, Malaysia or Cameroon. After an arranged battery of physical exams, and choosing Malaysia, he was to secure a passport, and report to his staging in Seattle in late June.

Jimmy McCleary, aimless and abandoned, claimed, "You're truly fucking nuts."

* * *

One April evening Mabel sat in the middle of their living room floor, going through her store of *National Geographics*, searching for references to that far-off land. She found four, and carted them off to work, after she and Truman poured over them at home. Angela repeatedly praised his decision with cow eyes. Kyle grew sick of it. The following week brought a second phone call. Again no names, but no giggling listening-in either, supporting the calling heart.

"Who could it be?" asked Mabel.

"Still wouldn't say," said Truman, cleaning the coffeemaker to brew a fresh pot.

"Think she knows you're going away?"

"She didn't mention it. If she calls back in July, we'll know."

"What does she ask about?"

"Crazy stuff. This time it was, who would I have like me, really like me, if it could be anyone?" he replied, as he reached for the dish towel.

"Oh my, Truddy. Who'd that be?" Mabel straightened with interest.

Truman was drying the glass pot. "I suppose someone like me."

"She'd be a dreamboat." Mabel beamed. "I'll bet she's not taken."

Meanwhile, in the mail, literature began showing up in big official envelopes from the Peace Corps, Washington, D.C.

Truman and Mabel studied these essays and commentaries regarding Malaysia. Mabel reminded him that he was always welcome home should he ever wish to bow out. "After all," she said, stunning him, "you'll have a lot of money waiting for you."

"What do you mean?" Truman asked.

"All your monthly food and clothing allowances from D.Y.F.S. since you moved in with me, honey."

Truman seemed confused.

"Remember our first summer together, when I sat you down here in the kitchen and explained it to you? That I'd support you myself, putting it all in the bank?" Mabel swelled with pride.

"How much is there? Can I ask?"

Mabel whispered, "A little over $26,000. Every penny of it yours, Truddy. It's been eight years, you know. Maybe money for college. What do you think?"

"I don't know, Mabel." A farm struggled to materialize in his mind.

* * *

By late May Truman's senior portrait bumped his eighth-grade graduation, gracing Mabel's living room, sharing the hinged dual frame with Fritz in uniform, taken just before he left for Korea. The irony dawned on Mabel. Having already lost one love to the distant East, she'd quietly separate the two pictures, lying to Truman about low flying transports rattling the two men of her life. Truman hadn't asked.

Then June blurred. A third telephone call came. Truman hung up on it. The migrant help at the farm went wild by radio one night as Panamanian, Roberto Duran, beat up Sugar Ray Leonard in Montreal, as pretty Angela worked herself around Truman's farm work almost daily. Kyle put up with it.

One late afternoon, Truman covered his Dodge Dart, to be stored atop blocks behind tractors in Chet's lower equipment pole shed, longing for this final walk home through the thickening springtime growth of the track bed. Angela offered to drive him, but Truman declined. She'd never kiss him, so he chose the one that would.

A day later he happened upon the old man next door, sitting childlike in the middle of his lawn, cradling the stillness of his dog. Truman approached the fence that separated their yards.

"Buddy's gone. Ole Buddy's gone." The old man wept.

That same day, Truman stood before his monkey bike, hanging from hooks in Mabel's garage, examining its rusty spokes, airless tires and forgiven front fender. Its childhood's work concluded.

Then more distant guns in the night, as Truman walked alone. No one was home at the Ferguson trailer. All was dark, even the trees.

Then Mabel that final morning. Both of them nervous. Truman with a large, single piece of new luggage, nearly a trunk, bought at Sears, working it out through the banging of their back screen door.

CHAPTER 9

Oct. 9, 1980

I'm getting a bit more settled. The first few days took me through a ringer though. Jimmy would flip with all the staring a white person gets here. My dreams at night are crazy, too & I can't seem to wake up in the mornings, or stay awake in the evenings. I don't know why. I just get so sleepy so fast.

This job might be some fun though with these (about a doz.) kids & two Malay ladies. Oh—a song just came on the radio that reminds me of that "You're Only Lonely" that I liked so much last spring. (It's funny how you can tell anything to a journal. I even feel guilty if I don't write for a week.) Anyway—to my job—I'm still not sure what all I'm supposed to do. That Azman guy (I guess he's my "host country boss") just smiles a lot, calling me Mr. Truman whenever he sees me, which is seldom, so I've just started cleaning the place up. There's trash & shit all over. Someone's been using the grounds as a dump!

I still don't know all the kids' names. Ramasami & Lim are always happy to see me though. Both were afraid to come outside at first. The two ladies are Fatimah & Zurina. Only Zurina (the older one) will talk to me, but we can't understand each other anyway.

I've also seen that Singer guy again. He waved first, so I waved back. We're getting along pretty good.

* * *

So Truman spent his first week dragging trash from the high weeds, creating huge piles in front of the modified six-bay garage. As he worked above the quiet pull of the Pahang River, his disbanded training group exchanged fast letters, and phone calls, where they could be made, for much needed support.

Ramasami, the ragged Indian boy, and Lim, a stout little Down Syndrome Chinese girl of twelve or so, tentatively ventured outside to help in the chest-high growth that had taken over the grounds.

Lim, sweating profusely, uttered no words of any language, baring a toothless, gummy grin at the end of her drags, pointing proudly at their growing pile. She also feared the small closed-up structure at the rear of the property. Ramasami, who eagerly courted Truman and the teachers a month before, jabbered a constant-rolling Tamil that no one understood, occasionally barking out, "Good morning!" to Truman in the crisp English he parroted from somewhere. But he tired fast in the equatorial heat and had to be led inside from time to time, where the others hobbled and shrieked en masse to the dark safety of the kitchen to Truman's every entry.

Twice, Truman peeked around the corner at the brown children, most in rags, at least two nude. With each their panic rose, driving smiling Truman away, out past the lone naked boy who slapped at his head and spun to the energy of the others. Truman learned his name, too, was "Azman," and thought it funny. He also wondered why the other Azman, who ducked in and out, from time to time, couldn't seem to answer his desire for a rake and shovel from anywhere.

That first week, Truman's piling of trash eventually peaked, elongating the mouth of the pitted driveway, to what he figured to be two truckloads of tin cans, lengths of wood and pipe, automotive parts pried loose from the earth, and whatever else Fatimah and Zurina had taken to winging out into the chest-high growth.

Resting, with his two helpers, he also learned the name of another scrambling about inside. A young Malay girl, Normah, dutifully dragged off by a friend in their escapes, was stricken with cerebral palsy. She was fourteen. By Truman's second week she ventured questions in a Malay jumbled with palsied contortion and laughter. She thought Truman was a hoot.

Outside, Truman rested in a spot he cleared beneath the reaching tree that a month before made him think of the climatic dog party ending of *Go Dog Go!* He also took his two helpers up into Kuala Harap's two intersecting streets for Coca Colas.

Ramasami was wild with joy, lashing out "Good Morning" amongst his rumbling Tamil to any passerby. Chubby Lim clung wide-eyed to Truman, peering suspiciously about the two streets, the people, and the thin vapor of diesel that hung in the air, never seeming to dissipate in the heavy heat.

American John Singer, from a distance, once saw the new guy with his two retarded children in tow. He smiled, kicking his motorcycle into life.

* * *

Meanwhile Truman searched for a place to live, while permitted to stay his first month at the local government Rest House, at the opposite end of the T that made up Kuala Harap.

He found two rooms for rent in his second week. One a windowless back room behind a herbal medicine shop, where he'd share a bed with a Malay boy about his age. The second sharing a flat with two Chinese men, father and son, filthy with grease, apparently mechanics, and arguing with one another at the inquiry. Suspicious of an oriental Jimmy and George McCleary, Truman declined that one as well.

With grinning Mr. Azman still tight-fisted over money for tools in his gracious Malay manner, Truman golfed his way back and forth across the property, leveling the high grass in two days with a rusted sickle he found in the small structure at the rear of the property, perhaps once a tool shed, and terrifying to little Lim. Ramasami was thrilled with the activity. Stout Lim, in time, was happy that Ramasami was happy. Normah cocked her face into asking Truman what he was doing as he rested one afternoon.

Bound to her broken wheelchair, the young girl exploded into palsied hilarity as Truman explained, in his limited Malay, his intentions of building a playground, not realizing his literal translation meant wishing the kids to have a place to play with dirt. But she stilled herself, as best as able, when the older, more talkative caregiver, Zurina, asked Truman if he was a Christian, an inevitable question Truman and his friends were lightly warned of in training.

Sitting inside, and sweating from work, Truman stabbed in his infant Malay, "I never go to the churches in America. The Christian mosques, if that's what you mean."

Zurina repeated his "never." "*Tak pernah!?*" She peered intently.

"Tak pernah," he confirmed, proud of his Malay. "I don't know what I believe. I don't think about it much."

Zurina's aging, cocoa-smile went wide, exposing pearly-white teeth. In a Malay too quick to understand, she asked, "Would you enter Islam?"

Truman grasped for his pocket translation dictionary. His wet hands spotted the pages as he thumbed. Zurina's "enter" tripped him up. "Spell *masu*, please," he asked her.

Zurina's grin stayed wide, without a trace of shame. "I was never schooled. Fatimah!" she called to her younger helper. "Spell masu!"

Broom in hand, the younger woman obliged. Truman caught the meaning, "enter Islam."

He smiled to the older woman. "I don't know." He wished to be inoffensive. "Probably not," he substituted for "never."

"Marry a Malay girl. Live in Malaysia." She beamed, in the dark heat of their indoors.

Normah's broken wheelchair nearly toppled with the twists this idea prompted. Ramasami and Lim hopped in delight. Something good must have happened. Truman's scar tightened with his smile.

He rose, thinking of Angela for some reason. At the modified garage door that slid sideways, like a cage on a track, Truman turned. He called to Normah, in her wheelchair, struggling in Malay, "I understand now. Miss Zurina wishes to marry me."

Normah contorted all over again.

Quiet Fatimah, back to sweeping, broke her silence with something directed at the older woman, which Truman couldn't understand.

Zurina fired back fast at her partner, and turned on the squealing youth in her wheelchair. Then she seized a broom of her own, chasing Truman out into the tropical sun, away from the clamor behind.

* * *

Across the following days, Truman set fire to the growth about the home with manageable burns, scorching the ground, ridding it of entanglements of brush and weeds.

It was hot work that had him shirtless, in jeans and work boots, chasing stray flames in the breeze, beating at their edges with a sack he found and soaked in a drum. He rested between burns that turned the downed weeds and brush into heavy gray smoke, lifting out over the lazy Pahang. The ash and charred ground left behind more trash: undetected hinges, broken glass, nails, silverware, and lengths of twisted angle iron and more.

A letter from Ben found him, with two more, one from Mabel and another from Mrs. Van Heflin. Ben's invited him to a hastily thrown together reunion for those of their training group within reach. Mabel's was warm and curious. Caroline Van Heflin's trickled with farm news, and Angela's fall semester. Chet wished him well in his wife's handwriting.

Back in his Rest House room, Truman penciled out a timetable for his first six months to submit to Azman, wishing to please his new boss who wondered aloud at all the piling and burning going on. Truman worried over the legality of his burning, a notion that never occurred to Azman, who commented, smiling, "After all, Mr. Truman, no one ever sees this place. Do you not think so?"

Truman was pleased, however, with his own planning, engaging him when he needed engagement. He eagerly sketched out his first three months into cleaning inside and out, sorting the useable from the trash, inventorying everything. His plans leapt into begging for scrap lumber from a nearby mill toward building a playground with an outdoor fort, maybe even a tree house in the spreading of the great tree, thinking of those crazy dogs and their cars. He penciled in a garden, a good painting for everything, and clothes. The kids needed clothes. Perhaps a drive of some sort.

Through December he felt good, but January and February spooked him. After all, he wasn't a teacher. In his dim room at the Rest House, he struggled over this final phase of implementing something educational for the kids. He brainstormed over materials, wondering what the kids might already know, trying not to let his sweating smudge his spiral notebook purchased for the job. Beneath the slow cutting of his ceiling fan he wondered which subjects, and for whom. After all, spinning-Azman was practically a wild animal. Then he calmed, figuring to spend these first three months reading through the material he gathered traveling with the teachers. And Ben and Andy had faith. Wanting the job was half the battle.

Two days later, after a brief entry of despair, Truman wrote:

Oct. 15, 1980

I thought I'd write again because things seem to be on an up-swing. I'm tolerating all the staring & at the Home I feel like I have some direction. It may become my home, too. I'm thinking of moving into the shed out back. It's got a water pump & I could run power out to it. It's half the size of the milking parlor (and a hell of a lot shabbier). It'll be cheap & I don't feel like living with a local family of any race. Azman said I could, for a monthly donation & as long as it was ok with old Zurina & Fatimah. I guess it was.

As for the kids, the crew-cut boy, Salleh, still runs around nude—always hiding from me & usually crying. (They say he can't speak.) Ramasami has become my little helper. He wears rags, never shuts up & must be 10 or 11.

As for news—Iraq & Iran are still hard at it, over 2 weeks (some don't think it'll last with Iraq pretty much on top). I read that Reagan has the edge over Carter with 3 weeks left. (I used to not care, but the P.C. office sends us free Newsweeks—so I'm learning.) (God knows there's nothing else to do around here!) Kuala Harap is lifeless after 9:15 or so, except for the two lines of shops down on the highway that are open all night for the buses & lumber trucks that rumble through. (I guess we're at a handy halfway point.)

I'll close for now, shower up—again—which means dumping pails of cold water over me—& head down to the highway for some fried rice & a beer at the one Chinese shop I like. A monsoon shower might be coming. The sky's been darkening & blowing nice & cool from the east. I hope I get caught in it. It'll be like the good old track bed days!

* * *

A week later, Azman the boss presented himself upon the charred grounds of the Home, smiling with news. Truman's shirt was undone, and soaked with his slinging of trash from the shed out back.

"Our District Officer has seen your plans. He has allotted 1,000 ringgits for your project."

Just a touch under 500 American, Truman figured, picturing rakes, shovels, shelves of paint and assorted tools. He flushed with pride, his plan acceptable. He was a bit grown up.

Azman, dressed neatly, and grinning with the discomfort he felt around Truman, explained, "It'll be a week or so before money can be released. You will be required to keep appropriate records of all expenditures." This spooked Truman back into boyhood.

"Come to my office first of next week, Mr. Truman. Ask to speak with me," he said with a slight bow, bringing his left palm to his breast, the Malay courtesy. "Carry on." He smiled, turning back to his Toyota parked in the pitted driveway.

Truman, having decided to live in the shed out back, was cheered into renewed vigor. The "appropriate records of all expenditures" concerned him, but at least he felt some settling-in.

After lunch, Truman strode up into the two streets that made up Kuala Harap; there were two competing hardware shops. The larger appeared to have better prices. Truman learned it did so to stay afloat. The Chinese proprietor wasn't as popular as his Malay counterpart down the street.

From out front the two shops looked identical to the fifteen or so others that shaped the T of Kuala Harap. With their steel-curtained doors, opened for business, and cluttered with merchandise, all were two-story row structures with overhanging second floors shading stained sidewalks beneath. These sidewalks were separated from the street by gutters so deep and wide that one had to take a decent leap to clear these municipal necessities of a rain forest town. Truman made the hardy strides, unknowingly drawing further attention to himself, as no Malaysian would do likewise unless caught in a sudden downpour. He bought a yardstick, rake and shovel from the Chinese shop. He was watching his money.

* * *

The days following Azman's visit rolled by with more cleaning, raking and grading, and, of course, more planning as a new piling of trash grew out front.

Indoors, Truman also began playing with the children, noticing Ramasami and Lim's wanting more. Speechless, and nude, little Salleh joined in the whacking around of an old tennis ball. Truman insisted he wear shorts, which he would for a time, before shedding them. Later that week, their indoor hide-n-seeks, with Truman always "it" proved too much. Normah toppled twice from her compromised wheelchair. Ramasami experienced some sort of brief seizure as little Salleh, naked, struck Lim with a stick. The new game also acquainted Truman with Kumari, a large, unattractive Indian girl of at least sixteen who served Normah as her wheelchair pusher. Kumari also hobbled to safety as a giant compared to the others in Truman's first days about the trash, as well as in his subsequent hide-n-seeks, abandoning her post behind Normah's chair, leaving poor Normah to squeal and convulse alone, pointing with a palsied finger to Truman's whereabouts. To Truman's untrained eye, Kumari's one side, beneath her ragged dresses, appeared paralyzed. She smiled, half-sided as well, often at nothing. She slobbered when happy, and she smelled distinct from the general wretchedness of their converted little home.

Mail came. A fast note from Dave, the farmer, and a lengthier one from Ben, both covering the weekend get-together Truman missed. The two views of the same party humored Truman. The group's support for one another apparently came as sharing one another's postings, rehashing cultural differences, and scrambling into ill-thought intimacies beneath the covers of darkness, alcohol and loneliness. Ben's letter also alluded that big Dave Hayden may have reached new heights of offensiveness. Truman was moved to write to Mabel and Jimmy McCleary. His aunt would read hers several times before proudly passing it around at her office. Jimmy would never receive his. He and his father were gone, lured by a woman, back up into Pennsylvania.

Then three weeks into his assignment, Truman wrote in his journal: "The hardest day yet . . . the goddamned people here . . . the staring . . . can't understand a fucking word anyone says . . . this fucking dump that no one cares about . . . Azman ignores me . . ." and so on. This entry came after a day of burning more trash, fixing up his shed out back, with the kids a nuisance, with strangers enjoying calling him "John," and the heat, the relentless heat bearing down on his self-doubt.

Before going out for his supper, Truman bathed long from chilling buckets of water. Another *Newsweek* arrived. He set it aside, gathering himself for a brisk walk along the village trails he discovered encircling Kuala Harap, down to the East-West Highway and back to the river road, to arrive by sunset through the growth behind the Home. His evening visit surprised the kids, and Zurina and Fatimah. This pleased him. He later apologized in his journal, bathed again, and strode off into the night for the shops along the highway that lived off the traffic and community by day, and the loggers and the buses by night.

Through the lit shops that lined the two-lane highway, cars shot by amongst the trucks that rumbled forth from the jungled night.

Truman, in a T-shirt, clean jeans and in work boots, crossed the road and strode up to the Chinese shop he liked. Jumping the gutter, he entered the light and sat at one of the half dozen Formica tabletops. Two Indian men occupied a corner table, drinking and rumbling happily in Tamil. Ceiling fans cut at the warm air above as the Chinese keeper and a boy stacked boxes, conversing in Chinese, to Truman a sing-song hacking of sounds, one subordinate to the other.

The boy saw Truman and strode to his table. "No *Engris*," he pointed to his own mouth.

"*Boleh Melayu kah?*" Truman asked, proud of himself.

"Oh, very smart," the boy responded in Malay, wiping his hands on his apron. "What will you have?"

"Fried rice, and an Anchor beer," answered Truman, enjoying his limited command of Malay.

"Yes, John!" the boy snapped in English as he spun about.

Truman let it go, noticing John Singer out in the night air, approaching the same late-night shop.

Taking a single step up into the kedai, Singer noticed Truman as the Chinese boy hurried Truman's beer to his table. Singer nodded. "Hello, fellow."

"How do you do, sir?" Truman answered, rising too fast to this young man somewhere in his twenties, an object of his curiosity for several weeks.

John Singer, at six feet, was taller than Truman, which made him something of a slender giant in Malaysia. Buying a pack of Winstons, Singer was sandaled, in shorts, exposing thin legs with muscular calves. His flowery shirt was baggy and untucked. Light freckles covered his arms and face. He combed his brown hair straight back, like Andy's, which had him, too, raking his fingers back over his head in lieu of a comb. His initial demeanor warmed Truman. He packed his cigarettes with several hard taps upon the glass countertop, then turned about.

"So, you're the new guy in town?"

Having sat again, Truman straightened himself. "That's me. For a couple of weeks now." He leaned back for the boy, quick with his fried rice, smiling broadly with both Americans in his family's shop.

"Care to join me?" Truman ventured.

"I could do that," Singer replied. "*Satu lagi. Air batu juga*," he spoke to the boy.

Truman silently translated: One more. Ice, too. He liked this foreign language stuff, a lone measure of himself amongst his disbanded training group.

John Singer pulled up a chair opposite Truman's. He noticed Truman's scar, but kept to his eyes. "So what do you make of our little town here on the banks of the mighty Pahang?"

"It's a quiet one. I'm still getting adjusted, as they say. I'm stationed down by the river."

Stationed, thought Singer, before his soft, "*Terima kasih*," as he casually thanked the Chinese boy for his beer, and accompanying glass of ice. Studying his foaming beer, John Singer continued, "I've seen you around town, with a couple of youngsters in orbit. About the second or third time K.L. called to remind me of you, and of some home for the handicapped project."

"It's down by the river. You have to pass the bus station and the mosque up in town, and then keep going, down around the hill. It's an old converted six-bay garage, fenced in." He was pleased with the recognition.

Singer drank, then wiped foam from his upper lip. "It's a cinder block thing, right? If you keep on going, the road narrows into a trail, skirting the river until it meets the East-West Highway, maybe a quarter mile down."

"Yep! That's where I've been, burning brush, whacking weeds, slinging trash and playing with the kids."

"Are you a teacher, or a social worker or something?" Singer asked, kicking back.

A bat fluttered through. Truman dipped his head. Singer smiled. "You're going to love this place." He drank long from his glass, working his freckled Adam's apple. He looked out into the dark heat of the night. "I sort of do." Then kindly, "I'm sorry. Go on."

So Truman explained, too much, that he was something of a farmhand, but not a college farmer, like Dave Hayden from training. He continued, cautiously, about the Agricultural Youth Extension opportunity possibly not really existing.

Singer laughed. "I believe that."

"Well," Truman answered, "we had this teacher trip, back in training, and here was this place in this town, and I felt like a guy without a job, so why not give it a wing?"

"I'm impressed," answered Singer, claiming the next two beers. Two beers later, he explained his own job as an accountant with the Department Of Forestry as Truman claimed New Jersey as home, learning John Singer's to be Buffalo, New York, the bowling capital of the world, "and windier than Chicago. That's a fact," John Singer added.

They talked of Kuala Harap, one eagerly, and listening, the other in jest and quiet reflection. Truman wondered of the "lone guy" stuff he was warned of, but thought better not to ask.

By midnight, an aged Chinese woman replaced the boy, as the two Indian men began quarreling over something. Singer called last round, claiming to be tired, yet pleased to have met Kuala Harap's other white guy. Truman wanted to ask if they could get together again, but John Singer did it for him, pulling back his hair: "I'll swing by the Home, or whatever it is, sometime soon. See you then."

As the elderly Chinese woman counted their bottles, Singer asked Truman, "You need a ride back to the Rest House?"

"The night air will do me good," Truman declined. "Thanks."

With a firm handshake, that took Truman aback, the two departed at the dark highway's edge. John Singer, helmetless, flicked a Winston butt out into the night as he kicked his motorcycle into life. Then he was gone, east toward the river.

Truman crossed the highway, for the darkness that blanketed Kuala Harap. Walking up into the sleeping town, he spooked a tailless cat. He also looked up, and thought the night sky incredibly starry.

* * *

Oct. 25, 1980

I'm in a bus heading back from K.L. I got my final Rest H. reimbursement $ & I'm sitting next to a guy who must have fish in his bag. We're crossing the mountains (very pretty). It's hard to believe they have monkeys & lizards & shit in them. This bus driver (like everyone here) drives like a madman.

I'm finally living in the shed behind the home. It's not too bad—except for the mosquitoes. I have to burn those coils, like in training. I've got the rest of the place all tore up.

The ladies cut off all Ramasami's hair. He looks like a little brown, scarred-up dickhead, mumbling & chattering away. Little Salleh also got the buzz, but looks cute pitching his little naked tantrums & biting at the others.

Still 10/25—later at night at home (bus ride a bitch)

I got home to a letter from Angela (waiting in the mail). She loves college & has all these new friends. She didn't mention Kyle & I don't know why. It was a nice letter, though—fresh & clean. I'll write back real soon.

John Singer came by, as he said he would & I was happy about that. I showed him all around the place—sort of proud & sort of not. Zurina made a big fuss over his fluent Malay & he was real nice to the kids (the ones who didn't bolt). Of course, he was already known—in a way—to Zurina & Fatimah. We're getting together tonight for a few beers—should be fun (me & John, that is).

Oh yes, down in Batu Pahat—where I stayed with that Malay family (& where we watched those guys hopping around on toy horses), a bunch of whacko fundamentalist Muslims attacked a police station hacking up everyone in sight with swords & machetes. (Even a pregnant lady got it!) It's all over the New Straits Times. *I guess they caught them all. It's strange to think that those kooky fuckers were down there hatching their scheme while I was down there wandering around, holding in a big shit!*

Well, all's nice & quiet inside the Home & the bugs are singing so pretty outside. (Last night I could hear Azman hooting & spinning away late at night. I guess the girls & the kids are used to it.) A monsoon shower slammed us a bit ago & cooled things down. I have a sore thumb thanks to Ramasami's help & I've discovered that little Lim steals fish from the kitchen & hides them beneath her bed & eats them at night—SCALES & ALL.

We also have a hen & 3 chicks hanging around. I hope they stay. The mother's missing half her feathers. She came to the right place!

CHAPTER 10

November 4, 1980

I've run out of work until shiftless Azman lets go of any of that 1,000 ringgits.

This morning Ramasami & I cleaned out the bathroom. (For people who detest pigs, they sure do live like them sometimes.) Our toilets, though, are regular ones—I guess left over from the British—not like the others here—porcelain holes in the floors that you squat over, that Dave called post-bender launch pads. Here at the Home, these people stand on top of these regular toilets, squatting over them—no one sits—not even me—too filthy.

Last Sunday John & I rode about 15 miles south of here to a little town he knew of (smaller than Kuala Harap & all Chinese) & started on a drinking spree that lasted until 12:30 at night. The town was Menkarak, south of here following the river & then through rubber plantations until you come to it. It reminded me of one of those dusty towns in Hang 'Em High *or* High Plains Drifter*—only surrounded with jungle and plantations. I hope we go back. It was a lot of fun. He & I are getting to be pretty good friends. Like me, his mother died when he was little (he didn't say of what), but his dad raised him (pretty old now & still up in Buffalo). He sort of joked that his "Barlow" brought him up.*

As for everything else, the Home & the town & the people & my little shed are getting better. Having John helps. I do like that slow, muddy river & the cooling rains & these nutty kids. Ramasami still loves helping & he pushes Normah now (in her wheelchair—but she doesn't trust him—who does?). The kids are also starting to roam outside a bit & that makes me happy. The elections back home are tomorrow. I guess Reagan has it. John says not to fear—big Teddy will save the day in '84, if he can avoid women, parties & 60 Minutes.

* * *

Days passed without tools or money. Truman kicked around for more cleaning and burning as every day's afternoon downpour ended his work, falling in heavy sheets through the trees, cleansing the little town above and pelting the river below as it moved, bound for the South China Sea.

Three goats wandered in. Truman wished they'd stay, not realizing someone owned them. He also patched the wooden fence that corralled their parched acre, using as a hammer a pulled-up piece of heavy angle iron against laying-around bent nails. He was thinking of the kids, who were beginning to venture some. Zurina hotly protested his closing the gaping holes. Fatimah stayed quiet. Normah howled in delight, later costing the cerebral-palsied girl a couple of slaps.

John Singer swung by on his cycle, usually about suppertime as their friendship quietly jelled. One evening, with Truman a little down, he suggested the Kedua, a coffee house amongst the row of shops that lined the highway. Truman hadn't noticed it.

Once inside, Truman grew happy. It was dark, and cooled with air conditioning. Along one side ran a bar like any nicer one in New Jersey, Truman guessed. The tables and the booths were clean and orderly. Smiling Chinese waitresses stood at the ready in dandy blue uniforms. They were the only women there.

"I had no idea Kuala Harap had a place like this," said Truman.

"Nearly every town has one, if there're Chinese around. Mentacab has two, ten miles from here."

A waitress approached, beaming at Singer. "May I bring you a jug and menus?"

"A jug of Carlsberg. Thank you." Singer smiled, directing Truman to a nearby table lit with a stubby candle.

"Do they all speak English?" Truman asked.

"Enough to get by, I imagine."

The girl brought their pitcher of beer that the two wouldn't have to touch with their waitress nearby. "So this is a coffee house?" Truman asked.

"Yep," replied Singer, as he raised his glass to drink long.

"I heard of these places in training. That guy Dave I told you about, talked of one in Melacca he used to hit."

Singer lit a Winston, then nodded, acknowledging a well-dressed Chinese man behind the bar.

"Who's that?" Truman asked.

"The boss. Everyone calls them 'Captain' for some reason."

"If this is a bar, then—"

"It's not a bar. Not in Malaysia. This is a coffee house. Bars here are shadier. At best, massage parlors with whores as masseuses." Singer smiled. "Like that one in the trio of shops up by the bridge."

"The Alpine Bar's a whorehouse?" Truman asked eagerly.

"Well, in an under-the-table, under-the-law, sort of way. This isn't Thailand or anything."

"Have you been there?"

"Once in a while. It's not a good habit."

"What do they do?" Truman leaned forward, smiling.

Singer glanced at the waitress shadowing their table. Misreading him, she pulled her lighter from her apron that matched her uniform. Singer waved her off.

"So sorry." She smiled, eyes to a squint.

"Jesus, Truman, calm down." Singer smiled.

"Just curious. There's got to be something to do in this town."

"Not much, Truman. Anyway," Singer continued, "it's just a grungy bar with these throw-away women as barmaids, except they sit with you, and flirt and shit while you drink outrageously expensive beer. If you want an *urut*, Malay for massage, you pick your girl and you go upstairs, to some little room, and she'll give you a half-assed backrub topped off with a hand job."

"Do guys fuck 'em?"

"Some of the girls. The cripples and the twice-divorced, I suppose," Singer replied. "I'm sorry. That's not very nice. Anyway, if that's what you want, you have to be clear about it in the chummy stage downstairs. If the girl you're with isn't interested, she'll direct you to one who is."

Their squinting waitress approached, emptying their jug into their glasses, then hustled off for another. Singer wanted to know about the funny name of New Egypt. Truman couldn't explain it. Then they talked of the cute waitresses, then of the elections back home. Singer knew Carter was gone when he heard, broadcast from the Voice Of America, that the campaigning President lost Florida.

"It's not true south," Singer explained, needing someone to listen, "with a good deal of Reagan's peers out-to-pasture down there, but it spells doom for Carter."

As the sun fell outside the big circular window of the Kedua, Truman told John Singer of his shyness toward him weeks before. Singer confirmed that he didn't wish for the clinging of a new volunteer, but added that he was certainly enjoying their young friendship. He angered, though, when Truman told him, "I was sort of warned away from you, by that Bruce Statton fellow, in the van returning from Penang."

Singer drew hard from a fresh Winston. "You're deemed a fucking recluse if you don't have your head up some other American's ass half the time. You'll see." He exhaled. "A handful of nice people, and a couple of dicks will sprinkle through, wanting to stay a night or two, then off to fucking talk about you, or your job. If you don't hit their parties in Kuala Lumpur, two or three straight, speculation will have you married off to a local, or half-crazed."

Then Singer changed the subject. "So tell me about your work," he asked.

And Truman did, as honestly as he could.

A jug later, with a polite bow, their uniformed waitress lit John Singer's last cigarette, ceremoniously handing them their bill on a decorative, stainless steel plate.

* * *

Two days later, Azman showed up at the Home. The kids were sitting for lunch. Truman was wiring the seat of Normah's wheelchair with twisted lengths of clothes hanger.

Ramasami, yammering, ran to Encik Azman, pointing to Truman, the wheelchair, and over to Normah, who sat off in the cooler darkness upon the smooth concrete floor.

"Yes, yes, I see Mr. Truman fixing the chair," Azman said, wasting his English, patting the boy's head without touching it.

"We're just wiring it up a bit," Truman reported from his kneeling position, working an unruly length of wire.

"Why are you using a clothes hanger?"

"It's all we've got." Truman smiled, with three final twists.

"I see."

From the shadows, Azman the crazed resident, came up fast, bow-legged, shorts undone, barefoot and circling. He slapped at his head, shrieked and ran off.

Azman the sane, recoiled. "Oh my. That one is quite wild. I believe he may be dangerous. Do you think it so?"

"The girls and the kids aren't afraid of him." Truman stood. "I really don't know what's the matter with him. He hasn't done anything dangerous, though."

"Well, Mr. Truman, we have your 1,000 ringgits. At my office. You may begin withdrawing in 100 ringgit amounts. I will require your records periodically."

Truman brightened, but steadied to the "records" idea. He had forgotten to ask John Singer about it. "Thank you. I mean, terima kasih for your help."

"*Sama sama*. But you may speak English to me," answered Encik Azman as he turned neatly, keeping the other Azman in his peripheral vision as he strode out to his car.

* * *

With resources at last, John Singer provided Truman with a ruled petty cash book that took minutes to learn. "It's as easy as balancing a checkbook."

"Never had one. Only a savings account."

"Damn near the same thing," Singer replied.

Then up to the larger Chinese hardware shop Truman strode.

Tools came first, bought from the heavyset proprietor: two shovels, a heavier rake, paint and brushes and thinner, a saw, a sledgehammer, and a handle for a claw head rescued from the ashes. From the heavyset man's seeming wife, a silent, skinny woman, with an unusually hooked nose for an oriental, Truman bought nails of several weights, a bigger sickle, a trash can, pliers, and twenty meters of light rope. Not forgetting the kids, and happy to be working, he visited a shop across the street, manned by a jolly Malay and his own seeming wife, buying tennis balls to bat around, a tricycle, a wagon and two kickballs.

* * *

Nov. 18, 1980

Well, Reagan's going to be our next President. I don't know much about that stuff, but John is horrified. Ben (in his last letter) wasn't—he was more excited about the Sultan of Johor's birthday message in the New Straits Times *about being on guard against religious deviants. It was about those whackos down south chopping up those people at that police station.*

At the Home I've hit things with a big punch with all the tools & stuff I bought—except for two days ago when I took a cab to Mentacab for the hell of it. I saw a shitty movie, ate in this shop & then the next thing I knew, I was headed down this alley (on my way to the taxi stand) & I got real sick & started to shiver. I got so weak I had to kneel down & puke like crazy in this gutter (& boy did I ever!). Some people came by & I heard them say "dia mabut" but I didn't have any beer. It had to be that smelly fucking chicken that I figured to be some local recipe or something. Anyway, no cab would take me home but some guy (a big Indian guy) in an old truck brought me back here to K.H. I was almost afraid to go to sleep that night thinking I might even die or something. (I was sick as hell!) Anyway, John S. was out of town & I felt better yesterday just lying around in the shade—eating nothing.

Last night I dreamed wild stuff (maybe I'm still sick?). I went to sleep early after watching the big moon & the stars through my glassless window. I dreamed of Scotty Winslow & of being chased by dogs in my Dart that floated down the road unsteerable. Then I was at the track bed & a train somehow came along. I jumped on it & rode it back to New Egypt where Mabel & Angela were waiting for me. Mabel hugged me but Angela cried that she was stuck & couldn't move. (She could only lean way forward—I mean, really way forward.)

Anyway, I woke up this morning feeling much better. Some of those buffalos wandered by (working on the grass outside the fence). They didn't stare or ask me stupid questions about my name or America or Europe. Oh yes, 2 cats fought outside my window—that's what woke me.

The rain wails us pretty regular now that it's the season for it. It's crazy, hot as hell. Wham. It falls in curtains, then hot as hell again before it comes from nowhere to wail us again for good measure.

I still have no friends to speak of. Locals, that is, except for Zurina (bitchy lately) & quiet Fatimah. John's still out of town, somewhere over by Kuantan for his job. (That helps my drinking—but then again, I damn near died without him.) Ramasami likes smacking the tennis balls around with a piece of wood & little Salleh can't eat his rice w/o getting it all over his forehead.

Can't think of much more.

* * *

Near November's end, with the rains coming harder, Truman switched to painting and patching up indoors. He also needed more hardware to start his promised playground. His initial 200 ringgits ran out, and Azman became harder to find, claiming, when found, "Tomorrow will be better, Mr. Truman. Please return this afternoon," and so on, and grinning to boot.

Truman wrote in his journal of his growing disdain for his Malay boss, likening him to having a Boy Scout in charge, placing manners before decision. He was warned of this in training. He logged these thoughts along with his contemplating the upcoming Kuala Lumpur Thanksgiving gala, and a surprising offer to buy elephants from two youths late one night as he walked home alone. Singer straightened him out. The quick-talking teens were moving marijuana, not elephants.

The first weekend after Singer's return, Singer and Truman also weaved south again, for the secluded shops of Mengkarak on Singer's cycle. Mengkarak was haunting and perfect with its slow-moving people ambling amongst the livestock that roamed the single dirt street.

In their corner kedai, John Singer chain-smoked with his feet crossed upon a pulled-out chair. Truman leaned forward most of the afternoon, elbows on the table, listening to news from Buffalo, via a letter from a first cousin of Singer's, a college student several years his junior. There was a girl "with flesh the color of freshly-baked muffins." Elvis Costello came to town "dancing on his ankles." A mutual friend was "suddenly married off," the letter sighed, "pulled into the great domestic abyss." All this, and more, signed off with, "Shape the clay, cuz . . ."

The cousin didn't mention John Singer's ex-wife, a woman Truman didn't know existed until that afternoon, as Truman ventured thoughts of the ideal home—a farm snuggled off somewhere in New Jersey, surrounded by pines, blue skies, four seasons.

"You won't have shit, if you don't have love," Singer added.

With his shirt stuck to his back with sweat, Truman asked, "What do you mean?"

"I'm just saying, Truman," he said as he tapped another Winston from his pack, "farms and front porches and neighbors won't amount to anything if you can't share it."

Singer lit his cigarette, snapping his stainless steel lighter shut. "I mean a real wife. A good one. She wouldn't have to be beautiful, just true. Believe me. I know."

With this, John Singer shared his brief, lost marriage. Adding, "I don't like thinking of it, but I guess I have been this afternoon."

As a lone rooster and four hens made their way toward their kedai, scratching at the dust, Truman learned she was a college girlfriend. They married and shared an apartment for just under two years when things failed. They were house-hunting at the time. John Singer was in Malaysia four months later.

Singer laughed, swinging his muscular calves down from their chair. Condensate from their beers pooled on their table. "Let's talk about happy shit. Like a Mengkarak town meeting. Who's been eyeing Chow's young wife? And what about all the goose shit over at Lim's place?"

Truman brightened. They talked of Singer's recent trip to the east coast. Truman shared his boyhood window-peeking route. "We're all voyeurs." Singer winked. "Why do you think TV's such a hit?"

John Singer braved his way to Truman's scar, then listened to the story. "Let's send the Rowlands a postcard," he joked. "Really. It's not the alcohol. 'Greetings from the banks of the mighty Pahang.' "

Then their conversation edged sad again, at least for Truman, as Singer talked of another trip in four weeks. A month-long recreational jaunt over to Sumatra, then down through Indonesia, leaving Truman alone in Kuala Harap.

Truman wondered aloud, "Everyone in my training group talked the same way."

"You ought to consider traveling some, as long as you're here," Singer advised.

"I sort of figure I'm already on a journey," Truman replied.

John Singer, as drunk as Truman, smiled. A lone hen stepped up into their open-air shop, scavenging fast before being shooed off by an aged Chinese woman.

* * *

Two days later Truman bought a bicycle, a plain, straight-framed black thing, identical to nearly every bicycle in Malaysia. In the New Egypt of his childhood they called them English bikes, and quarreled whether each other's really came from England or Japan.

On his second night with his new bike, Truman spooked four teens on the narrow road that led up from the bridge along the river. Two jumped into karate-like stances. Truman wrote in his journal: "You don't see shit like that in Cream Ridge." He was on his way home from Kuala Harap's lone movie house, down on the highway, across from the Alpine Bar. He saw *Oliver's Story*, subtitled in Malay, and thought it stunk having seen *Love Story* on TV with Mabel. Late that night, he lay in his shed listening to the crickets, and to joyous laughter between Zurina and Fatimah within their own back room in the main building, having an unusually festive evening.

* * *

By November's end, Azman returned, roaming the grounds, inspecting Truman's progress before proclaiming more funds could be secured. He studied Truman's petty cash book, asking nothing of Truman, who learned later from Fatimah that his Malay supervisor thought all the painting and repair a waste of money. Hurt and angered, Truman wrote in his journal: "I still aim to clean this shithole up."

The next day, loaded with 200 more ringgits, Truman returned to the Chinese hardware shop up over the hill, buying light bulbs, more paint, three rollers, thinner, and a wire brush. He also tried to return the lighter of two shovels, which bent on him while digging a drainage ditch off the back of the building. The heavyset proprietor, Mr. Tan, went earnest, then angry, at the mere thought of what was being asked of him. Truman, caught off guard, apologized as best he could in fumbling Malay, interspersed with English whenever the man chose to use what little he knew, littered with a litany of "Johns." Behind him, the big man's hooked-nosed rail of a wife moved silently, as though never hearing any of it.

On his second trip, big man Tan wasn't in. So Truman apologized again to his wife about the shovel as he selected another. She answered nothing in return. From his cultural training, he thought her too young to be wearing her matching, pajama-like garb that the Chinese women, middle-aged and beyond, tended to wear. Maybe because she was a touch homely, or not too bright, as she tallied the costs of his new shovel, a post-hole digger, a level and a square.

* * *

Into December Ramasami and chubby Lim became Truman's near constant companions as he worked. Even Normah, in her good-enough-for-now wheelchair, pushed by smelly Kumari, joined them around the grounds, between the daily monsoons that ripped the skies, cooling Truman's digging, painting and light building. From an Indian friend of Singer's, who nosed around one afternoon, Truman learned that Ramasami wasn't just a bumbling fool, but was, ". . . perhaps a little stupid, but he's very much speaking Tamil." It made sense to Truman, for the boy was indeed picking up Truman's limited Malay, and bits of his English profanity from following him sunup to sundown.

In the meantime, Singer's impending traveling settled in Truman as a need to strike out.

"Make a few friends," John Singer told him. "Or take the journey inward. Learn a martial art, or to play the guitar or something. Hell, I've read fifteen or twenty books, novels and nonfiction things since I've been here. It's been a solace, and damned good for me."

"I've never read a book from cover to cover," Truman admitted. "But I might give it a try."

Late at night, Truman heard Ramasami hollering out from within the stilled darkness of the converted garage. Zurina offered it as proof that he was pig-crazy. Fatimah said it came in cycles, perhaps the moon, or ghosts.

A letter came from Angela. Truman read it several times across several days. She and Kyle were still together, but at odds. The farm was dull and she seldom saw Mabel, ". . . who must tote your letters everywhere," apparently producing them whenever the two crossed paths. Angela didn't write of the cold of the coming winter, of Halloween and Thanksgiving, of the chilly mornings out in the quiet fields, or if the help ever asked of him.

Then more heavy rains, as headquarters in Kuala Lumpur mailed out obligatory Christmas party invitations. In Kuala Harap, the only sign of the impending holiday came from a small pocket of Chinese Christians from Mentacab, west across the forests and rubber plantations, as Truman and John Singer managed to get together every evening, at least for supper, if not a few beers. They even planned a modest hurrah to last Truman his month alone.

With a growing coolness, Azman released more money. Truman spread himself out, patronizing the Malay hardware shop for more paint and two different weights of nails. Two days later, for lower prices, he returned to the Chinese shop for a hand drill, bits, hinges, and a series of nuts and bolts. Big Mr. Tan was helpful and congenial, perhaps having caught wind of Truman's patronizing his competitor, or content over the establishment of his ground rules regarding returned merchandise. Mr. Tan's wife spoke, too, quietly complimenting Truman on his Malay. With a quick, punching command in Chinese, big Mr. Tan sent her off for something in the back.

On his way home, bicycling carefully through the colorful pattern of Malay women sitting along the roadside, selling any-thing, Truman thought of the Chinese hardware couple. It dawned on him that the man's wife, with her sharply-bridged nose, re-minded him of a much younger girl in Jimmy's Alternative School. In spite of their separate races, they somehow looked alike. Then he thought of Angela's criticizing Jimmy's special school. Then Angela as a little girl, the clothesline, her Imlaystown grade school, one day Jimmy's school. He thought of that desperate day he bicycled there. Then Molly, his art therapist, almost startling him. For he could hear her voice as he meandered through the colorful, roadside women. If only Molly could see him now. How proud she'd be.

* * *

Dec. 6, 1980

Just a few quick notes. I'm tired as hell. One bad thing & one good one. First, John left town for a month. It was a bummer watching him take off. 30 days of K. Harap with all these Malays. We did, though, go on a bender that was a riot—embarrassing afterwards & pretty expensive. We wound up over in Mentacab slugging down some sort of brandy & then we made our way back to the Kedua & then down to the all-night truck stop.

Secondly, the good news. Things around here are picking up work-wise. With my new tools, I've got plenty to do. I've even constructed a bit of a shop here in my "living quarters" as John calls my shed. My lawn, too, is starting to take.

I've got sturdy shelves up next to where the kids sleep & more in the room where they eat which will be a classroom in a month or so. (I wish Azman—the one who dresses nice—would notice, or at least say something about it.)

Ben answered my last letter. It was nice after I feared boring him. He sent along a clipping from the New Straits Times *about an argument down in the Singapore gov. It read: "It's That Old Women In Politics Debate Again: Even If A Suitable Woman Is Found, Would Her Husband Allow Her To Enter?"*

Ben loved it. Maybe he's tired of all the "close proximity" arrests.

The kids are as warmed up to me as can be, I suppose. Even little Salleh is happy to see me. I guess he's the retarded type that's not funny-looking (if there is such a thing). Every once in a while—when Ramasami isn't howling—I can hear a ball bouncing around inside about 3 or 4 in the morning. I went out one night & peeked in through the caged door & saw little Salleh (in just a T-shirt) chasing one of the tennis balls around—all alone—with his tongue out & his little dick flipping about. I guess there aren't ghosts for those who can't imagine them.

CHAPTER 11

Dec. 7, 1980

I got my lst real haircut here, from some big hairy Indian barber up in town. He finished the job by cracking my neck with 2 swift jerks. Shocked the shit out of me!

A couple of nights ago I came back a bit loaded from the one highway shop about 2 a.m. (on the river road) & ran smack into 3 of those kirbow (sp?) buffalos. I have no idea why, in that moonless night, THEY went rumbling off from me & my rattling bike. I thought I was a goner.

I'm building a playground platform beneath the Go Dog Go tree. Ramasami helped me drop a 15 ft. beam on my foot. What a 'tard. Later though (after supper) I found him out there barking senseless shit to Lim as he drew lines & scribbles on pieces of scrap lumber (playing grown-up?).

For some reason I also thought a lot today about when I first got my monkey bike when I was little & how hard it was peddling through the sand back in Chatsworth. Maybe I'm homesick w/o John. I'll call Mabel in a few days.

* * *

The next morning Truman rattled his bike up into town for his breakfast and morning newspaper, to bold, front-page news. The familiar face struck him. The story was in Malay. John Lennon was dead, gunned down on the other side of the world in front of his wife and home.

Truman wondered if Singer had heard, for he owned several of Lennon's tapes, one a new release. Singer had also lamented, over beers at their truck stop, of the inevitable resurrection of the songwriter's career. "After all," Singer had claimed, "he was the angry soul of the fab four. You know what I mean? Paul's polar opposite."

Eating his breakfast, Truman then thought of Scotty Winslow's mother, her 45s, then one song, "Eleanor Rigby."

Returning to the Home, and sharing his news, Truman learned that Zurina and Fatimah had never heard of the Beatles, let alone John Lennon or Yoko Ono. Zurina, however, had cheerfully heard of Elvis Presley, and asked Truman if the two men were friends. Younger Fatimah, listening in, and taking to the New York City theme of the killing, asked Truman if he ever saw the Statue Of Liberty, believing it the tallest man-made structure in the world. Truman told her that he hadn't, although he lived within sixty miles of the thing, before correcting her, explaining Chicago's Sears Tower, provoking thoughts of Mabel. Fatimah remained skeptical, returning to her laundry.

Across the following week, Truman erected his combination swing set-fort beneath the shady reaches of the great tree. At the Chinese hardware shop he bought larger, flat-headed drill bits for the woodwork, more nails, hinges and another padlock. Another jaunt, to the Malay shop, after Zurina's urging, got him eye bolts, more thinner, and several lengths of light chain.

One afternoon, Azman, quietly nosing about, approached Truman.

"I wish to speak, quite secretly. Confidentially, if I may."

"Certainly, Mr. Azman," Truman answered.

"It seems that the girls, probably Zurina, are having guests. Male visitors during the night." Under the spreading shade of the great tree, Encik Azman added, "Have you heard, or seen, anything suspicious?"

Truman didn't need to feign interest. The subject had universal appeal, and at last his boss had something of an interest in the place.

"I don't know," Truman answered. "But I'll keep an eye out." He recalled Zurina's flustering at his patching up the gaping holes in the fence.

"Thank you, Mr Truman," Azman said. Then he paused. "I remind you, close proximity is unlawful in Malaysia. My office does not need to be involved in a police matter."

"I understand," answered Truman, thinking fast of Jimmy McCleary and their window-peeking route. Jimmy would flip. Pay dirt.

* * *

A week before Christmas, Truman called Mabel for the second time since he'd been in Malaysia, from a hotel desk in Mentacab, at 7:30 in the morning.

The liveliness of her voice surprised him, after waiting ten minutes for the overseas' operator to connect them. She had a bulk of ready news, her eager voice warm. The Van Heflins were fine. The farm missed him. "You wouldn't believe how often people ask about you, honey," she stretched.

"I think it's still your 'yesterday' here, Truddy," Mabel said, "and we're in this cold snap."

Truman tried hard to imagine New Egypt, 8:30 at night, dark and cold and blowing against Mabel's back screen door.

He tried to explain Kuala Harap and his job. She claimed pride, calling him a saint. He must have somehow misled her. Then came their good-byes. So hard that Mabel had to assign Truman to hang up first, sending herself, with wet eyes, to her coffeemaker, as young Truman turned out into the morning heat, for the taxi stand a block away.

Refreshed, Truman worked hard that day. A letter arrived from Ben, which helped. Enclosed was a clipping from the *New Straits Times* titled, "Our Way Of Life Better, People Told." Truman saw it a week earlier. A political bigwig down in Johor predicted the collapse of western civilization, appealing to Malaysian youths to not be seduced by ruinous ways.

Truman wrote back, regarding both Azmans, and of his jaunts up into town, Ramasami stumbling along, insisting upon greeting every passerby within earshot. He wrote of the same article, asking if Ben caught the one about campus dating at the University of Malaya. Apparently coeds, restricted from fraternizing after sunset, had been using the university library, and Kuala Lumpur's department stores for illicit get-together chit-chats.

But in spite of staying busy, the days before Christmas grew sad for Truman as he finished Zurina and Fatimah's clothesline after securing the swing-set crossbars off the end of the big fort. He also moved the mailbox from across the road, to the mouth of the pitted driveway, claiming he wanted no one crossing the road for mail, regardless of how little the road was used. In his journal, he wasn't quite sure why he did this.

Days later he dumped hard on his bike, short-cutting down a muddy hillside south of the bridge. A day after that he fell from the top of the framework of the fort, slamming hard upon stacked lumber below. Ramasami and chubby Lim were there, equally stunned. Thick tongued, chubby Lim hustled inside for the help that squealed and hobbled out from the back of the building.

Bruised and aching, Truman went out that evening for his supper, then two evenings more for a couple of beers. But the Kedua and the highway shops weren't the same without John Singer.

* * *

Dec. 27, 1980

Well, my 1st Christmas in Malaysia wasn't too bad. I spent it down at the Kedua. Surprisingly, a lot of people told me "Merry" or "Happy Christmas." Even strangers—I guess because I'm white.

Most of the painting's done. Ramasami's help was a disaster. (He's probably tough to trust with a dry paint brush!) I had a nice chat out front the other night with Zurina & Fatimah about the stars. I wish I knew more about them (the stars, that is). They call falling stars "bintang tahit" which means star shit or poop or whatever. I tried to explain what they really are but the girls didn't seem interested. It was fun though, with half the kids out there & all. Ramasami's a killer—staring up & yammering away—nodding his head & all like he understands everything.

Azman (the nutty one) is getting to be more fun. If I bring food back from lunch he comes around like a begging dog. I hate to admit it but after teasing him with it (saying "Back off, motherfucker, back off!"), it makes the others laugh because they don't understand the English. But I think maybe he can be trained like a dog (by using food, I mean—not rolling over & shit like that). We'll see. Back to Ramasami—the little shit can't share any of the new stuff— crams it all into the tattered bags he lugs around & hangs on his bedpost & guards. I felt like spanking him a couple of times.

The other day some toothless man up in town stopped me & asked me in English if I spoke English. I said yes & asked him the same & he answered, "Bukon, John," with a big grin. I don't know why he asked in the first place. I guess it's like that "Poly vue . . ." stuff kids say. Or maybe I'm getting to be a neighbor around here.

Big Dave wrote to me about the P.C. Xmas party I missed. He said it was great—he even "damn near got some white pussy." (John S. says he doesn't care if he ever gets the pleasure of meeting him.) Dave also wrote that people asked about me—which made me happy. (John will say that that means they talked about you as far as P.C. parties go.)

Well, Merry Christmas for now. I'm going to go out & get some fried rice & a beer or two.

* * *

Two days later the mailman peddled up out front on his red bicycle and jingled his thumb bell. "Mr. Truman!" he called out from his balanced load. "*Ada surat dari Amerika!*"

Three letters and a *Newsweek*. Mrs. Van Heflin wrote. So did Ben, and a fat one from Mabel, containing pictures, four pages of chat and a money order for $100 in U.S. currency. Two hundred and forty in ringgits hoped Truman, money toward a motorcycle, or a trip with John Singer. Zurina, wondering over the money order, asked Truman if that's what American money looked like. Truman told her, in Malay, "No, but it's good enough for me."

That afternoon he bicycled down to his Bank Bumi Putra, to discover that they wouldn't touch the money order. A manager, or somebody who kept him waiting for nearly an hour, briskly instructed him to visit another bank. "Somewhere else," he added in English.

"Would they help me at The Bank Of America in K.L.?" asked Truman, staying in English.

"Excuse me," the man spoke briskly. "I do not understand you."

Returning to Bahasa, Truman asked again. "*Munkin Bank de Amerika tolong saya dalam Kuala Lumpur?*"

"Yes. Exactly. And there is no need to speak Bahasa with me. My English is fine. Yours is not. Too fast. Have a good day."

So out Truman strode, into the strength of the midday heat, pissed off.

He peddled up into town, to the Chinese hardware shop. A group of Malay teens, not helping, called out a jumbled chorus of, "Hey, John." They were all over, these aimless packs of the well-dressed unemployed, seeking shade. These Malaysians bothered Truman the most. The idle young, near his own age, broke, with nothing to do, and having a ball.

At Tan's shop Truman bought more paint and thinner, a keypunch and a planer that Mr. Tan sent his obedient wife into the back for. Surprising Truman, Mr. Tan then barked in tough English, "My American friend, I invite you to a Chinese New Year's party on the roof of The Pahang Hotel."

Truman knew the building, Kuala Harap's lone hotel, anchoring the stringing of shops that lined the East-West Highway.

Truman thanked the big man earnestly, assuring him he'd be there.

* * *

Three days later Truman walked down to the highway, in clean jeans and a short-sleeved button-up shirt, scrubbed that morning upon the concrete slab of the Home's back porch.

Tentatively, he ascended the three flights of steps, to the hotel's roof, emerging through a doorless opening, amongst some thirty people milling about.

A big red sun lay on the western horizon. All were Chinese, save several Indians. Truman couldn't find Mr. Tan amongst the faces that looked to him. He approached a friendly looking group of Chinese men, introducing himself, asking for the merchant, Mr. Tan.

"Yes, yes!" bellowed the oldest of the four. "You're the new American. Mr. Tan said nothing about you, but you are among friends. How do you like our western-style party?"

Truman agreed it was nice as the four men described their Chinese New Year as something akin to America's Christmas. Truman recalled this from training. Politely, he asked for more, and got it, the month-long praying to lost relatives and friends, the preparations and the making of amends to the wronged. The skinniest of the four added, "But, John, this business, this night, however, is merely a party." Smiling so wide, Truman let the "John" slide.

And a party it was. There was beer, food and music, as the rooftop became more crowded as the sun fell, but still no Mr. Tan, legitimizing Truman. Some danced to the mix of Chinese music and western pop. Others drank and laughed loudly amongst the strung-up colored lights that lit their revelry above the highway below.

Truman, an object of curiosity, enjoyed the attention.

There were questions in fluent and struggling English, and in Malay, too, ranging from helmeted American football, to life in southern California. Truman knew little of the second, while happily fielding the questions he could answer, many rooted in misconceptions borne of syndicated episodes of *BJ and The Bear*, *Dallas* and *Eight Is Enough*. Truman's newest male friends wondered earnestly of the promiscuity of American women. Truman thought of Angela, on her holiday break, with winter's breath resting about the farm, angering quietly at their happy suspicions. Then a drunk Chinese man wanted a cowboy hat, at any price.

"One of your own. I will pay for, John."

Truman disappointed him, never having owned one.

Truman had given up on Mr. Tan when a young Chinese girl approached him, introducing herself as a primary grade schoolteacher over in Mentacab. Her hair was curled. Her thick glasses comically enlarged her eyes.

She gave her name. Truman missed it, taken aback with her. "I am a Catholic Christian," she added in the same breath, as though her faith was a part of her name.

But their conversation went clumsy, with Truman unable to define whatever it was he was up to at the Home.

The goggled young teacher, in her limited English, asked, "Did you wish to be a teacher, but were declined?"

"No. I'm kind of too young. I didn't go to college."

She countered fast. "I just became twenty years, and I am a teacher." Singer explained later that a barber with connections could teach elementary school in Malaysia.

She brought up Israel, a nation their Islamic government denied, one Truman only recently began to understand, having listened to Ben, and learned more of from the ramblings of John Singer. She demanded an explanation regarding the intimate American-Israeli relationship.

Truman, feeling the beer, offered the United Nations granting the birth of the tiny nation a generation before, along with any nation's right to deal with any other it pleased, knowing next to nothing of Jimmy Carter's lone triumph at Camp David.

"But the Jews have stolen so much land," she snapped.

"They were attacked twice. Won both wars," Truman replied, hoping he got the number right.

She went stern, big eyes and all. "They started the one fighting. How do you Americans explain that?"

"I didn't know we had to. At least not me, anyway," Truman tried to joke, having wandered into unlearned waters, political and social.

And as quick, their conversation turned adversarial. No exchanges of culture, their relative youth or ideas of future as she thanked him for their brief acquaintance, and excused herself back to her friends. Truman thanked her in return, then mingled, quickly tiring of the same questions. Feeling a failure, he slipped out, down the three flights of stairs, out into the night beneath the hoopla of the party above.

Restless, he crossed the dark highway for the shop where he first met John Singer. He sat alone and drank another beer, before walking home by way of the road that skirted the river. But up near the bridge, the Christmasy lights of the Alpine Bar caught his attention. The surrounding shops and lone theater were closed up and dark. The Alpine stood alone, twinkling in the stillness of the night, promising another chance.

Truman crossed the road, figuring himself brave without Singer. His nerves heightened, in spite of the alcohol. He jumped the wide gutter, and swung the door open, stepping into the dark room of booths.

He stopped. There was no lengthy bar like at the Kedua, only candle-lit booths. Toward the back, heavy laughter erupted at a counter beneath numbers suspended from the ceiling. In the smoky light, three girls stood about the opened-up wall.

One, with a tray of drinks, left the lit counter. Truman stepped toward a central hub of four booths in the dark room. Painted panels of plywood divided each. He sat in an empty one. A candle flickered before him. The tabletop was sticky. From nowhere a woman appeared, startling him with her cheery, "Hello. *Boleh cakap Meleyu?*" as she sat next to him.

"Boleh." He smiled back.

She was a Malay, and much older than Truman. He guessed in her thirties, but stabbed at twenty-five when asked.

Apologizing for not knowing English, she asked in Malay, "May I join you, and get you a drink?"

Truman asked for a Carlsberg, and her company as well.

In her loose dress, she swept off to return with his beer, revealing purposeful cleavage, bending over. Truman went shy. She sat close. She was brown and thick, her right thigh flush against his own. She asked nice questions, but answered none. Her breath smelled like nice medicine. Truman didn't believe her name to be "Jane," but her thigh, paying such attention to his own, felt nice.

She asked Truman of his wife in America, as she stroked at his near arm.

"I'm not married," he answered in Bahasa.

"I do not believe that," she whispered to his ear, as her other hand slid off to work, beneath their candle-lit table.

Truman's legs closed. He flushed. But Jane's hand stayed, claiming the ground. Her smile opened her brown face as she found Truman's growing content. She whispered, "What more would you like to talk about?"

Truman told her he was on his way home. He worked at a place she never heard of. She ran her nose and face along his cheek, asking, "Would a massage be good for you, my American boyfriend?"

Truman straightened, hoping to gain some control. "How much would it cost? I don't have much money on me."

"Thirty ringgits. Twenty-five for you." She smiled, pinching the inside of his thigh.

Masculine laughter erupted from another booth. Truman asked, "What do I get? I'm sorry. I never had a massage before."

"What does my boyfriend want?" Her right breast rested on his arm. Her hand stayed to his jeans.

"A massage, and whatever comes with it." He fumbled with the syntax.

"You can not enter me. I am a Muslim," she answered, before startling him with sudden English. "No intercourse."

Truman shuddered, for he had never even kissed a girl. "Oh no. I didn't mean that," he quickly apologized in Malay. "Just a massage."

"Follow me." She smiled, her near breast rubbing him again as she rose from their booth.

Once standing, she instructed him to wait, as she returned to the busy, lit counter. She spoke to someone, then #19, on the board above the counter, blinked out from a switch thrown from somewhere.

Taking him by the hand, Jane led Truman up a narrow flight of stairs, into the yellow light of a dimly lit corridor serving four equally spaced flimsy doors.

Incense hung in the air. She opened the third. A room divided by plywood, making two smaller rooms within. Strung up curtains served as entrances. The curtain to the left was drawn closed. There was movement within.

Steering Truman within the other, Jane told him, "Take off your clothes," directing his attention to hooks on the plywood divider. A thin mattress lay on the floor. She covered it with a sheet from a neat stack in the corner. A candle lit their space as incense burned from a holder screwed to the plywood divider.

Jane became businesslike, lighting a second candle. She handed Truman a towel, more the size of one of Mabel's dish towels.

"I shall need the twenty-five ringgits. You may cover yourself with this if shy," she stated, forcing a smile. Truman stood, half aroused, in his underwear, digging into the pocket of his hanging jeans.

"Should I take off my underwear, too?" he asked, handing her the bills.

"Yes. Then lie down on your stomach." She folded the money, tucking it into a small bag, new to him.

Truman lay on his stomach, trying to adjust the small towel, peeking behind.

Jane slipped off her dress in a single movement, up over thick thighs, wide hips, an older woman's torso and messed flowing hair.

His heart leapt at her near-nakedness. He didn't want to stare. He wanted to be grown up, with his masseuse above him, in her underpants and brassiere, large and conservative, like Kathleen Van Heflin's, but flesh colored liked Fatimah's and Zurina's on his new line, the only color he'd seen in this country. Nothing skimpy and flowery, as Angela's had grown up to be on another line across the years.

Jane eased her weight upon the backs of his thighs. There was tapping. Talcum powder, in a cloud, pervaded their candlelight. Her hands fell upon his shoulders, his neck and upper arms. "Big muscles. Very strong," she cooed.

She moved lower, working hard at the small of his back. More talcum flew. Then sounds from their neighbors through the plywood. Then on to the muscles of the backs of his thighs and calves as she moved, spreading his legs with her own.

"Roll over," she commanded, with a slap to his buttocks.

He'd get to see her, above him, in her underwear. His small towel moved. He readjusted it. "*Jangon malu.*" she said, smiling, asking him not to be shy.

Then more talcum powder, in shaking quick clouds, as she worked on the fronts of his thighs. Her brown heaviness swayed as she worked. She moved her kneading nearer his hardness that moved beneath his towel. Then up to his chest and shoulders. Then more talcum as her own underwear-clad privacy slid hard against his own.

"Do you like this?" she asked the side of his face.

"Yes. It feels very good."

"We're almost finished," she answered, startling him, reaching back to undo her brassiere, letting it fall to his powdered chest, revealing brown breasts that hung long and narrow, unlike the supported fleshiness of minutes before.

"May I touch you?" Truman asked.

"No. I told you." She began lightly dragging the weight of her breasts in circular motions about his chest and stomach, then off to the reaches of his outstretched arms. Truman tightened.

She worked low, corralling Truman's hardness between her breasts, again in startling English. "Want masturbation?"

"Yes."

"Twenty more ringgits," she said as she worked, one breast at a time.

"Yes. Boleh."

She turned, and reached to a box of tissues that Truman also hadn't noticed, jerking several free in fast tugs. Then off to work she went. Clinically knowing her job. Truman arched, the tissues smothering his joy, staying to soak his lessening throbbing.

Truman hoped she'd be smiling. But she wasn't, not until she saw him looking.

Suddenly she was up, her brassiere on and fastened in seconds. Her dark dress pulled over her head and straightened before Truman could get to his feet.

He fumbled with his underwear as she asked for the extra money.

"Can you wait until I get my pants on?"

"Yes. I am sorry." She forced another smile.

Shirtless, Truman counted the extra twenty in the candlelight, and handed it to her. Jane looked suddenly angry.

She snuffed the candle, and with a quick turn she was out through their curtain of a door.

* * *

Truman dressed as fast as he could, sitting on the mattress on the floor, tying the laces of his work boots. Their remaining candle illuminated the small room in an uneven strobe as he noticed the wastebasket to the side of their small mattress. It was half-filled with balled-up tissues. It sickened him. Their room, the plywood, the incense that cloaked and witnessed. Even the talcum, that felt so good minutes before, clung to him like hardened bad air.

He made his way out. Someone sneezed in a nearby room.

Truman descended the narrow steps, and looked for her, finding her fast through the darkness, with another woman and two Chinese men in a far booth. He wanted to tell her good-bye, or anything at all. Instead, out the door he went, into the starry darkness, hoofing it hard along the quiet East-West highway, heading for the bridge, and the rutted road beneath, away from the cadence of the Alpine's twinkling lights, not thinking of not tipping her. Not knowing how women like her say good-bye.

That night Truman's partially built playground rested in the starry darkness amid lumber and sawhorses behind the converted six-bay garage, as Truman dreamed of New Egypt's Wawa mini-mart. Of the parking lot, then inside. Floating. Everything brightly lit. He floated to the cash register.

Truman knew the lone woman before him, but not from where. She turned to him, speaking Malay. Truman tried to speak to the man behind the counter, but nothing came out. Then Truman was outside, crossing the Wawa's asphalt parking lot, behind the same woman. Soaking wet, she turned to him. "I'm Mrs. Ferguson, from the trailer park. You know me," her mouth moved, "from my bathtub. Would you be my Valentine?" Then she melted away.

Several hours later, long after the hot Malaysian morning reclaimed the sky, Truman stirred into wakefulness. His head hurt. The smell of a spent mosquito coil filled his nose. He couldn't recall lighting it.

He sat up and went for his alarm, but it had not been set. He went to his rigged hose shower. He bathed in the cold water, scrubbing away the talcum that clung to him in creased lines. Toweling off he discovered Ramasami, Lim, and Normah in her wheelchair, waiting for him at his door, having already started their new day.

By noon, while pondering a bench swing overlooking the river, he recalled his dream, thinking of the woman from the trailer park. He thought of Jimmy McCleary, then he wondered of the woman's voice in his dream, never having heard her speak.

* * *

A week and a half later, Truman wrote:

January 11, 1981

It's another Sunday & my spirits have picked up. I spent the morning over in Mentacab at their Sunday market, reading the paper & drinking coffee. A group of rubber tappers to the south claim to have been jumped & beaten up by soldiers. (They have these areas called "Black Areas" where soldiers patrol because of communists in the jungles.) Anyway, the tappers say these soldiers ordered them to strip & then they whacked them in the nuts & shit. I believe it.

The tappers were poor Chinese down near John & I's Mengkarak & the soldiers are nearly all dipshit Malay boys who (as Ben said) seem to be more homosexual than heterosexual (if that's the word).

Another story (I wonder if Ben saw it) was about a school up in Kuala Trengganu hit with mass hysteria. These school kids started screaming & stuff & their nuttiness spread. In training, they said sometimes even the teachers hop in on it! The Malaysians—all of them—blame it on the "spirits" & call in Bomos (like witch Dr.s) to do their thing. I guess after a day or two everyone calms down. I'd like to see one of these mass flip-outs.

Around here I've gotten a lot done & I've stayed sober since—you know who (enough about Jane). I did get to the Kedua a few nights ago & as I sat there I got pissed off thinking about Azman talking down to me lately, every time I see him. Jesus, I'm the one who came here & found these kids (half of them naked & sitting in their own shit & piss) & decided to help with toys & a cleaner place & a yard (half of them still have this awful skin crap on them) Anyway, I should try to calm down. I'm starting to sound like the other teachers (not that I'm a real teacher). I asked for this job & I should just do it, but I do wish Azman would appreciate it—maybe Zurina, too. I think Fatimah sees how hard I'm trying. The kids do & that's what really matters. I can tell they're having more fun. (Hell, at least they're not afraid to walk outside anymore—a few of them, that is.) Speaking of which, here comes Ramasami—yelling about something—with Lim behind him waving her fat little arms all around.

"Hey! It's John!! He's back!!"

CHAPTER 12

Jan. 16, 1981

A few days ago I put this up for John's return. Since then all we've done is work by day & eat supper & drink by night. I told him about the Alpine & "Jane" & how I felt all cruddy. He laughed & said it's supposed to be cruddy for nice guys at first.

Last Tues. or so, Zurina & Fatimah & I had a nice chat out back with the kids playing about. They wanted to know certain English words for this & that & they laughed, repeating them to one another. I learned again that Kuala Lumpur stands for "muddy junction" & Kuala Harap for "hope junction." (This place needs some.)

John bought another cycle—his 2nd since he's been here. I didn't have the $ to buy his old one (damn that Jane).

The playground's shaping up & so is my adjustment, I think. I like strolling up into town for a break, or for lunch. Little Salleh & Ramasami are afraid of the seesaws & of swinging too high on the twin swings. But Lim's a bull for punishment. Ramasami still squirrels stuff up in his plastic bags that he hangs from his bedposts. I went through one (to his proud joy) & found rags, bent nails & bunches of clothes. Then big old Kumari limped over to take a peek & he flipped out, grabbing all five or six bags before jumping on top of his unmade bed (a stand of sorts?).

I've spent more time out at John's kumpang house (kumpang means village—in case I forget someday) & that's been fun. He respects his neighbors (all Malays) so no drinking too much or pissing outside (except where you're supposed to) or drunk stuff in general. There're little kids EVERYWHERE. Even John can't figure out who belongs to who. Everyone's related & they even seem to switch houses at times.

Received Christmas cards from Mabel's office pals who I hardly know. One from Angela & one from her mother & Chet (just cards, no letters).

* * *

On the other side of the world, Ronald Reagan was sworn in as America's fortieth President the day after Truman and John Singer came off their reunion bender.

John Singer raved of impending political disaster. "After all," he said, as he chain-smoked, "the man's crowning achievement came at the side of a fucking chimpanzee. California probably ran itself on the backs of migrants, the aerospace technologies and the man's own proposed values, churned out as stories in Hollywood."

Truman, not feeling qualified to hop in, hoped he was wrong. But he was also happy, having finished his towering playground fort with its attached seesaw and swing set. The kids loved the ramp for the wheelchairs. To Truman's mild disappointment, they spent inordinate time simply hobbling up and down the ramp's planked length. The entire structure needed painting, which Truman decided to work around setting up the classroom inside, which quietly haunted him. For a first, he didn't mind Azman's reluctance to come up with more funds.

In the following weeks he and John Singer saw one another daily, for at least something to eat down along the highway, or over in Mentacab for a movie. Through an office acquaintance, John Singer was invited to a Hindu wedding, south in Kuala Pilah. He insisted on Truman's company.

"Sure, you can come along. Didn't you pay attention in training? They're nothing like in America. Besides," he furthered, filling his glass with his first beer in two days, "they're a hell of a lot cheerier than their Malay counterparts, and less organized, if you can imagine that."

"I just don't want to go all the way down there to get kicked out," Truman said. "I also don't have any nice clothes to wear."

"Don't need them. Just put a good buffin' on those boots of yours, and we'll both be shining in that crowd."

Singer wiped the foam of his beer from his mouth. "Not to mention, with two Americans in the crowd, fast friends of the groom, the groom will be the cat's ass."

Two weeks later Truman was amazed, marveling at the temple's colorful walls, the statues of multiple-armed deities, and the children that seemed to have the run of the place, chasing one another about the ceremony that ensued amidst clamor in general.

The bride was extensively and finely illustrated on every exposed part of her skin. Even her face was masked with the ornate detailing. Truman thought her beautiful, being so hard to see. At a seemingly high point, a small fire was lit for her and her groom to circle a number of times. Truman asked three people why, and received three different responses.

The affair lasted an hour, followed by a huge vegetarian dinner. Truman was glad he went, in spite of Singer and his getting caught in a tropical downpour on their cycle ride home, as they made their way north at a crawl up through the jungles and plantations drained by the slow-moving Pahang.

* * *

Three nights later, at the Kedua, Truman learned from a shy stranger that the Mentacab schoolteacher was ". . . interested."

"That is all I may say, my friend," the man offered. "She is interested."

"In what? Optometry?" Singer nosed in.

"I don't know," answered Truman, for the young Chinese man had returned to his friends after a slight bow. "Maybe she wants to chew me out again over the Jews and the Arabs."

"Barkis is a willin'," said John Singer, exhaling a drag from his Winston.

"Huh?" asked Truman.

"Nothing. You ever read *David Copperfield*?"

"No. Heard of it though."

"You ought to. Everyone should." Singer smiled. "So, what are you going to do, lady-killer?"

"Nothing. I don't even know her name," Truman said.

Singer smiled again, from something warm. Perhaps that Copperfield story.

"You have to take up reading while you're here, especially after I'm gone. That's my advice, pal."

"Did you hear something today?"

"No, not yet," Singer answered. "But that's not my point. You're missing out on a wonderful pleasure, and I keep telling you I'm leaving you my books. It makes me happy. It truly does." Singer leaned forward. "Take it up. You won't be sorry."

* * *

As January marched on, Azman ducked Truman's every advance concerning program money. Driven to do something, even schooling, Truman resented the boredom that crept into his days.

Unsettling dreams returned. Angela appeared, wishing to be touched, but too far off. In another, crowds of men beat upon struggling deer behind Chet Van Heflin's twin silos. Chet materialized, telling Truman that they couldn't shoot the deer because of their religion. Then rivers rampaged beneath bridges that swayed perilously above.

In the evenings, Truman listened on as a friend back in Buffalo urged Singer into reading books written by, or about, some clairvoyant named Edgar Cayce. John Singer declined, likening E.S.P. to venereal disease. "I'll attend to such things when I believe I have such things." He half-smiled.

Around the Home, the kids took to playing outside and in, with a nothing-to-do Truman, who spooked them with hide-n-seek, before horrifying them with "Wild Dog," a game he made up, where three safe spots were established within the open bay of the building. Truman, on wrapped hands and knees, ripped about, growling and howling after any child who braved leaving one base for another, running, hobbling, dragging, or wheeling. The kids loved it, save speechless little Salleh, who hid and wept uncontrollably whenever the game was played. Thoughtfully, Truman modified the rules, whereas Salleh became known as the only boy in the world whom the monster loved. By January's end, shirtless, or naked, Salleh rode the beast as it savaged the others.

But no money came from Azman, coupled with Truman's slow-growing ranks of Malaysian acquaintances questioning his job at the Home. Truman's explanations were interpreted as babysitting, or again as his wishing to be a real teacher, but unable or unqualified. One friend, a banana vendor, of all trades, asked Truman if he was handicapped himself, thus having nowhere else to be sent by this mysterious Peace Corps place. After a particularly trying day, John Singer reminded Truman of his Home's lawn that replaced the dump, and of the kids who now played inside and out, some wearing clothes. In a remarkable coincidence, Andy showed up, from Kuala Lumpur, reiterating the same, before treating Truman and John Singer to supper, and too much to drink.

In early February, Truman was invited to another Chinese New Year's party, hosted by a Rotarian over in Mentacab. Returning the favor, Truman invited John Singer, knowing he'd be welcome. Malaysians were like that.

Although not of the rooftop sort, the guests were again Chinese and Indian, but this time largely the middle-aged merchants and businessmen of the two communities. Mr. Tan of Tan's Hardware was even there, which pleased Truman. Tan was robust and loud with him, never mentioning the shovel, while demanding an explanation for the sudden lack of business. Truman cautiously explained his boss, Mr. Azman. Tan heartily understood, whispering, "The Malays in the local government are stupid and lazy—full of shit—as you Americans like to say."

To Truman's pride, John Singer worked the crowd well. Discussing politics, his working the books for Pejabat Hutan, and his upcoming transfer to Pejabat Haiwan, on the east coast, sometime in March or April. Truman learned of this the week before, and didn't like thinking of it. He also learned, from a thoughtful Indian merchant, some patched history of his little Home upon the banks of the Pahang.

The story was brief, and easy to imagine, some Good Samaritan's failure. The Indian gentleman fancied it now a closet of sorts for the Social Welfare Department, similar to, and as neglected as a place he referred to as "The Old Folks Home" up off the other end of Kuala Harap's T-shape.

Truman, unaware of the place, asked to visit it sometime. This excited the slender man, who introduced himself as Manium. He offered sharing the site with both Americans, if they'd take the time.

Then the party began breaking up in couples and small groups at a time. Several men planned to regroup in Mentacab's side street of late night kedais. An Indian lawyer, Mr. Tan, and another Chinese merchant asked "Mr. Singer" if he and his friend would join them at The Shamrock Bar, one of Mentacab's two Alpine-sort. Singer accepted immediately. The invitation meant the host would pay. Truman's training never dealt with massage parlor protocol. He had some culture to learn.

So off the five rambled, across the larger town, and into the candle-lit darkness of The Shamrock's booths.

Once inside, from an unseen head count, five girls intercepted them, leading them to a large booth in a corner, wiggling their ways in between the individual men. Big Tan roared with laughter, demanding an exchange of girls with his Chinese counterpart. He favored the full-figured Indian. Singer cut in, insisting upon the woman Tan neglected, defying any challenger. All were delighted.

A quiet Malay sat with Truman. She appeared closest to his age, which he liked, but she never said a word as she touched him beneath the table, smiling and nodding to his nervous questions. Drinks were bought and set about. Tan's merchant friend talked to a man apparently summoned, then off they went, in pairs as the rooms above became available. Truman whispered to Singer about money. Singer hushed him—it was on Tan's friend.

Once upstairs, events unfolded just as they had at the Alpine. In fact, so identical in sequence Truman wondered if the two girls knew one another across their dark worlds of candlelight, talcum and flesh. Then a difference. Islam didn't get in this girl's way. She offered intercourse, without speaking, gesturing his hardness toward her own rocking, underwear-clad vulva, flashing ten fingers five times. Fifty ringgits. Truman declined, still a virgin, his secret, as he lay still for the talcumed finale. Then akin to her Alpine sister, she finished, dressed, and vanished.

Downstairs Truman was apprehensive. Only the Indian and Tan's merchant friend remained. In time, Singer and Tan returned. Singer was sweating. Then all left, amongst handshakes and laughter, out into the night air.

In Kuala Harap, John Singer and Truman hit the all-night truck stop, where they talked of the Alpine and Shamrock Bars, of the girls' western names, and of how Truman might get used to the visits, if he cared to.

"It's just expensive jackin' off," Singer offered. "Once you understand that, or get by it, you'll have more fun. It's business. Nothing more. And a damn sight better than doing it yourself."

"I guess so." Truman half-smiled. "Mine never said a word to me. Just a lot of motioning around."

"She was handicapped, wasn't she?" Singer asked, leaning back in his chair in the night air. Three lumber trucks rumbled by, whipping up a hot wind, rumbling off into the night.

"Jesus. I didn't know that," claimed Truman.

"Maybe a mute. A cleft palate or something." Smoking, Singer exhaled.

"Jesus, John, I'm supposed to be here helping those kinds, not having 'em rubbin' me all up and down, and jackin' me off and shit."

"You did help!" Singer said, laughing. "By keeping her employed. She didn't ask to be your girlfriend, did she? Did you fuck her and not pay her?"

"No. Just, you know, what they do and all."

"Well, partner, I fucked mine. Not on Tan's friend's generosity, but just the same, she and I, we're both better off for it."

A cat slinked by, low-shouldered and fast, vanishing across the dark two-lane highway. Singer continued, "She's a tad richer. I'm a tad poorer, and happier for a bit."

Truman drank long from his bottle. Did Singer wonder him a virgin?

But Singer was looking after the cat. Then he turned to Truman at their little table in the night. "If you want to make love, you have to be in love. Everything else is just fuckin'." He appeared sad, forcing a smile to nowhere. "Just the same, fucking ain't too bad either."

Truman didn't know what to say. Singer knew this, and looked up into the starry night. He shrugged. "Believe me. I know. Come on, drink up, so we can get the hell out of here."

* * *

The Chinese New Year closed shops across both towns, most being Chinese-owned as their Malay countrymen went about their business, ever courteous of their Chinese countrymen.

These were slow weeks for Truman as Azman put him off again for money for school supplies. So Truman played with the kids, tinkered about and wasted his days. Zurina and Fatimah didn't understand. Singer reminded him that they were Malays.

One evening Truman even bathed in the river with the two women, when a friend of one showed up to watch the kids. Fully clothed, both women worried about discretion, while delighted to have Truman along sharing a bit of their kumpang life. He learned, as he had in training, how one could bathe cloaked in a sarong in mixed company. Quietly, though, he bathed again in the darkness of his shed that night, not liking the film of silt, real or imagined, left on his skin.

* * *

February 12, 1981

Got a letter from Ben yesterday. He spent Chinese N.Y. up in Penang with Jackie (a social worker up there). Also got a letter (business type) from Andy after he visited, inviting me to a mental health conference up there in March (a month after John leaves) all expenses paid. John said I'd be nuts not to go.

Around here still no $ to start stuff up again. I told Andy about it & he told me to write a letter over Azman's head to some Tuan Kareem guy at the state level in Kuantan. I'm going to do it, but I don't want to get Azman in trouble or anything—I just want something to do (even faking being a teacher). I'll let Andy see the letter first so I don't come off as a fool or anything.

I already wrote about my 2nd "urut" lady business. (I just flipped back a few pages & saw it.) Ramasami's been naughty lately, but the other kids have been good. Wacky Azman (the head-slapping, spinning one) is getting to be more fun. I'm certain he's beginning to understand a few things. He sure knows when I bring back food (spins & begs at the same time).

I bought 3 more cassettes. I have 5 now for the tape player I bought—but I mentioned that. One's a Beatles' collection & the other 2 are music of the 70's stuff. Every once in awhile there's an article in the New Straits Times *Sun. Ed. about sex or morals or relationships & there's always a penciled sketch of a European- or American-looking woman near the title. I wonder if it would piss off one of the races here if she were obviously a Malay, a Chinese or an Indian. (I'll have to ask Ben up in Penang.)*

About private stuff, there's a kind of cute girl who sells ice cream outside the theater along the highway. I tried to flirt with her over the prices of her cones—I don't know how I'm doing. (John noticed & teased me.) The night before last we saw some shitty Henry Fonda thing called City On Fire. *John carried on afterwards about Jane Fonda's bitching over her father never getting an Oscar. He said her dad should try co-starring with Soupy Sales in his next movie if he wants the fucking thing so bad.*

Oh—before I sign off—Ben wrote that he heard I was having trouble "adjusting" out here in K.H. (He was real gentle & all.) I guess John was right about P.C. gossip. I also dreamed of Jimmy McCleary the other night, being over here walking lost through the crowd at Mentacab's Sunday market. In real life, I coaxed a stray cat to stay here at the Home for the kids. (A little fish head goes a long way!) Normah loves it since it's taken to napping on her lap, so long as she doesn't rock her rickety wheelchair.

* * *

Azman was still giving Truman his smiling, "Come back in three days," runaround into late February. So Truman roughed out his letter, addressed to a Tuan Abdul Karim bin Abdul Kamarul, Director of Social Welfare, State Of Pahang. With Singer's help, Truman sharpened it into cultural sensitivity.

A week and two purposeful visits to the ice-cream girl later, a heavyset Malay girl from Azman's office showed up at the Home. She hustled Zurina and Fatimah into their room, ignoring Truman outside with four of the kids. Twenty minutes later she emerged alone, shyly informing Truman that Encik Azman had money for him at his office. He could retrieve it whenever.

Truman thanked her with a slight and sincere Malay bow. This took the young woman aback. She braved a smile, then turned and hurried away, down the pitted driveway. Truman strode inside for his list of school supplies.

An hour later he received an official response from the director in Kuantan, acknowledging his letter, and mentioning that he had personally spoken with Encik Azman, and that there'd be no further delays. The brief letter also noted that funds were limited. In English, the Tuan advised, "Be prudent."

Good enough for Truman, who wanted to head up into town to Azman's local government office for the money, but thought wiser.

That night a subtitled *Apocalypse Now* showed up in the theater down along the highway. Truman and Singer hit the late show, sitting so far down front that Singer talked Truman into moving back a few rows, ice cream cones and all. After the movie, and needing, "a mission," according to Singer, the two finished their night at the all-night truck stop, before spilling on Singer's new motorcycle at 2:00 a.m., down on the rutted river road, trying to evade three wandering kirbow buffalo.

Across the following days, Truman made numerous trips up into town for school supplies with his money from Azman. Tan's shop had little, but he patronized it whenever possible, showing the large man his various lists.

Big Tan, mumbling in English as he read, commanded his hooked-nosed wife in brisk Chinese. If they had it, she silently produced it from their cluttered shop. If not, Tan penciled out where the items could be found in some other Chinese shop, in Mentacab if need be. John Singer pointed out the quiet war.

At the Home, Truman's classroom took shape in the dining area to the right of the sliding-cage entrance. Here he arranged a desk before his new shelves, stocked with reams of paper, pencils, a tape dispenser, glue, staples, scissors, thumbtacks and paper clips—anything remembered from Chatsworth, New Egypt and Allentown High.

A week later he hit the local primary school, told his story and returned upon his bicycle, with a bundling of tattered schoolbooks from Darjah One up through Darjah Nine, in math, reading, health and science.

The kids, especially the brighter ones, beamed with the activity. Ramasami, though, grew naughtier as Salleh and Azman seemed to get better. One early afternoon, Ramasami teased Normah, pushing her in her wheelchair into a stumbling Kumari. Truman scolded him. Ramasami mumbled in Tamil, then pulled down his shorts and shook his dark little penis at Truman. Truman dropped the big letter "G" he was cutting out for his classroom alphabet, spun the boy around and kicked his ass like a punt. Ramasami's behavior improved immediately, at least for a while.

The next day Truman returned from town with toy cars and trucks, blocks of various colors and sizes, two kickballs and crayons and markers. The kids' excitement compounded. Truman inventoried everything, dividing the wealth between everyday toys and school supplies. Everything in its place, like a well-run farm.

Meanwhile, Fatimah and Zurina went silent toward one another. Truman, knowing little of Malays, and less of women, didn't try to figure it out as he and John Singer saw a subtitled *Rocky II*, and made it to a Malay wedding out in a distant kumpang. Truman thought the soft-spoken vows pretty, being exchanged upon the bed of the girl's kumpang home. That week he also buried Normah's cat that Azman managed to back over on their pitted driveway. Chubby Lim and big Kumari wept beside Normah. Truman promised a new one. The tailless things were all over the place.

Two nights later the power failed. Truman had a grand time haunting the home to the children's laughter, screaming and hobbling horror. He also wrote Mabel for money, perhaps a small piece of his own, asking, as though not yet entitled. John Singer was on him, asking one night at the more respectable Kedua Coffee House, "And that's another thing. When are you going to get your ass in gear and buy a motorcycle?"

"I have to write to my aunt about it real soon," replied Truman.

"Soon is right," Singer answered. "I'm not looking forward to riding back here every other weekend to visit your ugly mug. Not when I'm livin' all but a mile from the South China Sea."

Truman flushed, thinking of having to put his friend to any trouble.

Singer misread him, thinking of his choice of words and his friend's scar. "Come on, cheer up. You know I'd gas up the Honda and point her toward Kuala Harap any time either of us needed the other."

"You won't need to. I'll get on it," Truman assured him, as their perpetually smiling waitress topped off his glass.

Then an irritated young Chinese man approached their table, addressing Singer, smothering their warmth, complaining of a Jerry Lewis joke he heard somewhere that he felt a slur. Truman recalled the bit from the celebrity's signature telethon. Lewis likened the clattering of spilled silverware to a quarrel in a Chinese restaurant. Singer listened, then hushed to Truman about the road to hell being paved with good intentions. To make life easier he apologized to the young man, who was obviously well into his own evening of beer, strangers and mistaken cross-cultural wit.

The next morning, however, Truman's cheerful mailman, on his nice red bicycle, delivered a surprise.

"Encik Truman!" his mailman called out, ringing his thumb bell. *"Ada surat hari ini!"*

Without a return address, the handwriting upon the envelope wasn't Mabel's, nor Angela's, nor Kathleen Van Heflin's. But seemingly a girl's. He wondered of another volunteer.

He worked it open. The message was clumsy and brief, without the loops and strokes he associated with a feminine hand, yet feminine.

It read, every time he read it:

Hello Friend,

    Are you from Amerika or is it Urope? Maybe England?

    I am a silly girl. Why do you like those kinds of childrens you have with? Is it you have big heart?

    I will write again. My hope is you not think me foolish.

    You friend

* * *

That night Truman showed his letter to John Singer, raising Singer's eyebrows over fried rice. They pondered possible authors.

"Fatimah and Zurina can't be ruled out," claimed Singer.

"Zurina can't read or write a word, John," Truman said. "Besides, she's pretty old. And both know where I'm from."

"This girl's hardly a literary wonder," Singer answered. "And Zurina's not that old. Your home may be a ruse. And if so, it'd be the intellectual high point of the letter." Singer smiled, reloading his fork, then added, "There's the Kedua crowd, and, of course, the Alpine and the Shamrock. Did either girl mention your possessing a particularly handsome johnson?" He laughed.

Truman smiled, his own mouth full. "One claimed it was bigger than yours," he replied, scraping scattered rice into a more manageable pile at the edge of his plate.

Singer smiled. "That may be," he said as he studied the note, "but this could also be from someone you've never spoken to. Regardless, she's—if it is a she—is asking you one, two, three specific questions. Compelling your answers. Pretty neat."

"How? Think she'll write again?"

"Of course she will," answered Singer. "And quit scraping your fucking plate! It drives me nuts. She's obviously never had the pleasure of dining with you."

Their conversation turned to Singer's staying in the area an additional two weeks, which pleased them both. They figured the next week to be their last, with Truman attending the national conference in Penang the week after.

So the two pals worked by day, and drank and roamed the two communities by warm night. One morning, a baby elephant had wandered alone into the area. It was being held at Singer's government complex. Singer alerted Truman. With a quick appeal for an office Land Rover, Truman loaded up seven of the kids, and Zurina, too, to see the leathery baby that rocked softly beneath the tree it was chained to.

The infant giant terrified little Salleh, who wet his pants. Azman, indifferent, was hell to get into the Land Rover as Ramasami and Lim tentatively allowed Truman to set them atop the animal's back. Normah was so pleased to get dressed up to go anywhere that her palsied face contorted and flexed with giggly anticipation all morning at everything.

At week's end, Singer and Truman so assured one another of regular visits that it embarrassed both. Then Truman packed for his week north, for the island of Penang, stopping by the Kuala Lumpur office for two inoculations. Jimmy Carter and Walter Mondale's pictures still graced the large waiting area.

In Penang, Truman had never seen anything like the five-day conference. A good deal of his training group was there, on the same floor of the hotel, with hot water for all who dearly missed it. Even big Dave Hayden, part of the agricultural program, and having absolutely nothing to do with it, showed up, making no bones about it.

Into the afternoon of the second day of the sessions, Truman grew bored, while noticing that half of the other volunteers weren't even showing up, in favor of hitting the local shops and beaches. Andy, himself, showed up midweek, happy to see anyone, and young Truman, too.

There were movies to see, and shops to eat and drink in. Truman and Ben, with several others, took in a Bond film, then Martin Scorsese's *Raging Bull*, sitting too far back for Truman's comfort. Big Dave clandestinely arranged a trip to the bars in a shadier section of Georgetown. Hushed word had him managing marijuana from a rickshaw driver to boot. Truman declined, opting to stay with Ben and the teachers who attended half the sessions, to collectively surmise, somewhat accurately, that the bulk of presentations boiled down to grand goals, nit-picking for handouts, and always more time to pursue all aims and objectives imagined.

The six days occupied nearly five pages of Truman's early April journal, an entry chronicling Singer's final days in Kuala Harap, laying both friends in financial straits. The same entry spoke of an article in the *New Straits Times*: "Naked Couple Bound Over, Told To Behave." Someone's thoughtful neighbor alerted the Religious Police of an extramarital affair. Then the attempt on Ronald Reagan's life took an entire page. Truman first heard of the Washington shooting in the halls of their hotel. A volunteer he didn't know claimed that the President was only wounded. Ben scrambled for special bulletins broadcast from Voice of America. A cab driver assured a teacher that her President was dead. A teacher from the group before Truman's, rambled tearfully of everyone's having known of its coming, "You know, that calendar year thing, with election years ending in zero." She wept, likening Ronald Reagan to Kennedy and Lincoln, linking all three to something weird in the cosmos.

Truman, feeling bad for the old man at his job for just a couple of months, wrote in his journal: "The whole thing, though, seems to have happened to someone else's president in some far-off country."

He also wrote how he missed Kuala Harap, and the kids, and Fatimah and Zurina's moods, which were becoming the benchmarks of his days. But he didn't write of the two letters waiting for him in Kuala Harap upon his return.

* * *

He opened John Singer's first, who wrote of settling into the small royal town of Pekan on the east coast, before asking about Penang and wondering why Ramasami had a copy of Truman's Peace Corps' pay sheet crumpled in his filthy pocket when he stopped by to say good-bye. Singer closed, advising that a certain Mr. Yap, who frequented the Kedua, may be, "as well mannered as we've been accustomed to, and as fucking queer as they come/cum."

Truman's second letter was in that uncertain hand. The kids clamored about. They were happy to have him home. The letter read:

> *Dear Mr. Friend,*
>   *I have not seen you of recent days. I think you may write back to me. If this is so, take your lunch Monday at the kedai next to the bus stand.*
>   *If this is so, I send to you a address. This must be secret.*
>   *Also, why do you wear boots like soldier?*
>   *Please keep secret. Secret friends be nice, isn't it?*
>   *Your friend, (secret)*

Big Kumari leered close over Truman's shoulder, seemingly interested in his letter. Recalling that it was Sunday, Truman was happy that he didn't stay the extra day with Ben and two others to lounge upon the beaches of the Pearl of the Orient.

CHAPTER 13

April 6, 1981

Well, I taught (or tried to) for the 1st time today—actually for the 1st time in my life. It was disorganized & the kids had no idea what to do or how to behave & I guess I didn't either. Normah tried, but was wild with joy (at the idea of me teaching). Every time Ramasami said the word "cikgu" (Malay for teacher) she went fucking hysterical, slinging saliva from her crooked mouth. Salleh was as cute as ever with his thick tongue sticking out as he pointed at things he thought I wanted.

This was after 2 or 3 bad days of me losing my temper with the kids & with the town in general. I've been moody & having trouble sleeping, too. Maybe I'm still adjusting, with John gone & all. I should try to make some friends of my own, I suppose.

I've also made myself one of those teacher plan books out of a (I guess it's a bookkeeping ledger) thing I found months ago. I hope to plan out the mornings to get every kid working on at least something, & then devote the afternoons to getting them outside somewhere. I've even thought of taking them for a dip in the river—some shallow place.

Enough for now. I've got to hit the sack after lighting this mosquito coil, before I get carried off!

* * *

As Truman saw only the bumps and sputters of his little classroom, Zurina and Fatimah experienced the kids' anticipation every morning at breakfast, but said nothing.

Normah and big Kumari worked at their alphabet sounds. Normah easily outraced her hobbling friend, who pushed her about in her wheelchair in the classroom, continuing their locomotive relationship, as Kumari had no walker. In a few months this would dawn on Truman, sailing him into construction.

Ramasami hated counting, but traced his alphabet like a boy possessed, hunkering down over his paper, snapping one pencil point after another as his single simple-mindedness compounded. Truman even managed to lure whirling Azman into the classroom, baiting him with food and the simplest of directives. Fatimah and Zurina loved it. The microcephalic teen leered like a curious chimp, hooting and slapping at his head, before fleeing the room. Truman smiled. At least he wasn't knuckling. A bit at a time, like training a dog.

Then Truman took his purposeful lunch at the kedai next to the bus stop. He wouldn't write of it in his journal.

He left his bike behind, hoping to appear grown up. Walking up into town he kept his eyes forward, to not spook the eyes of the writer watching from somewhere. He wore a clean shirt, tucked in, and sneakers in place of his work boots. He chose the table closest to the mouth of the open-air kedai, and he ate slowly, widening the window of opportunity in case whoever got hung up.

Satisfied that he could do no more, he paid his bill, and emerged from the little shop.

Nothing askew. The heat, the blue sky, its billowy white clouds and the busy shops about him. A scattering of laughing children rose from somewhere. Filthy water from a hard rain lay deep in the shadowy length of a curbside drain. Before him, leaning bicycles supported more of the unemployed juveniles excluded from secondary school. One called to him. Then Truman passed through shy Malay women, sitting along the road upon spread newspaper and tarp, vending fruit. Then he walked alone, down toward the river, for the Home.

* * *

Several days later, John Singer wrote a delightful letter of sarcasm and affection. Best of all, he'd be returning to Kuala Harap, via cab, or his "luminous thumb." Cycle problems plagued him in Pekan. Then another letter, a single day later, in that laboring hand, addressed to, "Mr. Truman." She had his name.

A touch lengthier, this one recalled the first time she'd seen him, claiming it was close enough to find him "handsome." However, he would have found her "quite homely." Her long-hand, in blue ink, appeared rushed, writing of her recent "secret practicing of English language" as her writing suddenly leaned left for two and a half lines near the end.

This lengthier note picked Truman up, but its effects wouldn't last. That morning's schooling surged without reference points for its captain, excepting little Salleh, who loved sitting before the donated tri-podded chalkboard Truman rustled up. The lonesome boy would have sat for hours, just to participate.

Without insight, Truman thought Salleh disobedient. Chubby Lim, speechless with her mouth full of tongue, labored happily at her alphabet sounds in spite of her responses hardly varying from her lone several sounds. He wondered if he was torturing the poor girl, not understanding her desire for his undivided attention.

Singer, as foretold, dropped in one afternoon, which led to a late-night bender. He left the next morning from Truman's shed in a wailing downpour, for an eastbound bus, cranking Truman's bicycle through sheets of monsoon rain. He looked back, too unsteady to wave, as Truman marched through April, suspecting a girl in Azman's office of authoring his letters, then another, an Indian girl in a Mentacab cycle shop, where he'd been eyeing a Kawasaki. There were the two bar girls, one mean, the other silent. And, of course, the flirting-back movie house ice cream vendor, and maybe even Fatimah, the quiet, steadier of the two workers, but Truman had never heard her speak an English word.

Again, Singer suggested a stranger. The town was full of them. A day later, Truman roamed the Sunday market where he thought of Angela, who hadn't written in so long. He wished Chet and Kathleen's daughter could see him milling through the Malaysian crowd, on the other side of the world.

In his journal, he logged passing his Malaysian-written driving test. His New Jersey license wouldn't do, in spite of the nice people at Kuala Harap's district office liking it, passing it around for their peers to see. Instead, he was issued an "L" license, a permit, needing only a motorcycle to complete the process. He also wrote of his English that the kids were picking up amongst their daily lessons, play and walks. The same entry recorded a recent series of editorials in the *New Straits Times* calling for a ban on blossoming rock shows in Kuala Lumpur and Johor Baru, performances deemed contrary to Malay customs and morals.

An Indian dentist Truman met at supper one evening offered free services to the kids. All good will—nothing Malay about it. Truman leapt at the opportunity.

Normah went first. It was bloody, and years late. There was crying, stitches and painkillers. Fatimah came along, comforting Normah's palsied sobs. Zurina found it funny. The following entry ended with Lim's chasing a lone goat out through the front gate, beast and girl, one fleet footed in spurts, the other stumbling, straight-legged and squealing. Another writing chronicled an evening chat with Zurina and Fatimah, enjoying an unusually cool breeze off the muddy Pahang. The two Muslim women abhorred the sickly stray dogs that Truman pondered befriending just one of. Zurina was spooked by Truman's explanation of Western human burials—the costly use of strangers, dragged out for days, with no intimate gathering of bathing and wrapping the beloved deceased amongst family and friends, to bury him near home, in mere hours.

Truman closed, chronicling his recent late nights at the Kedua Coffee House and the cheaper Chinese kedais, eating and drinking with curious strangers who collected about the late-night haunts.

One late night, bicycling around the bridge for the river road home, Truman passed the Christmasy lights of The Alpine Bar. A woman stumbled around out front, trying to find her way back in. Truman braked his bicycle into stopping. From across the quiet highway, he watched her fall, then rise to kneeling, then lie back down on her back on the concrete walkway. Lit by the twinkling of the Alpine's lights, she vomited above herself in a heaving sick fountain. Truman heard the splats from his distance.

He breathed deep, wanting to help. Then three men emerged from within, laughing and conversing in Chinese. They dragged her back in.

Two afternoons later, while sorting and stacking donated surprise lumber, another letter arrived via his postman's jingling bell, two weeks past his purposeful lone lunch.

Truman's bloodied knuckles smeared an edge of the single page.

> *My friend,*
>
> *I was happy to see you at your lunch that day. I think heavy rain keep you away that day. So I also think too sorry because I can't write in smoothly English and feel shameful and sadness in this case because may be you be boring reading my letters. But you eat at that shop and I feel happy again.*
>
> *If you wish to write letters to me I happy to receive and to give to you address.*
>
> > *Kotak Surat #123*
> > *Kuala Harap, Pahang*
> > *Malaysia Berat*
>
> *I shall be going away for weekend, to see my friend in my hometown. I glad to meet with her in such long separation. Shall I find letter from you upon my return? (I only joying and hoping isn't it)*
>
> > *Yours sincerely*
> > *Your friend*
>
> *P.S. This must be very honest secret*

Truman read it three times. A post office box in Kuala Harap. If he could only trust that grinning bastard on his nice, red post office bicycle.

His soiled hands shaking, Truman folded the letter back into its envelope.

* * *

April 24, 1981

I finally got an address for whoever's writing those letters. (I haven't mentioned them in here (until now—you know—what if it leads to something creepy, or who knows what). I'm pretty sure I'm going to write back. I just have to figure out what to write. (I'll talk about it with John.)

Yesterday I bicycled out to Fatimah's sister's house for this big family get-together. It was nice but Fatimah ignored me & then turned up back here all proud & chatty that I went! I know I learned it in training, but it's still strange (these rules of friendships between the sexes).

Twice last week & once this week either Zurina or Fatimah has gone with me to take the kids for an afternoon dip in the shallow bend up the river a ways. It's fun building these little dikes to trap minnows (the little fuckers here actually bite) & just lying around in the warm water, playing with the kids. (We even got Normah's wheelchair in.) Azman won't go in deeper than his ankles & when you try to lead him in deeper he either tries to walk out on top of the water, or he flips WAY OUT into slapping at his head & spinning (what he does best).

Tomorrow I'm going to my 2nd Malay wedding (some friend of the guy who gave me my written driver's test—of course, I don't know him—or the getting-married couple). The more the merrier, I guess!

Two days ago I had a hell of a day with schooling. Zurina was a witch, time dragged, Azman shit out worms & I finally had to discipline Ramasami. I threw him out the front door & he fell & got a lump on his head. I felt like shit about it, but I haven't apologized. He was bad all morning & he knew it (and for the last 2 weeks, too) & he was hitting the other kids & he finally threw rocks at me so that was it.

All else with schooling is going good. I teach (or try to) in the mornings. In the afternoons I either work outside or I take the gang to the river—or to this park-like place. I also want to start an Arts & Crafts sort of thing. I've been taking poor Normah to the dentist. She's done now & Lim's next, then Ramasami. (That nice Indian guy will be jerking the teeth out of these kids left & right for a while. Azman should be the tie-down thriller though!) The kids are fine— still love my Wild Dog game & the river as a new place to play. I have to remember (according to John & Andy) that they never left the building before I came.

Got new lumber, too. Nice stuff donated by a sawmill some 8 or 10 miles east of here. Mr. Tan helped. Maybe it'll lead to another "urut!" Who knows? Just bring on the big titted babes for old Tan!

CHAPTER 14

May 7, 1981

I just got back from Kuantan where I met John for 2 days of boozing, shitty movies & playing at the beach. I hitched down & back. It made me think of Jimmy M. & our own thumbing around. John had cycle trouble again & was pissed off. We also walked out on a movie called New York's Killer Gold. *John said it was "the shittiest movie never edited."*

I got a letter from Ben & another from Dave Hayden, who wants to come to K.H. I guess it'll be fun. John's also trying to get me into reading. He says it passes time & it's good for you. Maybe that's how he got so smart. I told him about my "journal" & he was impressed. He said (like back in staging) that a lot of people start one but never keep at it—him included. It made me feel good. Anyway, he gave me a book called Great Expectations *& another called* Mr. Lincoln's Army. *I'll give them a try. Lord knows I might be going a little crazy all alone here.*

For the big thing—I wrote back to my "secret friend." I kept it brief. I don't want to spook her off. God I hope it's a HER! We'll see what happens.

* * *

Real farmer, big Dave Hayden, stopped by for three days of uncomfortable working, and, of course, for more drinking at night after supper. Hayden, keeping a nervous distance from the kids, cheered Truman with stories of his roaming the peninsula, from one American to the next. He figured Kuala Harap to be a painful hole, himself having forgotten what little Malay he learned. So he and Zurina hit it off grandly through his happy bellowing and posturing, each unable to understand the other. Quiet Fatimah avoided him.

Meanwhile, Ben wrote, abuzz with gossip. Mindy, from California, couldn't seem to keep her undergarments on her clothesline down in Johor. Someone kept stealing them. Some guy from an earlier group, perhaps Singer's, got beat up in a Kuala Lumpur bar discussing the Iraqi-Iranian War with a couple of guys who really did care, and tough guy, Danny Ianuzzo, from outside Chicago, applied for a marriage license four months into his assignment.

Truman shared this with Hayden, who laughed aloud. "The fuckin' little worm came here for a wife after all!" He belched, then added, "Jesus, Truman, you'll have to get married yourself to get some pussy around here."

An hour after big Dave climbed into a cab up in the T of Kuala Harap, barking happy commands to his Indian driver, John Singer rolled in. Singer could only stay the night. In his shed, Truman told Singer about Hayden. Singer was relieved to have missed him, He asked Truman, "Hear anything from your pen pal?"

"Got an address. A post office box. I wrote back," Truman answered.

As he was leaving the next morning, Singer lightly cuffed Truman's scarred side with the back of his hand. "Keep me posted, and be fuckin' careful."

With an affectionate wink, Singer kicked his repaired cycle into life. "Oh, yeah." He smiled above the rev of his engine. "This morning I kicked your bottle of V.S.O.P. while you showered. It's for your own good!" Then he meandered off through the ruts in the Home's pitted driveway.

"Prick!" called out Truman, laughing, with Lim and Ramasami at his side.

"Prick!" called out Ramasami, happily waving.

* * *

Later that week, Truman's little family gained another child. A thin Chinese girl named Yap. Truman, developing a better eye, knew she was mentally retarded, but didn't recognize her Down Syndrome without its thorough chubbiness.

Speechless and homebound, at eleven or twelve, thin Yap couldn't understand the simplest of Malay. Truman figured it'd come in time.

He also believed her arrival a vote of confidence from Azman. Actually, Azman would have referred her anywhere. A Malay assistant, stopping by with groceries, alluded to this. This hurt and angered Truman. Luckily, he received another letter that afternoon. A full page.

> *Dear Mr. Truman,*
>
> *Received your letter two days ago. Thank you to your reply. I'm so glad to received it and I readed it again and again that you wouldn't believe. I know you wouldn't do this silly thing as I do, isn't it?*

Truman noticed the contractions and was happy for her, as her letter went on about her having so few friends in this world, with no one to truly worry over her. *"May be I will tell you about my former life one day,"* it ventured, then: *"Have you ever lived in mountains of America? You so look like camper man from America television programs with boots and blue jeans and curls of long hair."*

Upon thanking him again for his *"secret writing,"* her uneven hand closed: *"I do think of you much and you should know this too. Very Truelly, Your happy new friend"*

* * *

Truman waited several days before writing back, needing the time, while waiting for the fleeting windows of being in the right mood. Life without Singer was tumultuous.

But he stayed busy, buying hardware from Mr. Tan, then lengths of chain from Tan's wife for the ladder he was affixing to the fort. A quick note from Singer cheered him, as did the new girl, skinny Yap. After helping him water the saplings he planted, he found her watering the swing set and the fort posts, understanding something.

Then gloom, a letter from Ben suggested a Peace Corps' rumor that had him drinking too much out there in the sticks. Jesus Christ, trying so hard to make something of this place, and being so alone, and then having his real bosses ready to send him home? Mabel would die. The feeling revisited hard several days later when she wrote, enclosing a money order for $500, U.S. currency, noted as withdrawn from his savings account. Faraway Mabel was dubious, requiring a fresh pot of coffee and several phone calls.

But Singer's reading helped. Truman finished *Mr. Lincoln's Army* in a week, learning more of his nation's civil war than he'd ever known, not to mention the joy of having read a book, which paled in his journal in comparison to his new motorcycle, a 125cc Yamaha, freeing him to cruise to Mentacab for his evening roamings. He also wondered if his secret friend noticed this new mobility.

At the Home, chubby Lim and skinny Yap became fast friends, and the funniest of enemies. Whether playing, or bound in confrontation, their discourse consisted of head tiltings strung with feminine sounds in varying degrees of intensity. Truman, with Normah and Kumari as a tickled audience, tried to sort their struggles as the kids worked daily with their alphabet sounds and numbers.

Truman also learned that his cycle rides couldn't cure the ills that his daily teaching and afternoon tasks kept temporarily at bay. His loneliness followed him everywhere through the warm nights, from one kedai to another, to a Mentacab theater, or weaving through the kumpangs that hugged the flow of the muddy Pahang.

Singer wrote again, which helped as Truman worked with the kids on papier-mâché masks beneath the shade of the great tree. Singer wrote of big Dave Hayden:

"The hypocritical fuck was on a fact-finding mission, out to K.H., and how do I know?" Singer asked. "Andy called my office in Pekan, and asked me what I thought. And shame on his drunken ass, too! How did I respond, you may wonder?" his note continued.

" 'Sure,' I answered, 'The kid has the same problem you and I have with the booze—our monthly allowance runs out too fast.' Good buddy, they'd rather have you going nuts, whacking your little Jersey dog against some rambutan tree before allowing that one needs a little recreation—especially we bastards who actually work!" Singer closed with: "Take it light, buddy. We're among those doing something. The ones who matter know it."

The next day Truman started Dickens' *Great Expectations*, finding it hard to read. He liked Pip, though, and had nothing but time to follow the boy's tale. Suddenly, Zurina brought up the Mentacab Chinese schoolteacher, the young woman keenly interested in American-Israeli policy. Truman had no idea what networking of busyness could have found its way to old Zurina, but at least alcohol wasn't worked into it.

* * *

A week later the Pope was shot. Truman's *Newsweek* offered an artist's rendering of his Holiness' damaged papal entrails. About Kuala Harap, acquaintances and strangers sought Truman's opinion. After all, the gunman was a Muslim and Truman, being white, had to be Christian. The popular John Paul II forgave his assailant, as if he could do otherwise. Truman thought the incident sad, while discovering that standing on his head drove little Salleh to new heights of little boy fear.

He wrote in his journal of the beautiful Malaysian sky in the evenings, rainless, yet rolling with thunder, huge and menacing. He didn't write of his crossing the open bay one evening, catching a slicing view of Fatimah through an ajar washroom door, washing her legs with her tattered dress tucked up under her chin. A moment of thick brown thigh. For a while he thought differently of her.

Then their Home gained another child, a boy, of about fifteen, half Malay, half Indian. Singh smiled constantly, embraced immediately by Ramasami, who led the boy everywhere, mumbling in Tamil with bits of Malay, about the playground and the makeshift classroom. This new boy spoke clearly in courteous, limited Malay. Truman thought him six or seven, mental age, a concept he learned of from a book he drummed up in training. The boy was also timely, being cordial and happy for a group visit to the Home, sprung upon an unsuspecting Truman. A dozen local teachers were to show up, to donate 500 ringgits in a day or two.

Truman sped to Azman's office for confirmation, and got it.

Angered, and unsure if he had a right to be, he asked his Malay boss, "Why did I have to hear of this from Normah, a child in a wheelchair, for Christ's sake?"

Encik Azman paused at the reference to Christianity. Then he smiled. "There is nothing to explain, Mr. Truman. There will be cameras. Please see that the children are bathed. You are dismissed."

Truman worked late that night, scrubbing and mopping, with faithful Fatimah. Zurina was supposedly at her father's kumpang home. The old man began falling ill two or three times a month about the time Truman moved in out back, patching up the gaping holes in the fence that surrounded the Home.

Sixteen teachers came the following morning as Truman was conducting lessons. Cameras flashed at a caring Encik Azman, flanked by four of his office's social welfare workers, all of them heaping affection upon the well-dressed children they couldn't have named if asked. Shortly, the 500 ringgits were ceremoniously handed over to all sorts of gratitude from the local government office, recorded in Truman's journal as "a good natured gang of Chinese giving a handout to a gathering of indigenous liars."

Then all left, except Azman, who complained of the smell of ammonia, and Ramasami's manners. Late that afternoon, Truman sat beneath the spreading of the great tree in the elevated fort the teachers were never shown. As the kids played below, he sat amongst partially painted papier-mâché masks, rereading a letter of Angela Van Heflin's.

That night, Truman awakened to nightmares. Within the darkness of his shed, to the smell of a half-spent mosquito coil, he fumbled in the dark, finding his extension-cord-strung-up lamp. His hands shook in the sudden light.

He dreamed of being in his shed, fully clothed, and slowly sinking into the concrete slab of his floor, unable to grasp at anything to arrest his descent. He tried to climb out of the concrete that wavered beneath him, swallowing him as close as paint. A harsh, barklike sound awakened him. A sound he didn't know the source of. Sitting upon his bed, with his feet on the floor, he looked at his own shaking.

Then he looked about, becoming aware of the crickets, re-calling pieces of an earlier dream that may have culminated into this terrific one. There was Angela, faceless and crying, blaming him for something. Then he was in Dale Rowland's home, in their living room that only Mabel ever saw. Mrs. Rowland cried at the sight of him. Dale appeared behind her, climbing stairs, getting nowhere.

Truman pulled on dirty jeans, then a sweatshirt over his head, in spite of sweating. He glanced about, fearful of sleep. He went to his hose-rigging and washed his face, then to his journal tucked beneath his lesson plans and ledger. He opened it, mildly pleased having reached triple digits. He wrote "103" at the top, then "May 18th—no—the 19th."

He wrote about the visiting teachers, and of his anger with Azman. He tried to describe how it seemed that only the kids, and sometimes Fatimah, seemed his only solace. But he couldn't place his tormentors, except his growing disdain for his Malay boss. Then he wrote fast of penning two quick notes to "Kotak Surat #123." Half an hour later, the struggles of Dickens' Pip put him back to sleep.

Like medicine, another letter came the next day.

> *Dearest friend,*
> *Hai! I worry about you last middle of night*
> *and could not sleep. Only listen to rain. I feel sorry*
> *to you if you have get angry with me. Furthermore,*
> *I do feel wonderful to receive two letters so fast!*

Sometimes I think of what be a wonderful night for me if me and my dearest friend can visit big city like K.L. isn't it. Have you ever visited Ampang Park or Zoo Negara?

Lastly, I got to stop now because it is late and I not sleep so well. I fear I not sleep well until you write to me again. When you received this last letter of mine, remember to write to me a long letter, okay?

Your friend, (dearest too I hope)
P.S. Do you have white woman American girlfriend? I wish to know.

* * *

Across hot days, Truman taught through the mornings, breaking in the afternoons for one project or another, or to take the children on one of their rickety meanderings up into town, or out into the surrounding kumpangs.

With corrugated tin he saved from the original rubble, Truman added a sunroof to the long swing he built overlooking the river. Fatimah and Zurina immediately took to it in the heat of the day, catching the breezes that swept off the Pahang as they mended clothes, or simply chatted away. In school, little Salleh, shirtless and barefoot, made great gains following two- and three-part commands. His classmates cheered his accomplishments. As quickly, Zurina had him hustling laundry back and forth to the line Truman strung up months before.

In his evenings Truman finished Dickens' *Great Expectations*, but didn't understand the alternate final chapters until he saw Singer again. In either event, poor Pip never got his Angela. Nearing May's end, Truman reflected on being nearly a quarter of his way into his tour, a year and a half lying before him, not counting his three months of training. He wondered if he'd make it. His loneliness had no Mabel, nor Chet Van Heflin proud of his work, as the reflections of John Singer had left town with Singer himself.

A television was donated by a lone returnee of one of the Chinese teachers of weeks before. Truman, with his hair growing into a wave, was thankful, immediately setting to work at a makeshift aerial attached to existing rabbit ears. He also penned a thank-you note, in duplicate for his boss's office. Malaysian television began airing at 4:00 p.m., to sign off at 11:30. Subtitled *Dallas*, delayed a year from America, was hot.

So was *Eight Is Enough*. Fatimah, though, got hooked on subtitled episodes of *Little House On The Prairie*. "Nothing for the government censors to edit there," explained Truman in Malay, "except an occasional pig."

Dallas, on the other hand, was cut to ribbons, like most of the movies at the theater along the highway. It was usually Bobby Ewing or Ray Krebs, inevitably kissing one buxom woman or another, unfitting to the standards of the religious do-gooders.

One afternoon, while building an indoor, four-kid rocking horse, Ramasami, after watching some western, pestered an irritated Truman over how real horses fight.

Truman, in a sweat, answered, "They bite each other's dicks off. That kicking and bucking stuff you see on TV's fake."

"*Aie yoh!*" exclaimed Ramasami, covering his own crotch. Singh, his sidekick in retardation, did the same. Normah contorted, reeling hard in her wheelchair. Big goon Kumari, manning her chair, extracted a scratching paw from her dress, compensating the sudden jolt.

"It's true." Truman winked. "Why do you think they can run so fast?"

Fatimah, having overheard, smiled and dashed for Truman with broom in hand. The kids loved it. Another evening, Truman brought up a story he read in the *New Straits Times* concerning a missing Army recruit. The young soldier vanished sometime around 4:00 a.m. while guarding a rifle range. Local villagers blamed the "*orang bunyian*," the "night people." The villagers claimed these mysterious people appeared three or four times over the past ten years, abducting unsuspecting loners, releasing each after several unexplained days.

Zurina and Fatimah listened intently. Zurina asked, "What happened next?"

"I don't know," Truman answered, imagining the mild-mannered witch doctors he learned of in training. "It says here, local bomohs have stepped forward to help."

"Ah, *bagus*," breathed Zurina.

"Yes. How wonderful," answered Truman. "They'll find soldier boy now," he added, as their conversation ventured into the spirits and ghosts that sailed through the surrounding forests after the sun went down.

* * *

May 28, 1981

I was quiet this morning & sad & sick & tired of hearing Fatimah's and Zurina's fucking gabbing & laughing. I thought it was about me, especially after that visit from Azman's secretary, or whatever it is she does over there.

I've been working on the rocker every afternoon. I gave up on the horse idea & switched it to a 4-kid thing—2 on each side with a single bar across the center for them to hold on to. (It's going be a heavy prick—hope no toes get smashed.)

I also wrote the "long one" asked of me—to who-knows-who. I may stop writing about it in here (cover my ass as John advised). Last weekend I gassed up my cycle & cruised up into the Genting Highlands. It took an hour & a half to get there, but it was worth it. The place is a resort for the rich, I guess. (I hear they have gambling & expensive massage girls.) It's up in the mountains & the cool air smelled of New Jersey in the fall. It made me think of the track bed, & of cruising with Jimmy M. (I wonder what he's doing now.)

The river's been too high to splash in with the kids. We miss it.

I've been real angry, as usual at times—even thought of quitting.

(Later—same night—10:30 p.m.)

I strolled up front to hang out with everyone. I tried to explain to Fatimah & Zurina why I've been so sad. Fatimah thought I was mad at her, then Ramasami cut in with Zurina having to bathe for her friend who was expected. Fatimah grabbed him, to shut him up. I tried to explain that I didn't give a shit. Jesus Christ, I hope they fuck to high heavens, so someone around here's normal.

Anyway, I think I'll hop on my cycle & go have a beer somewhere.

One last thing—good old Singh (new kid) watches our TV like a madman. Car crashes drive him wild!

* * *

Two days later Truman received his next letter.

> *Dear Truman,*
> *Please this secret MOST OF ALL!*
> *I will be come to K.L. on the 31st of May.*
> *Maybe we can meet each other and have nice day?*
> *If you care to meet with me, please go to the big*
> *movie theater (The Lido in K.L.) at the end of*
> *Jalan Raja Muda. I will try to have brave enough*
> *to meet with you (no one know of me there).*
> *I wish we could go for jogging in Stadium*
> *Merdeka, as friends do there, like exercising on*
> *Hart To Hart American TV show. I have to tell*
> *you. I am not pretty. I also have pimples on my*
> *face, so you may scare and move from me at my*
> *sight.*
> *If this true, PLEASE KEEP US SECRET!*
> *Thank you very much for think of me. So I*
> *look forward to Sunday.*
> *Your friend*

* * *

May 30, 1981

So many entries lately. I've been doing a lot of thinking.

Maybe it's getting better. I talked again to the girls about missing home (NJ and Mabel) & how I'm sorry for whatever fix they're in, having to be here, & how I'd love to get this place into shape but it's taking time. They don't understand & I hate being seen as a fucking babysitter—especially after Azman stopped by to pay the girls yesterday, then asked me what the Peace Corps pays me for playing with these kids. (I didn't tell him.)

Also, I'm going to Kuala Lumpur tomorrow. Fuck it. I hope her complexion's not too bad. (Just kidding—it won't matter—any friend will do.)

CHAPTER 15

Sunday morning dawned cool and clear over Kuala Harap. Truman awakened to the haunting call to prayer half an hour before his alarm clock was set to sound.

His mosquito coil smoldered. He opened his wooden shutters to the coolness outside. A goat bleated nearby.

Truman bathed quickly beneath his hose-rigging. Then wrapped in a sarong, and dripping, he laid out jeans and a white button-up shirt, laundered the day before on his shower floor. He set aside his work boots, a belt, and white cotton socks, then a heavier corduroy shirt to cover his white one for the ride.

After quickly reviewing his laid-out clothes, he put on others, and strode out into the morning air, mounting his cycle for breakfast up in town. Motoring out of the pitted driveway, he recognized the goat, a white spotted female with two kids, about the area for a week by then.

* * *

Five hours later, in bustling Kuala Lumpur, Truman chained his cycle amongst dozens of others in the busy lot beside the Lido Theater. He had been in the city nearly an hour in an Indian kedai, a block away, where after the long ride, he ate lunch and washed his face and hands in their one-hole-in-the-floor bathroom.

A mass of people milled before the Lido in the early afternoon. The feature was *Grease*, subtitled. The theater across the honking street boasted *The Nude Bomb*, Maxwell Smart's ascent to the big screen. If not for her instructions, it might have been a tough choice.

Truman worked through the moviegoers, ignoring two "Hello, John." He bought his ticket and returned outside, beneath the theater's marquee in the heavy heat, buying ice cream from an aged Indian woman amongst the vendors, hoping to make himself visible.

Eating his cone, he realized his shaking, like prey, hunted, possibly stalked.

He rechecked his chained motorcycle, then the time. He moved with the crowd, inside the dark theater.

Moving with patrons down the aisle, he retucked his shirt. It was more crowded than he figured, possibly making him hard to find, so he paused just below the halfway point, before excusing himself, in Malay, toward an empty four or five seats in the center. Not his preference.

Shortly, the screen-sized stills, selling cigarettes, beer, cosmetics, and national pride ended, giving way for the coming attractions.

"*Akang Datang*" filled the screen. From New Egypt to The Children's Home, and back to New Egypt, Truman hated missing these tidy, action-packed sequences. In the Lido's darkness, he counted upon one or two of the Malay sort, stringing dramatic pleas and tears regarding village life, family and the dawning of the urban type. Just as certain came the Chinese clips, rapid episodes of kicking and chopping and magical leaps, all virtuous acts correcting oriental wrongs.

The house lights went low. In Malay, "Feature Presentation" filled the screen. Then new shuffling in Truman's row, to his left, his scarred side he worried.

He ventured a peek. The couples, triple dating, were rearranging, tickled to be together as the opening end-of-summer beach sequence flickered before the darkness, silencing the crowd.

John Travolta strolled hand in hand with Olivia Newton-John. Something about Australia. Kangaroos slipped through Truman's mind. Then new movement. To Truman's right.

His peripheral vision strained as his row adjusted, allowing a taller female. He couldn't tell if she was alone. Danny and Sandy exchanged teen promises on the big screen as the peristaltic movement worked inward, toward him. He stared straight ahead. The seat beside him filled. The woman straightened her skirt after she sat. She was alone.

Truman looked fast. A shudder raced through him. Mr. Tan's wife flickered to the musical, cartoonish opening credits that took over the darkness.

Tan's wife! Jesus Christ, of all places, trying not to panic.

She's fucking everything up!

Then: Tan's wife! Holy shit, trying to settle himself.

He leaned slightly away, rearranging.

The bridge of her nose flickered. On the big screen it was the first day of school at Rydell High. Danny Zuko was cool again.

Beside him, Tan's wife was a rail. Her neck thin above her slight bosom.

"Hello," whispered Truman.

She remained silent. Not a peep.

Then quiet he'd be as well, as Truman settled into his seat, occupying both armrests as the Rydell High kids reacquainted, singing and dancing about their lunch time, launching their senior year.

Truman enjoyed the film's lively soundtrack set to the moods of the story. He especially liked "Hopelessly Devoted To You." When Frenchy's hair backfired, turning pink to the joy of the audience, as Frankie Avalon descending heavenly stairs, sang of her mishap of choice, Tan's wife giggled.

Truman liked it, too, but not as much as the block and tackle sequence, working to song, lowering a new engine into the gang's dreamy red hot rod, before flashing back to Kenicki's junker they started with. Tan's wife wouldn't acknowledge Truman until the televised dance contest.

On the screen the camera swept the decorated gym, showdown its theme. The Asian audience cleanly missed the young girl reference to her name ". . . as in cherry" to the older emcee preying on her. Truman crossed his knee, bumping the thin woman's. He whispered an apology. She offered an uncertain hand from her motionless lap.

Truman welcomed the slender fingers upon his knee, placing his hand over hers. Their hands stayed so, until the Rydell gang danced and strutted through the movie's closing carnival. When Olivia Newton-John's Sandy braved into turning naughty, clad in black, Tan's wife turned her own hand up into Truman's, never saying a word.

The house lights eased on as Danny and Sandy's convertible ascended into movie-land blue sky, for 50's heaven. The thin woman's hand vanished as though wired to the same switch. But Truman was pleased as they stood.

He could look at her now, cueing her to her side of the aisle.

Turning away, she was nearly as tall as he. She wore a long-sleeved pink blouse, with ruffles at her cuffs and collar, tucked into a dark blue skirt. Her blouse was buttoned down her back.

Out into the aisle, they moved rearward for the exits, silent, as others gabbed in Chinese and in Malay.

Outside, rain fell in heavy sheets. Tan's wife stayed beside Truman. Around them, the scurrying crowd made fast plans. Some dashed into the rain for Datson and Toyota cabs in the honking traffic. The lines of vendors stayed put, dug in, in the wind-driven sheets, knowing the storm's brevity.

"Do you want to go somewhere else or something?" Truman asked her.

"I sorry. I do not understand your speech," she whispered, oddly tilting her face downward.

Truman spoke slowly, "Would you like to get something to eat somewhere?"

"Yes. Fine."

"How about across the street?" He pointed toward a line of kedais through the rain.

"Fine," she whispered, glancing to his handsome side.

Truman signaled her to wait, with his palm up. He bought a *New Straits Times* beneath the large veranda of the bustling theater, giving it to her with the Malay word for umbrella.

He smiled, and she smiled back, fast and crookedly, then gone.

"Follow me," he coaxed.

Across the street, amid clattering business, they sat at a small table against the kedai's greasy white-tiled wall.

Tan's wife ate sparingly at her fried rice. Truman, hungry, consumed his. She looked quick to his ordering a Carlsberg Special Brew, a product with twice the bite of regular beer. Truman needed it, constructing a story in his mind in the event that big

Tan himself might show up. The big man's wife, picking at her fried rice, hoped he'd place his empty out of sight.

"You look very pretty," Truman said, having never seen her dolled up beyond her Chinese-looking pajamas. Her face, too, was softer. Truman knew nothing of makeup.

"Thank you. I sorry for my very homeliness."

Truman couldn't find a single pimple.

Truman asked slowly, "Are you happy to be here?"

"Yes." She looked quickly to him, then down again. "Are you pleased, too, to have meet with me?"

"Very surprised, and happy, too. I had no idea," he answered, looking about the kedai, wondering of her husband, deciding not to ask.

She sipped at her water, then whispered, "I much fear you hope I someone with much more prettiness. Forgive me."

It was back to this. Truman should have paid more attention in training. It was culture to speak lowly of oneself, or of anything held dear.

"I'm happy about you," Truman assured her, before turning to the movie, something they had in common. "And I liked the movie."

"Yes, the movie nice, and the dancing very fine, indeed."

"And I liked holding hands," Truman answered her, emboldened with the Special Brew.

She kept her face down. "Holding hands was very fine, indeed."

After eating, Truman asked her if it was safe to be where they were, ". . . you know, like this? With you? Alone?"

"My husband thinks I have taken holiday with my friend, in Kelang." Her eyes and bridged nose went down again, near to the ruffles of her blouse. "I must return by 5:00 p.m. For return to Kuala Harap."

"Good then, we can go somewhere for an hour." He reached across their table for her hand. She surrendered her right one, upon the formica surface. "Would you like to?" he asked, her hand looking older than the rest of her. The hardware shop, he thought.

She took her hand back. "Yes," she whispered.

"Good! Where to?" he asked, thinking of a stroll. "We may need a cab. Kuala Lumpur has a helmet law, and I've got only mine."

"Do you know of a place?" she asked, eyes up, then down.

"Well, anywhere would be fine." He smiled, trying to cheer her. Things weren't going well. They had no plan.

"I know a place," she answered, leaning forward. "You must not enter me. I am married."

Truman sat silent. Then got it. Stunned.

"Whatever you want," he answered. "I just want us to have some fun." His voice cracked. "I don't even know what to call you."

* * *

The fast rain passed. Steam rose from the street and side-walks outside as Truman and Tan's wife climbed into a cab that Tan's wife hailed. She had taken charge. Her brisk commands to their Chinese driver startled Truman.

Honking and weaving, the old man led them around the high-rise downtown, northeast, into an area unfamiliar to Truman, surprising him when they pulled over before a seedy three-story hotel. The cabbie blurted Chinese. Tan's wife went to her purse. Truman interrupted in Malay, *"Berapa harga?"* he asked, taking out his wallet.

The cabbie seemed pissed. "Twelve ringgits," he answered in Malay.

Sort of inside, at an open-air counter cluttered with newspapers and magazines, Truman imagined himself in command. "I'd like a room," he said in his best Malay.

The aged, T-shirted Chinese man behind the counter answered in English, "How long you stay, John, today, or overnight?"

"Just this afternoon," Truman answered, suddenly thinking of Molly from The Children's Home. "We just need to rest and clean up."

"Twenty-five ringgits, John. Follow me." The old man rounded the counter, leading them up a single flight of concrete steps, their room key in hand.

At the first door, in a line of four, the old man worked the key hard, opening the smudged door inward, before handing the key to Truman.

Tan's wife slipped between them. The old man coughed, remaining posted at the door he held open.

"Terima kasih," Truman thanked him, pulling the door closed behind him, figuring the old man's muttering a reference to his dark deed.

Sitting on the edge of the room's lone bed, straightening her skirt, Tan's wife wondered why Truman didn't tip him.

* * *

"Well, here we are." Truman smiled nervously, walking to the side of the bed.

A ghostly daylight lit their little room from a single window of translucent glass, of horizontal slats.

"I still don't know your name."

Ling didn't care, pulling Truman on top of her on the small bed, hugging and kissing at his cheeks and neck.

Truman didn't know what to do. She rolled him over, and then back again, on top of herself, continuing her urgent kissing, everywhere but his mouth.

She rolled him to his back again, rising over him, between his legs, untucking his white shirt with swift tugs, undoing the buttons, popping one.

Truman rose to his elbows, trying to help. She pulled his shirt over his head, flinging it to the foot of the bed. Then she fell to his chest, kissing him down to his stomach, as she went to his belt, then to the waist of his jeans, then fly. Then she rose, her bony grasps pulling down his jeans and underwear as one, near to his work boots which he still wore.

Truman arched, helping.

"Let me take off my clothes," Truman said, when both seemed done, or not knowing what to do next. He was on his back. Tan's wife lay beside him, her head on his shoulder, only her blouse untucked.

As though a command, she rose and went to his work boots, which she untied and took off, with his socks. His jeans and underwear she worked over his calves.

"Now you," said Truman, smiling.

"No. We must not." She sounded startled.

"We won't," he answered, relieved of the task. "I won't touch you. I just want to see you. That's all. I promise."

"I am ugly," she whispered.

"I won't think so."

"I want you to be happy. Due to me."

"Then let me undress you, too, under the covers. I want under them anyway."

"Are you shy from me?"

"A little," he answered, for it seemed suddenly lighter in their room, their initial fury passed. He could hear traffic outside, and music from somewhere on their floor.

"Do not be shy," she spoke softly. "You very handsome."

"Well, I don't think so, and I'm getting under this blanket. I don't do this sort of thing every day. You with me?" he offered, opening the cover.

Under she went, skirt, shoes and all, with her ruffled blouse untucked.

Truman put his arm around her, learning her name, Choo Poh Ling as she seemed to relax, explaining her surname first, followed by Poh, then her proper name, Ling.

"Ling," said Truman. "I like it." He unbuttoned her blouse. "How about only your top? That's all. I promise."

She sat up, silent. He removed her ruffled blouse. Ribs showed, then the knobs of her spine as she briefly turned with his work.

"I am ugly," she reminded him as she lay back down.

Truman spoke low, "No, you're not." He looked to her chest, reaching to touch one small breast, cupped within her beige bra.

"So, I would call you Ling, right?"

"Choo would be proper."

"I like Ling better," he said, noticing her protruding sternum, central and rising, like a chicken's breast.

"You may call me Ling." She tightened to his touch.

He kept his hand upon her. A moment passed.

"It is okay. You touching me," she said. "What shall I call you?"

"Truman," he answered.

He moved his hand to her back, between bony scapulas, finding light acne.

She held still, looking straight up. Truman looked to her sternum, protruding sharply between the rises of the fabric of her brassiere hollowed to her lying down, little tents filling with her small flesh when she'd sit up or stand.

"May I know your age?" she asked, as Truman worked his hand beneath the center of her bra, for her rise of sternum.

"Nineteen."

"You must think me evil, so very bad, to be here with you," she spoke to the ceiling.

"No, I don't." He slid his hand to her left side, finding her small soft mound of breast. "How old are you?"

"I am shy to tell of my advanced age."

"Don't be." Truman propped himself on an elbow, moving to her other breast. He was becoming aroused again, and pleased.

"I am thirty. Twenty-nine in western way. We Chinese are one at birth."

Truman withdrew his hand. He kissed her cheek. "Ling," he whispered, as he went to the soft skin of her stomach. "I want to take your skirt off."

"You must not enter me. Please."

"Just your skirt. Nothing else. I promise."

"No. I am afraid."

"Don't be. Not of me." He wanted to tell her that he had never even kissed a girl.

"I won't do anything to make you not like me," he said instead. "I want to hug you, with just your underwear on." His hand went low, to the waist of her skirt.

She crossed her legs, working off her shoes.

Then she arched, undoing the back of her skirt, slipping it down her legs, beneath their thin cover. She pulled him close. Truman resisted, wishing to see her near nakedness. She stiffened.

"Very pretty to me," he told her. Her beige underwear was waist-high, like Kathleen Van Heflin's. Womanly.

He rose above her, looking below. Thinness prevailed, with the separate rises of her hips. She worked beneath him, ending his viewing, settling him just right for her hugging, slow rocking.

The music down the hall, and the traffic outside, faded away. Truman hugged her back, noticing his own sweating. He liked this singleness of private constant. He kissed at her face and neck, groping at her small breasts, as she worked harder beneath him, grimacing, sweating herself.

Tan's wife strained and grasped at his back and shoulders, arching hard, a secret of her own.

She went still, then hugged him, saying something he took as "my friend."

The traffic outside and that music from somewhere returned. Truman asked her to smile. She did. He liked it, and told her so.

"What would please you?" she asked.

"This. Holding each other, and I want you to talk to me."

She tried, going back to her homeliness, which Truman denied. Then she spoke of being a "lonely girl."

"I'm lonely, too. It's been my whole life, it seems, and more so in Kuala Harap."

She smiled, then squeezed his arms. "You have muscles like American mens on TV shows."

Truman liked this, thinking Bobby Ewing. Beneath their thin cover, she instructed, "Please keep purchasing your needs at my husband's store. But not speak with me, except with concerns of business." She squeezed his hand. "I shall like seeing your fine appearance. Will you write correspondence with me?"

He assured her he would.

She asked to get dressed. "Our time over. Would you turn from me?"

He did, losing her as she focused somewhere else, dressing in a minute. Truman stole looks, thinness and flesh, beige underwear and bones, prettiness covered fast beneath her ruffled blouse and blue skirt.

Then Truman dressed. His shirt and jeans went fine, but he fumbled with his belt and struggled with his bootlaces. Tan's wife stood quietly beside the door.

Then they were gone. Down the concrete steps, out past the mumbling T-shirted old man.

* * *

The sky was blue again out in the horn-blowing street.

Smothering heat laid everywhere. The steam was gone, giving way to diesel-fumed air. Truman tried small talk. Tan's wife didn't answer. Her chin was down. "We need separate taxis."

"If that's what you want. I had fun." He extended his hand. "You know, with the movie, and the meal and all."

She nodded his handshake away. She waved a cab. It wheeled in hard. She glanced. "Will you write to me first? Our correspondence?"

"Yes, I will," he said, his hands going to his pockets, for anything.

She glanced away, saying nothing. Then she climbed into the cab that weaved her away into the downtown traffic.

* * *

May 31, 1981
What a day. Wish I was better at that stuff.
Maybe I'll get another chance. Hope so.

CHAPTER 16

The bleating goat, with one kid behind her, worked through the lush growth between the Home and the river. Truman heard her the evening before, then again at sunrise.

Fatimah told him her other kid was swept away in the river, and that she was searching for it.

Truman felt for the animal across the following days, as he moved through Kuala Harap with a new confidence, and a new tension. His letters having led him to a hot dirty city, changing him, reborn as something else, evil yet wanted, welded into secrecy.

He returned to his A.M. schooling, his lunches up in town, and into the afternoons of his four-child rocker, woven into new thoughts of her. "Ling," he repeated in his mind, wondering what she was doing up there in her husband's shop by day, and in her upstairs home by night, her quietness having to be doing something. Would she ever tell? Would she fold from guilt? What of her differentness? Adultery, like stealing, or any crime, had to cut through the fabric of their separate cultures as certain sins should.

Maybe she wanted to be his girlfriend. There's a thought. A first girlfriend. Of course not really his, but whatever was? Not the farm, not Mabel's little home, nor even New Egypt, nor The Children's Home, nor old man Archer's home in the Pines, nor Allentown High School. Everything assigned, even the scar that clung to the side of his face. The only thing he never wanted.

* * *

June 7, 1981

First off—John stopped by & we had a great time down at the truck stop, over in Mentacab & then back at the truck stop. We saw ROCKY again, & I told him about you-know-who & he teased me about not getting her to go all the way. He kept at it & I couldn't make him understand. I sure as hell wasn't going to tell him about me (you know—the big "V" word). (I also wrote to her—as asked— but I didn't know what to write.)

Anyway, John came & went. The kids have been fun & trying hard at their schooling. (I still feel funny saying that that's what I do.) I've spent too much $ lately. Ben wrote to me about a 1-year party for our training group in a few months. I'll try to go. He also sent an article from the New Straits Times *about the arrest of some guy in Johor Baru who kissed a girl & dashed off into the woods. (Holy fuck! If ___ was a Muslim, they'd hang both of us!)*

I also got a letter from "real" teacher, Jacki. She's hanging it up & going home. Ben said she wrote to everyone in our group. (She added for me to watch my drinking. Jesus, I'm not the one giving up & heading home.) Besides, she hardly spoke to me back in training.

* * *

Truman wrote Mabel a lengthy letter, pondering the thinning of his mail, save hers. The next night, early in his sleep, he dreamed of returning home, forgetting to pick up his readjustment pay. Mabel floated about her kitchen, uncaring, packing her station wagon to go someplace. Then Allentown's offensive guard appeared, the pisser in Jimmy's sneakers, then Jimmy McCleary, who wanted to go out riding around.

In the heavy heat of wakefulness, things went easier, the kids back to routine. Even Fatimah and Zurina got along. One afternoon Singh and little Salleh were naughty at the river. Truman wrote in his journal of ". . . chasing wet go-tards along a sandbar of a jungled river."

He finished his four-child rocker, sweating the day it'd crush little brown toes. He laid out plans for a big sand box surrounded with painted planks serving as bench seats beneath the shade of a corrugated tin roof. Then a package arrived from John Singer. Enclosed were two novels, The *Catcher In The Rye* and *Walden II*, along with a warm letter.

Singer commented on Truman's last letter, written too late at night. "Did someone run off with your favorite memories? Was it that hardware harlot?" Then he commented regarding the rumors of their drinking. "You should be proud. How is it that so many (including big-shot Andy) know what we've been up to? I guess we're such cool fucks that people make us their business."

He mentioned the books, then invited Truman to Pekan, "my quaint little royal town," before mentioning that he also heard through the same grapevine, that a certain "Jackie, of your illustrious group?" suffered from some sort of vaginal virus or STD or, "who the hell knows what?"

Zurina asked what was so funny. Kumari and Singh joined Truman, laughing and nodding in confused ignorance as the mailman's bell sounded out front, returning, rattling up the pitted driveway. Truman had one more.

"Mr. Truman. *Ada satu lagi!*" he said as he huffed and puffed and smiled.

"Terima kasih," Truman thanked him, noticing the woman's childlike handwriting upon the envelope.

> *Dear Truman,*
> *Received your last letter Thursday and sorry to*
> *reply you late because just don't know what should*
> *I say to you. You seem you have start to get fed up*
> *on me. Why? Have I done something make you*
> *mad on me? If I did so, let me know, okay? I will*
> *change my bad character in future.*
> *Sincerely, Ling (as you say you desired)*

Truman folded the letter carefully, then walked to the side of the building. He looked up into the deep green of the trees that separated his little Home from the town above. A new happiness surged within, in spite of the deepening deceit, in spite his having no idea what she meant.

* * *

Mid-June was kind to Truman. At the river little Salleh and Azman stayed upon the sandbars whenever Truman was in the water, fearing his rhythmic Jaws cadence, the wet cousin to his indoor Wild Dog.

Up in town one early afternoon, a taxi struck a young boy. From inside a kedai, the skid and light crash sent a chill through Truman, reflexively thinking of Singh and Ramasami, both developing healthy senses of wandering. That evening he wrote a deliberate, warm letter to Tan's wife, thinking of her as underneath him, then imagining her thin hand retrieving his letter from her post office box. He wondered of her face reading it, within or above her husband's cluttered hardware shop.

In one of those early days of June, Truman met a government official, an Indian. The quiet man introduced himself as, "Mr. Martin." He paid for their lunch, genuinely concerned for Truman's "project."

Truman liked this older man immediately, and invited him to visit the Home. In Pekan, with John Singer, Truman realized that Mr. Martin, denying race and culture, for some reason looked remarkably like an imagined grown-up Scotty Winslow. Maybe it was the bones in his face, or his gestures or smile. Truman cheered, picturing Mr. Martin taking a grass-staining slide.

Then Truman grew irritable. One afternoon he walked out on the kids, striding up into town, leaving Singh and Ramasami staring at homemade flash cards, blowing any sounds to please their stormed-off guru.

Work on the sand box held him together, though, leading him to Tan's Hardware for new bolts. But Tan's wife was too good, never acknowledging his presence, rearranging inventory along a wall as her robust husband counted change.

The Catcher In The Rye helped. Truman couldn't put down Holden's chronicle of his own despair with everyone being such pains in Holden's ass. He liked Jane Gallagher, too, with her tears lost on a checkerboard, somewhere in America, years before.

B.F. Skinner's *Walden II* chased close behind, filling Truman's sweltering void between work, crummy movies down along the highway, and solitary beers in dirty kedais. Skinner's story saddened Truman. Even scared him a bit, for Truman loved America and didn't need to read such a scathing review of its culture by someone so smart, while living in a land where western values were hurled upon weekly. Truman wondered if Skinner's *Walden II* really existed. He'd have to ask Singer in Pekan.

* * *

June 22, 1981

Just got back from Pekan & happy as hell to see the kids & Zurina & Fatimah. I needed it—two nights & a day of boozing & just being around John. I had to thumb it down though—fucking battery's dead in my cycle.

I started down at the bridge & got picked up in about 10 minutes (just beyond the sawmill where some fuckhead workers hooted & jeered at me like I was some hippie traveler or something). A Chinese guy picked me up. He spoke no English or Malay—just "Kuantan" where he left me off after a terrifying ride, passing on curves & at the crests of hills. (He even threw us into a skid over chickens.) But Pekan was great. Smaller than K.H. & dead after 6:00 p.m. It's surrounded by kumpangs clear down to the sea & back up to the Sultan's palace, which was huge and white. Seeing John was what I needed the most. We partied from Friday night until Sunday morning.

Friday night we talked about everything until 4:00 a.m, playing music the whole time. I felt proud talking about his books (but he knows more than me). He told me not to worry about Walden II*—he says you can't domesticate people like barnyard animals. He said we're too aware of $ & most of us are "in heat" most of the time anyway & besides, the Russians have been at it since 19-whenever and are miserable as shit.*

Saturday we loaded up & hit the beach (miles & miles of nobody—just sand & waves) and swam & had foot races. (He also questioned me about you-know-who & teased me some.) Back in town (Pekan) we let some old Indian guy drink with us & he apologized for stinking (which he really did).

Sunday a.m. we hit the Kuantan bus station for a bus for me to K.H. John held up my bus while I found a place to piss long & clear, in some ratty (I MEAN real rats) alley.

Two hours later, I'm here in K.H.

* * *

Truman's next journal entry was filled with warmth for the kids, the progress of the sand box, and what little he knew of Islam, which he supposed made Fatimah and Zurina so kind most of the time. He penciled in Ben's plans concerning their group's one-year bash less than a month away, including their training. Then he switched tablets, to write quick to Tan's wife, telling her that he thought of her more and more.

Happy again, his A.M. schooling went well, as he again noticed the blue of the Malaysian sky, its billowy white clouds and the ever-present deep green of growth everywhere.

His sand box, empty but finished, was a hit as an open-air playhouse. Rough plans for a merry-go-round churned in Truman's mind. The central rotating hub was the puzzle. On one of their afternoon wagon-train walks, Singh defecated in his pants. Ramasami scolded him sharply. Truman intervened as Singh began wiping himself with his dry right hand. Normah contorted and howled from her wheelchair, steadied by an oblivious-to-the-hygiene-crisis Kumari, who dug deep into her own dress, preoccupied with some condition of her own.

On another hike, little Salleh and crazed Azman sat down on an active mound of hard-biting ants. Both leapt and danced in turmoil. Azman spun like a top, slapping at his head, then Truman's. He even cried a little, while being picked clean. It was the first Truman had seen him do it.

The Blues Brothers, subtitled, came to the theater down along the highway. Truman treated Ramasami and Singh to an early show. The rampaging car chase through the suburban shopping mall brought the modest crowd to its feet. The three of them stopped at the ice cream girl's stand on their way out. She was all smiles, innocent of earlier suspicions, grinning wide, waving good-bye to him, and to Ramasami and Singh.

The following afternoon they splashed in the river. Skinny Yap speechlessly imitated the Jaw's cadence, terrifying Salleh. Later that week, Truman secured the use of a local primary school's lawn mower, then solved, in theory, the hub problem of his mind's merry-go-round while leading his trailing of retarded children past an abandoned rear axle and differential assembly in the high weeds behind the bus station. The following day he happened upon, and cussed out a small circling of Malay boys torturing a lone puppy. In school, Yap, the shark, took a keen interest in Truman's scar as Singh shit himself again. Zurina wasn't as chari-table as Fatimah. A *Newsweek* and two letters came. Truman set one aside. The first was from Kathleen Van Heflin, with pictures and all. Truman felt guilty, thinking of her womanly underwear. In two photographs Angela looked awfully pretty, but confused or sad. Maybe she had to pose, wishing her mother didn't make her do it.

The second letter read:

> *Dear friend Truman,*
>
>   *How do you do? I feel disappointed that I can't speak with you recently. I wish you have enjoyed your trip to Pekan. (I hear from customer that the European one who plays with kids went to Pekan to stay with the gone one.)*
>
>   *I look forward to meet with you again in K.L. on other weekend.*
>
>   *So please write to me and let me know if you choose to want to meet with me too.*
>
>   *That is all.*
>
>   *Yours, Ling*
>
> *P.S. Think of you always and hope to see you soon.*

That night in his shed, Truman dreamed of being shot in a dark hallway, several times in the chest. The lack of pain surprised his dreaming self. He couldn't decide upon last words, then realized no one was around to hear them anyway.

* * *

July 5, 1981

It's been a week since I last wrote to my "friend." I still feel odd in front of her husband. Kind of bad—I mean—you know—slimy or something.

Schooling went downhill for a bit. I had to collar Ramasami for slamming down my toolbox when I told him to leave. (Fatimah understood—Zurina didn't—the bitch. She went on & on singing some made-up song about how Encik Azman is so nice to these kids— to get under my skin.) A dip in the river with the kids made everything better. We trapped a bunch of those biting minnows. They'd kick the shit of New Jersey's.

I also ran smack into John S. up at the taxi stand yesterday. I had to laugh. He said all he had to do was stand around long enough in this town & sooner or later I'd be along, & maybe with 'tards in tow. (He meant it kindly—he was on his way to his Close of Service conference in K.L.—over a year for me—just 2 more mos. for him)

I found out some Jr. Rotarians are donating a sliding board in a few weeks. I'm glad. People are noticing the place, & it'll be used.

That Mr. Martin guy came by & I showed him all around. He then took me up to this old folks' home that I didn't know existed on the other side of town. They were all old Chinese men in this barnlike building off the edges of the Chinese section of houses. I'm thinking about taking the kids up there on one of our hikes.

* * *

Truman had his sand box filled one midmorning, puzzling the children, and Zurina and Fatimah, who thought it fine the way it was. Shrieking and hobbling about, the kids got a bigger kick out of the dump truck that delivered the sand. Singh wet himself over the snorting spectacle.

Two afternoons later, Truman marched seven of the kids up through town to the barnlike barracks housing the aged Chinese men. Once there, he relaxed and strolled, cot-to-cot, observing how his kids mixed with the aged men. He swelled with pride.

Ramasami was a gem, confident and cordial, leading skinny Yap, greeting and shaking hands with the toothless and tired. Singh and Salleh froze with fear, having discovered a sleeping dog off in a corner. They kept the animal's slumber in check throughout the visit. Chubby Lim remained quiet, sitting on an old trunk with her hands on her knees. Normah had to be coaxed into the structure, wheelchair and all. Big Kumari, smirking and limping, worked her amongst the trunks and bed spaces to Truman's cues.

They stayed an hour. A journal entry reflected the smiling of the aged men in the dusty darkness, Singh's whisperings regarding the sleeping dog, before fabricating that it was suppertime, and that they'd be late. Truman finished with, "Maybe I found something these kids can do."

That night he also wrote back-to-back letters to Tan's wife, and felt reckless for doing so. Her response was nearly as prompt. At a full page and a half, her lengthiest to date, it read, amongst other things:

> *Anyway, I'm so glad to have received your letters*
> *and I think it much better to have received it*
> *everyday if I may . . .*

And:

> *I do not know why I am so anxious to hear from*
> *you, you know something? It remind me of not*
> *much time for us to see each other. Only 1 year and*
> *several months for you to live here. I think maybe*
> *10-15 dates for us and then you will receive back*
> *to America and forget about me. I feel sad when I*
> *do think that.*

Closing with:

> *I haven't angry on you because we can not*
> *meet with me around K.H. so stop worried about*
> *that. Lastly, send to me more letters. Also, how do*
> *you find my English language? Is there any im-*
> *provement or more worse than before? Please tell*
> *me truth so I can get improved in future!*
> *Your secret friend, Ling (as you wish)*

* * *

So across July, Truman wrote back, about the kids, and about seeing her in her husband's hardware store, so pretty on a ladder, or making change, so emotionless it confused him. He wrote how the Muslim-fasting month quieted nice Fatimah, as it morphed Zurina into a raving, nasty thing, until they could eat and drink after sundown. John Singer wrote how the author of the Koran, God or otherwise, when exempting the poor, the children, the warriors and the travelers, should have sympathized a little more with the temperamental.

Truman attended his training group's one-year reunion party, and shared it with John Singer. There was booze and food, shop-talk of good placements and poor ones, a couple of new loves, some hip Malaysian acquaintances, and really cool new friends from previous and subsequent groups.

Bruce and Andy showed up lugging softball gear. Truman was thrilled. By the second inning he was discovered and moved to plug his team's hemorrhaging at shortstop. At their makeshift plate he arched the ball deep, quietly enjoying the other team's outfielders backing up to his occasional at-bats.

In the relaxing that followed, he learned from Ben of the Malaysian Youth Movement's calling for a prohibition of Gideon bibles being placed in the hotels of the cities, deeming the practice a covert missionary activity, according to the *New Straits Times*.

The next morning upon his return to Kuala Harap, Truman learned that Azman, the well-dressed, remarked in his absence that Truman did "donkey's work." In his journal, Truman labeled his Malay boss, "an ignorant, propped-up pig-fucking Muslim."

Then a package from John Singer arrived, containing a copy of Carl Sagan's *Cosmos*, with an attached note:

> Hello, my friend,
> My confusion has dissipated. My hope satisfied. I am at peace. Allow Sagan to be your guide.
> Hugs & kisses, queer bait!
> JS

* * *

In the evenings, Truman returned to spending time up front with the girls and the kids, teasing Ramasami a bit too much, hugging with Salleh, and chatting with everyone.

One night he dreamed of being in a church all night long, having to stay awake to watch over the kids as they slept. Bats fluttered in. He moved around within the high darkness, locking windows and doors materializing before him. Then an opened door appeared, with a harsh noise from beyond. He froze, fearful. Chubby Lim appeared beside him, her thick tongue protruding, pointing toward the same door. Truman let her enter first because she wasn't afraid. He heard a sound, like an animal's, then awakened in the dark of his shed, ashamed of himself, his pulse racing.

By July's end Truman found himself swept up in the Hari Raya spirit, warmly awaiting Islam's Great Day, closing their month of fasting. Schooling strained, but playing with the kids upon the sandbars of the river didn't, nor did their wagon-train hikes up into town, and down beneath the bridge and beyond. Spinning Azman was bitten by a territorial goose. Salleh, backed up by an assertive monkey, fell into a muddy ditch as inch-long leeches continued to find chubby Lim. Skinny Yap, speechless, with lots to say, began to pick up Malay, largely through her justifiable fear of Zurina. And Truman ran into Tan's wife at the bank up in town. She exited as he entered, never looking at him. He awaited her next letter.

He also tried to telephone Mabel from a hotel in Mentacab, but something between there and Kuala Lumpur was down. The kids were his solace, dancing to his radio to mournful Malay pop. Most bobbed in place. Singh was the best, Ramasami the most alarming, jerking and shaking about, as Azman, sensing hoopla, hooted and spun like a top off in a corner.

On the day before Hari Raya, Truman happened upon Fatimah weeping beneath the great tree out back. He had just returned from buying the abandoned differential gear he found a month before. She claimed she was okay. On his desk inside, he found a letter from her. It explained their Muslim Great Day, and it asked forgiveness for anything she might have said or done. Later in the day Zurina did the same, verbally, as she could neither read nor write.

* * *

Aug. 6, 1981

I had a good time at John's over Hari Raya. I spent way too much $, but it was worth it. The best time was at the beach on our cycles & having our stupid contests—foot races & coconut shot puts (puts or putts???), etc. John even brought a cleaned chicken he bought. We cooked it over a fire at the edge of the palms. All day long we chased crabs, ripped around on our cycles, talked, swam & never saw anyone else—not even a ship or a boat—just sand, palm trees & pine trees. I now sit here in the Home—returned this morning—no kids—no Zurina or Fatimah—just these little birds that are always here. They fly in & out through the caged door, folding in their wings for a long flap until they're through the bars.

Watching the kids leave for Hari Raya was pretty & sad (got all of them out to one reluctant relative or another). One by one they left in the office Land Rover with me watching with an unexpected feeling in my chest. I really do like the little shits.

Lim left laughing & jumping up & down in the back seat. Ramasami & Azman together. Ramasami packed 4 plastic bags of clothes (his & who knows who else's!). Azman (the kid, not the asshole) just looked bewildered. Normah left howling with delight. Singh, smiling hand-in-hand with his mother. When I called Salleh, I believe every bone in his little body jerked at once, rattling the loose ones in his head. He looked scared climbing into the Land Rover— next to big old Kumari who sat there all stupid-looking (scratching away at one of her big tits). Yap was the last—her eyes swollen with tears. She was walking around the place feeling forgotten.

Funny enough, I, too, got into the Harai Raya spirit these last two weeks. I guess from all the pretty lights & the thoughtfulness from all the Muslims, all the Raya cards about (like Xmas cards), going to see John & of course, the nice words from Fatimah & Zurina.

Back to Pekan, I knew that Azman's home (the jerk, not the spinner) was nearby so I struck out to find it (being in the spirit) & found him & a house full of Malays (family & neighbors). Azman was surprised & I have to admit, very kind to me being there. (I think my being an American, and his being "my boss" made him the cat's ass for a bit.)

Before leaving Pekan, John & I went out (hungover) and had a nice breakfast in an unusually cool morning to say good-bye once again. I rode straight home w/o stopping & the jungles seemed very pretty in the cloudy morning. When crossing the bridge here in K.H., I saw about 100 people crowded below. I suspected a drowning & was right. They were searching for a Chinese boy who fell in while fishing. The odd part is there were vendors with their carts down there along the riverbank selling drinks & quay. Wherever there's a crowd, I suppose.

I visited Normah's house in her kumpang & was surprised how young her father was. (His 2nd wife wouldn't allow Normah on the rotan furniture so she stayed on the floor. I saw her wheelchair outside, but didn't ask.) I also visited Fatimah's & had lunch there—

parents very old & very nice—village about the prettiest around! I went to Zurina's, & on this rutty old dirt road, I saw a Honda Cub dump with—no shit—5 people on it—2 little ones were crying loudly. Zurina's house surprised me—very poor & falling-down shack on stilts. Only her father (aged & crippled) & a sister lived there. I ate there, too. Her younger sister (a grownup—older than me) served me—bending over & over again with sparkly beads of sweat on her chin & nose & neck & nice brown cleavage. Anyway, she looked awfully pretty for a homely woman working over the open firebox in their little shack of a home.

Well, it's getting late in the morning & hot again as usual. I'm still all alone. I'll kick around, waiting for the kids to return. Maybe I'll plant another tree. I also have the merry-go-round centerpiece (bus axle) out back & I can start on that. It'll be the most challenging thing to build so far (& the most fun).

* * *

But Truman didn't write of John Singer's divorce, disclosed on their second day on the beach. After Singer had teased Truman about Tan's wife, Truman had his thoughts toward an eventual wife, something Singer once had, something Truman could only imagine.

"You're taking your time. You could be on it by now," Singer chided, sitting beside Truman in shade at the top of the narrow beach in the furnace of the midafternoon.

"Is it cool, though? You know, having a wife?" Truman asked.

"It depends on who you marry."

Truman mirrored Singer's sitting in the sand. "It'd just be neat having someone all the time. Someone who depends on you. Sex whenever you wanted."

"Whoa, young buck!" John Singer laughed. "There's not a lot of that going on. Even around here. And if it's a chore, who wants it?"

Truman dug his heels into the sand. "Well, I've never been married or anything."

"Apparently not." Singer laughed again.

"What was it like for you?" Truman asked. A clean line of wave rolled and peeled itself upon the desolate beach before them.

Singer watched it. "At first it was good. Or at least I thought so. Back then. Looking back, though, I guess it was never any good. But I tried awfully hard, trying to convince her that we were okay. You know, happy together."

"Then what happened? If I can ask," Truman shied.

Singer smiled toward the sea. "Sure. But I'll need another slug of that brandy you've been making love to."

Truman, eager for the tale, handed him the bottle.

"Whelp, old friend." Singer winced from a good swallow. "I met her in college, my sophomore year. And I chased her and chased her until I caught her, or convinced her, or something, to marry me." He pulled back his hair with his freckled free hand. Looking to the wind and the waves, he continued, "And then she married me, and we bought a small house, in East Aurora, outside Buffalo. Something else I talked her into—her parents, too. For I was still chasing her, you see, still hard at that work of convincing her that we were happy. And a few seasons passed and she got pregnant. I thought we did anyhow, and, of course, I had to chase her some more, into being happy about it. And then the baby came. A little boy. A little mulatto." He smirked. "The little bugger ended our marriage."

Singer wiped at his mouth with his wrist. "No. I'm sorry. She ended it, or I did, or everything did." He drank again, keeping his gaze to the sea. "Or better yet, I suppose I ended our marriage, years before, back in college, when I knew damn well that I was working too hard. Lord knows I've had plenty of time to fucking think about it."

But Truman was lost, tripped up in "mulatto." Handicapped maybe? Thoughts of Ramasami and Salleh flashed by. "What do you mean?" he asked. "Was something wrong with the baby?"

"Well, yeah!" blurted Singer, with a sudden laugh.

"I'm sorry. I don't know what mulatto means."

"It means the baby was the product of a black-white union." Singer smiled quietly, again toward the sea. "She fucked a fucking nigger, Truman!"

Truman went silent. John Singer nudged him.

"Don't take it wrong. I'm not mad at you. I'm just still mad about it . . ." his voice trailed off. "And I shouldn't say 'nigger' either. Sorry. Some black guy. It's just she got all swept up, like a dumbbell, in this guy's smooth-talkin' shit." He paused, his heels deeper in the sand. "And I guess, I wasn't man enough, or husband enough, or whatever, to keep her home in that way. Whatever it was she wanted, or needed, I didn't have. I've come to understand that. Malaysia's been good to me that way."

"Some surprise," whispered Truman. "I'm sorry to hear about it." And he was, too, as well as amazed. John Singer getting burned.

"Geez," Truman added, "you must think I'm a fuckin' dirt ball. You know, with Mr. Tan's wife, and her being married and all."

Singer smiled, gave him a shove. "Fuck, no. Not at all. Christ, Tan's about as faithful as a rooster." Singer lit a Winston, snapping his lighter shut. "No, Truman. No two are the same. Not in the whole world. Each has its own reasons. Believe me. I've had two years to ponder it. It's at least one thing I know."

Then he looked to Truman again, and smiled. "Tan's likes his women big breasted, right?"

Truman smiled back, his pardon granted. "Yeah. He likes 'em big." Looking at the same waves, he thought of Tan's wife's own small breasts, separated by that hard rising of sternum. Funny how Singer conjured chickens.

"And it's not the same thing," Singer continued. "You were approached. You didn't weasel in on a life someone else was trying to build. Know what I mean?"

"I think so." Truman was relieved. "It sounds like she didn't even warn you."

"She claimed it was a onetime thing. Just at a time when we, or me, anyway, was hoping for a baby. I guess she figured it'd have to be mine. And you know, Truman, believe it or not, I still feel sorry for her. You know, with her secret hope and all, across those months. A pretty big one to worry over."

"Did it matter that the guy was black?" Truman asked.

"Fuck, yeah. It shouldn't have, but it did. I guess it's really a blessing, though. Imagine if she laid some white guy. It could have become the deception of a lifetime. Anyway, she cried. I cried. It was embarrassing and humiliating—for both of us. I left her for it. She pled, but not long. We got a divorce, sold the house, and off I ran to Malaysia. To here. To this fucking beach, with you." He laughed.

A sand-whipping breeze swirled around them. "Geez. I thought I had it tough," Truman answered.

"Tougher than me. Having no parents was not your own fault. I fucked myself trying to will myself on someone else."

Truman stared out to the sea.

"Life isn't fair," Singer added. "Both of us had parents die. That kid hurt you. You hurt him back. I tried to make things wonderful for a girl I adored, and wrecked us both. Jesus Christ, have another drink. On me." He grinned. "You're the only friend I've got on this beach."

"You, too, John." Truman smiled back. "And just for us I've got another bottle. Hid it good." He rose, for his pack strapped to his cycle.

"You're a fucking genius!" John Singer called to him through the wind-blown sand.

* * *

An hour after Truman closed his writing, omitting Singer's brief marriage, a quick note arrived in the mail. Truman was alone, working on the merry-go-round. As his postman's red bicycle weaved away, he read the uneven hand that gave the name of a hotel in Kuala Lumpur, a block from Stadium Merdeka. The note was brief, suggesting an "all night visiting" a day away.

Truman's next journal entry was two days later, dated Aug. 8 (late at night). He was cautious, writing "she" or "her" in place of Ling.

This entry chronicled his long cycle ride through the cooler mountains, for bustling Kuala Lumpur. Then the small balcony off their uncarpeted sixth-floor room. Unwritten, was fast rolling around, the first clothed, the next naked. Little talk. Then none at all, then sleep.

She woke him in the night, his journal reflected, her thinness, steering him, knowing what to do, seeming so distant that it concerned him, as though she were alone in their room. "V word no more," he wrote.

Then she joined him on their tiny balcony, for the twinkling of the city's lights in the middle of the night. He wrote of their brief words, but nothing of the smell of her hair, nor that of her sweating skin. He didn't write of her ribs, nor of her hard rising of sternum between small breasts. He wrote nothing of her working beneath him, as he wrote of her broken English on the balcony, of her wishing "for some person in this world to have love for me, so I shall not be alone."

His entry closed, mentioning their morning, their subsequent shyness in the daylight that sliced into their room. Her dressing fast. Her head down and hurried. Out into the gathering heat of the new day in Kuala Lumpur.

Each for separate paths home. Across the mountains, east for Kuala Harap.

CHAPTER 17

Truman weaved through the jungled mountains, knifing the cooler air of forever green hills, returning to Kuala Harap, ascended to a higher club.

At the Home, he went to work, cementing upright, into the ground, his rear axle-differential gear to serve as the merry-go-round's central hub, after digging a tremendous hole. Letting it set for a couple of days, he went to work on its circular platform carriage. He couldn't decide what to call it in his daily plans. He built it pentagonal, and mostly wooden, with steel rods supporting its circumference above spokes of lumber supporting planks for seats to come in his mind's eye.

As he worked, several of the kids returned from their holiday. Skinny Yap took it bad, screaming and sobbing and clinging to an adult brother, who had to wrestle her from his little blue sedan. Her pain pained Truman as she ran after her brother's car, dragging her tattered laundry bag as her brother's Renault rounded the end of the drive, up into town. Truman caught her and walked her home, trying to console her as they walked. Out by the gate she stumbled and fell upon the broken asphalt, adding to her sobbing.

Truman figured she'd sit and cry it out. But Skinny Yap simply rose, soldiering on, lathered in tears and snot.

Truman wrote of her cheering later that evening, to the return of Singh and little Salleh. Singh sported a new hat. "You should have seen the fucker!!" he wrote. "Holden Caulfield would have been proud." Salleh, though, returned with a toothache. "Oh boy, here we go again," he wrote before turning his pen toward a separate letter for his friend in the darkened town above.

He thanked her for her kindness, pondering how she'd read that sentiment. He mentioned the city's lights from their little balcony, feeling the urge to tell his truth, the two of them forever married in at least that way. Instead, he wrote that he was sorry they didn't really talk to one another, especially in light of their letter writing, which was becoming easier. He signed off, calling her "very pretty, and very special."

* * *

Four days later she responded, along with a *Newsweek*, and a letter from Angela. What a bounty!

Ling's letter read:

> *Dear Truman, My special friend,*
>
> *Even though your letter arrive a bit late to me, as I estimate, I happy to received it. Okay? By the way, who was that beautiful girl over in Mentacab this week? I hear of a white woman who stays two days. Is she your girlfriend who come from America? Some people think so. I hope you do not share your holiday with her. I more wish that we may meet again on the weekend of 31st August. It is near my birthday. I don't wish any gift, but hope that you'll come down to K.L. to meet with me again and we can go for a show and have a drink and talk as you wishes. Do you know something? I think of you a lot and that's some that we can talk about. I want talk to you as you say, but I worried that you'll feel mad on me for talking wrong.*
>
> *Thinking of you so much,*
> *Your special friend*
> *P.S. Write if we may meet near to my birthday.*

Then Angela's letter, a wonderful five pages. Truman swelled, for it started well.

"Dear Truman," she wrote in her leaning to the left, looping hand of purple ink, "the heat and the humidity of this summer around this boring farm means you've been away for a year now. I can't believe it! We all miss you so much!" as her purple lines stretched to meet her anticipated margin. And why the "we" wondered Truman.

From there, Angela's letter swung back into the weather, then over to her concluded summer classes at Mercer County Community College. She asked, and answered questions about herself. Then she asked questions of Malaysia, but all too pointed, trying too hard. She wrote of friends from high school, then new ones from college, all in tidy fashion. The horse race of her life well under way.

She apologized for not writing sooner, joking of his falling for some exotic oriental girl, so far from home. Truman felt teased, thinking of sternum. Then her purple ink gained strength, as though put down for a time, going back to her college friends. She couldn't wait for the fall. College was nothing like Allentown High School. She'd be starting her junior year up at Montclair State, a regular four-year institution. "One FARTHER from home!!!" she wrote.

Then carefully, she led into a new boyfriend. Kyle didn't work out. Truman didn't care. Her purple hand looped and slashed on. The new guy was some Jake Goodwin, also transferring to Montclair, and "Mom and Dad aren't too pleased." They didn't understand. "But Mom at least tries. Neither know him like I do," she added, as her flight of purple thought hurried with determination. "Jake has insights and plans. He's an ambitious man."

Angela, head-over-heels, had lost some of her sensitivity since once laboring over drawing a boy cutting grass too near a hungry robin.

* * *

August 16, 1981

 I wrote to my friend & she wrote back as quickly as I hoped. I also got a letter from Angela a few days back. It was sort of dopey, but it made me dream of her. We were at the farm & she wouldn't speak to me until we were on the track bed (my old walk), & then she told me I could touch her from the waist up, but her new boyfriend showed up (sort of faceless). He had buddies who came out of the brush. I told her I wasn't afraid of them. The guy shook my hand & then showed me a Corvette (his I guess). Anyway (real life now) I drank a bit the next night & wrote a bit of a mushy letter to her. I don't feel bad about it though.

A load of Jr. Rotarians swung by today to help clean & do what they could. (I got the merry-go-round painted.) The one guy (their "leader" he told me) was surprised at Azman's (all the kids are back now) behavior across the 3 hours they were here. Christ, the kid's been doing that for 15 years or so.

I also saw a movie called Death Ship *tonight. It sucked—I walked out—some big ship drifting around through fog for an hour & a half.*

* * *

Then Truman marched his stringing of kids back to the old folk's barn.

Again he was pleased. The aged men grew chipper, gave the kids water, tied up their flea-bitten mutt and passed out cookies. The next afternoon, after schooling, Truman marched his gang farther upstream, to a new sandbar, to play the afternoon away in the cool passing of the Pahang.

The merry-go-round was a hit. As the kids howled, Ramasami took something akin to a seizure, chubby Lim vomited her supper and little Salleh, brushing aside Lim's mess, demanded more. Azman, who should have been a natural, stood fearful from a distance. Skinny Yap sang a wordless melody while riding. For some reason, Zurina hated the song.

Then Fatimah fell ill. Something she ate she claimed. Truman found her in the kitchen, her eyes swollen with tears. Two evenings later, as Truman hung around her and Zurina's room, Ramasami entered and kicked over a box. Soap and toothpaste fell out, along with a generic brand of sanitary napkins. Zurina gasped. Normah convulsed in delight from her wheelchair.

"*Apa ini?*" asked Truman, teasing the two women.

"*Tiada*," fired Fatimah, snatching the box.

A single napkin fell from the opened box. Zurina recoiled. Truman was quick. Ramasami stared, ignorant.

"Apa ini?" Ramasami asked.

"It's a little mattress, Ramasami," Truman answered the boy in Malay.

"Ah." Ramasami peered, nodding. Normah went wild, jerking in her chair.

"You're very bad!" exclaimed Fatimah to Truman.

Truman pressed on. "They're mouse beds, Ramasami. Zurina's too kind. She puts them out for the mice that I try to catch, so the little devils have a place to sleep."

Both women laughed, the joke turned to the boy, as Ramasami studied the single white napkin, nodding away.

"Zurina will need it now to put out for her little friends," said Truman, taking the pad. "Sshh! It's a secret," he added, patting the boy's head.

"Sshh!" Ramasami answered, darting an eye toward Zurina.

Truman, proud of himself, thought of it again that night in his shed with his journal upon his lap, believing he made it up.

* * *

As August worked on, one afternoon Truman learned from Mr. Tan, of all people, while purchasing nuts and bolts for imagined monkey bars, that Encik Azman of the Social Welfare Office claimed at a recent function that the American was doing "donkey's work," to everyone's amusement. "The fucker likes that term," Truman reflected in his journal.

Big Mr. Tan, smiling with the news, slapped Truman on his back as he left the cluttered shop. His thin wife behind the counter penciled upon a ledger. Truman already knew how Azman felt about the Home and the kids, but now Mr. Tan, too, and having fun with it to boot? "Not a good day," he wrote that night.

* * *

Big Dave Hayden, burly farmer at large, made the *New Straits Times* as a space-filler for a moving violation somewhere south in Johor. A judge let him off, mitigating his selfless service to his host country. Truman wrote to his secret friend, agreeing to meet with her at month's end in Kuala Lumpur. Two U.S. Navy fighters downed two Libyan fighters in the Gulf of Sidra, a Ronald Reagan pledge fulfilled. Visiting born-again Christian Indians asked if Ramasami could visit their Sunday School. Truman quickly agreed, having read of "mainstreaming," figuring the boy could exercise his Tamil for a change. It lasted two Sundays. Happy as a lark to go, Ramasami had no interest in an active, personal Saviour.

Then John Singer arrived one Friday afternoon, out of the blue, weaving up the pitted driveway on his cycle. A Winston clung to the corner of his mouth. Truman was overjoyed. They started that evening down at the truck stop, before hitting the Shamrock in Mentacab, the massage on Singer. Truman asked for, and got #19 again. He declined "intercourse," not sharing the offer with a generous Singer.

Then back to Kuala Harap, to the Kedua Coffee House, they talked of Singer's final three weeks. Truman missed him already, and told him so. At closing they returned to the truck stop. At 3:00 a.m., two drunken Indian businessmen joined them. President Reagan came up, then the Gulf of Sidra incident, and then hushed tones of the unspeakable tensions between the rich Chinese minority and the much larger, and poorer, Malay ruling class. One of the men left for home as the darkness blued in the horizon to the east. The remaining man wept to Truman over an unresolved family matter as John Singer slept, sitting in his metal folding chair, his freckled face and throat exposed to the dawning sky. By 7:00 a.m., Truman woke him to return with him to Truman's shed behind the Home.

By early afternoon, the kids harassed both into skull-splitting wakefulness.

* * *

Aug. 26, 1981

I just entered yesterday, but I felt like writing again. I've been real up & down lately. I'm going to miss John when he goes & I've gone & agreed to spend a weekend with Ben down in Seremban. I feel bad about it, with only 3 weeks left for John. But spending 2 days with Ben will be nice, too. He'll have all the training group gossip (except for anything about me). He'll also like hearing about my job. I told him I'm just trying to teach the kids to read & write & counting & adding & subtracting. (With the real retarded ones it's obeying commands & dressing & undressing & stuff like that— Azman's doing the best—he still slaps his head, but he stops long enough to shake your hand. Normah's really reading well & even Singh has his alphabet down.)

Back to Ben—when I leave his place it'll be to meet ____ in K.L. (I won't tell Ben though.)

Around here, me & the kids have been swimming a lot & hiking about town & down beneath the bridge & beyond. I even got Normah's wheelchair through the thicket down behind the theater. Salleh's been picking on Lim (hitting her with sticks & shit), then he tried it on Yap who made angry sounds & then slapped his face—that was that!

The kids are getting the hang of taking off on long walks to get out & goof off. I'm proud of them. They even fuck with the goats & the geese we come across, except Salleh. He bullies Lim, but fears most everything else—even roadside equipment we've happened upon. All the kids are leary of stray dogs (all over the place).

* * *

Final letters were exchanged between P.O. Box #321 and the riverbank Home.

The Southeast Asia Hotel it'd be, their best yet, with air conditioning, carpeting and hot water showers and western-style tubs. They planned movies, like a real date, as Truman quietly appreciated her writing: "Do you know something? I do really disappointed if we would not meet this time. Maybe laugh on me, but this truth I feel."

On alternating afternoons, his climbing monkey bars took slow shape as Truman planed and sanded the edges of the two-by-fours, thinking of splinters. He also needed more nuts and bolts. Tan's wife worked alone. Two Malay men were off in a corner debating something as Tan's wife placed Truman's change in his hand, never touching him, barely catching his eye. He wondered how she could have written that letter.

That night Truman dreamed of falling from the merry-go-round, for some reason inside the open bay of the Home. The walls were an even soft blue. An oblivious Zurina was sweeping the floor near an empty wheelchair. The kids gathered around. Truman, feeling no pain, couldn't move. He tried to speak, to warn them of never approaching a wounded man. It could be dangerous, and they were so innocent and ignorant.

Shaken, he woke up, relieved he could move. Outside his shuttered windows all was dark, and still and cool. He wrapped himself in a sarong, and took a bottle of brandy out into the starry night. Up front, the Home was silent. He breathed deep of the tropical night, thankful it was only a dream.

The next day, from a ratty motel along the highway, he telephoned John Singer's office in Pekan. It was a sad two-part conversation, and Truman ran out of change. Singer called him back. They talked of Singer's time remaining and of Truman's squandering it in Seremban.

"You know, John. Where's your best friend when you need him?"

Almost a chat between lovers, Singer consoled, "We'll have our blowout. I've got the master plan."

* * *

Three days later, Truman packed three days of clean clothes and strapped his backpack to his gas tank, striking out for Seremban.

He chose the rural route, south through the forests and sprawling rubber plantations, bound for Kuala Pilah, then west for

Seremban, bustling compared to Kuala Harap. He weaved through the shade of the Triang Road, a meandering, pitted two-lane effort the British must have hurried with. Hard turns were banked perilously the wrong way as repaired buckles and folds snuck up where hillside drainage was little considered. By the time he stopped in Kuala Pilah for gas and coffee, his back ached. The remainder of his trip though was beautiful, motoring through shaded forests, slowing for grazing kirbous between roadside stands manned by nothing-to-do Malays, set to the hues of the waning day. Just before sunset, Truman cruised into Seremban.

Following Ben's directions, he found Ben's home easily. It was small, set upon a recently poured slab of concrete in a Chinese community. No stilts for these Malaysians.

Ben also had a television, so that night they watched *Dallas*, with a good deal of the rest of the nation who had electricity. The popular series, akin to *Flamingo Road*, was another sterling example of homespun American values, a year behind its production in the United States.

The following morning was more of Ben's life, up early, a big breakfast and then off to his government office, where he did his civil engineering, mostly irrigation systems. Two small dams had him excited. Then they shared an early lunch before returning to Ben's row home for a quick farewell. Maybe too quick, Truman sensed, earnest to gas up, bound for Kuala Lumpur.

* * *

The ride north was faster, on better roads linking the western coast of the peninsula. Traffic slowed only once, around a head-on between two large trucks. A blood-soaked body lay bent upon the side of the asphalt. It bothered Truman into slowing, but not for long. He didn't wish to keep her waiting.

And patiently she waited, on the steps of the Southeast Asia Hotel.

Truman, deep within the big city, saw her immediately as he rounded the corner. She held a small bag and didn't wave, but smiled, which relieved Truman as he parked and locked his motorcycle. She wore a yellow dress he thought others might find funny-looking, which he found pretty for the same reasons.

The lobby was as nice as any Mabel might have taken him to, had they ever traveled. From behind the polished wooden counter, a well-dressed Chinese man gave Truman their key for room 904. Again a view, thought Truman. Ling remained behind him, across the lobby, too close to a potted plant.

The elevator ride, their first, was quiet, with an equally quiet Chinese couple on board.

There were two beds in their room. Truman tossed his backpack upon one, as Tan's wife placed her bag at the foot of the lone dresser. Truman opened the shades. "Come here. Have a look. It's nice."

She came, and stood beside him, silent.

"Thank you, Ling. You know, for coming here and all."

Staring out through the glass across the city, she replied, "You welcome, and I thank to you for meeting with me."

* * *

Truman showered long, basking in the hottest water he could stand. He came out clothed, planning to ask her which movie she'd like to see, but finding her within the covers of the one bed, tucked up to her chin, peering out at him. He sat down beside her.

"You want to do this first?"

"If it pleases you."

Truman was equally surprised to find her still in her yellow dress, straightened neatly beneath the sheet and cover. Shortly, though, he was happy, hot-shower clean, against her bony frame, so pretty to him. But he didn't last long, and he apologized, asking her how he could please her.

"I wish to be hold to, and to talked to."

So he asked her where she grew up, and about being little there. He told her of America, at least his New Egypt, his aunt and the farm. She smiled, so Truman smiled, too, propping himself on an elbow beside her as she stayed flat on her back, her legs straight beneath their sheet and cover. He complimented her prettiness. She denied it, closing her eyes. Then he teased her.

"Hey, are you by any chance Japanese?"

She stiffened. "No. I am Chinese, of course."

"I don't know. You look a little Japanese to me." He smiled, touching her cheek. "We can't tell the difference, you know." Then he feigned concern. "Oh no! You're not Vietnamese, are you? We hate those pricks!" He laughed, rolling to his back.

"I am Chinese. Why do you tease me?" she asked, straight-faced.

He again propped himself, placed his free hand upon the rise of her own hands, and clasped upon her stomach beneath her sheet and blanket. "Because I want to. You're my girlfriend," he said, smiling, "for as long as we can. I'm your boyfriend, aren't I?"

She smiled toward the ceiling. "It would please me to be your girlfriend. How should I answer when you do tease?"

"Say, 'Oh, shut up, Truman.' Or, 'I've had enough of your shit, young man.' "

"Shut up, Truman," she tried it out.

"There you go, Lingy. Now we're talking." He grinned.

"I have nuff of shit, Truman," she ventured.

"Good." Truman pulled her closer, both of them happier, before deciding on a movie, then rising to dress, backs turned, before heading out into the muggy streets below.

They saw *Stir Crazy*. Truman thought Richard Pryor was a riot. They ate afterwards in an Indian kedai, Truman heartily, his accomplice sparingly, taking great care to not soil her yellow dress. At eight, across town, they saw *The Blue Lagoon*, holding hands and sharing popcorn over this story of children's paradise. In a slow spot, Truman brought up *Grease*. At another, in the darkened theater, Ling whispered, "Does you girlfriends in America look like Book Shield?"

Angela's smile fleeted by, then more foolishly, Molly's.

Not lying, he whispered, "You're the prettiest one I ever had."

She squeezed his hand in the dark, then placed it upon the lap of her yellow dress.

* * *

That night Truman opened the windows of their ninth-floor room, liking the sounds of the traffic below. He talked her into showering with him. She insisted darkness. They compromised, leaving the bathroom door ajar. Knifing thin light ignited their translucent shower curtain and wet bathing.

In bed, her brand-new pajamas had packaged creases.

To his pointed question, she answered, "Our meeting is safe. My husband believes me in Kelang with my, how do you say, I think, foster sister?" This woman, Truman learned, was the lone surviving remnant of her life before Kuala Harap. "From my childhood," she added.

"Well then, we're at least a little bit alike," Truman said. "I was half-raised by an aunt. Second half. But more about you."

She answered that her husband's family was from Kuantan, "On the east coast. He spends much time there." Truman sat up to that. "His mistress resides there as well," she added, "near to his family. With her own home, tending to his other hardware shop."

News to Truman. So much so that he had to laugh at her asking, "So, you are certain, you have no wife or girlfriend waiting in America?"

"I have no one," he assured her. "Does it please you? I mean that nicely."

"How so? I am sorry. I do not understand."

"Just you. You're my only girlfriend."

"I may be too evil to be so," she said in their darkness. Then Truman asked her of children.

"My husband, who I must not challenge, says failure is mine. It is a situation of great shame to his family."

"I'm sorry to hear that." Truman tried to console.

"I am not so certain as my husband and his family." Shyly, talking to the ceiling, she added, "I have birth control for use in our friendship," to which Truman didn't question. Good thinking.

Then Truman slept deeply.

Tan's wife beside him, in pajamas she bought in Mentacab, then hidden from her husband, watched him for a while. The warm air of the Kuala Lumpur night pushed lightly at their curtains far above the dirty streets. Truman had wished the window to be open.

CHAPTER 18

The next morning, Truman returned eastward into the cooling hills, passing climbing lumber trucks, yielding to racier taxis and sedans.

In the wind of the ride, his thoughts wandered from Ling to John Singer, from the kids to Zurina and Fatimah. He slowed through the highway's lone tunnel, then plunged out into blue sky. Before him the rear of a large truck swerved across the dual lanes.

Its tires locked, disappearing within blue smoke igniting up from the rolling asphalt. Truman swerved, braking hard. The truck jackknifed, then popped up violently. A thunderous bang, ramming an oncoming lumber rig.

Keeping his cycle up, Truman braked harder, gearing down, around the swirling clouds of dust and smoke. Tires rolled to his right. Twisted straps of steel slid across spreading beads of glass. An oncoming car stopped. Lumber rolled left, halting a bus. Truman pulled over. A sedan passed him, around the collision.

Aware of his own pulse, oddly at the nape of his neck, Truman wondered of those who had to be dying. Malays hurried out from the right, from beneath roadside trees. Impending hysteria. It's always in the *New Straits Times* in these rural areas. And they were warned in training. Truman looked back to the steaming stillness of the entangled rigs. A body slumped through a hole that was a windshield. Truman worked his foot at his gearshift, chiding his cycle into movement, his heart pounding. He eased up on the clutch, merging into the traffic feeling its way around the mess.

For twenty miles he was cautious, and then he was back up to sixty, seventy, and eighty miles per hour, and still being passed, his mind strolling from the Van Heflins' Cream Ridge dairy farm, to the passing rubber plantations and jungle, to John Singer's final weeks, to his friend sitting beside him in the dark theater. How she held to him. Her slight smile seldom offered.

* * *

Two days later, Truman received a letter from each friend, along with a *Newsweek*.

He read Singer's first.

> Dearest Truman,
>
> Just a quick note to cordially request that you come to Pekan (our Sultan's hometown) this coming weekend.
>
> I've cancelled my previous arrangements, enabling us to pound our respective livers and central nervous systems.
>
> Don't make me come hunting for you!
>
> Hugs, John S.
>
> P.S. I have a bed and a bookcase for you. A friend of mine attached to Pejabat Haiwan says he can deliver both to the big K.H.
>
> P.P.S. Save your fucking money. We're going to Penang at the close of my tour. I'd hate to spend it with a lesser friend (but WOULD).

Singer's best friend grinned.

Then Ling's, in her uncertain hand, nearly two pages, all three times Truman read it. She recalled their late-night city view, and their teasing, before wading into why they became friends to begin with, writing of loneliness, suspecting in a year he'd return to his America, forgetting his lost friend.

Mid-letter she veered into Truman's work, and what her husband thought of it. "So why is it you do this?" she asked, before suggesting he desired to be a real teacher. Damn her. But he couldn't as her pen continued, ". . . the sadness of our situation. If you were a Chinese I sure you are falling love on me but so I do not realize how you feel over me." Closing, she added, "I rather we see each other in our secret ways until our last day for you return to America. Please do not misunderstand seeing me. I think of you since you left me our last meeting."

Ramasami quarreled with Yap beside him. Truman, rereading, understood little, but appreciated the urgency. He sorted for music, something hungry, something Springsteen. The only problem he sensed was her being married.

* * *

A week later:

Sept. 7, 1981

It's Monday night. I gassed up & dashed off to Pekan, then stayed an extra day to renew my cycle license, as long as I was so near Kuantan. It was a good & a sad weekend. Pretty soon John will be gone. We drank & ate like pigs & hammered out plans for his final week. He's calling it, "The Furious, Futile Final Days." I sort of can't wait & I sort of can.

The weekend was a lot of nice talking, going swimming again, probably drinking too much & listening to cassettes (which I'll inherit the load of). Now I'm home, with a plugged-up ear & a shitload of laundry soaking in two buckets.

We talked of this rumor about the Peace Corps pulling out of Malaysia next March due to budget cuts in D.C. (It'd send me home 6 mos. early.) John says we're all assured our regular tours. Oh yes— we went to a fire walk! (a Chinese ritual) where these shirtless guys in trances go goose-stepping over a bed of hot coals about 10 yards long (pretty long I thought). Anyway, I don't know how they do it, but this one big fat guy must have panicked because he really hustled along, then fell face-first plowing up a furor of coals in front of us. (John said Pete Rose would've been proud.) I know it's bad, but it was pretty funny (I still chuckle over it—am right now), because it was dark out & these other guys –his pals—went in and rescued him & then they stood him up & the poor bastard looked like a Christmas tree with the glowing coals stuck all over him. (You had to be there—I'm laughing right now!)

I also talked with John about how even ___ made me feel crummy about my job & not being a real teacher. I wrote her back today, with the stuff he told me—how I NEVER told anyone I was a teacher in the first place & besides at least I'm doing something for these kids that no one else in K.H. will do. (Malay or Chinese or Indian or whatever—this stuff matters to these people—they're fucking keeping score all the time!)

It was sad when John & I left each other in Kuantan. Sounds a little queer, huh?

Anyway, aside from laundry, I also came home to the gang here— all HAPPY to see me—Zurina & Fatimah, too!

* * *

The following week Truman accomplished all of his planned exercises in his A.M. schooling. Midweek, he and his stringing-along kids explored the Chinese cemetery downstream from the bridge.

Foot paths wove about the cemetery through overgrown weeds and gnarled brush, nothing like the manicured lawns back home, even the one deep in the Pines, which Truman thought of, moving the kids through the rises of monuments erupting from the growth, all of them frightfully foreign, many with burned-out sticks of incense affixed atop them. Some supported pictures, Truman assumed of the deceased. The kids quieted, stumbling upon the rotting mass of a dead cow, too gone to smell.

On their way out, as the wind picked up, poised upon the horizon were three large dogs watching their hobbled weaving through the thicket. Backed by darkening thunderheads, Truman thought their breathing postures pretty. Then he thought of Mabel's *National Geographics*, reminding him of where he was with his young life. The scene frightened Normah, as it disarmed Ramasami and Singh, and terrified little Salleh. Truman felt good and strong, reassuring them of safety with him.

That week they splashed in the muddy Pahang, and again visited the Home of the aged Chinese men. Ling wrote, too, asking forgiveness for the job insult, ". . . feeling shame to talk with you with poor English. Perhaps that was the mistake for I would never wish to insult to you." She also asked to meet him at the Jalan Pekeliling bus station, in Kuala Lumpur on the 19th, signing off: "I hope you can come meet with me on that day. We can go for a movie or have walk together."

The following week more hiking and swimming took over the afternoons as the monkey bars sat out back, half done beneath the spreading of the Go Dog Go tree. A fast note came. It wouldn't be Jalan Pekeliling, ". . . but back to S.E.A. Hotel . . ."

Superman, The Movie came to Kuala Harap. An excited Truman treated the kids. The cinema's manager, seeing their famous little trailing-in-line at his theater, wheelchairs and all, let them in at half-price, next to nothing as Malaysian movies go.

Ramasami, Singh and Normah loved it, or at least being there. Salleh feared the big room after the lights went out. Yap sat quiet throughout as chubby Lim couldn't shake her concern for an insistent barking dog carrying on somewhere outside. Waste-of-a-ticket Azman squatted upon his seat in the dark, transfixed to the swirling ceiling fans far above. Truman worried for the boy's neck, but quit caring by the time teenage Clark's earthling father's heart failed him in the barnyard driveway.

That weekend, John Singer's next to last, put Singer in Ipoh, closing out business with his Pejabat Haiwan office as Truman had his own day trip, meeting Tan's wife at the Southeast Asia Hotel, where he secured his cycle for the day. Ling, wearing the blue skirt and the ruffled blouse she wore nearly four months before, was already there, out front, as still as a mannequin.

They ate first, where Truman called their day, "our big date." "No sex," he whispered, reaching for her hands. "We're starting over. Boyfriend and girlfriend. Secret ones, but good ones, holding hands, hitting the sights."

"As you wish so," Tan's wife answered.

They took a cab to Ampang Park, a smaller shopping mall, where they strolled four tiers of air-conditioned shops and restaurants. Truman talked of Burlington Center, its Sears, one of three anchors, and more of his Aunt Mabel, who wrote recently of a new mall going up near Freehold. Then he talked Tan's wife into ice cream cones.

Ling led Truman through furniture, then women's clothing. Swimwear made her shy. Her oddly bridged nose stood out to him just then.

"Would you swim with me some day?" Truman asked, retaking her hand. "You'd need something pretty to splash in."

She held up a one-piece thing, purple and white and modest. "You shall have to keep it for me. Hiding at your place, you understand?"

The thought warmed Truman. His smile tightening his scar, he said, "I'd like that."

She found her size, bought one, then rolled it tight and tucked it into her purse.

Truman brought up Subang International Airport, a thirty-minute cab ride away. Ling thought it odd, but agreed to watch the jets landing and taking off from the heat of the windswept balcony.

In the open air terminal, they ascended the steps to the balcony. A heavy concrete eave, counting on torrential rains, reached over them. Standing next to one another, Truman ventured the grace of the large jets. They talked of what they knew of the nations they hailed from. Truman brought up the floating military transports of his youth, then spoke of John Singer's impending departure from this very terminal. Tan's wife thought it sad, and said so.

"I wish your return further away. Only twelve more months. Small time for our friendship," she said, as both peered into the hot afternoon air over the runways.

"That's a year. A pretty long time," Truman replied to his friend beside him. She was reluctant to lean upon the concrete.

Then they turned and went back inside, where above the open air terminal Truman stilled, stopping Ling beside him. Below was Andy, of all people, chain-smoking, milling amongst others. He waved to someone across the crowd below. Truman followed his wave, finding Bruce Statton, the country director, working his way toward Andy.

The thought of explaining Ling to them jolted him. He pointed the two men out to her. Then he calmed, being above them.

"Do you wish me to leave, for you to be with your American friends?" she asked.

He reached for her hand. "No. We're on our date, remember? They're only kind-of friends, anyway."

"What to do if they ask of our being together, if they see?" she whispered, the bridge of her nose downward.

"I'll tell 'em we're friends. It's none of their business."

Then it became clear what the two men were doing, side-by-side, smiling.

They approached a customs entrance at the south end of the terminal where a stringing of Americans appeared, smiling, toting carry-on luggage, jelling as a group amongst handshaking and more smiling. They were the last of the Peace Corps' training groups. Truman read of their impending arrival two weeks before in a P.C. bulletin.

"I can't believe this," he told Tan's wife. "Do you understand coincidence?"

"Are you sure you wish to be near to me?"

Truman laughed. "Fuck 'em. They got enough to do now, lying about how happy they are to see everybody, before having to answer a boatload of stupid questions, like if they can still use their U.S. money, and why the hell not. Then what food will make 'em shit themselves and so on." He laughed.

The milling assembly moved like an amoeba for the baggage claim where a year before Truman stood at the same circular band of turning steel, his suitcase opened, socks and underwear out for the ride.

"Many pretty American womans," said Ling.

"Why do you keep saying things like that?" Truman asked.

"I am sorry. I just think for now, maybe you wish to be with friends down there. Not up here with me."

Truman turned to her. "Look over there. There's a nice group of Chinese people. They're having fun. Maybe you'd rather be with them, instead of with me."

"I see. I am sorry," she offered.

"Don't be sorry. It's just not every American is my friend. For instance, there's this one guy, Dave Hayden, who came over in my group. More of a farmer than me, and at first I thought he was pretty neat and all, but now I think he's an asshole."

Tan's wife stood silent, puzzled with the term's literal translation.

"Anyway, I talk to him and all, but I wouldn't go running to him. Do you know what I mean?"

"Yes. Not all Americans like each other."

"Do all Chinese like each other?"

"No. But we like each others better over we like Malays," she answered. "But why is it you do not like this farmer?"

"He's a big mouth with no job and proud of it. I guess he just bombs around the country, gettin' loaded and hittin' the whorehouses and stuff." He paused, knowing what he knew of her husband, as the Americans below steered one another through the terminal for their bus to Kuala Lumpur.

On their own bus for Kuala Lumpur, Tan's wife discreetly dug into her bag between them. She slipped Truman her smaller bag of her balled-up swimsuit.

In Kuala Lumpur they ate lightly at an Indian kedai, then said good-bye for separate cabs, Tan's wife for the Jalan Pekeliling bus station, Truman's for the Southeast Asia Hotel, to retrieve his cycle.

That night in his shed, Truman thought of her bony hands, then of her lipstick after their long day, how it covered only the outer halves of her lips. She had no mirror.

He checked for anyone outside, only the songs of the bugs of the night. Then he dug out her swimsuit, carefully inspecting the small cups for her breasts, then the fabric reinforcement in the crotch. He flustered, then carefully rolled the garment back up and rebagged it, hiding it within his shirts. He lit a mosquito coil, and darkened his shed, wishing they'd found someplace to slip off to.

* * *

Azman stopped by in the middle of the next week with a Malay field worker, a potential new resident and, apparently, the young Chinese girl's parents. The kids were afraid of the child. Singh retreated. Ramasami circled. Yap and Lim teamed up, hooting to Truman, pointing at the girl, demanding explanation. The girl's parents, visibly upset with their daughter's manic conduct, cued her while apologizing to Truman, who insisted in his best Malay, "At least she's smiling. Somebody's doing a good job."

They never saw the child again. Truman worried the fault was his.

By mid-September he finished the wooden monkey bars, painting them orange. The kids climbed cautiously. To Truman's delight, two boys from up in town discovered them and played on them daily, one with remarkable finesse. Truman also mowed his improving lawn with the borrowed mower, the morning after he saw a subtitled Robby Benson movie, *Walk Proud*. He thought it sucked, and wrote so in his journal.

Two days later he wrote of little Salleh's growing self-confidence, and of Ramasami's love of splashing in the river, jerking about in glee whenever an afternoon swim was announced. In their morning lessons, Normah advanced to DarjahTiga, a third grade reader, then leapt the fourth to struggle proudly in a fifth grade text. Truman was happy for her, documenting her success. Even happy-go-dopey, shit-in-his-pants Singh had his alphabet mastered and could count to twenty-two, at which point he drifted into random numbers and letters alike, stabbing happily at whatever might exist beyond his personal, cerebral summit.

An angry Truman recorded in his next entry that the Chinese girl was denied by Azman, who thought her too aggressive, without seeking Truman's opinion. His single year of experience, and self-assigned readings, had her as Down syndrome, slightly palsied, mentally somewhere between Yap and Singh, a good notch above lovable, trash-eating Lim. He wrote on, hating Azman's perpetual Malay smile when lying, and his shameful thinking that he knew the Home better than Truman. He didn't write he felt like quitting, or asking for a transfer, and a good thing, too, for that same evening, while hiking with the kids, a tormented Yap flung cow shit into the face of a deserving Ramasami. Truman decided to stay.

Meanwhile he and John Singer wrote back and forth nearly every day. Truman missed him already. One letter swelled Truman with happiness, labeled, " WARNING—ITINERARY OF THE FURIOUS, FUTILE, FINAL DAYS!" detailing the holiday Singer lovingly envisioned for he and his young friend: bars, whores, beaches, books and movies. Truman wrote to Ling about it, omitting one ambition. She wrote back, happy for his happiness, signing off: "Do not forget about me and our friendship!" A slight pang stirred in his chest.

Truman's cycle broke down, putting him back on his rattling bicycle, which he didn't mind, until dumping again, down along the highway. He skinned up his forearm, an elbow and a knee, much to the interest of skinny Yap who harbored a keen fascination for all cuts, pimples, abrasions and surface maladies in general.

School chugged along. Truman mowed again, thinking of Van Heflins' lawn, figuring it the smell of the freshly cut grass, and wrote so in his journal. He built more shelves for the toys that trickled in from donations, accompanying the small treasures the kids dragged back from their excursions—sticks and trash and pretty rocks.

Late in September Fatimah considered another job. Truman feared Zurina alone for any length of time. Then came three cool days, back to back, making Kuala Harap lovelier in the lesser heat. On the twenty-second, a new boy was dropped off. Raj was his name, an Indian of eleven or so, of normal intelligence. His crippling from the waist down was a cruel snarl of lower spine and atrophied legs. His young face was handsome, with features much smoother than Ramasami's.

Truman, of course, had no clue what process of admissions delivered the boy. An aloof, smiling Azman told him, "All is proper. Quite fitting."

"A little history might help. That's all," Truman said, constructing a bed from his store of broken ones.

"As I said, all is proper. That is all you need to know, Mr. Truman."

Three days later his Malay boss asked him, "What else can these children do besides making noises and climbing around on these things you build?"

Truman was finishing a ribbed washboard for Zurina and Fatimah so they wouldn't have to labor over the broken slab of concrete out back.

"Well, read and write a bit, dress themselves and eat like people, or at least a few of them," answered Truman.

"Could you teach them to sing, and perhaps dance, for an upcoming government function?"

Truman stood, wiping sweat from his eyebrows. "First off, I can't do either myself. Look, I offered to come here to help out, to make a decent home, and to teach whatever I can to whichever of these kids can learn. I'm not creating a circus act out of 'em."

"I do know," Encik Azman answered, "that other programs, for these sorts of children do this sort of thing. It is very nice."

"Good. You have office workers. Let them come down here and do it. I'm sorry, but do you remember all the shit and the piss and fearfulness of only a year ago?"

"I see, Mr. Truman," answered Encik Azman, before he spun about, striding away, smiling. As though aware, Tan's wife's next letter came that afternoon.

From up in town, she wrote of seeing him on his bicycle, and of their having watched the jets together, while hoping to swim together soon. She wondered if he, too, had a swimsuit, and worried over it, "... more too shy if yours is tiny one such as Bobby Ewing's on *Dallas* American television show." Jesus, thought Truman, thinking of Bobby's speedo, before reading how she wished to meet with him, "in K.L. Friday evening, October 9, after your good friend's departure? I need answer quickly," signing off: "You are my dear one. Ling"

He wrote back fast, and dreamed that night of being in a long hallway by a lone drinking fountain. He tried to drink but found himself surrounded by people who were talking about him, and he didn't know why. Upon awakening he recalled Mabel and Kathleen Van Heflin in the crowd. It was just 4:00 a.m., but he thought of breakfast for he was hungry. Then he wished John Singer would write. After all, Tan's wife just had.

* * *

Across the end of September, Truman got agreeable Raj settled in. He wired and bolted together a quick wheelchair for the boy from pieces of chairs stored out back. He'd reconstruct a nicer one after Penang. He started and finished Graham Greene's *The Quiet American*, compliments of John Singer. In his journal he figured Greene to have been fond of and cared for by an oriental woman as well, noting where Greene's was fascinated with the British monarchy. His own savored her fictitious American rich, her Ewings of *Dallas* and her *Hart To Hart* couple.

Truman wrote on in anger: "Azman has pig shit for brains," reminding his journal, in parentheses: "I mean the better dressed one." He wrote of two stories in the *New Straits Times*, one titled "Government Bans Two Books and Five Documenets," all seven contrary to the interest of Islam and national security. The other, "Dirty Ways Some Writers Use To Boost Book Sales," reported sex in novels to lure readership, warning Malaysian students who studied abroad of this literary corruption of the West.

Truman closed more mellow, reflecting how much he found himself smiling at, and with the kids, recognizing their needs to be touched and played with. He noted the friendliness of Kuala Harap, for a cabbie had pulled over, informing him that he saw John Singer, who he couldn't name, days before, loaded with bags cutting through town.

Truman pictured his friend, in town just long enough to switch cabs for the opposite coast, looking at Kuala Harap for the last time. He wrote in his journal: "Me, too, in another year. Still far off."

* * *

Oct. 11, 1981 (Sunday night)

This will be a long one. It's been 10 days & Penang & everything else & with John being gone. It all started 2 Fridays ago with Zurina demanding I go see Azman about something. I was itching to get out so I just left—fuck him. (I like the "spinning" one better anyway.)

Friday afternoon I hit K.L. in a palm-oil tuck (I hitched) & found John at the S.E.A Hotel (thought of you-know-who). We lay around, rung up beer, then decided to hit a movie. John went out and was victorious on a ___ run. (This is whole new thing that I was afraid to write about in case anyone ever got into these pages. I have ___ a couple of times & at first was ashamed of it—but it is pretty fun, except for they'll lash you or hang you for it in this country—I'll hide this journal pretty good!!)

Well, we got so much into talking & stuff that we missed seeing Joe Don Baker in Walking Tall *so we headed out for The Ritz, where we were earlier & we sat near the jukebox & sort of watched everyone. I heard a commotion, then screaming in the next room & I looked & to my horror a man swinging a huge meat knife came crashing into the room. An Australian man I was talking to minutes before got brave & got stabbed in the stomach. The man (with the knife) went through the swinging doors & and then there was screaming outside & then all quieted down, but I tell you, I about shit my pants. In a while John got to talking to this old lady named Ruby (a big fat Zurina type).*

By this time it was dark out & I went outside & strolled up this alley beside the place to look around & the alley was dark & streaked with K.L. city lights. Quietly milling about were these women who I thought were whores. One followed me back out to the street saying something, but she stopped & wouldn't come any farther (like the lights of the streets were her limits). It turned out they were "pundans" (men dressed as women—Whew! Close call).

Ruby then took us to this disco a block away & they had these girls sitting in a line of chairs & the men had to buy tickets to dance with them. I just sat & watched. Some of them were pretty wild dancers. John said if he had to pay $ to dance he'd go ape-shit, too. We left, laughing like hell about something & we walked old Ruby home—to some slummy area not far off. John tried to talk her into something for 50 ringgits, but to no avail. (She was strictly 100 ringgits so we returned to the S.E.A.)

Sat. morning we got up, packed & went to Pudu Raya bus depot & took a bus to Buttersworth. Nice trip for such a long one (6 hrs.). I ate like a pig all day. We hit Penang, got a room, got ____ again (I swear every trick-shaw (sp?) driver on that island has ____ for sale or knows someone who does) & then we drank & went to a whore-house. I had an older Malay, named "Janet" (although she couldn't spell it). John took an Indian woman & came back all wet & sweaty & quiet about it. This may sound weird, but I thought he looked pretty cool all soaked with sweat & I wished that I looked like that for Ling. (I know—weird—but I did think it.)

Sunday morning we got up, ate & went & saw Charles Bronson in "Death Hunt." Shitty tough-guy stuff but beautiful mountain scenery that looked so cold, & I liked those parts. We hit the room & got ____ again & went & saw ANOTHER Bronson flick! (Border-line) Then we hit a bar & then came home & I puked all over our dumpy bathroom. I cleaned it up & crashed until morning.

Mon. morning we grabbed a cab & went out to the beach— drank & swam & foot raced & wrestled. Some world travelers gave us some flack that night, which is rare—they're usually quiet people.

Tues. morning—swam & went back to town & found (amaz-ingly) the same trick-shaw driver we had Saturday night—so more ____!

Went back to Hong Kong Bar & some queer liked John & that was funny as hell. He offered John money!

Got our pictures taken, of all things, in one of those dopey booths (received them in mail back here in K.H.—kept John's—Zurina wanted mine so I gave it to her).

(Back to Penang) Asked for another whorehouse & we got Janet's so we asked for another (and then another weirdo thing happened—but I'll write it anyway). Arrived at the place & it was empty except for the working girls. Well, one older Indian woman's smile (and non-smile) reminded me (for some reason) of Mrs. Van Heflin (super nice Kathleen—Angela's mother & Chet's wife of all the sick things I've done). She sat with me for a bit & after a few beers I paid for 30 minutes & beneath me she became Mrs. VH for a short while. (I know, pretty sick.)

Wednesday a.m. Got up & got ___ & went to beach again & saw an Aussie girl & her baby get all stung up by a jellyfish they waded into. Then we went to town & crossed the strait on a ferry & found a shitty hotel in Buttersworth.

The next day (Thurs.) we thumbed to K.L. and got there by 4:00 p.m. In K.L. we got caught in a downpour as we tried getting a cab, & while looking about, my eyes jerked back across the street to a motionless RUBY—staring at us expressionless—John & I went wild laughing—we were in K.L. for the 15th round!

Again got a room at the S.E.A. hotel (of course I thought of ___). We hit the Rex again & finally went and saw Joe Don Baker in "Walking Tall." It was hilarious. John wondered if J.D. Baker was an asshole in real life as well.

We closed out at the Rex & the next morning John packed his bags. We ate big & John gave me 75 ringgits to stay the night in K.L. (I told him about ___.) We got a cab & laughed & talked the whole way out to Subang Int. We had 45 minutes to kill so we walked outside for our last time together & strolled through some weeds & then we went back inside & shook hands & then John was gone with a wave.

His last words were: "Watch your back with this ___'s wife thing."

I went back to K.L. & got another room in the S.E.A. & by early evening I found her in the lobby. We were happy to see each other. I marveled again at how skinny she is. We ate by candlelight in the room—her idea—saw it on "Hart To Hart." We stayed in the room until we slept. I was beat & she was very nice. It was the nicest time yet. She talked more. Boy, do I like her. I thought of many things as we rested and talked before sleeping.

Mostly though—John was gone. Best friend I ever had—Scotty W.—then Jimmy M.—then J. Singer.

CHAPTER 19

Truman enjoyed his open-windowed, windswept bus ride home. With each turning of the East-West Highway, he was happier. Kuala Harap was home.

Up in the old part of town, he slung his bag over his shoulder and headed down into the turning of the riverside road. With the Home in sight, he headed behind, wading into the green of the riverbank growth, through the fence behind his shed. He dropped off his bag to sneak up on the Home.

In the heat of the early afternoon, no one was outside. Truman hit the back windows first, growling and making catcalls.

Kids stirred. Cries sounded out. He heard Zurina's, "Truman bali!" Normah squealed from her wheelchair.

From an adjacent window, Truman whispered loud in Malay, "It is I. The ghost of Truman who died in Panang."

"It is Truman!" cried out Fatimah, from the kitchen, amongst scrambling. Ramasami yelped. Shirtless Salleh bolted by.

Truman headed out front to the sliding open cage. A hero's welcome home. Several wheelchairs, Fatimah, retarded children, and Zurina, hobbled and scrambled out fussing over their wandering adulterer.

Truman smiled wide, happy to be back. The kids were lovely, from devilish little Salleh to big old, scratching-away Kumari, the eternal hygiene mess.

A *Newsweek* awaited him, along with a newsy letter from Mabel, and a warm one addressed to "T. Kramer—The Best Friend I've Had In Some Time," from John Singer, postmarked Penang, thanking him in advance for those "furious, futile, final days."

Truman tucked all three away for later, charging his children with an immediate *Walk About*, paying homage to one of Singer's recent literary bequests. After requisite exchanges with Zurina and Fatimah, he led his trailing of wheelchairs and youngsters, with new boy, polio-stricken Malayless Raj, down along the river, beneath the bridge, up behind the theater, to loop back around for the Home, in time for supper.

* * *

That evening Truman plunged into constructing a ramp, with sturdy handrails, enabling Raj to toilet himself, unemcumbering fumbling Ramasami or Singh of placing Raj's bare butt wherever they could. Asking Zurina or Fatimah to help with the boy's toileting would be too much.

That night he wrote a long letter to thin Ling about caring and confusion, groping with each, a sister of the letter he mailed to Angela weeks before, two letters needing to be written, but sent to whom from a boy awakened to desperate, uncertain hunger.

Truman sealed the two-and-a-half pager, then settled into a left-behind Desmond Morris book. "He's no Sagan," advised John Singer, "but not bad at all."

Closing his week, Truman finished Raj's *tandas* ramp, swam alone in the river and took Raj, Ramasami and Lim to the Sunday market. Raj, in his thrown-together wheelchair, gaped. Lim clung to Truman amongst the strangers. Ramasami tripped and stumbled about. The four snacked on fried bananas, then milled happily through the wares: the fish, the clothing, and the pirated and legitimate cassettes. Truman was home again.

* * *

By mid-October, cooler monsoon air graced the skies by day as a waxing full moon dressed it by night. Truman got his cycle back, having finally paid for the carburetor work. Crippled Raj caught up to Ramasami in recognizing his alphabet with appropriate sounds, as Singh and Ramasami loved Truman's flash-card sound game, but remained unable to string together anything into the reading of words.

Then Azman showed up, majestically driven in the office Land Rover through the torrent of a monsoon shower, accompanied with a Malay office girl and a bent-up Indian child, a little girl. A new resident. A vote of confidence.

The young girl spoke no Malay, like Yap and Raj before her, having come from a rubber plantation and denied schooling. Her name was Kamala, prompting Truman to think of graceful deer in the distant savannahs of Africa from some forgotten issue of Mabel's *National Geographics*.

Of eleven or twelve, she was wrapped in a blanket, wearing only soiled green gym shorts beneath. Her hair was cropped to a crew cut, and she was visibly frightened. Several large boils flared up from the brown skin of her thighs.

After brief words, Azman, his office girl, and their driver were gone. Truman, with Ramasami's interference and Raj's help, discovered that she indeed spoke Tamil, and was frightened, whisked away from the only three rooms she had ever known. Truman noticed her one leg appeared useable, with the other a near bone, having permanently curved her spine through a hopping loco-motion she managed across her young years.

Raj's budding Malay told everyone that someone had died, and that the girl was hungry. Truman, through Raj, assured her she'd be cared for and dolled up from the stacks of donations he kept in storage. He told her she'd learn Malay and be taught to read and write, wishing up through the colossal rain that fell again outside, that Tan's wife, then fading away Molly, could witness him doing his job.

* * *

Oct. 17, 1981

It's about 9:00 p.m. Today we got everything done in school & this afternoon I took Normah's wheelchair down to the cycle shop to be welded. (I'm building a third for Kamala from my spare parts— she's really taken to the A.M. schooling routine—must know 20-30 Malay words by now). I took Ramasami, Lim, Singh & Salleh with me. We had fun.

2 days ago Singh got into a bees' nest while on a hike. I had to run into the swarm & carry him out. Both of us got it pretty good— him crying a good deal. Kumari (stingless & rubbing away at her big tits) cried, too.

I've been irritated lately with Fatimah & Zurina. They don't like Raj & Kamala talking to one another in Tamil. (I've got to do something about Kamala's boil situation—she's got 6 goose-eggers.)

Still waiting for my friend's reply to my last letter. I catch myself waiting for the mailman's thumb bell every day.

Last night I stopped for a beer, then went & saw this "Salem's Lot" movie down at the theater. Scared the fucking shit out of me!!! Especially the kid floating outside the window & tapping on the pane. Whew!!!

I started reading "Lord Of The Flies" thanks to John. I like it (poor fuckin' Piggy). Around here I cut the grass & we've hit the Old Folks' Home again. We hit the river, too. I got the smarter ones into seeing things in the clouds above. Kamala liked it & (according to Raj) saw a big chicken lying sideways. Normah laughed to that & said it was a house with people on the roof.

I have enough work to do for another week or so. I've been feeling sad at times & I've had trouble falling asleep. Oh yes, I saw in the New Straits Times *another acid-throwing fit. Some Indian guy getting back at his wife for something. 2nd or 3rd time I've read of that nuttiness since training.*

* * *

Several days later in the clean air after a downpour, the office Land Rover pulled up again. No smug Azman, just the same office girl, delivering a severely cerebral-palsied Chinese girl, as though she were delivering a sack of rice.

This girl, of twenty or more, figured Truman, suffered an affliction much more debilitating than Normah's. Even her eyes appeared bedeviled with her erratic muscular spasms. And she was ugly to boot in her dirty flowered dress that didn't conceal long breasts that swayed and jerked with her torso. Skinny and pale, when placed on the floor, she looked almost crustacean, and in pain, even when nearly still, which was seldom. Only the peace of sleep, Truman learned, kept her palsied storm at bay.

That night, alone in his shed, Truman recoiled from his own repugnance. Despair pervaded his attention. He missed John Singer. He looked about his room, at his things, tidy and innocent. He looked to where he hid her bathing suit, and thought of his lust for another man's wife. Suddenly he felt helpless, wanting to be extra kind to his few possessions as though they suffered with him.

The following morning they named the new girl, simply, AhSoh, or "woman." Coiled on the floor, she wrenched in apparent pleasure.

Yap loved her, petting at her scraggly hair like a dog. Chubby Lim circled in delight, pointing her out to anyone. Zurina wished nothing to do with her. Truman couldn't read Fatimah. He felt good, though, that afternoon as it became apparent that the girl, or woman, understood what was happening as he prepared a bed for her, then picked through donated clothes, holding up colorful garments that made her squeal, and chubby Lim applaud.

Two letters came in that afternoon's mail—one from Angela, the other from Tan's wife. Not the first time they arrived as a pair. He read Angela's first, saving the second for a more thoughtful reading.

Angela's was long enough, but again written with caution; then Truman remembered his last letter to her. Her pleasant hand looped about over their respective youth on the farm, her parents, and of college life with all its work and discoveries. She again questioned Truman of his work, and of the people and so on, before closing with her own solidifying relationship with her new boyfriend, who her parents still held in unreasonable suspect.

The thin woman's letter didn't grope at all. She was happy about his long letter, and she apologized for his having to wait for this reply. She wished to hear of his troubles. "Isn't it you like to let me know? If so, I can please share it with you, okay?" before speaking to concerns regarding herself with, "After the last meet we had I am fine. You shouldn't worried about me. I take good care for myself."

In her second page she wished to know if she added to his troubles, or was it his distance from home, or having to live in Kuala Harap. She also disliked the town and was "quite fed up on it" not knowing what to do with herself until: "I happyer here since I know you." Then she signed off: "I wouldn't and never shall be mad on you for feeling confused. I miss our meeting. Thinking of you at all times. Ling"

That late afternoon, after a good supper, Truman took a slow cycle ride south along the river. He thought of her clothes, how she put them on, of her shy smile. The monsoon air was cool. He thought of her soft words, her hard sternum. He smiled, thinking of her watching her American television shows. Some twenty miles south of Kuala Harap he stopped to look at the river, then parked and swam in its slow passing in his jeans. That night in his shed, he wrote her again. A love letter.

* * *

Several nights later he awoke, unnerved. He tried to read but couldn't. He tried to sleep, but grew angry. He turned to his journal, labeling the entry, "Oct. 24th," then "Oct. 25th," factoring the time of night.

Seemingly forever removed from the cycle ride he took the evening before, he wrote of the emptiness John Singer left behind: "These days are getting blotchy or something." From laughter with the kids, to the dreadful quiet times alone. He longed for the cleaning and burning that occupied his days a year before, tasks with immediate purpose and ends, but he couldn't find the words.

He thought himself disgusting, and tried to chart change. AhSoh needed a wheelchair. Zurina, her unfinished cart to haul wet clothes out to the lines he strung back in simpler days. Then he fell asleep, an hour before sun-up, just before the haunting Islamic call to prayer sounded out from the town above.

* * *

The remainder of the week, to Zurina and Fatimah's delight, Truman finished their *kerata kein,* as they called the laundry cart he thought looked too much like an elevated playpen on wheels. Ramasami coaxed Singh into it and got whacked by Zurina. She knew what was hers. Truman used a lengthy afternoon for a hike with the kids, avoiding the recently swelling river, reserving the following days for reconstructing two more wheelchairs from spare parts, one for Kamala, the little Indian girl, the second for AhSoh.

The job required welding, another fun walk for the kids. Then hardware, fun for Truman, if it wasn't for boisterous Mr. Tan, who insisted upon his needs. But the next day he needed clamps and nuts and bolts, as Deepavali, the big Hindu holiday, brought soldiers with gifts to the Home. He waited until they were gone.

Three Malays mingled within Tan's cluttered shop. Truman exchanged pleasantries, rounding up his needs as Tan's wife emerged from the back, never acknowledging his smile as she turned to the Malays. Truman milled at the counter. Maybe it was his last letter, the heartfelt one.

Shortly the three men came up behind him. Ling went behind the counter. She spoke to Truman matter-of-factly, in Malay, "Can wait for me to take care these items?" Truman nodded. Glancing to the Malay men, she said, "Your other item in back of shop."

As soon as the men left she calculated what Truman owed, then bagged his hardware. Handing him his bag, her thin hand caught his. Her voice went so low Truman thought others might still be in the store.

"Can you return to visit me this night? I am alone until tomorrow evening."

"Yes," answered Truman. "You mean here?"

"Yes. I shall unlock back at 8:00 p.m. Can I expect you between that time and 8:15? It shall be quite nice," she sped her request.

"Okay. Are you sure?"

"Yes. Thank you." She took her hand away. "I see you then."

* * *

That evening, after showering and putting on a nicer shirt and his cleanest jeans, Truman left on foot, up into the town after sunset. Above the darkened, battened shops, lights shined through the closed shutters of the second-floor living spaces.

Truman cut into the darkness of the alley behind Mr. Tan's side. A cat with a gnarled tail slipped out of a wooden crate just before the shopkeeper's back entrance. The door was open.

He entered. Ling startled him, from closeness.

"Ssh. Follow. Up these steps, and quiet."

Truman felt his own heart, ascending the narrow flight, behind her. She wore black slacks, sandals, and a different white blouse.

At the top of the steps he removed his work boots, sorry for the lacings. Her home was neat and clean, in spite of walls in need of painting. A rotan coffee table sat between a rotan sofa and an accompanying chair. Mr. Tan's, figured Truman. The TV, turned off, was aimed at it. Black and white photographs of aged people hung on one wall above a shrine of sorts. Truman had seen the like in other Chinese homes. There was a stack of *New Straits Times*, and another of magazines, in Chinese characters. Several calendars hung on separate walls. Again not surprising. A mat on the floor centered everything. The hall that led to the rest of the flat was dark. Truman's thin friend vanished into it.

He remained standing as she reemerged, smiling, carrying a tray. Hot tea for her and ice and soda and compound brandy for him. Her skinny arms protruded from the sleeves of her blouse.

She set the tray down and rose to Truman. With a quick, uncertain kiss, she whispered, "Thank you for your latest letter, and for coming." Truman liked her warm breath. "My husband shall remain in Kuantan until tomorrow night."

She went on. They could visit and talk, perhaps of his feelings, then watch *Laverne & Shirley,* then *Hart To Hart,* two more of her favorites, then whatever he'd like.

"I need we must be very quiet," she added seriously.

"We will," Truman agreed. He could hear the neighboring family through the thick plastered walls.

The alcohol calmed him. They sat upon the short sofa and talked of their letters and of the jets of Subang International. Then it was time for subtitled *Laverne & Shirley.* Truman wasn't crazy for it but he liked Lenny, the taller of the two stooges. In this episode, one of their more tender outings, Lenny fell for a retarded girl, not knowing her to be retarded.

Hart To Hart followed. Ling sat closer.

"I wish, since meeting you, we could be like the Hart couple in America."

Hart To Hart, like popular *B.J. and The Bear,* was another wonderful example of life in the United States. Truman thought of Singer's thoughts, at least the sons-of-bitches love each other. Unlucky for them, homicides follow 'em wherever they go.

Tan's wife, though, loved the commercial-free forty-five minutes, holding Truman's hand, encouraging him to relax, asking him to tell her something nice.

The episode closed. The Harts caught their man, an enraged secret lover, yet charming business associate. Who would of thought? The news followed: *Berita Negara,* delivered by professional-looking Malays. Midway through, Truman and Tan's wife were embraced on the sofa.

Then she excused herself, working free from beneath him, to darken the room to the wavering glow of the TV, before stripping the small sofa of its cushions, placing them neatly upon the floor.

As they went to the cushions, on the news something was happening in northern Africa or southern Europe. Truman was nervous, but hungry for her. With the sharp bones of her movement beneath him, he opened her blouse, finding her small breasts. Then their lower selves came together.

Truman was quick, and felt bad about it. She told him it didn't matter. He kissed the bridge of her nose, then dressed himself.

"I should go. We're stretching our luck."

"No, no," she hushed, half naked. "Stay some of the night with me."

"I can't. Not in your house. Ling, this is bad enough," he said, motioning to their cushions on the floor, then to the brandy behind them.

"Please! I wish you so bad. Just sleep me a small time."

"Sshh!" hushed Truman, kneeling, tucking his shirt.

"I'll bring out blankets. Are you hungry?" she asked, as she fumbled for his hands that worked at his shirttails.

"No. We'll get caught. I'd love to, you know."

"But I now have love with you. Do you know?" she blurted, beginning to cry, tightening her mouth, closing her eyes.

Truman covered her mouth. "We have to be quiet."

"Just hold to me."

"Okay," he whispered. The TV news went to small dams built south in Johor.

But in the same glow, they coupled again, their cushions sliding and separating with new vigor. Then rest, catching their breaths. Then more of her pleading, "Stay with me some of this night," sadder and louder.

Truman made promises, explaining his fears. He had never seen any girl or woman at the edge of themselves, her stricken demeanor lit by the haze of the TV, her wet face, her hard-breathing ribs.

"Be patient. There'll be other times," he said, as he helped her dress, whispering devotion. "Be patient. I'll write to you every day if you want. Do you really love me?"

"Yes." She nodded tearfully. "And writing every day shall be fine. And I shall practice at patience."

Truman stilled.

"Again, Ling. I have to know. Do you really love me?"

"I do. I have love for you."

"I love you, too."

She kissed him hard. He liked it.

"Then have faith in me. I must go now. I love you. I really do."

In minutes he descended into the darkness of the back steps.

He peeked into the stillness of the alley. Nobody. Then he strode off. A crashing sound stilled him. From back in Tan's house.

Then a singular yelp, or shout or sneeze. Then silence.

He listened, edging the shadows of the alley. Then more sounds. Glass, broken or kicked. Her tea arrangement. Or his brandy set-up. Then nothing.

Truman stayed still. Had someone been in there with them? Behind closed shutters, a sliver of light snapped on next door. It had to be her. There was no one else. A spill, or more despair.

He stood still, then strode off into the night, watching dark corners and piles of crates and parked trucks, feeling like a coward when startled by a lone goat upon the river road that led to his Home down below.

That night upon his bed, Truman read long, then showered beneath his hose-rigging, trying to rid himself of feeling. He read again, then he went for his journal.

* * *

Late Sat. Night

   I can't believe what I just did. I'm very scared for her. I have to keep reminding myself that THERE WAS NO ONE ELSE THERE BUT US!!

   I wish she were mine. I'd take good care of her. I really would. I hope so much that she forgives me & hasn't snapped or flipped out. What a fucking mess.

* * *

An hour later, he stole off by route of the riverside road for the all-night truck stop. He drank alone, and heavily, throwing up on his way home.

By the call to prayer, just before dawn, Truman slept in his shed, still dressed. Outside his glassless window, a neighbor's hen and her five chicks pecked away at the fried rice of his second vomiting.

CHAPTER 20

Truman calmed the following day. The neatly dressed police weren't swarming the small community, nor did Zurina, nor Fatimah return from their errands up in town with news or curious questions.

In his journal, he wondered how something so creepy and bad could be so easy. Over a year into his assignment, he leafed back through his pages to October of the year before. He smiled, reading his own words regarding an elusive John Singer, seen several times, yet left alone, heeding Andy's advice.

Then he wrote, logging Singh's fainting to the tearful openings of Kamala's festering boils, after consulting a government physician, a soft-spoken Indian over in Mentacab. With Fatimah's help, he proceeded upon the job himself. Pus and blood and tears were everywhere. Lim and Normah cried, too, for their new friend as Truman administered the first of the kind doctor's antibiotics.

He then wrote of a failed effort to telephone Mabel from the hotel down along the highway. Then he wrote of the kids again, having learned AhSoh was thirty years old. Zurina hated her, but the poor, gnarled woman loved being spoken to, patted on the head, and said good night to. Her twisted mass upon the floor convulsed whenever Truman entered the open bay of the Home. But he didn't write of this as his writing veered to two residents of the old Chinamen's barnlike home wandering their way to his when he was off on an errand. They may have molested Yap or Lim. Fatimah stayed away from it. Zurina was a volcano.

"*Dari rumah orang tua!*" Zurina shouted. "*Sangit jahat! Paling jahat!*" She spun about.

"Very bad. The worst," Truman agreed. "What'd they do?" he asked, calmer.

The older woman flustered, claiming it was too evil to say, so she demonstrated, grabbling her own breasts and jiggling them.

Jesus, Truman thought, this culture's a funny one. So he asked questions more pointedly, discovering that Zurina never actually saw any of this, but Lim and Yap told her so. Of course, neither child could so much as utter that they were thirsty without stabbing at approximations. And each feared the older woman who could ape them into anything short of intelligent discourse.

Truman felt bad for all around. He wrote they'd have to not visit the place for a while, after everyone was getting used to each other and enjoying it.

The next day brought a letter from the shopkeeper's wife. She apologized for ". . . my bad conduct. I do hope you are not feed up on me. Only if I could give to you the titles of me to talk about . . ." Truman figured she screwed something up from her translation dictionary. She closed: "I am very lonely until we have our meets."

Truman wrote back fast. Forgiveness was easy. He wished no pain, especially on account of himself. Then he wrote to Mabel, imagining New Jersey's cooler air, turning October's reds and oranges, a dark Halloween wind, and for some reason, the framed black and white stills of long-gone Fritz.

The next morning, he awoke from a dream about a girl he often saw about the halls of Allentown High School. She was cute and quiet and little. Then dogs appeared along the growth-laden track bed, then Mexicans, jewelry, and firemen. At his midmorning break from teaching, he tried to reassemble the dream into order, but couldn't.

* * *

He tried calling Mabel that following Saturday night from over in Mentacab, and got her after a twenty-minute wait. Their thirteen-minute conversation cost him 138 ringgits. It was a clear one, though. Mabel's voice loving, excited and concerned. She recognized his voice immediately, surprising him. Thoughtfully, she asked after the children, and then of his health, before pausing, choking up, apologizing. A cleaning man she hired hauled off his old monkey bike.

"I'm so, so sorry, honey. Oh, Truddy, I truly am," she pled.

In the heavy heat of the Malaysian night, Truman pictured Mabel, on the other side of the world, her arms birdlike, phone in hand, coffee brewing nearby, delivering the tragic news. He smiled. "Don't worry about it. It's not like I've been dying to ride it as soon as I get home."

"Oh, 'home', Truddy!" It rang so nice to her in her own early morning. "I tried to get the man to find it, but he said it was gone for good. I'm so sorry. I really am."

"Don't trouble yourself," Truman answered, meaning it, before passing along hellos to everyone, before both closed with a mutual, "I love you," so unexpectedly that both were embarrassed, yet warmly pleased.

Their conversation left Truman pensive. Over several beers in a kedai, with a flickering fluorescent light above him, he thought of Tan's wife, then of his old monkey bike. That sharp fender. Then back to her warm breath, her straight hair, nothing done to it. Then old man Barlow Archer, the deep sand of his cluttered backyard when the bicycle was new. Then mother. "April," he whispered. Her illness. Practically all he remembered anymore.

Leaving his motorcycle parked, he walked the two blocks between the sizzling of the late-night stalls, for the Shamrock Bar. He asked for #19. She came to him through the dark, an Indian woman this time. They must not stay long. He paid for the massage, but nothing else, thinking of other things all the short while.

He wouldn't write in his journal for another two weeks.

* * *

Nov. 17, 1981

All's well, I suppose. I feel better about Ling & me. I've also wondered about the rumors of us going home early due to cutbacks in the P.C. It's been a while since I wrote & a lot has happened.

Most of all (the week before last) when I was up in Tan's shop for pipe, hacksaw blades & fasteners for a better walker, Ling waited on me last & then motioned for me to follow her into the back. Well, I did & she led me back around a corner of boxes & crap & we started making out!! It was real fun though (standing up and making out against these boxes). (Tan was in Kuantan.) She even laughed a bit & left me there as she tended to customers we heard coming in up front. Then she hustled back & we went at it again. We got all sweaty, hugging & stuff (reaching into each other's clothes and all).

The next morning (a Saturday) I thought about her for almost the whole ride to Ben's to stay over with him. He wrote, asking me to call him at work & I did & we set up this spur-of-the-minute visit. It was fun. (I never told him about Ling though.) We drank Carlsberg Special Brews & he showed me his growing collection of newspaper clippings that he thought was a riot. His latest additions from the New Straits Times *were about actresses & factory girls posing nude for pictures & how some were caught as others were tricked into it at parties—all illegal, of course. Another was called: "One Wife It Is Come March—Polygamy Outlawed For Non-Muslims" meaning next year the Hindus & the Chinese can't have more than 1 wife. (Maybe Tan should reel in that Kuantan babe pretty soon.)*

Anyway, back to Ling—on my cycle ride down there, while cruising through all those pretty plantations & villages, I daydreamed of what it'd be like if we just ran off & lived in one of those lonesome villages (except our neighbors would be Malays & where would I work?). Back to our messing around in the back of her shop, I don't know what was so nice about it. Maybe the smiling. I really liked turning her around & pressing against her with her hair in my face—but mostly it was all the hugging & sweating so much. Before I left (all ruffled up), she asked for K.L. the next weekend (which was this past weekend). We did meet & we had a lot of fun for a day. We even hit Zoo Negara, which was pretty sad compared to the Philly zoo from our nutty visits when I lived at The Children's Home. (I felt real bad for this black guy and his family—maybe he was a diplomat or something—but these fucking Malay zoo workers (of all people) kept calling out to him, "Hey, Kunti Kinti!" (from "ROOTS"—on TV a few weeks ago—what fucking dicks).

Back in the city, Ling remembered a place where I once tripped & almost fell down (2 mos. ago) and laughed about it—although she didn't back then. Anyway, it was fun being together. We also hit a McDonald's that opened in K.L. & I'm still convinced it's the best fucking food in the world.

Back here in Kuala H., everything's going okay. Me & the kids went on a good long hike Mon. afternoon & got treated to cokes all around by some traveling Chinese businessman who saw our little caravan down by the theater.

Then last night this cat that's been hanging around invited his friend into my shower area for a screeching, fur-pulling tussle over who knows what.

* * *

With half of November passed, Truman buckled into routine.

From John Singer's loot, he began reading Mark Twain's *The Innocence Abroad* and liked it, especially Twain's observations of traveling companions starting journals to document their adventures, with few having the discipline to keep after them; another indicator, from a great writer's comments, of being a little bit special.

But his nights remained stormy. He dreamed Ling returned with him to America, and as she rode with him on his motorcycle out Route 537, toward the farm, dark waters flooded before them, sliding across the road carrying trees and furniture. They turned back and found themselves in a restaurant, sitting near Mabel and Kathleen Van Heflin. He tried to hide Ling, sending her to the bathroom. When she didn't return, he wandered out into the parking lot to find the children of the Home scattered about looking for him. Lim and Singh were crying. Normah and Kamala were frightened, sitting tightly, sharing a wheelchair. Truman rounded them up as spooked deer ran by crossing 537, nearly struck by suddenly-appearing large trucks. He called for Ling, then saw her, her back turned. Then he jerked awake, feeling a heaviness in his chest in the darkness of his little shed.

By day, Truman finished new crutches and a walker, the second more popular with big Kumari, who hobbled happily across the open bay within. But it was only a game to her, as she preferred propping herself behind Normah's wheelchair, enabling walking while providing propulsion for her friend.

One evening Truman went down to the theater to see *Elvis*, starring Kurt Russell as the legendary king. He wrote in his journal: "Either the movie was pretty crappy or Elvis was an asshole." He didn't write of sitting at the truck stop afterwards, drinking a beer beneath the starry night, thinking of Scotty Winslow a childhood ago, and of Scotty's mother and her 45s back in New Egypt.

One afternoon a gathering of Chinese Methodists stopped by the Home, questioning what the place was about, who oversaw it and what was Truman's role in it. Truman solicited their help in the form of toys or clothing from their friends in Mentacab. But their interests turned to Truman's own religious convictions, stunning them as none.

Their missionary response was fast. One whipped out a *Plain Truth* magazine, insisting Truman take it. Over the head of a butting-in Ramasami, the cover story read: "A Gorilla Speaks Out Against Evolution." Truman read the article that night, and was disturbed after having enjoyed Carl Sagan. Wishing he could share it with the more critical eye of John Singer, he mailed it to Buffalo. A month later, Singer responded, returning the article as well, having highlighted and labeled the sweeping generalizations beyond its starting gate conclusions, each in italics or bold type with multiple exclamation marks.

Truman imagined his wiser friend pulling hard on his cigarette, critiquing the text, writing back in his own neat block printing: "Well, Truman, it basically claims that the great Charles Darwin was a fool and a liar. His peers, past and present, worse, and that men are men and monkeys are monkeys, goddammit, and that we were all created and it's proven by being written in the Bible. And if you don't believe it then you should be reading yours, you foolish boy! Ever wonder why these types of mags are free in such discriminating locales as 24-hour laundry mats?"

Truman missed his friend.

* * *

Later in November, well-dressed Azman visited the Home, requesting a look at Truman's books. Truman's homemade teacher plan book, styled after glimpses he stole from teacher desktops back at Allentown High School, didn't interest his aloof Malay boss. He dismissed his plan book with a smirk.

"I do not see the need to be teaching these sort of children. No, no. I mean your ledger for spending is what I wish to inspect."

Fine. Truman was equally proud of that book, kept secure in his desk and managed as a petty cash book, like the checking account he never had, taught to him by John Singer a year and a week before. The next day Truman learned that Azman was leery of a possible visit from that Tuan Kareem bin somebody from the Kuantan office.

One night, about 10:00 p.m, someone and his friends threw rocks at Truman's shed. Truman was shocked and angered, entering the event into his journal as an act capable of any number of the town's numerous, unemployed, unschooled, aimless grinning teens. Sheepish and giggly, still calling out, "Hello, John" from their numerous shady hangouts. Truman had long since ceased giving his real name.

In school everyone progressed, except Ramasami and Singh in their reading. Between them they had down six sight words, sharing two, like buddies, but neither boy could phonetically decode anything as they leapt happily into unbridled guessing beyond their big six. Normah, and new boy Raj, got a kick out of it as a recent afternoon doll-making activity was going well. Truman wasn't crafty, but he discovered cutting out any number of identical patterns, stitching their edges to mates until only an opening anywhere remained, to pull them inside out, then stuff them with the endless rags all over the place, before deciding on features for a face.

To Azman's relief, big-deal Tuan never showed, but Truman's strange dreams did. One woke him in the dark stillness of his shed. He was in his Dodge Dart in front of Mabel's house. Jimmy McCleary appeared, rooting through the glove compartment. Then Mabel, at his window, asked him why he worked with children, sadly telling him to not touch the little girls. Then they were at the farm. An ugly man chased Chet Van Heflin and struck him over the head in his wife's kitchen. Truman chased the man, calling for Jimmy to help, hoping Jimmy would get to the man first. The ugly man turned and lifted his club. Truman awakened, startled, his darkness smelling of mosquito coil.

Two days later, Truman wrote kindly to Ling, settled into whatever it was they had. The very next day he received his second letter from John Singer. Buffalo, New York, again the postmark.

Truman read it eagerly. More visiting with friends, something that wouldn't mark his own return. The women were still beautiful, ". . . not that the Asians aren't," wrote Singer, "but somehow more varied—with bigger tits—hate to write it—and with levels of conversation almost unheard of with Malaysian women." Television was still inane, ". . . but what a fucking cable menu!"

Singer asked of the kids and passed on his regards to Fatimah and Zurina, and both Azmans, to a chuckle from Truman. Before signing off he asked: "What's the standing of your ___'s wife thing?" reminding his pal to be careful and to keep the calendar in mind.

The following day Truman received another letter from Tan's wife, confirming an overnight in Kuala Lumpur. She wrote that his last letter made her very happy and that she: ". . . have read it many times before destroy it." And she asked: "Do you know how long we have not meet each other after that last meet we have?"

Her handwriting, like a boy's trying to be careful, suggested the Southeast Asia Hotel and McDonald's, and the airport if he wished. Apparently watching the calendar herself, she closed: "I think only another 10 months for you to stay in Malaysia. I like to know how do you feel, if happy to return to America or not?"

By month's end Truman was just happy to get out of town, away from a protracted struggle of some sort between Fatimah and Zurina. The two had quarreled before, but this one had no end in sight as they moved about their chores, eyes tight with pursed lips. Truman wrote in his journal: "If they were cats, they'd being moving about the place with arching backs to the mere sight of one another."

In the same entry, he chronicled little Salleh again being frightened by a lone monkey on a recent hike, and that he himself made Singh cry in school and felt terrible about it. He wrote of arranging medical check-ups for each of the kids over in Mentacab. Big Kumari went first, and didn't pass the hygiene test. "Poor girl was red flagged at the inspection station," Truman wrote. The concerned Indian doctor: ". . . the sort with a turbin and beard . . ." prescribed a daily salve with a frequent changing of the underwear she didn't own, to arrest whatever it was she hosted. Naturally, back at the Home, Fatimah and Zurina, still at war, refused to have anything to do with the girl's problem. In the same entry Truman cussed them both: ". . . along with their goddamned religion," frustrated that he'd never be permitted, nurse-like, to help the hapless goon of a girl.

Four days later he was happier.

* * *

Nov. 29, 1981—Sunday night
Well I feel better, even though my cycle just cost me 75 ringgits. My weekend in K.L. was fun. We again stayed at the S.E.A. (hot water & tub!!) & saw For Your Eyes Only *(a Bond movie) &* Clash Of The Titans. *Ling loved her "frying horses" as she says it. I also bumped into 2 other volunteers (from my group) in the hotel lobby (I was alone on a beer run). There was a party somewhere in town.*

___ & I slept together holding hands. I liked her shyly apologizing for "having period time." We talked more & laughed over how she writes to me. She told me she writes her letters first in Chinese to get her feelings across, then translates into English. (I had her write

*in Chinese for me on the hotel stationery & it looked real pretty—
she did it so fast.) She also told me that she'd like to be able to watch
me writing letters to her from within my shed at my table.*

*I really enjoyed eating egg burgers & watching James Bond with
her skinny arm through mine. In the morning we talked a bit instead of bolting, & then we split up to head home separately. On the
ride home, I was enjoying the cool day going up into the mountains
& then my sprocket went on me—a mile short of the fucking tunnel
& I had to crawl along & then get pulled along by some nice Chinese
kid, clear to Bentong. I was so pissed off the first half that I thought
of beating somebody up, or terminating early, then finally I cooled
off. Eventually I was able to laugh about the jam I was in.*

*In school things are all right (Fatimah & Zurina are still lock-
ing horns), and we got a new kid, a Malay boy (the girls are happy
about that). He's about 12 or so. He carries a white bag at ALL
TIMES with clothes & shit in it & he won't sleep near a window or
the door ("takut hantu" he tells me). I guess some of the retarded
ones are also afraid of all the flying-around ghosts.*

*Salleh doesn't have his screaming fits anymore like he used to,
but he's scared shitless of the stuffed alligator I made (our stuffed
dolls—I painted blood dripping from its jaws). Raj has got to get
over pitying himself getting him by (he's learning Malay real fast
though & so is Kamala—her sores are all healed up & her hair's
growing out).*

*I heard Jackie's going home early from her placement in Johor
Baru due to medical problems. Some psycho from another group also
got packed off—I guess for being nuts. I've got to control some of my
wild daydreaming about Ling lately (& my "really nutty" night-
time dreaming), or they'll be packing my ass off, too.*

CHAPTER 21

Going into his second December, Truman wondered over his ten months left.

Maybe a hundred more pages of journal. Nearly a year, for the kids, his Home and Tan's wife, his first real girlfriend. Plenty of time for loving other people's children and another man's wife.

Truman found joy in new boy, Kordi. On their hikes about town, Kordi harbored an intense fear for cars, even parked ones, toting his ever-present white bag. And geese, too, probably a sound disposition. Some could be nasty.

Kamala and Raj remained quick learners, able and willing and thankful for Truman's routine.

Only Mabel seemed to write anymore, with New Egypt news, some gossip, the weather, and her own busying about, which Truman enjoyed, especially how she still missed him, and of her deep pride: "Oh, honey—every single day . . ." which called into question, in the unquiet of his mind, his fondness for the shopkeeper's wife.

Then Andy stopped in, with two trainees, both men in Special Education, one headed for Johor Baru, the other for a site in Kuala Lumpur. Truman felt as though he had to explain himself, as he broke from routine, quietly trying to recall them from the milling crowd at the airport.

"I'm not really a teacher, you know. I do a lot of things around here, stabbing at schooling every morning."

Andy cut him off. "Both trainees were briefed about this site, Truman, and of your fine work. The K.L. office is very pleased, and much satisfied."

Throughout their visit the teachers were cordial and appreciative, very kind to a showy Zurina, and playful with the kids in orbit. Surprisingly, all three took Truman up on a swim with the kids in the unusually shallow river. Relaxing upon a sandbar, they also decided to stay the night in Kuala Harap's lone hotel down on the highway. Andy welcomed the idea. Any exposure to field experience was good for the trainees, who tended to not wander far from their training groups.

That night they drank at the Kedua Coffee House, then cheaply at the all-night truck stop, beneath the cooling stars, most of it on Andy. They talked of Malaysia, of special education, of their trainee friends, and of the great trainee concern for how fast or slow Truman's own tour was passing, and of what may account for whichever answer he might give.

"Are you lonely out here?" the younger man asked.

Truman's thoughts lingered to Tan's shop. "Sometimes. But I do enjoy the kids, and Fatimah and Zurina."

"Do you visit or hear from other volunteers?" the older one followed.

Truman smiled. "Some. And you hear stuff and you meet from time to time."

The talk turned to specific disabilities and handicaps, with appropriate interventions and instructional methodologies, things Truman knew little of.

"I'm just a guy with a job," Truman answered.

Both apologized.

"Don't be sorry. Not for me. This place is my home. At least now. I even miss it when I'm gone from there. It's hard to explain. I really don't know why this one or that one can't walk or talk. I just tend to the place. Do whatever I can."

Andy leaned forward, his elbows into tabletop condensate. "This, my friends, is a picture of a Peace Corps volunteer," he proclaimed, a bit drunk, pulling his dark hair over his head.

Truman suddenly felt shy, thinking of the twinkling Alpine Bar, two hundred yards up the moonlit highway. He thought of Tan's wife, and asked that they change the subject.

The next day in his journal, he entered his own pride for the place and the kids, supposing either of the two trainees to be better suited. He closed, writing of Kamala's catching up to Raj in reading. He'd group the two in a day or so.

He dreamed of Ling the next morning, just before waking. She was in a room with him, but talking to someone else. He saw her the Sunday before at the Sunday market, from a distance, wearing a dress he hadn't seen before. Truman liked it, and wrote so in a letter. She answered, promising to wear it: ". . . in our next meet, when that should be?"

He wrote in his journal of looking for Christmas cards over in Mentacab. He came home with a *Blondi's Greatest Hits* tape instead.

He wrote of Zurina's recent nastiness for the kids, especially poor AhSoh whom she'd only sneer at. He wrote of Zurina's thrashing Singh and AhSoh with a broken broomstick after catching loopy Singh looking into AhSoh's unbuttoned blouse, at the dangling ugliness of the poor woman's breasts. Truman intervened. Singh and the crippled woman wept upon the concrete floor.

Zurina barked, "They were about to make love."

Truman wrote in his journal: "Singh's too stupid, AhSoh's too crippled. Islam's a FUCKING DISEASE!!"

Then he wrote of his recent bad haircut, before confessing that he too was recently short with Ramasami and Singh when they got stuck in their lessons. He closed, detailing Zurina and Fatimah's impending trips to some bomoh downriver from their kumpang. "Some sort of witch doctor check-up. Hope it works!"

* * *

Ling wrote again, a thoughtful one, with no clandestine arrangement. Truman treasured its commanding ownership of himself. Her unsteady hand demanded an explanation of his recent American visitors:

"Three I heared. Were any of these peoples American womans?" her pen pointedly asked. "That shall hurt me if prettier girl should take you from me. There is so few months left for our meetings before you return to America isn't it?" Then she puzzled him. "We may not meet for a time as the shop is very busy. Please do not worry on me, or think I not like to meet with you. I so like to see you in Kuala Harap and at the Pekan Sari Market. I hope you will not mad on me if we have no meets for a time. Please understand. I do much feel love for you and wish to meet again soon. Please write. We can write letters all we wish."

So Truman wrote. Her bathing suit could wait, his visitors were men, and didn't stay long, a relief to himself as well.

As steamy December marched on, rainy and hot, Truman hiked and swam with the kids. He tightened wheelchairs and constructed toys and games. He also happened upon Zurina denying AhSoh dry clothes in the washroom, kicking her for being naked and crippled upon the floor. Truman quarreled with the older woman, feeling abandoned by younger Fatimah, who wouldn't step forward.

On the other side of the world, an aging Muhammad Ali finished his career with a fight billed as "Drama in the Bahamas." Truman read of it in the *New Straits Times* breakfasting up in town. When he showed up for schooling afterward, chubby Lim, with Singh and Yap, were running two goats off the property, in happy, retarded vigilance.

As angry as he was with Zurina, Truman rode both women off to that southern village, every other night, on the back of his motorcycle for whatever service their bomoh provided. The waxing moon reached down through the canopy of the trees hugging the river as they skirted the waters of the Pahang. It was easy to forgive. Zurina clenched her thighs tight to Truman as they made their way through the darkened villages.

At Kamala and Normah's urging, Truman and the kids started new dolls. Truman also made up two sets of playing cards, one a Malay equivalent to Go Fish that translated as *Main Ikan*, the other, for the brighter ones, a Malay answer to Uno, which he called, appropriately, *Satu*. Both games were hits with those able to play, mostly upon the flooring of their shady fort beneath the reaches of the Go Dog Go tree. However, Truman noted in his journal: "Raj is a cheating little prick in Main Ikan," once the polio-stricken boy discovered that lying propelled one's position in the game.

At mid-month, spinning Azman was taken home for a weekend, a shocker for Truman who had never known a visitor for the hooting, self-slapping boy. Several days later Azman was deposited without affection upon the rutted driveway, and visibly sore from being rightfully circumcised.

The boy's parents had, however, reported to the other Azman how manageable their son had become since they last saw him. He dressed himself, followed simple directives and shook hands, albeit a bit too much. His shy mother asked the well-dressed Azman when her son would become normal.

Feeling like a real teacher, Truman swelled with pride, hoping to keep his temper in better check, especially with getting-naughtier Ramasami and Yap. He wished he could spread his intentions to Zurina, who pulled Kordi's ears the next day, and to Fatimah, who was worked into a frenzy a day later over Kumari's insistent scratching at her itching breasts. Truman felt for palsied Normah. From her wheelchair, sensing a thrashing, she pled her goony friend to stop.

In his shed, Truman wrote to and received loving notes from up in town. A week before Christmas, she sent a card she found over in Mentacab, a Vermont-like scene, early morning following a heavy snow. She mentioned their diminishing time left and: ". . . near one month since our last meet," hoping for patience, before returning to Truman's great holiday. "It's confuse me to wish Christmas to you as you told me before that you do not go to Christian church. Anyway, the snow look very soft, and I hope you will like this card from me."

Truman did, and wrote back so. Lonely for her, he added that he missed her too, and that he loved her, ". . . so very much."

* * *

A week and a half later, Truman wrote in his journal:

Dec. 25, 1981, Christmas night
    Sort of sad, but very nice, too. I'm really trying to be more devoted to the kids & I think I am.

This entry begins about a week ago. It certainly hasn't felt like Christmas. I did get cards—Van Heflins', Mabel's, 1 from Ben, a screwy one from Dave Hayden (he hit everyone in our group). I sent one to Mabel, another to Angela (a calmer thing this time) & one to Ben & a long one to John S. I'll bet it's cold in Buffalo—I like seeing winter in movies that pass through here.

Fatimah & Zurina have been themselves—lazy & moody—fun sometimes & then pains in the ass. Fatimah told me Kumari likes being filthy because all "orang Inida suka koto." (Indians like being dirty.) I felt like telling her that all Malays are stupid & lazy. For example, I heard the one old guy at the Chinese old man's home got put in jail for brewing his own booze. The poor bastard must be 85, one-legged & owns nothing but rags & now he sits in a jail in Kuantan—Islam is glory—God is great. Down with America!

To happier things—while on a hike Singh shit himself again & crazy Kordi lost that fucking white bag & flipped out.

Some Catholics from Mentacab came over (honest to God—it sometimes feels like we're the Mayberry of Malaysia & Mentacab's Mt. Pilot) & put on a Christmas party for us. It was fun.

Later in the day Yap came back from a home visit & of course we couldn't get her out of her family's car. She kicked & screamed. I never saw her that bad. I told her sister's boyfriend to drive down by the bridge & we'd get her out down there. We did—to her sister's embarrassment & pleadings for Yap to behave—all to the delight of 4 Malay teens watching on (with nothing else to do, the jobless fucks) who I told to get lost (because they were laughing at all of us. I also called them "dog fuckers"—a religious insult—more rocks to come?).

I felt so bad for poor Yap & I promised myself never to lose my patience with her again (but I have). I just want a nice home for her.

After returning home I sat with her overlooking the river until her crying went to a whimper, then she began to mix, then Fatimah twisted her cheek, calling her "paling jahat" (the worst) as Zurina ran off a string of shit about her being bad & Chinese & who knows what else. NO wonder the poor thing hates it here.

There was one cool day where I took a cycle ride south. As usual I thought of Ling & worried why she's not so hot to see me these days. This thing sort of snuck up on me—how much I like her & all.

Oh yes. 2 days ago, Ramasami found & brought to my attention a big weasel or otter-type animal lying around out back—real sick-like. I tried to run it off (thinking of the kids). It wouldn't go, so I hustled the kids inside & went back & killed it with a shovel & tossed it into the river.

* * *

Truman didn't write of his Christmas that swelled within. Instead he sat down with Fatimah and Zurina, to unload how he felt about them, the kids and the Home.

The three sat in the women's tiny room. Zurina surprised him, attentive, smiling, bowing to his thoughts, as Fatimah sat there, disappointing Truman. He hoped the opportunity would mend their fences.

That evening he forgot all about it, seeing the movie *The Gods Must Be Crazy* down along the highway. The South African film, taking the nation by storm, was filling theaters everywhere. Truman loved it. A laugh a minute from his lone seat, front and center. He treated himself afterwards to a couple of stiff Carlsberg Special Brews. "A beer to punish Colt 45," Singer once quipped. "The white trash and the brothers back home would guzzle the stuff."

* * *

An irritable cat Fatimah had been keeping died. In tears, and carrying a ragged pillowcase, she approached Truman. He assured her that he'd take care of it. In his journal he wrote: ". . . so I pitched that miserable thing into the river, too."

Then he telephoned Mabel, but couldn't get through. That same day, the Mentacab Methodists returned, extending belated Christmas wishes while seeming more concerned over the Muslim diet being imposed upon all the kids, Malay or not. "Hardly the greatest of the kids' problems," wrote Truman, "or those nice Methodists', either."

Then Ling wrote, ending a two-week wait.

A confusing page and a half, expressing: ". . . evilness and these bad meets of ours," his diminishing time, his being so close, and yet so far from her. Her trying hand, translated from her graceful Chinese, wrote of her guilt, yet asked that he think of her and write to her. She wrote of ancestors and shame, placing all blame on herself, a spiritual thing her English couldn't harness. Reading in his shed, Truman didn't care about dead people, not hers anyway. In closing, she repeated: "Please write letters to me. I know our letters are bad, but maybe we have our bad meets for a while longer."

Truman wrote back that night, as understandingly as he could, with her skin, and her attention swirling through his mind. He wrote slowly and unsurely, after coyly getting out her modest one-piece bathing suit, envisioning the knobs of her spine, the smell of her sleeping, groping about the evolving terms of their friendship.

Three days later he remarked in his journal his new patience with the children. Gnarled AhSoh loved his getting the kids dancing to John Singer's tape player. He invented, for Raj, Kamala and Normah, the "ball-bearing shuffle." He closed, writing of the return of the Mentacab Methodists, appreciative of their soon donating of a brand new wheelchair. "For the little Indian girl over there," one said as two pointed out for Truman, "not the Chinese one on the floor," as menstruating AhSoh dragged herself, in a long smear across the floor, toward the joy of the others. "Fatimah was little help," wrote Truman.

Into January, Truman learned from giggling Normah, that little Kamala had dreamed of him, calling him "*cikgu*" or teacher. He swung Kamala up into the air, hugged her, then flashed back strong in his mind to another school, deep in the Pines of New Jersey. A teacher came to mind. She kissed him, and he didn't know why.

Another afternoon, he learned Kumari's father was his own Indian barber up in town. He was surprised. The next night he saw and enjoyed a Robby Benson movie, *One On One*, though he cared little for basketball. The night after that, while writing to Tan's wife, Truman pondered the near-nothing he knew of his own ancestry: Mabel, his father's lone sister, then his mother, who came to him, in recollection, sitting in her wheelchair, speechless, slowly looking about. Seemingly in black and white, moving incomplete, like an old 8mm home movie.

Another night, he started his first Hemingway, *A Farewell To Arms*, again Singer's. And he liked it, with time on his hands, and with his thoughts of Tan's wife. He also cut the grass and made a new burner barrel from a 55-gallon drum he sort of stole from behind the gritty bus station up in town. In his latest *Newsweek*, the year-end roundup issue, there was a picture of a woman lying naked, coiled within a large snake. The photo startled an unsuspecting Zurina, prompting her to turn away, then look once more, mumbling something incoherent.

Meanwhile, the *New Straits Times* was enjoying a righteous weeklong heyday with World Book-Childcraft International Of America, for an offensive passage in one of its children's publications depicting Malaysians as living in trees, fearful of animals. Truman endured reaction in the shops where he ate, and down at the Kedua Coffee House. To one heated Chinese patron, a fed-up Truman, retorted, "Jesus Christ, the people at that company already apologized up and down to your government. And how 'bout you guys, thinkin' America's nothing but a vast land of sex and murder and endless fuckin' cowboy hats, and whatever else you see and believe on *BJ And The Bear*. You should watch the goddamned *Waltons*."

The man calmed. But his friend took over, with better nonsense, cheering Truman with a story going around town concerning long-gone John Singer. Apparently Singer embraced Islam and changed his name. "Like that Cat Stevens singer," the quieter man claimed. Then it got better. "We hear your friend now resides in Hong Kong, with an obese Malay woman."

The following day the Methodists returned with a smug Azman, two of his office girls, and the local district officer. As it turned out, the good Methodists had owned their promised wheelchair for some time. Everyone simply awaited the appropriate fanfare of opening the truck of the minister's car, with cameras flashing, for him to hand the chair to the district officer; from him to Azman the well-dressed; in turn, Azman to an office girl for her to drop it on her own foot, before struggling with it, handing it to Truman. Then finally, Truman, to Kamala, the cute Indian girl.

AhSoh, knotted in sitting and bloodless, watched from a shadowy corner. Only Truman looked to her.

* * *

Jan. 14, 1982

The 8th was a national holiday for Mohammad's birthday—a day off for everyone except poor AhSoh, who Zurina slapped around for being crippled or ugly—for Mohammad's birthday present. The poor thing (AhSoh, that is) did get some visitors the other day. It was nice seeing people being nice to her & fussing over her. (They were Indians—Chinese would have wished her well & tossed $—Malays would have simply stared like puzzled chimps.)

Ling & I have been writing about once a week. It's nice but still no visits (or "bad meets"). I don't understand it. In one letter she forbids me to see other girls—American or Malaysian (as if either are all over me) but says she "permits me to go to the massage bars if I wish."

An old Indian lady dropped by to snoop around. I asked her in Malay if she spoke English, & she answered in English, "Of course. I am Roman Catholic." She also asked me why some of the kids are dirty. I answered because some of them play in the dirt & that she was seeing them prior to washing & that she was complaining to the wrong person.

On a hike, out of the blue, Ramasami got all excited about having pubic hair & asked me if I had some, too. Normah overheard &

squealed & bucked in her chair like a nut. Nitwit Ramasami was delighted, claiming that she must have some, too. (Ass-beating waiting to happen?)

I also think Ramasami & Singh have hit their limits in school—just can't get them to count any better or learn any more words. Maybe I'm doing it wrong, but Raj & Kamala are taking off & Normah's up in a Darjah 5 reader now.

Before I hit the sack (to read some "A Farewell to Arms" which I like) that one fucking bum tried to scoop leftover rice from my plate down at the kedai behind the highway. I flipped out & told him to eat it like a dog. I shouldn't have, but I'm sick of him (don't think I wrote of him before).

* * *

That second January, Truman continued schooling the kids in the morning as they hiked after lunch, or worked on puppets instead of dolls. From *Newsweek* he learned the earth was spinning 1,000th of a second slower due to the rising oceans beating upon the shores of the planet, and one night he took an interest in a lunar eclipse, while drinking alone at the truck stop. It was red and slow and pretty. He thought of Bob Dylan's "cold bloody moon" from John Singer's left-behind *Street Legal* tape.

Two days later Truman walked in on Azman and the girls, obviously discussing him, for they quieted quickly. That same week he was taking the kids on motorcycle rides down along the rutted river road. Even Azman the crazed climbed on, grunting and gurgling, able to say, "bye-bye," as Truman and the shopkeeper's wife exchanged letters, in spite of her seeming to not see him as he twice purchased goods at her husband's shop.

Big Mr. Tan, joyfully ignorant, remained loud and carefree, tending to Truman's needs.

One afternoon Truman took eight of the kids to see *Superman II*, which arrived down along the highway, after working the large cities, and on the heels of its predecessor in Kuala Harap. As before, half the fun was getting there. Again, Azman was transfixed to the slow-moving ceiling fans. That night Kamala and Normah, with great joy, reported to Zurina and Fatimah, Truman's rapt attention to the intimacies exchanged between Lois Lane and the man of steel.

Truman felt good for a while, and wrote so in his journal. He received a long letter from Angela. A friend of hers had a baby. Angela wrote of her friend's trials and courage before going into her own plans and recent past. She had a run-in with Kyle, forever out of her life, a high school thing, what a foolish pursuit. Jake, the college kid, had everything. "Even Dad's coming around," she wrote.

Ben wrote, too, twice. His second contained a *New Straits Times'* clipping, "King Cobra Case Takes New Twist," the third in a series that Truman was also following regarding a cobra encountered by rubber tappers in Bidor that incited strange dreams and behavior from those the snake came upon. The police were baffled. Bomohs were consulted. Truman, reading beneath the shade of the Go Dog Go tree, smiled, thinking of the wacky snake that hypnotized Mogley in Disney's *The Jungle Book*. He wrote in his journal: ". . . these fuckers ought to be living in trees."

By month's end, though, his moods swung again, feeling at a lost with his job, the kids, the little town, and being so near to her. He wrote to her about it. She took it wrong. Three days later, she blamed herself and their "so bad meets." He wrote back as fast, trying to correct her.

His nightmares returned across nights of poor sleep. He arranged more dental visits for Raj, Kamala, and finally, the worst, Azman: a wild, strap-down ride. The kind Indian dentist excused his Malay assistant, who feared the boy's terror.

The coming and going of the Chinese New Year made things better. Visitings at the Home left the children rich with new junk and plenty of candy. Then a tape came from John Singer, from the cold winds of Buffalo.

Truman wanted to send one back, immediately, perhaps even taping Azman's return to the dentist for a slice of life from his little madhouse by the river. He didn't, but he got the kids on the tape, and Zurina and Fatimah, too, who wished to know what was said in English to Truman from Singer, and from Truman back to the grainy voice within the recorder, all that was left of his dear friend.

By January's end, Truman entered into his journal Salleh's sudden, expanding vocabulary, eight words, crystal clear. He had plans to meet with Ben, which he needed, and he wrote of the shopkeeper's wife, and of finishing *A Farewell to Arms*, then back to his friend again. He was certain he loved her, ". . . and pretty ashamed of myself for it." Then he mixed the great novel in with the quiet woman. "Of course it makes me think of her, when I'm trying not to. I'd certainly row a boat across a lake for her. I sure would."

He closed his three-page entry with: "Now, of all songs, that stupid 'My Eyes Adore You' song by Bobby Vinton (or whoever) just came on (on one of my oldies tapes). I must have been an ass for liking Angela for so long. I hope someday I can find someone like Ling—I'll keep her for sure."

CHAPTER 22

In an impulsive burst, Truman sawed out and framed a new window into his shed. No need for glass panes, not with home-made shutters for the rain, and mosquito coils at night.

February 4th, Truman entered into his journal: "I write from my new home. It makes the place sunnier in the mornings and cooler at night."

As he worked at his window, the kids clamored about. Raj and Kamala helped from their wheelchairs. Ramasami, with nails tucked between his dark lips, strutted about, waving random-lengths of wood, snapping irate commands at Singh and Kordi, who stayed close to Truman's tape player and their community tray of leftover Chinese New Year candy.

Then Truman received an invitation to a party celebrating Andy's termination. He decided to go, held at Bruce Statton's nice home in suburban Kuala Lumpur. Ben would be there, too, and Truman liked Andy.

One evening he took another long ride south, through the villages on the opposite banks of the river. As expected, no power lines, no police, so no helmet. And no shops, just winding, rising and falling dirt roads, from one village to the next until invited into a home for supper. The rural Malays were like that, and Truman accepted, becoming a small celebrity. Word spread out into the trees to homes he couldn't see. Colorful visitors came by. Most claimed to have seen him one time or another, upstream in Kuala Harap, a near city to these people of the quiet green of the forest. These people who overfed him, happy to have him in close person, delighted with his accented Malay.

On his slow ride home, beneath the stars through cool night air, he felt guilt for the things he had written of the Malays and Islam. He made a note to keep his frustrations with Zurina and Azman out of his broader opinions.

At the Home, Truman wrote of Kordi fitting smoothly into the routine, without any special friend. The boy kept a smiling outlook on everything. When happy, he leaned inordinately forward, sometimes having to take a step to keep from tumbling. "He walks around the place as if trying to look around corners that don't exist." That same week, Ramasami made repeated claims that gnarled AhSoh carried a load in her pants. Zurina flipped to the possibility of having a mess to clean, as well as to the notion of Ramasami's having snooped about the crippled woman's backside. Upon investigating, Truman discreetly discovered an ugly lump. The kids clamored about. AhSoh hated this particular attention. Perhaps a protruding coccyx, more likely a callous of her life of dragging herself about. Regardless, it was just there, and Zurina and Ramasami could rest easy. Truman wrote in his journal: "The poor girl's just a tad uglier than we thought."

* * *

Truman's other life wouldn't stir until the tenth, when invited to a post-Chinese New Year's party at a place known as Mrs. Low's Rice Outlet. Truman was familiar with the business, two miles west of Kuala Harap, toward Mentacab. The invitation came from nice Mr. Martin, who assured Truman he was more than welcome.

This much quieter affair than the rooftop curiosity of the year before hosted nearly all Chinese, with a sprinkling of Indians. Most were older married couples, and nearly all, as far as Truman could determine, were established business people of the area. The building was a single floor combination warehouse-home, with the home in the rear. The front two-thirds, the business, was partially cleared, providing room for two tables of refreshments and the milling crowd.

Mr. Martin never showed, but Mr. Tan and his wife did. Truman, feeling alone, was eventually approached by the curious and the well-meaning. He even managed a few commitments for the Home, most notably, basal readers in Health and Science from a local primary school principal. He wrote in his journal of the women segregating themselves, and of seeing Ling, three or four times. He knew her dress from his distance with the men, and he was childishly jealous of her jocular, heavily drinking husband.

The next day the thin woman consumed a portion of his next entry, hoping for better times. He reflected: "There's only 7 and a half months left for us to know each other." In the same entry he wrote of the hoopla of papier-mâché masks with the kids. After painting them, little Salleh wet himself from fear. Superstitious Kordi couldn't straighten himself for days. Truman also chronicled Yap's sudden poor complexion, and some new thing Ramasami and Singh had for one another's rearends. Zurina was certain of a love interest between the boys. Truman didn't know what it was. Even mild-mannered Fatimah favored a quick thrashing over Truman's more cautious reminders of appropriateness he leveled at the two silly simpletons.

The following day, three days after the rice outlet party, the mailman's ringing bicycle brought new hope.

> *Dearest Truman,*
>
> *It is very hard for me to wait for your letter but I am still happy to receive it. Thank you.*
>
> *There was something bad happened but don't worried please, okay? I am sure will over come it. Sometimes I wonder why should I living in this world without any parents and family love when I facing some problems, but I always take it easy after I have soft my problems. You have your kind aunt so you know of this too.*
>
> *Truman, I do enjoy the meet we have in Zoo Negara and also the nice sleep together. I still can remember you answer me by this, "I already did" while I asked you to hold me tight. So you see, I remember every word you said. And there's why of course I remember you tripping on the step one year ago. Ha Ha!*

I think of you much and then to see you at the party makes me ask myself so much. I ask why we never hold hands when walking (while on secret meets).

Is it because Americans don't really like to do so even they love each other? So why not let us show each other the "Hart To Hart" couple way (TV show) Okay? Moreover, since you'll be back to America on October, please let us enjoy ourselves to have more sweet memory for then? Maybe you thought I am a old minded Chinese and I'll feel shy if we do so in front of people, right? I'm not the Chinese you think of. Okay? Let us try it, okay?

I like to tell you something else. Do you know why sometimes we never talk much to each other? I have feel that we seldom close to each other because we do not know about the character and hobby we have, so sometimes even if we wish to tell or show our feelings to each other, it is hard for us, right? For example, I like to tell you something about my job, my life in K.H. and about my childhood life to you but I worried that you not be interested to hear about all these, so I don't know what and where should I start? I think maybe you also think same way. So I hope we'll soft this problem when we meet again, okay?

That's all for this time. Please write and let me know any idea for us in this problem, and when you can meet with me, okay? (do not forget to give me a kiss when you come to me, okay?)

Please take care of yourself. I miss you too.
    Ling
P.S. Please send my request to your aunt.

* * *

Feb. 14, 1982 (Happy Valentines Day)

I already mentioned that nice letter from Ling. I wrote back that night saying that talking more would be nice. We've agreed to meet again. I'll have to wait for when & where.

Went to Andy's party at Bruce's house. Arrived cold & wet & pissed off (got lost in K.L. rich section after checking into some fucking rat hole to clean up). Everyone (or about everyone) got all drunk. I hung around mostly with Ben & got snotted on by some girl I sort of flirted with. Nearly everyone crashed there at Bruce's. I left (or should I say busted out) at 4:30 a.m. after being eaten alive by mosquitos—the place was locked up like a goddamned fort. Anyway, Ben found a flame who he wound up with. A bunch of people argued about the music choices. One guy claimed to be a child psychologist & another guy didn't believe him so they argued about that. (I steered clear—I'm not a real teacher either.) Big Dave H. was there, all loud & nuts—carrying on about all the white pussy in one place— wonder if he got any?

Anyway, it was pretty fun. A bunch stayed the next day for a touch football game. I thought about it, but at the rat hole I bummed out & headed for home at 6:00 a.m. (did hit McDonald's for breakfast—holy shit, what good food!!!).

Stopped by Batu Caves outside of K.L. to see this Indian-ritual stuff—amazing dancing—arrows stuck through tongues—great big Mummer-like get-ups HOOKED to the flesh of their chests. I felt like I was in a Nat. Geographic *and not hungover, mosquito-bitten & anxious to get home.*

Back here all is well. Teaching is fine. Yap is up & down from sad to super naughty to just plain shit-ass silly. Salleh & Kordi are getting into little stare-down scraps. Neither knows what to do next over the toy trucks they both think they own. (One of them should just put on one of the masks we made!)

* * *

Quietly, Truman turned twenty, wondering over his seven months left. For so long, he simply figured he'd just return to the farm, but he wasn't so sure anymore. Then Ling wrote, like a potion sweeping future away.

She wrote of her feelings, surrounding the holiday most dear to her. She also got wind that a friend of hers was getting married. "Registered," she wrote. She wished her friend well, ". . . with much more good fortune than I have had," before mentioning the zoo, and how she wished for pictures of that "wonderful meet." Then came their next meet: "This weekend if possible, come to K.L. to book a room and see me. Buy something from our shop, and nod yes to me. Also, can you shave off your beards for me?"

They met that weekend, with neither able to afford the Southeast Asia, settling for a place on the south side of the city. Tan's wife wore the dress she wore at Low's Rice Outlet party, as asked.

They purposely held hands through the shops at Ampang Park. Truman strode as tall as he could, maintaining the inch he had on his thin friend. In no time their handholding became natural. Truman asked Ling, "Why do you wipe your hands so often?"

"So my hands are agreeable for you." She kept her handkerchief in her purse.

"They're very pretty," he answered, raising the one he held, kissing it, surprising them both.

They talked that night of her patting at her upper lip as well, with the same handkerchief, cleansing beaded sweat. Truman liked the subject. "Why do you Chinese women avoiding tanning?"

Ling liked the conversation. "We do not wish to be dark of skin. We wonder over your white womans wishing to be so."

During their loving she remained quiet, but claimed she liked it, especially, "holding to each other," afterwards. Except when Truman, up and about, discovered they could see into the neighboring flats. He wrapped her in a blanket and led her to their windowsill. Maybe they'd see a murder or a beating. Who knows?

Instead, there were kids and steaming kitchens, and the hanging of wet laundry. One family watched TV. Truman enjoyed the clandestine closeness, and their whispering as they watched. Sharing her blanket, Tan's wife enjoyed Truman's pleasure. Truman felt it, too, for in the middle of the night he awoke and went alone back to the window. And he didn't like it. Returning to Ling's bony hips and shoulders, his mind slipped back to New Egypt, to Jimmy McCleary, and the smell of the pitch pines the two boys climbed to watch the woman in her trailer rise from her bath. Then Ling's thin arm reached for his hand to hold. Shortly, Truman was asleep.

* * *

Back in Kuala Harap, a stomach virus wrenched through the kids. Normah was first, heaving and lethargic, then fish-stealing Lim, who should have been first. Then Singh and little Salleh. Kordi fell next, and behaved as though dying. Ramasami, jerky and impulsive, soldiered through, as did big Kumari and AhSoh, neither gaining any new attractiveness. Crazy-as-a-loon Azman spun and yelped his merry way around the place, apparently immune to the contagion. "What a kid!" Truman wrote.

Truman took only Ramasami and Singh to the clinic. The doctor, a Malay, prescribed the same medicine to the lot, site unseen. Truman also wrote of finding the source of recent foul air, a dead dog some twenty yards beyond his much-repaired fence. "I set fire to the fucker twice," he wrote, "with stacked wood & all, & there was still more dog to go, so I let him cool & pitched what was left in the river (glad we swim upstream)."

None of the kids died. Schooling returned, and on their first hike that week Truman's hobbling gang happened upon another dead cow, bloated and stinking down beneath the bridge. For some reason Singh cried. A day later a cheerful Zurina told Truman of a dream she had which placed him in a fast red car down in the Pekan Sari marketplace. Truman dreamed, too, of ice-skating, alone and far, across a vast frozen lake, to come upon a cabin where he happened upon Mrs. Ferguson, the bathing woman from the trailer park. She took his hand, led him to an old sofa. He touched her. Her breasts were pointed, and as hard as wood.

Then depressing days crept in, prompting a dark journal entry. "February 26th," ending with, "Jesus, I'll read this in 1989

& think I had a shitty time over here. It's not that bad. I just miss you-know-who."

A letter and a package from Ben lightened him, with Ben's take on Andy's party. Ben also complained of his own social life before giving great praise for an included book, *The Russians*, by some Hendrick Smith fellow. Good. Truman finished *A Farewell to Arms* and needed something worthy to follow, for the love story invoked thoughts of purpose and desperation. "I'd steal Ling if I could," he wrote. "I'd row a boat for her clean to the South China Sea if I had to."

His next entry was cheerier. He appreciated poor AhSoh's smile within the twist of her face. Yap, lovingly took to shadowing him. Kordi reminded him of a chimp in clothes, and a damn sensible one at that. On a hike, Salleh walked blindly into a deep ditch. "Vanished," wrote Truman. "Just vanished from sight, to climb up & out—all fucking frantic & bug-eyed." The entry closed, though, with Zurina beating a stumbling Kumari with Truman's yardstick. "Jesus Christ," wrote Truman, "& these people keep asking me if these kinds of kids are dangerous. Hell, I have to protect them from the help."

Three weeks would pass before his next entry.

* * *

March 21, 1982

It's been some time. This one will have to be sketchy.

Raj & AhSoh's tandas ramp never worked out so I built them a "potty"—real low to the ground (whore Zurina says she'll "never" empty it). I have & Fatimah has, too, before we found out that Ramasami loves the awful job. (I'd teach him to wipe AhSoh's ass but Zurina would have a fucking stroke.)

I got Xmas $ from Mabel & turned it into ringgits. I bought binoculars & got drunk. I'm saving the rest for a Kelang getaway with ___. We've been writing often & her last letter was real nice. She mentioned her "frying horses" from that stupid movie. She also wants to take pictures this time (she'll be in her swimsuit for a first), *but I think it's pretty risky. The letters back & forth are bad enough, but I did like her writing that she didn't want to forget my "handsome appearance" after I leave. I wrote that I wanted pictures of her, too, & she wrote back that she's too ugly. I wish she'd cut that shit out. I know it's the culture & all but it irritates the hell out of me. Anyway, I can't wait for Kelang.*

Around here we've been hitting the river a lot. Normah cut her foot & let me carry her home. I was surprised. One afternoon we had such a good time that I kept them out until 7:00 p.m. We built sand castles with moats & everything.

Oh, another letter from Mabel came after the $ one. She has a "special friend" that she felt she had to tell me about. She met him through Chet & Kathleen VH & he's in the ag. business somehow (probably a salesman). Anyhow, she thought I should know & she says it's nothing serious (which means it is). He's from "a nice family down below Mt. Holly"—other farmers.

Back to around here. I wanted to note all the margarine Zurina & Fatimah put on their bread. Food must slide through the Malay gut. The planets lined up & the world didn't blow up or anything. Everyone believes that kind of shit around here (all over in the New Straits Times—*even a full front-page story from a " prominent astrologer"). (Ben's probably broke buying up issues.)*

There's talk of a recession back in the States. Fatimah's friend from somewhere dropped off 7 chicks in a box for her to take to her family. Kordi & Salleh love them. Like back home we call them "peeps"!!

* * *

Near month's end, Truman saw *Gone In Sixty Seconds*, a B-film about stealing cars, that he walked out on, enthusiastically endorsed by four people—Ling, by letter, included. Meanwhile, Zurina and Fatimah quarreled for nearly three days by Truman's reckoning, as he read into Mr. Smith's *Russians*, enjoying it more than he thought he would.

In his journal he wrote of Salleh acquiring the chimp-like mannerisms of Kordi, before writing of stargazing with the kids, out front with the dark Pahang sliding by down over the bank. Truman laid out blankets to lie on. Fatimah and Zurina joined them. Yap lost interest quickly. Chubby Lim never gained any, taking to the long swing in the dark. Ramasami wouldn't shut up and Kordi fretted ghosts. As a group, they caught three falling stars, one so brilliant and reaching, that solemn Truman wished it were only he and Ling lying upon the cool grass.

* * *

Then came Kelang. Taking a cab, he met Tan's wife in Kuala Lumpur where they took a bus to Kelang. Another cab took them six miles south, to an older beachside hotel, their one-night getaway.

Their small hotel was an aged, thick-walled inn constructed by the British a hundred years before. Vines climbed the outside of the structure across peeling green and blue paint. Inside, a pillared central room was swept with the swirling of equally spaced ceiling fans. The airy rooms upstairs hosted wooden beds. Two bathrooms, one for each sex, served everyone from opposite ends of the central hall. The proprietors were an aged Chinese couple who asked no questions.

Their room was cool through the night, with their two windows kept wide open. Ling was shy about her swimsuit late that Saturday afternoon. To Truman she was lovely, all bones and knobby knees. She could swim, too, in a cute, progressive slapping at the water. Being in the Straits of Malacca, there were no waves to speak of as they played. Distant ships wavered upon the hot horizon. In the cooler evening, they held hands along the same stretches of narrow beach, passing only chickens and the play of Malay children.

They talked of going into town for a movie, but settled for staying in their room. "This is better," Ling said, "for have good conversation."

Lying on their hard bed, they talked of their separate youth, and of their secretive six months left. For a coy first, they talked of what felt good for one another, and they hugged and smiled over their own beginnings, nearly a year before. They smiled over her first letters that started it all, and of how she still had to translate from Chinese script.

"I like picturing it in my mind," Truman told her.

"How do you mean?"

"You know, working away at your letters twice, taking your time to do something for me when I'm not even there. It means you like me!"

Ling smiled. "I do. I have love for you."

"I love you, too. Now tell me something about myself. Anything."

Ling liked this. "You have boots like soldier, still this time, as with first time I saw you. Now tell me something I may know about you."

Truman pulled her close. "I read your letters over and over again."

"Because you have love for me?"

"Yes. Now tell me, too. I need to hear it."

"I shall never forget you. I love you and I shall always wonder of what happiness you have found in America."

"I don't want to talk about that," Truman told her. "I hate the idea of you in Kuala Harap without me."

* * *

The following night he wrote in his journal how much he cared, and how pretty she was in her purple and white bathing suit, and of how he didn't care if she was funny looking to others.

Alone in his shed, he paused, thinking of her as a little girl, teased and shy, coming of age, all alone at twelve or so, for she had shared this with him.

He penciled the quick math of the years in the margin. She began blossoming, a Malaysian world away, as he puttered around upon the soft pineland sand about the cluttered home of Barlow Archer.

CHAPTER 23

Then April, the first of six months left, a quarter of Truman's way to go, framed as farming. He could sow and tend, but for the kids, Fatimah and Zurina, and for the thin woman up in town, little time to reap.

On a hike he coaxed chubby Lim into wrestling Azman. She tackled him, laughing. The spinning boy freed himself and cried, slapping at his head. It was the second time Truman had seen him cry. Not proud of himself, he nearly did, too.

And there were love letters, back and forth as the kids lined up for their motorcycle rides. And in the cooler heat of the mornings, AhSoh still yelped and contorted upon the concrete floor to Truman's entrances. Then came a big Peace Corps to-do for the human services related volunteers, meeting personnel from the government's Ministry of Social Welfare.

It was a strange trip. Truman felt out of place at the a.m. session, amounting to a great deal of affected awe for the stuffy Malay officials, interrupted with smiling break-time conversations of one-upmanships between the volunteers themselves, many of whom Truman didn't know. He missed John Singer, and was happily stunned to find Tan's wife motioning to him from across a Kuala Lumpur street, a block from the building during a noon recess. She had decided to surprise him.

Over lunch she claimed, "I do disappointed that we can't have a sleepover, or not even a return to Kuala Harap together."

Truman, happy, yet fearful of being seen, skipped the second afternoon session in favor of a brief aloneness.

They slipped off to McDonald's, then strolled through Ampang Park before seizing a brief hour of intimacy at a cheap hotel. Lying upon the sheets afterwards, they talked of her pretty bones, and of his sad scar. Of the growing wave in his hair, she told him, "This needs cutting, to not look like hippie man."

"Hippie man? I wish I was. At least I'd be something."

"Do you mind private question?" she asked.

Truman smiled. "Go head."

"Why are you like a Muslim? I only know Malay word, *sunat*."

"Circumcised, you mean." Truman grinned, having first learned of it himself at The Children's Home, where some boys weren't. He was left ignorant until a health class at Allentown High School. He thought of his mild-mannered Phys. Ed. teacher, Doug Hunt. "Supposed to be hygienic," Truman said. "It's a cultural thing, I guess. I'm kind of used to it, if you know what I mean."

They talked of his time left, and of getting any meetings they could, aiming for one sleepover per month until he left at the end of September. Truman didn't write of this the next day, favoring recording a dear classmate of Ling's, another little girl years before who sprang into tears whenever Ling did. Truman pictured the two, skinny and little and timid amongst other uniformed little girls at the Sekolah Chinese she attended.

He also didn't write of witnessing a Chinese man being run over by a municipal bus shortly after he left Ling. The hot air at the intersection. The shouts. The swirling scene. Truman felt a fast sorrow for an imagined wife and children, waiting in vain for this man to return to their home.

He also didn't chronicle his cycle ride home, up through the highlands where he stopped to swim in a roadside stream that tumbled cool, where he fell asleep in an abandoned hawker's stall that for some Malaysian reason didn't seem out of place next to the mountain pool of nowhere.

Truman awakened to a spattering of rain upon the tar-papered roof. He thought "tent," but had never owned nor slept in one. Sitting up, surrounded with wet greenery, he listened, trying to figure out why it sounded so pretty, before rising and making his way through the wet growth for his cycle stashed beside the East-West Highway. The sky above was cool and gray.

That night, in his shed, he dreamed of the thick sleeves and backs of the canvas slickers that hung, waiting for rain, in Chet Van Heflin's milking parlor.

That same week they hiked and swam. Clothes were donated. Truman smiled at matching bright yellow shirts for Singh and

Ramasami, likening the two boys to lovable, dumb bumblebees. ". . . stingerless things," he wrote: "friendly—one dumber than the other."

Then Ling wrote, a long one: "I do disappointed we couldn't return together but do not feel sorry. It is our situation." Again she mentioned pictures, and Truman's appearance as "a handsome smart guy." Extending a previous conversation, she wrote of favorite memories, watching Truman shave, his underwater swimming in the straits of Malacca, their "first kisses we have." She closed: "Does your beloved aunt know anythings of us? Now I thinking too much of you!

"PS #1) Do you think we have still our language problems or is this problem is getting better?

"PS #2) I forgot favorite memory of all! I remember after that night together I have wrote Chinese sentences for you which means 'I love to spend overnights with you' so you may see how I write my letters to you at first in Chinese to make to English."

* * *

April 10, 1982

All's good—not counting a ripper of a nightmare I had which I knew I was going to have before falling asleep, because I couldn't keep my mind off weird things like ugly faces & flashing lights & shit. I felt like I was going nuts & that's what my dream was, too— I think.

Zurina & Fatimah have been pains, mocking the kids & teasing AhSoh & Kumari & Raj. (Raj is spoiled though, wanting everyone to pity him & he's got to get by that & I should help him do it.)

I've been thinking of New Egypt a lot, of going back & of what I'll do. I could work at the farm & probably will, but I've been sort of fantasizing about going to college—maybe for Sp. Ed. (On long cycle rides, I daydream about being a teacher—& about Ling, too.)

I caught Zurina one night (a few nights ago) in the classroom, all alone, trying to read one of the Darjah One books. She wasn't at all the witch that she can be. I asked her if she wanted help, but she hid the book in her lap. Fatimah (usually the nice one) was mean-while whacking Yap about something—I think she left the mandi *room shirtless, or some other Muslim crime against fucking every-thing.*

About my K.L. trip—meetings were boring, but I got a nice surprise visitor (I don't know how she got away with it). She made everything happy for me—as usual. She might be changing me, too, because at this meeting with the hotshots, I met a new volunteer (here 9 mos. or so), very plain & in her 30s, I guess. I thought she was prettier than the others.

* * *

As Truman's nightmares gave way to kinder dreams, Salleh on a walk again found himself pinned between terrors, this time in the cut of a ravine between the breathing stillness of a large lizard and the manic posturing of a lone monkey. Truman won-dered in his journal of the workings of his little mind, prior to his high-stepping, straight-armed escape. He wrote: "Routine is back."

On a group swim, Truman lost his keys out on the sandbar of the unusually low river. He returned an hour later in the same hired boat, beneath a darkening, churning sky. The pilot, a boy, expressed concern. Truman dismissed him, searched for and found his keys. Then he sat upon the exposed sand in the ensuing cool downpour, feeling a sudden sadness and awe for the beauty of his own Malaysia, the villages behind him, the sky above, and the rooftops of Kuala Harap before him poking above the riverbank trees.

Two mornings later, an editorial in the *New Straits Times* angered him, claiming America a land and people without cul-ture. Several pages beyond, four Malays were arrested for *khalwat,* or close proximity. The four seventeen- to twenty-one-year-olds had carelessly picnicked alone, or at least they thought they had. Then Ramasami hustled in from outside.

"Teruman! Orang putih datang! Orange putih!"

A white person. A world traveler, figured Truman. Some fucking hippie steered my way by a well-meaning cabbie, needing to discuss his ten cool days bumming around.

In minutes the man entered their sliding front cage. "Hello. *Ada cikgu Truman desini?*" the familiar voice called out.

Truman rose fast. It was good old Danny Iannuzo, tough little man from Illinois, once a student teacher in a suburb of Chicago.

Truman was suddenly proud of his excited kids hobbling about. Truman had seen Danny only twice since swearing-in a year and a half before. He'd lost weight. He looked good, and, of course, he was married to a Chinese girl. As they shook hands, Truman recalled the things said behind Danny's back throughout their training, long before.

"So what brings you by this neck of the woods?" asked Truman.

"Traveling up the east coast. Had to cut back by way of the East-West Highway, for Ipoh up north. I figured I'd drop in." He looked about. "Holy shit. This doesn't even look like the same place."

Truman was confused. Then he said, "Oh, yes," recalling Danny had been with them that first time Truman himself had seen the place with their vanload of reluctant teachers.

"I've been punching away at it. Let me show you around."

Danny followed, with his stuffed backpack over a shoulder, nodding and commenting all nice things. His admiration was sincere, and Truman took it so. In time, he hinted staying the night. Truman happily agreed, and settled the older teacher into his shed out back that he apologized for. "It's not much, but it's home. I like it."

Danny thought it lonely. "It's peaceful," he said, not mentioning his quiet respect for this kid who had lived this way for so long.

The girls were happy to have a guest, especially Zurina, who fell all over Danny with quays and tea. Danny was taken by a quick swim in the river with the kids. Digging his toes into the sand, and surrounded by splashing, retarded children, he assured

Truman that neither he, nor any teacher, was experiencing anything quite like this.

Sitting in the same sand, he explained his young wife as being on holiday with family in Trengganu, on the east coast.

That evening the two ventured to livelier Mentacab, to eat frog, fish, chicken and rice, in some curry Danny was familiar with and asked for. Truman enjoyed his company. His edge was gone, smoothed away by life in Malaysia. He boasted of nothing as the two began drinking with no worthwhile movie in town.

They talked of other volunteers, who lived with who, and of two others who had also married Malaysians, a man from Missouri and a woman from Delaware. Later in the night, four soldiers joined them. Being Malays, the soldiers couldn't lawfully drink, at least not in public. Their Chinese proprietor was discreet, offering a back room. Three of the soldiers were sergeants. The fourth, a major in civilian clothes, and speaking crisp English throughout their spirited drinking, reminded his American friends of his college degree. He used the word "fuck" clumsily and frequently as they drank, ". . . but never in the company of women," he proclaimed. By midnight, he wished to compare penises for the sake of racial curiosity, before slurring his regard for the University of Malaya.

* * *

Truman wrote in his journal of Danny's second day. It was unusually cool and breezy. Dark skies churned overhead. Earlier that morning, Danny even taught with Truman. Both had a nice time, especially with little Salleh, who recited the sounds of his alphabet in spite of his plateaued eight-word sight vocabulary. Kordi identified Danny as, "*Suda tua. Ada rambut uban,*" mistaking Danny's light hair as a mark of advanced age.

Walking through the little town above the Home, Danny talked whimsically of the odd weather, likening it to an autumn, wishing for a discreet flask of whiskey and an embattled thirty-yard line anywhere in America. Truman tried to listen, but thought other thoughts. He liked football, but they were passing Mr. Tan's hardware shop.

Across lunch, the two spoke of their six months left, one more certain than the other. Upon returning to the Home, Truman hid an arrived letter from Ling. She wished for "hugging and kissing, with hope soon." That night, Danny's last, became worthy of an entry itself.

The two started their evening down at the truck stop, deciding again upon Mentacab. Danny brought up the notion of a bar, to which Truman, wondering of Danny's wife on holiday, and of any gossip finding Ling, declined as too costly. But half a bottle of Johnnie Walker Black Label later, he changed his mind and led his guest up through the several streets to the Shamrock, wondering if #19 still worked there.

In no time, in the smoky darkness, Danny had #6 upon his lap. Appearing Malay, she claimed to be an Indonesian, from Borneo, a Christian, enabling her to drink alcohol and work in a place like this, boasting of being Catholic to boot. A stout little Chinese girl sat with Truman, claiming, incredibly, to be, "Jane, as with your actress, Miss Jane Fonda." She beamed in the candlelight. Truman, laughing, introduced himself as, "Henry, like her dad."

"So pleased to your acquaintance, Mr. Henry," Jane said. "Shall you treat me to a drink?" she added, slipping her thick arm through his, working a soft breast into his upper arm.

"Keep it cheap, Jane." Danny smiled for him.

Then a booming, "Hello, my American friend, so good to see you!" sounded out from a smiling Mr. Tan, emerging from the shadowy single flight of steps.

Clinging to the shopkeeper was a young Indian girl, very dark, and visibly drunk. Her buttoned blouse skipped a hole at her bosom, exposing a small triangle of herself to the flicker of their booth's lone candle. Shortly, a well-dressed Indian man joined them, an associate of Tan's. "Next round on me! Bottoms up!" he boomed.

Danny was cordial, introducing his date. A sad-looking Chinese woman sat down with the Indian businessman. "Much too skinny," Tan said, grabbing at her, jerking his drunken Indian girl into a brief swaying beside him.

All laughed, arm-in-arm, in pairs. In time, Danny's #6 and Jane gave up on the two Americans, favoring Mr. Tan, who gamely courted a threesome, whispering and laughing about prices with more sober Jane.

Low on money, Truman got a ready-to-go Danny out into the starry night, back onto his cycle, and back to Kuala Harap, to the truck stop where they began, never learning if the merchant's heroic endeavor ever materialized.

The next day, with Danny long gone, Truman entered the events into his journal, from Iannuzzo's surprising entrance, to his leaving by cab, the both of them hungover in the heat of early day. He wrote of Mr. Tan with the drunken girl, and of the money he wasted. "We should have stayed at the truck stop," he wrote, "where we started and finished." The very table at the Kuala Harap truck stop where he and John Singer once drank a night away with a domestically distraught Indian a year before. Truman recalled the man's concern for his family, and Singer's sleeping through the slow dawning of the new day, his whiskered throat exposed to the cool sky, an unfinished beer before him.

* * *

Truman answered Ling's latest letter, pitying her for her husband, wanting to correct things with his own devotion. The next night a gloomy storm rolled through, staying long into the evening. Truman told ghost stories to the kids. Fatimah and Zurina listened in. Everyone loved it. Visitors came another afternoon, Malaysian Boy Scouts from Mentacab. Yap and Ramasami fought over the distribution of candy.

A fast week snapped by, bordered with letters from Ling, the first returning the anguish of their affair, the second coordinating another night visit above the hardware shop. Tan was bound for Kuantan early the following week. Truman was to stop by the shop for his final nod on Tuesday.

On a hike, Ramasami stepped on a nail. There was swimming over the weekend, then schooling, and Tuesday with her nod, whispering, "10:00 p.m. Be careful."

Truman, wearing aftershave, felt like Christmas for some reason, and wrote so in his journal. The alley, wet from a fast rain, didn't smell as it usually did. Ling was at the back entrance, silent and patient. There was more TV, and drinks and sandwiches. "The American way. For you," she told him.

In time she led him into the dark hallway to a small room up front, and said, "Made special for our meet."

Diagonal light sliced through slatted shutters. Truman saw that the room was used for storage. There were more magazines, newspapers, boxes and sewing things, with a hustled-up bed nicely made in a corner.

She woke him just before 4:00 a.m., whispering the time. "Don't dress. Not yet," he whispered back, as he slipped into his nicest jeans and shirt. Then he lay her back down, beneath the reaching of the unchanged diagonal streaks of light, lightly touching her ribs, then her breathing rise of sternum. "I love you," he whispered.

"I am in love with you, too," her voice spoke.

* * *

Moments later he slipped out into the cool night, without a sound, making his way through the dark alley toward the bend in the road, for home.

In the dark quiet of his shed, an hour before the first call to prayer, Truman lay awake. A mosquito coil burned nearby. He was recalling another darkness in another time, old man Barlow Archer leaving him and his mother's half of their shared home deep in the Pines.

Up in town, his thin friend also lay awake in a darkness of her own, pierced with diagonal rays on the small bed she prepared. Nestled in crumpled sheets, her face was wet with sorrow.

* * *

April 27, 1982

This had to be the fastest month yet. Just 5 left—under 1/4 of the way to go. (I shouldn't make it sound like jail—it's not—besides, where am I being sprung to?)

Azman, suddenly giving a shit, wants the Boy Scout letter that I lost so I had to scrounge up their address. I got letters (on the same day again) from Ling & Angela. I wish Ling's was a little mushier. Angela's was all springy—about her super boyfriend & how badly she needs her upcoming spring break.

Also got a letter from Mabel (a few days later). Nice & newsy, talk of work, the Van Heflins, my trusty old Dart waiting for me & New Egypt's springtime (no word about her "new friend").

UMNO kicked ass in the national election here. That was an experience. The people are very secretive about how they vote. UMNO has these slick ads on billboards & on national TV about how they give huge shits about everyone who's not Malay.

School's been fun & so have our walks. Took the crew down to see "Fame." I moved Normah & Kamala (& big lug Kumari) off by themselves to better enjoy the movie, sparing them the fools surrounding me. I could hear them howling & carrying on like hyenas during the sexy dance parts. I learned later that night (from equally hysterical Zurina & Fatimah) that Kamala & Normah were watching me watching those same scenes—saying I was watching intently as the birdbrains around me carried on (Azman, Ramasami, Yap, Singh & the gang). They're little devils—like seeing Superguy a ways back!

Got a lot of reading done. (I've written to Mabel & Angela about this new—hobby?—& hoped I wasn't sounding like I thought I was a hotshot or something.) Anyway, I read "How Children Fail" by this John Holt guy (gift from Danny I.) & felt how I've been nasty to little Raj. I'll do the best I can. I also finished "Will" by G. Gordon Liddy (left over from John Singer's inheritance). The guy's a fucking nut! (Liddy—not Singer) But I understand all that Watergate stuff a little bit better than I did back in high school.

One night I dreamed of an electric chair here in Malaysia (mounted in a moving bus late at night). Nitwit Jimmy McCleary really did whatever it was he was accused of. It's funny, though, when relaxing or resting these days & I think back, it's not so much to Jimmy or the farm as it is to my younger days of Scotty Winslow, baseball, my old monkey bike & summertime in New Egypt.

Well, enough for now. I'm tired & I should read a bit. (Oh yes— I dreamed one night of finding books in a ditch. They were all wet & I felt panicky, even though they weren't mine or anything.)

* * *

Near April's end, officials from the Department of Social Welfare, from Kuantan and Kuala Lumpur, showed up with brief notice to tour the little Home by the river. To Truman's delight the surprise visit came to Encik Azman's seldom-seen anxiety. Azman the sane, raced about, kind to Truman, wanting something showy. Again, could the kids dance or sing? Could we cover the rotan furniture?

Truman was angered and happy. The children were clean and playful and learning at their own paces. Teasing his boss, he suggested spinning-Azman leap through a flaming hoop as Ramasami unicycled about, juggling. "While you and I befriend the big brass," he taunted in Malay, knowing Azman preferred English at a time like this, especially while being made sport of before his usual allies, Fatimah and Zurina.

The party of four came, spending all of a half an hour. Sensing disaster if Azman talked too much, Truman took over, introducing the children, one by one, their classroom and their sleeping and playing areas, inside and out. Sensitive to culture and rank, Truman falsified ideas and consent, ennobling his supervisor. He cited the use of the gracious community, which was true, the shops and the kindnesses of the surrounding villages on their hikes, toward the goal of normalization for these handicapped children. Well-dressed Azman beamed.

Piling into two cars, the big-guns left, promising to have the pitted driveway paved. Several days later Azman received his glowing report, and thanked Zurina and Fatimah up and down, pissing off Truman. Several days later their driveway was paved, to the hobbling, retarded delight of the watching youngsters. Truman noted in his journal: "Singh literally shit his pants as the dump truck snorted hard, raising its bed filled with hot asphalt. Salleh hid behind me. Ramasami bossed everyone around as Kumari lumbered off somewhere, shrieking (big left boob in hand, eluding Zurina, chasing her with a broom)."

Truman related these same events to Ling, in a long letter. He also wrote of receiving his Close of Service conference notification, from Kuala Lumpur, mailed to those remaining of his original training group. It'd be late in May, in the Genting Highlands, a bastion of fine vacationing in the mountains, tolerated by the Islamic government for its revenue. Included was an itinerary of sessions across three days, with bits of noteworthy events and volunteer activities throughout the country. One caught Truman's eye. Reckless, jobless, big Dave Hayden was involved in a motorcycle accident, and was expected to recover shortly. All were thankful it wasn't worse.

Tan's wife, sitting on boxes in the back room of her husband's shop, read of the asphalt driveway, the kids and of this conference thing in the mountains they'd crossed numerous times for one another. She folded her letter carefully, in the heat of the back room, and tucked it away. She patted at the sweat of her upper lip, then more at her forehead and neck, counting out the five months on the bony fingers of her right hand.

* * *

Schooling and venturing went on. There was painting to be done between tropical downpours, and repairs to the fencing and the much-played-with dolls. Zurina and Fatimah tussled again, quietly at first, then feverishly, about something Truman couldn't sense the bottom of. Zurina enlisted the sympathy of Kamala and Normah. Fatimah went silent. Truman sensed a long one.

Raj developed a toothache. Truman had it repaired, which meant extracted. They splashed in the river and schooled by morning as Truman, by night, drank alone down at the roadside tables of the truck stop. One afternoon he saw a horse, his first in Malaysia, a big fat white thing tied to a tree behind Mentacab's smaller theater. Another night a militant Malay, with two friends, joined Truman for supper, demanding a quarrel concerning Israel's occupied territories. The outspoken Malay was kind at first. Truman didn't care. The heavier of the angry man's friends wished instead to discuss the subtitled film, *American Gigolo*, showing in Mentacab, cut to ribbons. Truman confessed not knowing any beautiful American women, back in New Egypt anyway, needing to employ male prostitutes as dashing as Richard Gere.

Little of this appeared in Truman's journal, sparse for a few weeks as he and his thin friend worked like patient thieves, by mail, silently arranging an east coast getaway mid-month.

Their wishing was the island of Tioman, a south sea paradise. Three or four days would be lovely, but impossible. Kuantan had to be skirted. They wrote of Mersing, a quiet coastal town that launched for the islands, but available alibis restricted that distance.

A single night it'd have to be. Meet in Pekan, John Singer's old town, then ride together to somewhere, anywhere south on that beautiful coast.

Anywhere was Sungai Kecil, a coastal Malay village, where they stopped to eat. Truman asked the two teens waiting on them for a local hotel, or government rest house.

"Oh no. Our kumpang much too small," one replied, over his brother in rapid Malay, before going on, increasingly excited over their uncle's house on the beach.

An older woman was called out. The cook, Truman supposed. She was heavy, and impressed with Truman's fluent Malay. She grew as animated as the boys, sending one off on a rickety bicycle, into the lush green.

The kid returned, sweating with news of their uncle's house on the beach on the northern edge of their village.

"Can stay in this house as long as you wish. Very cheap!" His beaded face beamed.

With Ling's quiet nod, they were led to the house, a hundred yards from the surf, nestled beneath swaying palms. Only the neighbors' foraging chickens and roaming goats were about. Truman paid the boy who asked no questions.

Ling again wore her modest purple and white one-piece bathing suit. Truman again thought her pretty. He tried not to laugh as she apologized for covering herself in a white cream before going out into the sun. The heavy-duty sunblock transformed her into a bony, ghostly thing. Although loathing the idea of tanning, she more seriously couldn't risk explaining tan lines.

"How to say where these marks come from, you know?"

Truman felt bad for not thinking of it himself. "I'm sorry," he replied, reminded of the shopkeeper who had that access.

"It is not often," she said softly. "But I may not deny him. It is in darkness, but I cannot take chance."

Truman's journal reflected better times. The fluttering bats, the friendly Malays, and their quiet meals in the two kedais that made up less than the dozen shops of downtown of Sungai Kecil. Truman read his *New Straits Times* in the shade of the palms in the morning. They talked of the seasonally expected sea turtles, graceful giants of the surf, up from Australia or was it Indonesia?

They listened to the predawn clamor of the gibbons the next morning, along with the Islamic call to prayer, sung out from a crude P.A. system strung up somewhere in the surrounding trees. Their togetherness hit quiet spots. The thin woman assured him they did not mean uncertainty. She blamed her poor English, but shouldn't have. Truman loved the love, her hips and her sternum and that bridge in her nose, moistened in the cream that refused to come totally clean. Tan's wife loved holding hands, walking along the beach, into the evening.

* * *

In his journal, Truman wrote of their departure, farther north in Pekan, Ling to a bus, he to his stored motorcycle, for their separate homes in Kuala Harap. He stumbled in his writing, pausing, his thoughts upon her womanly mound rising up from her thinness. This warm preoccupation embarrassed him. He wasn't sure it was proper. If a real man would chronicle it.

His 75-watt bulb dangled above to the sounds of the crickets in his shed. He wrote of their talking about his four and a half months remaining. He wrote of his ride home, westbound across the East-West Highway, of how he grew happier, weaving nearer to Kuala Harap. Home. Four and a half months of it.

He wrote of killing his cycle up in town, coasting down and around the bend in the river road. He wrote of sneaking around the building, through the high grass about the fencing, then up to an unsuspecting window—Kordi's—for catcalls, then ghostly cries. Growing-tall Yap saw him first. She squealed and ran to the back door to hug him. No one was around so he hugged her back, firm with happiness. Then he let her go, culture was every-where.

His entry closed with Zurina and Fatimah's telling of how Singh, after quarreling with Ramasami, went to the river road and called out for his return. The two women, getting along now, held hands and laughed, telling the tale, imitating the weep-ing boy.

He reached up from his writing and snapped off the single bulb that lit his room. He undressed, Ling long washed from his skin. His journal lay closed upon his small table.

CHAPTER 24

The following day Truman and Tan's wife wrote fast letters to one another.

Truman penned his impulsively, during the swelter of lunch. The thin woman penciled her Mandarin draft while her husband was out, tucking it into the pocket of her pajama-like garb between patrons.

Truman wrote of their flutter of evening bats, and of their swimming. Ling's thanked Truman for their affection, then wandered into the marvels of America, ". . . your Grand Canyon, and that special mountain with your past leaders carved into." Both letters, mailed within the same post office, closed with wishes for another meet.

* * *

Later in May, Truman read in the *New Straits Times* of efforts to curb prostitution in Sumatra. Effective that month, married men caught soliciting prostitutes would be arrested and released only to their wives, or mothers-in-law. Ben read the same article. "Sweet Jesus!" Truman murmured to himself.

Another evening, down by the highway, Truman ran into two world travelers. He ate with them as invited, but declined further company after discovering they didn't drink. Then he bumped into a lean, dark Indian man of about thirty, who drank a good deal.

The man's name was Singam. He worked for Felda, a government agency regulating, among other work, the clearing of the rain forests, replacing them with little prefab Levittowns on stilts. Mr. Singam, prone to staring off, angered fast at little things, and needed the ear. Truman, his drinking partner, was a sympathetic judge in exchange for the company. This first night, they discussed Truman's work with the kids. Singam reminded his new friend that he had generated a bit of modest fame about

Kuala Harap and Mentacab as something of a Pied Piper of the youthful lame. Truman also learned of displeased territorial monkeys returning to their cleared ranges to attack hanging laundry and unwatched Malay toddlers, before knuckling hard back into the thick green trees. Truman thought of Mabel's *National Geographics*, then Marlin Perkins, then finally his own neglected clothesline. Before departing, soothed with alcohol, Singam and Truman talked of women, whispered of Malays, and wondered of the brewing international trouble in the Falklands.

One morning Fatimah became enraged with Truman over sarcasm taken seriously. Zurina was overjoyed. On an evening cycle ride to Mentacab, then south, over dirt roads yet traveled, Truman stopped several times on high ground, marveling unexpected beauty. So much forest, so few people. A column of smoke appeared motionless in the distance, a single pillar above the wave of deep green.

Truman's journal reflected a wonderful out-of-the-blue offer from the staff of a Mentacab clinic, wishing to host a beach trip for the Home. Truman liked the idea. So did Fatimah and Zurina. A bus was needed, and parental permission wherever attainable. A series of cycle trips would do it. One trip had Truman writing in his journal: "May 22nd—ADOPT RAMASAMI?!?—Jesus Christ!!"

Truman cut and retied the clothesline with hardware bought at Tan's. The big man was there, angry with three patrons over something. His thin wife waited on Truman without so much as a glance. That night Truman dreamed of her legs, the tops of them.

These same days Truman cuddled with little Raj after a particularly rough hike. The polio-stricken boy cried that Truman didn't love him like the others. Truman wrote: "I didn't think it showed." At the river, Normah pledged Truman to secrecy, telling him of the return of Zurina's night visitors. One man scared her, stopping to look at her as he crossed the open bay in the dark. Truman didn't know what to do.

Then Mabel wrote. It was springtime in New Egypt, and "so, so pretty." Her friend's name was Ken Herndon, a widower with two grown children. "My son's a grownup, too!" Mabel's handwriting quipped. "You'd like him, honey. He inseminates cows all over N.J. and Delaware and up in PA., too. I've told him all about you, and how proud I am!" She penned the letter on her kitchen table, to a fresh pot of coffee, thinking she wouldn't marry until after Truddy came home and got settled in.

The grass needed cutting, and Truman killed a huge snake out by the side of the building. It, too, sailed into the passing river. Two days later, before leaving for his Close Of Service conference, Truman received a troubling letter from Tan's wife.

She leapt into not acknowledging him in her shop the day before: ". . . so I think you might be mad on me for this. Anyway, I would to say sorry to you for that day and hope you wouldn't be mad on me any more when you have this letter."

Then news and more sorrow, and then hopelessness:

"I have think a lot our relationship. So I think that we should not have hugging and kisses too much, otherwise we will get more hurt when we depart coming September. When you are free. I hope we can still be meet each other again but maybe no more sleeping together, okay? In fact every time after a nice sleep together and when you leave me back to Kuala Harap, I feel hurt because I know I shall never have you. Please know I do have love you so much."

* * *

May 31, 1982

It's after supper & I'm writing from inside the Home. My Blondie tape is playing "Call Me! Call me!"—my favorite. Ramasami's arguing with Singh about a tennis ball throwing game they're playing. Yap & Lim are watching me & Kordi's somewhere hollering. Azman's sitting Indian-style (American-style) and rocking to Blondie. (I should turn it up!)

It's a hot fucker outside & sometime today I have to mail in my passport for its last renewal. I hoped for another letter from Ling since the C.O.S. conference but none was here. Her last letter was pretty confusing about "not so much" you know what. I wrote back, agreeing, but I hope it isn't so.

On my way to the C.O.S. weekend, the ride was cool going up into the mountains off the highway. It grew foggy, winding up the weaving road. Made me think of late spring around New Egypt— didn't seem like jungle—just cool & green. Anyway, the conference was kind of boring & kind of interesting. Andy's back in the country & was there & was one of my roommates (a good one, too—along with Ben). It was good seeing Danny so soon (everyone still thinks he's an asshole—not me). He roomed with Dave H.—who really is. (Word had it that Dave also had dope so I guess he was a popular asshole.) It was nice seeing all the others though. There're 12 of us left. 2 are staying—extending, they call it. Another one is staying but to work at a hospital in K.L.

As for the sessions, I liked the "Life Profiles" one best. It was the first time I really had to sit down & think about & then write about the stages of my life. It brought back Mom, nice old Barlow, & the first & last times I saw Mabel. Of course my scar & how I got it & then Dale Rowland & The Children's Home. (I even wrote about Molly, the art lady—who I loved—her & her big knockers.)

It's 10 minutes later—Ramasami cracked Singh with a piece of wood so I spanked him with it. (God, sometimes I'm more & more like Zurina.)

Anyway, back to C.O.S. Of course, I wanted to put down Ling but we had to share our "life sections" so I couldn't—but she's pretty important to me—more than my job or the kids, I hate to admit. She'll be the toughest part about leaving.

I felt real good though with everybody—not like my dopier time of 2 years ago. Played good softball, too & felt strong & handsome (too much listening to Ling?).

On my way home, I ran out of gas & was given some for free by this real nice Indian family along the road. The Brits kicked the shit out of the Argentines down in the Falklands. The people here are split on it. I guess they feel closer to Argentina (the lesser developed country) than to their old colonial masters. One guy (when it began) pointed out to me how much bigger Argentina was in size so they'd have to win—like nations were kids in a schoolyard—dumb fuck.

Little Raj is silent-treating me, but the others are glad I'm back. Dreamed last night of wild circus rides. Ling was on one & fell off, but I couldn't move. Then I was at the farm & no one was there— then this blonde lady danced around me, saying things from behind a painted face.

Oh yes, Salleh has a crew cut thanks to Zurina. Kind of cute but it pisses me off anyway—reminds me of when I came to this place— all rags & stink & shaved heads—girls, too.

Singam (my new buddy) swung by. I was glad to see him. He wants to get into one tonight. Fine with me. I liked our last outing. What a hoot drinking & talking with him. He once ran amok with a big stick through a Mentacab hotel—I once beat up a football player in a locker room—just drunk talk.

This morning on a hike down by the highway, we got 4 free watermelons from a truck that pulled over (curious over the white guy with a stringing of crippled kids). On the way home Singh pissed himself & Ramasami dropped one of the melons. Sweaty Lim tried to put it back together (probably wanted to hide the thing under her bed). (Also made me think of Humpty Dumpty!)

Before I went to the C.O.S., I drank with Kumari's dad (the barber) & met her mother for a 1st. She's real dark & looks sad & once pretty. Kumari favors her Dad.

* * *

Two days later, Truman's next letter came from up in town as a cool storm brewed. Truman took it out back in the gusty air, sitting upon the merry-go-round. The sky swirled above.

Dear Truman,
 I thought I want to wait for your next letter then write to you but then I think there's things of which I have to tell you.

*I have think it over after which you told me is
right. I do seldom tell you how I feels toward you.
So do you like to hear about it?*

*The time which we have is so nice and so happy
especially that night we have in that kumpang
house by sea. There was so wonderful, so nice and
the candle light maked you look so handsome. Oh I
hope we can just lying on the bed there forever but
unfortunately I can't have you in my life much
longer?*

*By the way, I would like to tell that my husband
due to go to Kuantan second week in June for two
to four days, so do you like to see me again? And I
think you'll be welcome to me to stay over night
with me. Maybe we can have more nice time
together? Anyhow can you reply me whether you
can stay here, okay?*

Hoping that we can hold each other nicely.
Love you, Ling

Truman read the letter three times. Chubby Lim sat beside him, curious, her thick tongue protruding from her happy face beneath the dark sky, flashing in the distance. Truman was happy, and stayed so across the next two weeks, anticipating promise.

He schooled the kids, swam with them in the river, and hiked with them to the old Chinese men's home on the other side of Kuala Harap. There were permission forms to be gathered for the beach trip. One afternoon he took off far, thirty miles to the east, to Raj's rubber plantation home. The crippled boy's father surprised him, very kind, small and weathered, seemingly frightened of an equally gentle Truman. Raj's home was small, two rooms. His thin father, once handsome, had a face so familiar that Truman warmed to him immediately. In light of his recent difficulties with the boy, Truman felt good running the errand. On his cycle ride home, it occurred to him that Raj's father resembled the possible adult version of a Puerto Rican boy who lived across the hall from him at The Children's Home back in Mount Holly, taking his thoughts to Molly, the art lady, and her kindness. Truman wished she could see him now, weaving beneath stretches of shaded jungle, on the other side of the world.

Late that week, Fatimah slapped around Yap for again leaving the bathing area nearly naked. Unusual for the quieter of the two. The next day, Zurina spat in AhSoh's face for spilling her breakfast. Not unusual, excepting it outdid the hot cocoa in the crippled girl's face of several weeks before. Pretty little Kamala caught up to Raj in his fourth-tier readers, pissing Raj off. Normah leapt to Darjah Eight across her subjects, as Truman's journal reflected the joy of Salleh, illiterate, yet so far from his days of being a naked, urinating, fearful thing a year and a half before.

Truman continued his cycle rides for the kids upon the pitted riverbank road. He met with Singam, daydreaming of Tan's wife and meeting her anywhere, as he and Singam drank and talked. A reoccurring visage had he and Ling swimming in the Pahang, kissing and holding to one another in the warm pull of the river.

The Kuantan beach trip was a howling success. At the main beach, their original destination, with their wheelchairs and mass hobbling upon the sand, they drew an uncomfortable crowd. Angered, Truman ordered all back to the bus, to drive north, seeking a coastal village where they could play in peace.

A journal entry chronicled Truman's likening Kumari's lying at the surf's edge to some sort of large, beached sea mammal. Wheelchairs rested hub-deep in the surf. Zurina and Fatimah played and laughed in the waves, fully clad in the dresses they wore day to day, the modesty of Islam making both women achingly prettier. The rhythmic waves bathed the children. Truman closed his entry with: "Singh (of course) had to shit himself. Kordi never left the water. I had to spank Ramasami before lunch & spinning-Azman never went in more than ankle deep & never sat down on the bus—not once for the 2 hours there & 2 back."

* * *

Truman received a tape from John Singer, recorded across three weeks. Singer had moved east, to Rochester, for a better job and something of a girlfriend. Truman wrote back, feigning surprise that Singer wasn't at a mosque in Hong Kong.

That afternoon came the nod from the thin woman as Truman shopped for paint and a roller.

Head down, counting change, she whispered, "Tonight. After 10:00 p.m."

Truman killed the time in Mentacab, seeing *The Champ* with Jon Voight. He'd write in his journal: "Sad, sad mother that one was." Then back through the night air, to sleepy Kuala Harap, to park down at the highway, to walk up into town, to slip into the damp alley, staying at its edges.

She made up the same room, leading him directly to it. In the familiar diagonal light, she whispered, "Tonight only. My husband due to arrive on tomorrow. It is sad. Do you think so, too?"

He did, tasting her breath.

In little time beneath their single sheet she was rising fast and hard. Truman felt bad for lasting for so little of it.

She clung to him. "It is okay. It makes me happy."

Slicing rays pierced the small room. Ling rose up into that light, naked and bony, moving for a tape player she arranged. "I wish to listen to my sentimental music songs."

Truman liked them as well, especially the *Superman* song, "Can You Read My Mind?" Toward the end, he whispered, "I wish I could save you, Ling."

"I wish that, too. I also wish we had pictures of our beach last month before. I would hide them, and save them. After all," she spoke to his chest, "it is only three and a half months left for us. Then you'll be gone to America, and I shall be sad and alone."

"Don't think of it now," Truman said.

"I am sorry. All I ever wanted was to love someone who loved me, too.

Then Ling fell asleep. Truman slipped out shortly before 4:00 a.m.

Back in his shed, within crickets and darkness, he relit a half-spent mosquito coil and climbed into his bed. For the first time since arriving in Kuala Harap, he wished he had more time left.

* * *

The following night, beneath his dangling bulb, with Singh and Kordi playing in his room, Truman wrote in his journal:

June 16, 1982

All's pretty good lately. Zurina's been mean to me for 2 days & I'm sort of worried about it because I have no idea why. My friend & I didn't get our 2nd night, which was sad. Another will come. (Kordi & Singh are in here now. It's bedtime for them. I'll take them up front when I'm done.)

I took a long (real long) cycle ride down south, way past Mengkarak (after having supper with Singam—turning down a good drunk—have to save my $ for my friend). Oh, I saw The Champ over in Mentacab. What a sad, sad mother that one was.

Anyway, I needed that cycle ride south. It was very pretty, taking my time cruising beneath the trees along the river & all. On a straight stretch, I saw a dark cloud waving over a field toward the road ahead of me & WHAM—I hit it broadside & blew right through it—BEES—fucking bees in a huge swarm. No stings though. Miracle!

* * *

As Truman wrote, a Chinese family in sleepy Kuala Harap, adjacent to Tan's hardware, tried not to listen to the crashing-about din through their common wall.

It was an uneven, heightening fury from sweating Tan, spattered with his wife's blood.

In their central room, Mr. Tan breathed hard, waving a letter before his wife who wept, lying crookedly across their rotan sofa. New blood seeped from her mouth.

Her husband hollered again, a stringing of Cantonese. His wife's writing, in Mandarin, pointed Chinese.

"Do I have business with him?" Tan hollered, slapping her face.

He stepped back, breathing hard, reading aloud from her letter: "I have thought a lot about whether I should tell you how I feel toward you, because I can't have you in my life."

Tan screamed, "Whore! Whore!" in his Cantonese, before reading: "Do you remember that night in my house and we held each other and talked until 1:00 a.m.? Oh, I have such a foolish love for you."

The big man spun hard. "In my own house, you dog! You childless dog!" He pulled her from the small sofa to the floor, to her hands and knees. He stepped back, then kicked her in the ribs.

* * *

In the quiet of his shed, Truman wrote on in his journal:

Anyway, I brought my binoculars for stopping here & there. At one stop I watched a village across the river (Oh no—Kordi & Singh are now pretending to read. Singh's looking at wildman Liddy's Will. *Kordi's mumbling to an upside-down* Newsweek.*) Back to the river— I watched some Malay girl bathe like they do—in her sarong, all soaking wet. She certainly couldn't see me, but she looked so pretty, all wet in their slow way of bathing. Made me think of Ling.*

* * *

Up in her home, Tan's wife convulsed on the floor, moaning, groping for anything to cling to.

Her husband circled, uncertain with his work.

He knelt, and read from her Mandarin words: "I know you will surely write a letter saying you can't make me happy due to our meets. Sometimes I think silence is beautiful too, isn't it? I have done swimming and I would learn bowling for hoping I can meet with you to enjoy these things together."

Her husband hissed, "You're an evil thing. An evil childless dog from hell." He spat a large, loose spit that strung across her hair and face. Then he bent to her, pulling her up to her slippered feet.

"Evil!" he screamed to her face that glistened bloody sweat. He ran her into the near wall, smearing the faded plaster with the blood of her broken nose.

Then he threw her to the floor again. "Read to me, whore. Read your words to your shameless dog lover."

Blood streamed from both nostrils, covering her mouth and chin, blotting her torn blouse. Through sobs, she quietly read, "I never have any family love and even don't know how family love looks like. I always hope that I can get a man who really loves me, take care and concern me."

Big Tan wrenched a leg free from their overturned end table. Ling turned, pleading in her husband's Cantonese.

"Shut up and read it to me," Tan demanded.

"Please. I can not."

He bent and grabbed her bloody head and pulled it back. "If I had acid, I'd throw it in your face." He hollered a meaningless cry, swinging the table leg across her face.

The fleshy smack jolted her head. Her bloodstained letter fell from her hands. She coughed hard, expelling a tooth, then another with a fresh heave of blood, then vomit.

"I beg of you. No more," she pled, instinctively in her childhood's Mandarin.

* * *

Down over the riverbank, Truman wrote on:

Farther on down the road, I thought I heard something in the jungle or somewhere so I stopped & took off my helmet & shut off my engine. It was a P.A. system asking in Malay for everyone to clear the area. I later (today) learned these were Army maneuvers.

I turned around & stopped at a village for a drink & was taken by some guys to this place called "Frog Rock." (The angle to the "Frog" had to be really, really right!) Then I asked around & got all sorts of wild guesses about how far south I was from Mengkarak (from 10 batus to 25). I bought another snack (from a one-eyed deformed guy—so much for getting away from the job).

Anyway, from there on back I got real sad thinking about leaving. It was weird how it crept up on me—all these thoughts of Ling & the kids, these forests & back again to Ling as I drove nice & slow.

* * *

Up in town, the big man strode off into their small kitchen.

His wife, shaking, reached for her unfinished letter, crumpling it against her bloodied blouse, trying to tuck it away where it should have been all along. Then glass broke in her kitchen. Still on the floor she tried again, and again missed her blouse.

The big man emerged with the neck of a broken Pepsi bottle in his grip.

He grabbed her by her hair and jerked her back over her haunches.

Tan knelt over her. "You ugly, childless dog," he whispered, tearing open her blouse.

He pulled at the center of her beige bra, cutting it with his broken bottleneck, exposing her heaving sternum and small breasts. He spat upon her bosom. "Let us see," he uttered in his Cantonese, "how your dog lover likes your new appearance," as he dug the broken bottleneck into the giving-way flesh of her left breast.

She arched away. She made an animal cry.

"Hell," he screamed, "you and your family belong in hell!" as he spat at her new stream of blood, turning his bottleneck clockwise, digging into her bosom, holding to a fistful of her hair.

Then he pulled its jaggedness away, throwing it behind him, striking a calendar, freeing it from the wall. His wife stayed on the floor. Her crumpled letter in her hand.

"Out," he told her between breaths. "I'll kill you if I ever see you again."

* * *

In his shed, beneath the single dangling of his light bulb, Truman wrote on:

Well, the kids have stopped their fake "reading" & are now scrap-ping over my tape player. Maybe they want a "sentimental" tape. I'll get them up front before Zurina comes nosing around.

Oh yes—one last thing—when I ate with Singam (my new friend) the other night, he asked about John Singer!! Then told me he heard John was really a C.I.A. agent & got transferred to Vietnam or China & that his name was really never John Singer but something else & that even I didn't know it!

Jesus Christ—so goes Malaysia.

An hour later, as Truman readied himself for reading and bed, the lone figure of the shopkeeper's wife shuffled slowly along the gravelly shoulder of the East-West Highway, moving unevenly through moonless, starry darkness.

Occasional cars and large trucks blew past her, the flash of her figure in their lights taken as a lone villager.

She carried no bag as her partially cleaned face swelled, as she clung to her bloodied left breast.

She wept off and on, moving west toward Mentacab, then Bentong, intending the spine of the mountains for the great city beyond.

Kuala Lumpur. The Oz of Malaysia.

CHAPTER 25

The next morning Zurina was better. It turned out Truman's calling her *jahat* several days before infuriated her. "Jesus," he wrote, "ill-tempered is far from the worst I could call her."

Then their Home got a new child, another girl, a nameless Indian about three years old, brought in by Azman and a new office girl. Truman couldn't see anything wrong with her. An orphan of sorts, gathered Azman. The girls, especially Normah and Kamala, got a kick out of dressing her up. Truman called her Little Jeannie, after the Elton John song that was popular his senior year in high school. With no apparent ties to Islam, the name stuck.

Then Truman wrote lovingly to Ling's post office box, his Close Of Service conference fresh in mind. Any meeting would do, even seeing her busying about her husband's shop. He almost floated the idea of exchanging letters after his return to America.

Schooling went well as the heat of the dry season settled in. Mail came, but only a *Newsweek*, a letter from Mabel, without mention of her friend, and another from Angela, a benevolent effort Truman wished she hadn't felt compelled to write. Fatimah returned to her village for two days that stretched into five. Zurina was uncharacteristically good about it. In the faraway Falklands, the Argentines, harshly disciplined, surrendered to the British.

Mostly though, Truman wondered why he hadn't been written to. He couldn't recall anything to account for this nothingness for over a week. So he wrote a second letter, lighter on emotion. Then he visited the shop, two days in a row, picking up any little thing. Big Tan, robust and jocular, attended him both times.

* * *

June 27, 1982

It's only been two days, but I've been down. Even a good swim hasn't done it for me. I got War & Remembrance *from Jackie at the*

C.O.S. It's a fat prick but goes fast. She said it's a sequel to one just as big. I'm learning about the big one (WWII) though. I hope Pug's ship does well. (His wife's been fucking some scientist on the homefront—but I can't bust on that.)

Anyway, about being bummed—it's got to be about not hearing from my friend. I think about her all the time, like some kind of nut or something. I wonder if I did anything wrong & if so—what?

Around here, Fatimah's back & everyone's happy. Zurina was nearly out of rope. What a bitch. She told Azman that I've been mean to the kids in school. (I've been short-tempered—but far from the spitting & throwing shit in their faces that she's done. I feel bad even writing this—like we're all dipshit Azman's older kids assigned to look after his younger ones—none of whom he cares about anyway.)

About the kids—they're all fine. Lately big Kumari's been lots of fun. She's changed a bit & wants to be a part of everything in her big old limping-buffalo way. I saw the movie Night Hawks *down by the highway. New York in the background made me think of going home in a few months (even though I've never been there—it's close enough though). (Stallone was better as Rocky.)*

The big news around here is the one new guy worker at the office (Malay, of course, & chubby & courteous as hell—I think Fatimah's got it for him, too) dropped off an old lady (35 or so) with her 2 kids. He said we're just a temporary place for her. Zurina doesn't like her & Fatimah's quiet about it. The lady's very quiet & says nothing to me. I fixed up two beds but she sleeps in one with both of her kids (boy 10 or 12—girl 3 or so). I think Zurina's problem is her night visitors will have to duck the lady—or maybe Zurina will have some competition!

* * *

It'd take another week for Truman to discover that Azman knew nothing of the woman with her two children. Angry and embarrassed, Azman grilled Truman at a kedai where they bumped into one another, after Truman's mentioning the woman's son wishing to hop in on the A.M. schooling.

"I'm happy to include him," Truman reported. "He's a good little boy."

"What boy, Mr. Truman?" Azman asked, tilting his head.

"That new woman's kid. The lady Khairol brought down to us a week ago. He told us she was nothing special, telling the girls, *'Tak makan bunyak.'*"

"He told them to not feed who much?"

"Her and her kids, I guess," Truman answered, as he sniffed Azman's sniffing a rat.

"I shall see to the matter at once." Azman straightened.

And get to it he did. Stout Khairol's head didn't roll, but he must have gotten it good for Fatimah literally hissed at Truman for letting it out. Zurina applauded his diligence. Naturally, this ignited another range war between the two. Truman concluded in his journal: "Jesus Christ, you never know what the fuck is going on around here."

Apparently the whole thing was concocted by new man Khairol, for reasons Truman would never learn. The woman, deemed unstable, probably a relative, bathed her little girl five or six times a day, outrageous even by tropical Malay standards. If the child cried for any reason, it was off to the mandi. Her son, on the other hand, warmed Truman, being almost noble as a lone, wished-for sane one in his little family. But Zurina thought him evil for not fasting during the Ramadan month that began during their brief stay. But Truman liked him. He played hard in the river, fetched tools, smiled wide, and took to moving occupied wheelchairs like a child in dire need of being useful in exchange for the shelter and the food he knew his mother couldn't provide.

The following week Truman drank too much with new friend Singam. He also approached Azman with the idea of their little Home also serving as a temporary shelter of sorts. From his years of loose attachment to New Jersey's Division Of Youth and Family Services, Truman periodically received requisite literature concerning such places meant for children not blessed with an Aunt Mabel of their own. Arriving soon after the second Dale Rowland incident, Truman supposed the mailings reminded him that his aunt could run him off at her leisure. In time, Mabel intercepted his mail, sparing herself her little boy's quiet spells.

Azman listened, then claimed he'd get back to him.

* * *

June turned into July, with no word from, nor sight of the shopkeeper's wife. Truman worried in his journal and on his hikes.

He led his hobbling children to the old Chinamen's shelter, and to the river and beyond. One evening, while watching horseplay in the fort beneath the Go Dog Go tree, Truman told Fatimah, "Just watch. Someone's going to fall."

Luckily it was Ramasami. His upper lip swelled tremendously. Kamala likened him to a duck, and by the next morning everyone was calling him *itik*. By that afternoon, Ramasami took to carrying a stick amongst the snickering. Zurina, Azman and Azman's dutiful office girl thought he fractured a bone in his upper jaw, requiring medical attention. Zurina favored her kumpang's bomoh, who didn't work until sundown. Truman offered a good old-fashioned fat lip, writing: ". . . maybe these guys never saw one. The Malays are like that. They're gentle, in at least that way. Still learning, I guess."

Across the days, Truman followed Pol Pot's visit to Kuala Lumpur, representing his Khem Rouge, butchers one in all. His *Newsweek* told him so. In the same issue, diligent censors took the time to blacken out the buttocks of two naked swimmers photographed for an article concerning liberal beaches in Italy.

Into July Truman watched his mail, as political scandal ripped through Kuala Lumpur. A certain Datuk Mohtar, Minister of Youth and Sports, was arrested for murder. Truman, following their politics, noted in his journal: "The man's rival, Dr. Mahatir, is probably shitting raw power about now." John Singer would have been proud. Singam, who ate with Truman twice that week, didn't care. On their second outing, Truman nearly shared his recent venturing into Mr. Tan's hardware shop, once to nose around, a day later to purchase nylon rope to change the girls' clothesline.

Chubby Lim helped. Truman worked slowly, knowing the line would last well into the next rainy season. Long after he'd be gone.

Then local Rotarians swung by with gifts and heartfelt comments for his obvious dedication. Several mentioned they figured the place to be abandoned, until a year and a half ago. One claimed to be a resident of Kuala Harap. The urge to ask of "her" rose hard in Truman. Of course he couldn't.

In the evenings he took his suppers down along the highway, followed with peaceful cycle rides. He read on in *War and Remembrance*, enjoying subsections supposedly written by some fictitious Nazi commander illustrating the German point of view. Another night, when suddenly sad, he wrote a third letter to Box #123, trying to be big about whatever it was that was happening.

Then he drank again with Singam. It was mid-July. Truman wished to meet his wife and kids.

"I promise this to you, sometime to come," Singam said.

"I'd like that. I really would," Truman answered.

"I prefer my evenings out with my American friend. You can understand this?" asked Singam.

Then a handful of the Rotarians returned unexpectedly, bringing clothes and a used television. Then a reporter from *Asiaweek*, tipped by someone who saw one of Truman's lurching-along trailing of youngsters down along the East-West Highway. The reporter was on his way to Kuantan to cover the much ballyhooed arrival of the great turtles.

But no story materialized. Truman's journal instead reflected Ramasami's biting Lim's big toe over her blocking his view of their new television. The gang was watching a subtitled episode of *Laverne & Shirley* in the midst of the grueling month of fasting, making Fatimah so sad, and Zurina much faster to anger, as each day was another of still no word from her.

After sundown, when the women could eat and drink, Truman revisited their shrieking game of Wild Dog. He also noted Yap's recent thickening into puberty. On a hike she also, uncharacteristically, defecated in her underwear, beneath her tattered blue dress. Singh, a great shitter himself, had harsh words for her. Yap cried the whole way home. Zurina was unusually kind about it. Ramadan's close was only days away. Truman's spirits, too, picked up from the festive mood that swept the land. Hari Raya. The Christmas of Islam. The clearest of windows into the Malay soul.

Much more than the year before, Truman thought deeply of this. He asked Fatimah and Zurina of this day of theirs. They happily obliged, telling him, one early evening, of their mutual devotion to Allah—their blessed, one and only Almighty God.

The kids were about them that cooling evening of togetherness. A scattering of the neighbor's hens pecked at the lawn. In the distance, two small boats slowly crossed the river. Above them, tall columns of clouds, thick and white, reached so far up into the sky that the blue above them seemed forever far off.

* * *

Eight days, and another resident of the Home later, Truman wrote:

July 22, 1982
It's the 1st day of what's supposed to be Hari Raya, but no moon last night so it's delayed a day. The Home's strangely quiet w/o the kids. Left here is Kumari, her mother, AhSoh, Little Jeannie & the new girl. (All others we got home—Zurina & Fatimah are home, too, so Kumari's pretty mother's here. Azman's plan & a nice one, too, for Zurina & Fatimah.)
This new girl is maybe part of the idea I gave Azman. She's younger than me—maybe 16-18 & very dirty & pregnant & crazy as anything & probably more unfortunate things. She's here ONLY until the cops can figure out where she came from. Anyway, she has no name (or gives none) and has bugs galore in her mop of black

hair. She mumbles nonsense & smiles & laughs at nothing & once in a while rubs up against me & even the kids. Zurina says the spirits got to her. Fatimah's not sure. I don't know, but she doesn't seem retarded & something's surely wrong with her.

I've also thought a lot about Ling. Too much. I really miss her & I feel real shitty about it—I guess I'm getting dumped.

Boy, I must have been here a long time. The final week up to Hari Raya felt so nice (while last Christmas came & went w/o being special). I, too, got caught up in all the lights & the candles out in the villages. (All the visiting will be nice, too.) Singam wants to get together (not for Hari Raya), & that'll be fun. He's like a kid, like me, except all grown up & married (hard to explain).

I also started a "talking board" for AhSoh. Got the idea from some stuff Danny sent me. I'm using pictures from my Newsweeks & gluing them on a piece of thin, sanded plywood. There'll be 36 altogether for her to point to when she wants to say something (pictures of food, water, anger, a toilet, etc.). She's all excited because she knows it's for her. (Maybe Zurina will hate her a little less if we have some idea what the fuck she wants when she gets all contorted & loud. Hope she doesn't get whacked with it after I'm gone.)

With just a few of the kids here, we still took our walk. Kumari's mother even came along. It was real nice returning in a cool drizzle for a change. (Kumari's mom got all wet and pretty—what a shit I am.) It also reminded me of home—a long soft rain—no sudden downpour as usual (back home—oh, what to do?).

The kids' leaving was sad & happy (as it was last year but more so now with just 2 1/2 mos. left). Little Salleh was sadly the last to go—wandering around with just a shirt balled up in a plastic bag with him trying like hell to get on every Land Rover load. Yap had tears of joy climbing into her father's truck. Fat little Lim howled toothlessly. Ramasami was serious as shit in the same load. He did look nice though, in a clean shirt & trousers & shoes (& different colored socks).

* * *

July edged to its festive end, lonesome for Truman, spiritual for the nation.

The kids and Zurina and Fatimah came back from their surrounding villages as they had left, one by one, and in small Land Rover loads. Considering past returns, Yap took hers well. A quick illness then swept their numbers, laying the kids low with diarrhea for a day or two. Truman wrote of it in his journal, and of his own quick temper. "Geez," he wrote, "I don't know what it is. It's got to be my own end looming closer, and they can't even see it!!"

He tried to call Mabel, but no one was home. Needing varnish for AhSoh's talking board, he hit Tan's shop and was surprised to be tended to by a woman he'd never seen. She was nice and very happy to be introduced to the big man's American friend.

"My merchandise have built everything at his little river home," Tan boomed. "This one always comes to my shop. Isn't that right, my friend?"

"Oh yes," Truman replied. "What would I do without you?"

That same week, Truman flared at little Kamala and Raj in their reading. He paddled Ramasami and Salleh, probably too hard, for repeatedly stealing sobbing AhSoh's talking board. It turned out Zurina was behind it for sport. "Islam's a fucking disease," he wrote in his journal, before crossing it out, then adding, "Sorry—but Zurina IS a fucking pig. Wish the crazy girl would whip her ass (she's still in orbit around here)."

* * *

On a better note, Truman was invited to Kumari's village home by her barber father. Truman wrote of getting drunk with the big man, but not of his cycle aching with the barber's 300-pound carriage over the trail that meandered between rice paddies and stretches of tall trees. Nor did he chronicle Kumari's silent mother, glistening in sweat to the flickering of their battery-powered fluorescent light that weirdly lit their shed-like home as she served, then cleaned up after the two. He thought of her walking through that drizzling rain two weeks before.

Ben wrote, entangled in a sticky thing with another volunteer, a girl from another training group, possibly pregnant. They intended to travel to Singapore to see to the matter.

Then the police showed up midweek for the crazy girl, having found family of sorts. Truman was invited to ride along in their marked Land Rover, evidently liked by one of the three officers.

Their ride south took them far below Mengkarak, into the forests beyond Truman's farthest cruise. The ragged, pregnant crazy girl bounced and swayed with the ride, grinning to the hot wind. It wasn't even a kumpang they finally came to, far off the main road, just a sparse scattering of half-deserted homes deep in the lush green of the jungle. With no sign of economy of any sort, Truman wondered why these suspicious-looking Malays were even here.

The three policemen questioned a reluctant, shirtless man.

They learned that the girl had three children and that her elderly husband was gone. Up north, Trengganu, the shirtless man heard. No one knew anything of her own family. Her husband's family, still about beneath the canopy of these trees, wanted nothing to do with her. "That was their house," the shirtless man said, pointing toward a half-fallen hut overgrown with the jungle floor that took only weeks to cover anything.

The older officer thanked the man, then motioned the crazy girl toward her abandoned home. "*Jalan, jalan,*" he ordered.

So off she walked, angling toward the half-fallen structure, then away from it, smiling to herself, dirty and ridden with her lice, and swollen with child.

"That's it?" Truman asked the younger officer who liked him.

"Nothing more," his uniformed acquaintance answered in his soft Malay. "She's crazy. Nothing we can do."

Leaving this place deep in the forest, Truman jostled about in the back of the crawling-along Land Rover thinking of the vastness of this jungle with so few people. He wondered if the girl would fall to safe hands, for she'd surely die if left alone. For several days he saw her in thought, crazy, laughing, flickering away into the growth.

* * *

Two days later, in Kuala Harap's post office, Truman quickly peeked into the little glass window of Box #123. All three letters were there, leaning against one another like forgotten friends.

The next night, while drinking with Singam, he could stand no more.

"Singam," he asked, "do you know the merchant, Mr. Tan?"

"Yes. I am not fond of him. Why do you ask?" Singam answered tightly.

They had been at their table a while. Condensate pooled about their bottles and glasses.

"I don't know," answered Truman, pouring another beer. "I buy most of my supplies there, and I've bumped into him, you know, here and there."

Singam, smoking, leaned forward. "He has a big mouth. And I do not like that."

"I don't know about him," Truman answered, "but his wife, that quiet woman who's always in his shop, she seems very kind."

Singam motioned with a quick hand, pulling them together over their table. "This is between you and I, yes?"

"Of course. You're my only friend in town." Truman smiled.

Singam smiled back fast. "Thank you. And you are mine." Sweat beaded his dark forehead. "She is gone. This is a small town. He ran her off." He pulled hard on his cigarette, then exhaled. "For having taken on a lover." He smiled again. "Hard to believe, isn't it? She was so, so homely, as you may say."

Truman tried to right himself in the night air of the little kedai. He swallowed hard, noticing the pooling condensate between them, then the slow turning of the ceiling fan above. He drank long, composing himself.

"You never know, I guess," he answered his lone friend.

CHAPTER 26

Truman then lived his days in despair for his friend, plagued with the pain of possible discovery.

By nights, his pre-sleep ghosts surfaced, a happy-sad parade dancing about the image of cast-off Ling. The crazy girl of that distant forest. His own mother, silent in her wheelchair, pushed by a watching-about Barlow Archer. Art lady Molly was saddened, disappointed. Both Dale Rowlands, the bully, and the afflicted, slunk about the edges, joining the dance about the run-off woman.

Work became therapy, A.M. schooling, packing everything in, to lunch fast to get the kids out, hiking, swimming, to the aged Chinamen's home. Anything to keep his demons at bay, for a new one hopped in, appearing as ugly Kumari's sad mother, cast sweating in the humming glow of a lone fluorescent lamp.

Molding new evil, he imagined Kumari's mother's nakedness wanting to comfort him as her drunken husband slept, a poorly planked room away. He fought it off with more cycle rides, out into the cooler villages. One trip pleased him, to Zurina's when he knew she was there. The older woman was surprised and excited. She and her younger sister filled his rice with greasy fried eggs and pieces of chicken. Their aged father, crippled and confined to the front room, begged for medicine from the young American. Truman, in a staying pain himself, apologized for having none.

There was a story in the *New Straits Times* concerning the Islamic pitfalls of being adopted. Thinking of Mabel's love for him, Truman tried to pick on it in his journal, but couldn't. After discussing it with Fatimah, and a freshly returned Zurina, he saw only more of their Islam, overbearing, beautiful, a comprehensive recipe for all of their living. He could hardly argue.

Twice he drank heavily, and shouldn't have. A day after the second, he road south along the river and hated himself for bringing his binoculars, hoping for the distant bathing girl.

He turned back to the kids, their loving natures luring him in from despair. Kamala, and especially Raj, grew dearer in their

A.M. scholastic toils. Memories of little Salleh's single-packed shirt battled off his ghosts, as did Kordi's imagined ones. Singh dependably soiled himself on a walk to the cooling river, blaming his own shit on Azman, faithful head-slapping spinner, following their trailing gang in his own loose orbit.

In early August, Truman furtively checked Box #123 a third time. All three letters remained, entombed tracks of his thievery.

* * *

August 8, 1982

Zurina's been an angel since I visited her home. Maybe she was the kumpang hotshot for a day, with the white guy & all. (For a change I was proud of myself for not having dirty thoughts about her sister's cleavage bending all over the place.) (I've been something lately—I hope I'm getting better.)

There's been a big deal in the 10:00 p.m. news & the New Straits Times *about the Israelis defacing the Muslims' 2nd most holy site & of more need to help the Palestinians. (Christ, the other Arabs have all that oil $ & land—let those fuckers give something up.) Anyway, there was no mention of a Muslim shooting the Pope or that it was probably a Jew (or Jews) just as loony who damaged that place they're flipping over.*

The other night I caught Fatimah with her teeth out (almost scary). I didn't even know she had fake ones & then I began teasing her, starting all my Malay words that began with "s" with the "th" sound. She took it rolling with laughter & that surprised me—we all howled. I could learn something from her.

Well, I finished AhSoh's talking board & she loves it. I then built the "Fabulous Flying Machine" in just 2 days. (I've been on fire for a bit, trying not to go nuts.) It's actually a go-cart with wings & a tail. The kids love it, but maybe a bad idea. (The wing tips clip the shit out of nearby ankles & Lord knows very few around here pay much attention to anything.)

Took a real nice hike yesterday (Normah's chair needed welding)—8 of us went & we stopped for sodas as usual. Zurina & Fatimah have been very nice lately—to me & the kids. I wonder if they can tell that I've been sad lately—with 1 month & 3 weeks left, & having done what I did.

I got loaded the other night with Singam. (I listened & waited, but didn't venture near it.) (My letters are still there—good news for me—I don't know what it means for her.) I try not to think about it too much—dreamed of her again. We were down by the theater & went in to see Raiders of the Lost Ark, *but quarreled. We left & suddenly she was far off down the road & I couldn't move to catch her. Then fucking Jimmy McCleary showed up in my Dart that turned into a tractor, saying that he got a job here, too. So much for that.*

My favorite old jeans finally died. I brought them here (2 years ago) with my new ones (bless Mabel). I was going to cut them up for patches, but I pitched them in the river for the fuck of it. (I remember when they were brand new & I wanted Angela to see me wearing them around the farm & all—what a nitwit I must have been.)

Anyway, I had a nice time with Singam, as I started to say. We arm-wrestled (let him win—kedai boys watching) & I harassed a world traveler. Singam couldn't believe that I'd pick on another white guy. He was some hip, cool know-it-all, so I became a laughing "steer-fucking Texan who lost his way!" & so on. It was a riot. Then some Chinese guys traveling to Kuantan joined us & it was fun all around (for me anyway—Singam should loosen up—he's a pretty suspicious guy).

I've been working as hard as I can at school, & I guess I should go ahead & write this down. I took a fast (sort of desperate) ride to K.L. Sunday, just to ride around to our old spots. I just had to look.

* * *

As Truman wondered where Ling could have gone, his fear of her husband hardened into New Egypt resolve, a short crowbar hidden in his shed, a length of chain tucked away in his desk.

Two days later his cycle broke down a mile south of the East-West Highway. Walking it home, he thought of her smiling while window-shopping in Kuala Lumpur, then splashing in the waves upon the beaches of Port Kelang. That night, lying in bed, waiting for sleep, she reclined with him, reaching for him with her bony arms, wearing only her modest Asian underwear.

Several nights in a row he drank too much, one night with Singam, the next two alone. The last took him to Mentacab, for a movie that he walked out on, to venture up to the sparkling lights of The Shamrock. Amongst the darkened candle-lit booths, he waited for an older Chinese woman, who turned out much thicker than his lost friend.

Upstairs, amid the plywood and the talcum, he said little. She called herself "Tina." In his journal he called himself "a drunken fool wasting \$ & pretending crazy shit," not chronicling her heavy flesh beneath his own of sweat and brandy as they coupled in the powdery candlelight. He wrote of being unable to recall leaving Mentacab, just windy stretches of the ride home. He remembered, but didn't write of the woman's hairline scar across her forehead, at his own chin as he worked above her. He never saw those of the stretch marks splayed about her spongy lower abdomen. Scars of the heart. Efforts of an earlier lifetime.

In the second week of August, Truman sobered, finishing *War and Rememberance*. Not even Pug, commander of battleships, could keep his woman. He started Dicken's *David Copperfield*, thinking a classic might help. He also received notice of his waiting readjustment money. Another reason to travel to Kuala Lumpur.

At the Peace Corps' headquarters, he ran into a girl from another group he'd met a year before at a party, then married Danny Iannuzzo, extending his tour another year, feeling as though he had to explain it to young Truman, who listened courteously over a late lunch, itching to get to his hunt.

Alone at last, Truman drove slowly about the city, several times about the shops of Ampang Park. He circled out to Zoo Negara, and twice by the new, much touted McDonald's. He swung by both of the city's busy corners of theaters on opposite ends of town. Dark heads bobbed everywhere, the taller ones of women gaining his attention.

Then he happened upon their first hotel. He stopped out front. A woman occupied the open-air desk. He recalled *Grease*, the shiny engine descending from the block and tackle, pretty Frenchy with her screwed-up hair, their ratty little room, then Ling as a stranger, rushing, clumsy and silent, a year and two months before.

He worked his way to the edge of the city for the mouth of the East-West Highway. Loaded with cash, he pulled over. He looked behind him. The sun setting over the city. His eyes blurred, thinking of the blemishes she needlessly apologized for.

* * *

That same morning, across jungled mountains, Ramasami, with Singh in tow and Kordi in orbit, marched the flying machine to the top of the curved hill.

Ramasami's shouts of joy silenced once his speed picked up. His hands on the sled-like pull ropes froze as the winged go-cart sailed off the curve of the hard-turning road, descending into a three-quarter barrel roll, like a Libyan MIG hitting the Med, Truman supposed that evening, dragging it back to the Home with its broken wing and cracked fuselage, with no black box revealing the truth.

Passing Malay teens found Ramasami. Singh was crying nearby. Kordi wasn't far off, with a keen interest in chickens scratching at roadside weeds. By the time Truman returned, Ramasami had already been to the bomah under Zurina's directives. He sported a crude splint, lathered with leaves and a heavy grease of some sort.

Truman remained quiet, figuring to fight the fight later. And what a fight it'd be. Zurina pledged never speaking to him again if he took the boy to the clinic east of Mentacab. Even Fatimah hopped in. "*Tak boleh campur ubat!*" as the bomoh advised, protecting his handiwork. But off Truman and Ramasami went, with Ramasami riding between Truman's legs, half on the motorcycle seat, half on Truman's pillowed gas tank.

The little hospital was dirty and busy. Tailless cats wandered outside open windows. The x-rays were conclusive, dual hairline fractures midway up the ulna requiring a stripping of the bomoh's work to fashion a cast locking the elbow. Truman recorded Ramasami crying as the Chinese doctor worked fast. He didn't write of holding Ramasami, comforting him, nor of recalling another little boy once wondering of rooms designated for the dying struggles of rabid humans.

Home with a casted Ramasami and a silent Zurina, Truman tried to not live by the routine of the mail. He drank some with Singam, but stayed in, too, playing with the kids, and reading thoughtful stretches of *David Copperfield*, loving another boy from another time. "Good old Peggoty," he wrote. That night he dreamed of loose dogs chasing deer behind the Van Heflins' central barn, catching one to tear it apart. Kathleen Van Heflin wept nearby. The following weekend he ventured again to Kuala Lumpur, cruising the bustling streets of the tropical capital.

Then he rooted for young Copperfield's loving Dora and her dumb dog Jip, as Traddles was a better friend to Copperfield than Jimmy to himself. And, of course, the kids. He sank himself into their play and need of his attention, more planks of his creeping despair. He didn't know how he was going to leave them, a concern that first surfaced back in March, then stronger in April, happier days of his other, clandestine affection, with an endless half year remaining.

* * *

Aug. 17, 1982

Pretty slow week for how fast time's been going. Thurs. night was clear & starry & we lay out back & watched for falling stars again— me 6—Raj 3—Fatimah 4—Zurina bitching & mumbling some horseshit inside—Kamala and Normah maybe 5 (if not lying)— Salleh, Kordi & Lim a big goofy 0.

Went to lunch on Thursday & returned to find Singh whacking AhSoh on the head with one of the strings of counter beads I made.

I tossed him out along with the counter beads I made. I'm so sick of everyone hitting each other lately—it turned out Zurina was in on it. Jesus Christ, there's no talking to her. An hour later she threw water in Yap's face over something.

Got my cycle ignition fixed again & still no word from anywhere & I checked the P.O. Box two more times—no change—all 3 still there. I've been real sad about it. It goes away once in a while, but never for long.

On a hike this week Singh & Azman made me laugh over sudden barking dogs that leapt out from an alley at the edge of town over by the aged Chinamen's home. It was like the old days of me first getting them out & herding them around. (We've come far—they're more like normal kids now—dressed so much nicer & staying together & playing as we go.) Anyway, it was funny as hell.

Oh yes, brief letter from John Singer. (Jesus, I've got to write him.) Advised me to lay off the booze. (He knows the feeling at the end, I guess—boy o boy, if he knew MY ENDING. I won't tell him, though.) He also claims he's finally settled in. It's been nearly a year. That girl became a steady one.

Thurs. & Fri. work went good. I fixed the one toy shelf & tightened the laundry cart screws & lines for Zurina, who's finally cooling off over Ramasami's cast which I painted & put all the kids names on it. (He knows them by location at least.) Good old Singam stopped by & we had a few but I didn't go for the ripper—instead read David Copperfield. Steerforth fucked up as bad as I did.

Lastly, something's cooking with Azman (the employed one). He was kicking around here last Sat. talking to the girls & then Normah & Kamala started crying (Normah like she was dying). Then he told me in his pansy-nice English "Not to worry, Mr. Truman, not to worry." Like a big brain, like his was on the fucking job. Here I was working all day on a Saturday (a fucking nightmare for a Malay!).

I'll try to cheer up. So long.

* * *

Aside from brief comments and notes, three weeks worked by before Truman wrote in his journal again.

These were days of working and wondering, keeping a fix on the calendar. Weeks mattered, not months, as he had accustomed himself. Truman marveled over once thinking in terms of years, always one and some fraction, then one, then most of one. The days of John Singer seemed a brief boyhood.

The mentally able of the children, all three, grew sad, with Fatimah and Zurina, to Truman's final weeks of service. The retarded were medicinal, a safe means for discussing the impending separation in terms of their own unawareness of it.

There was a dental appointment for Truman, arranged and insisted upon by Kuala Lumpur. Truman had one cavity. Twice he circled the city's dirty outskirts that late afternoon, aching new pains.

Days later he drank too much with Singam, over in Mentacab, and witnessed a frightening fight with broken bottles between two middle-aged Chinese men. He never wrote of it. Instead, he noted Azman's recent musings, germinated from the Kuantan office regarding converting their little riverside Home into a library. Poor Normah. Distant, dirty institutions for one and all of her doomed little family. Truman's repairs, green lawns and thorough painting might have done them in. That evening Truman motorcycled fast, south along the winding river road, beneath the canopy of tall trees, beholding the tropical beauty of Malaysia, cursing the visions of distant others.

A visit was planned, possibly establishing a board of visitors to govern the premises in conjunction with the Department of Social Welfare, hopefully to determine a just fate for the renovated property, as Zurina and Fatimah fought over something unrelated. One called the other bodoh. Truman noted: "Sometimes both of them are equally stupid." He road to Mentacab the next night, then south. "Beautiful," he wrote. "A crescent moon, and so many stars above the distant fires of clearing land."

At a Sunday market in Mentacab he bought a jacket he fancied himself handsome in, for October back in New Egypt, when the turning leaves would blow and fall as the chilling nights ate into the shortening days, all to the distant guns of Fort Dix. That afternoon he went and saw the movie *Airborne Disaster*, realizing he'd already seen it, titled *Black Sunday*, renamed to lure the Asian audience that lined up and howled at wreckage in general. He recalled the mall chase sequence in *The Blues Brothers*, the Kuala Harap crowd wild on its feet.

Then Mabel wrote, a touch insincere, regarding his homecoming. "Oh, everyone can't wait . . ." and "We're all so anxious to have you home . . ." Chet Van Heflin, of course, held a job for him where Truman didn't care to be a boy again. Maybe he'd try another farm, somewhere else, if this secret college idea didn't pan out, and how could he break this to Mabel? Meanwhile, Angela and Jake were anxious to see how much he had changed. Jake had grown on Kathleen. Chet needed more time. Mabel saved the best for last. Ken Herndon, more than anyone, wanted to meet him, "and has been waiting right along with me, Truddy. We're marking off the days. Please know that 'our' home, honey, is still 'ours.' " Never mentioning her taking down and packing away Fritz's assorted frozen expressions, hoping her boy wouldn't notice.

The expected visitors came and browsed about. Truman was cordial. With them was some Yang Berhormat Mohamed bin Sudin, "The Respected One-somebody," Truman reflected in his journal. They stayed all of twenty minutes, before the Yang Berhormat passed out the candy Azman purchased for Truman to store for the visit. "Just more craziness," Truman noted on his pages that chronicled his working his little Home into the first week of September, when the young police officer returned, the one who invited Truman to accompany them deep into southern forests, returning the crazy girl to her village.

The entrance of the uniform startled him, his crime with Ling never far off.

Then he was happy, recognizing his brief friend, near his own age, sharp-looking in his beige khaki trousers and tapered light blue shirt. "A perfect fit," Fatimah commented, "like on *CHiPs*," a recently popular, subtitled American import she especially liked. Quietly, Truman did, too.

The officer smiled back. "Hello, my friend," he spoke with soft English. Then he motioned Truman outside, where he mixed his limited English with quiet Malay. "Yang, ah, girl, the crazy gila, as one may say, girl *yang kita* return to village last time. Boleh remember?"

Truman answered in Malay, "Yes. What about her?"

"She was found dead in a well in her village," the young patrolman eased, switching to Malay. "Possibly foul play, or perhaps the spirits."

"I see," Truman answered. "Very sad. Were you there?"

"Yes, I was. Nothing we could do," reported the young officer.

Then they chatted, overlooking the peaceful pull of the Pahang. The young officer bid Truman farewell, never mentioning the pregnant girl's leech-ridden nakedness, nor her ragged mop of hair streaming water as her corpse turned, raised from the well, revealing her open mouth, streaming more water. Then her open eyes, kissed with madness, even in death.

CHAPTER 27

Sept. 11, 1982

Only 3 weeks left of Kuala Harap & all that's here for me.

It just keeps getting sadder. Now it's the kids & the girls (not like last month when I thought only of my friend—who's still gone). I hate to think of this place without me—the kids wandering around— no hikes or swims or schooling. The retarded ones make me sad in a different way—like when I'm gone how Kordi calls out for me when they're scrapping—only next time I'll never be back.

Drank again with Singam & found out he owes $ around town & in Mentacab, too. I guess he runs these tabs like me & John S. used to, then lays low. He grumbled some shit about daring anyone to try getting it from him. I finally met his wife (the 3 of us) over in Mentacab. She was chubby & pretty & had big dark eyes but never looked at me, & goofball Singam answered everything for her. Any- way, she left (I guess prearranged) & Singam turns around & wants to hit a massage parlor! Christ, he should go home & fuck her! (A nut like him is lucky to have such a nice wife.)

Last week I mailed my 1st box of stuff off to Mabel's, & I guess my house, too. It was sad to see all my things go (she'll be surprised at all the books). Anyway, I felt even sadder seeing my last 3 letters still in "her" box while there.

Got another (& probably last) letter from John S. from America. I must have told him more than I wanted, or meant to, about Ling because he mentioned relationships & what love maybe really is. He wandered a bit, then apologized. He didn't have to. He's still the best friend I ever had. Anyway, he was saying that love is just a cozy thing between best friends. I think he was trying to say that we love people who make us feel okay, or maybe pretty darn good about our- selves because we sort of believe them more than we believe ourselves about ourselves. Get it? I did, & then lost it & then got it again. I guess it's the same for all sorts of love. I know the kids love me & it makes me feel like their dad (if that's not too silly), & I know how I felt with ___ even when I wasn't with her (esp. so!). Anyway, he says there's plenty more back in America. (He's just trying to help.)

Bought one of Ling's tapes—sentimental songs—listen to it when I shouldn't.

I heard Azman told his one office boy that I was lazy. He's one Malay who's a rotten, worthless pig-fucker (and there's a few of them over here). Sometimes I hate him so much I can't even think about it.

* * *

Like water approaching falls, Truman tried to pace his days into proper farewells for those in the two towns who had gotten to know him. He thought of penciling a schedule but didn't, and should have.

He bought film for out in the villages and around town. There was the old Chinamen's home, Fatimah and Zurina's neighboring riverbank kumpangs, the children of his Home, and who knows whose goats he'd grown so accustomed to. He snapped photographs of the theaters of both towns, but couldn't capture how once inside, one was at liberty to indulge in brought-in booze and food. For a Muslim country, they were awfully tolerant in some ways.

He tried calling Mabel several times, but no answer, after timing each twelve hours ahead of New Egypt's Saturday and Sunday nights. Another night, he kept the kids outside until after 11:00 p.m., playing and talking and looking at the stars. Zurina was with them, and warm about it. Then Fatimah came out, too. The next day he telephoned headquarters from Mentacab and canceled a nicely planned lunch with himself, Azman and a headquarters' representative, refusing the phoniness. He hated Encik Azman. He had also heard, and logged, that the "respected one," who visited two weeks before thought the Home stunk. Zurina found this out. "It was an AhSoh accident," Truman wrote. "But the Yang Berhormat was a Malay—too fucking stupid to see the barrel past its saddest apple."

Truman bought more film for his small slice of the East-West Highway, his shed of a home, and so discreetly, that seemingly forever damp alley that corralled the main streets of the T of Kuala Harap. "I still wonder about her several times every day," he wrote on the 19th of his fast-collapsing September, before penciling about a kind letter received from the Mentacab Rotary, an official five paragraphs of sincere appreciation: "It was a privilege having you work in our community of Kuala Harap for the past two (2) years." He had ". . . proven yourself a credit to your profession, spread rays of hope and love to our unfortunate, and contributed toward the promotion of better understanding for not only the handicapped but also the people of Kuala Harap as a whole . . ."

Truman appreciated it, and thought of his C.O.S. conference, that weekend of resumes and references. Maybe he could get another from headquarters.

* * *

His journal was up to page 277. He took to flashing back. John Singer always pleased him, sometimes making him laugh aloud. But her earliest letters were in there, too, hidden, laying in wait amongst the pages of Singer's drinking and caring.

In the quiet of his shed, he read of the kids growing and changing, having to comb through the second half of their "meets," surfacing anywhere and everywhere, stinging from his own longhand. So he switched books for the kids, whom he'd soon never see again, wandering through his makeshift teacher's plan book. A progressive chronicle, safe from the thin woman's reach.

With Singam, he closed the Kedua two nights in a row, their uniformed girl smiling at table-side, pouring beers, and lighting Singam's cigarettes.

On the 22nd he entered in his journal foggy inscriptions, certain only of leaving. The quick lines, written to the lesser light of a recently screwed-in 40-watt bulb, the only one on hand, passed over his packing two more boxes to mail to Mabel, a quiet inventory of things squirreled up over two years, stuffed and taped to the ever-present smell of after-sundown mosquito coils.

His notes did, however, record his daily pilgrimage to the vast burnings, south of Mentacab. By day, the smoke rose in distant columns, merging as a single gray mountain of southern sky. By night, the burning was haunting, silent flames licking skyward from downed forests, giving contour to the rolling land in the dark of night.

He didn't write of straddling his turned-off motorcycle, in awe of the distant scene before him as he beat back thoughts of how lovely the children danced, especially Yap and Singh the day before at the Home at an impromptu picnic hosted by visiting Chinese Christians. This time Catholics.

The next night, he returned to the distant flames. Then he stopped in Mentacab to call Mabel in faraway New Egypt. He called from the open-air hotel desk. Again no luck, then he strangely fell asleep in the chair lent to him. No alcohol in him. Just deep, heavy sleep.

* * *

Sept. 21, 1982

Took a hell of a long hike today. Azman was all tuckered out with big fish eyes, heading straight for water (with the others) when we got back—squealing lightly—not understanding lining up. Zurina's been nice. Maybe she's thinking like me—departure coming too quickly!

I've been very confused—not making definite plans for a return trip. (Everyone else, I hear, has these pretty neat travel plans. In a way, I just want to head home.) I've been getting these weird feelings. Like flashes of things—the breezes, the smells around the farm, the sounds of the cows, my good old Dodge Dart! (hope she starts!), the rec. fields where I played baseball as a kid (wonder what Scotty W.'s up to—see?—there's another). And, of course, the track bed. I plan to walk it as soon as I get home. I hope the leaves are turning & the wind is blowing. I'll probably start thinking about the kids or

_____ & maybe even cry (almost have a few times lately—got to keep it together)._

Ramasami got his cast off. That was fast, too. He was so scared I had to hold him down. School's been good. Maybe it's the end in sight for the smarter ones. I also took Singam down to Mengkarak for a one-horse-town drunk. He didn't "get it" & thought we were wasting our time. Not me. I like drinking where there're goats & chickens wandering about (reminds me of Butch Cassidy & the Sundance Kid _when they were in S. America), beautiful & good for me (missed J. Singer)._

I went to the Sunday market for new clothes for home—found nothing—may wait for Burlington Center on a Dart run—only 2-3 weeks away. Unbelievable.

Had a surprise lunch date invite from the guys at the cycle shop on the highway. (They've taken enough of my $.) It was fun, even though it was all in Malay between me & them as they yammered away in Chinese amongst themselves. One guy asked me about John Singer & if I heard the news of his real ID. Next night I watched the kids as Zurina & Fatimah hit the movies to see some popular Malay flick. (I can see it now—torn-apart kumpang love—tears & wailing all the way through—a Bobby Benson-like Malay in the lead.) Anyway, they came home all happy & lit up about their movie. I felt like kissing them both for everything. As for me, I fell asleep to my tape player on a blanket out front. I've been real sleepy like that lately. Out of nowhere. Bang, zonked out!

Oh yes! A day later they both came to see me (very seriously) about the Malay lady who sells ice cream at the theater (the one I used to flirt with over a year ago) & how she told them I've been meeting her under the bridge & behind the theater. What a fucking nut!! Just my luck, my stories won't be as wild as John's—but I shouldn't complain—as long as the "real one" stays down.

I also saw Damian III, The Final Conflict & it sucked. I liked the 2nd one best & I think so only because of the wintery scenes (imagining the cold again)—except for that fucking kid under the ice!

Dreams have gotten crazy again, too. Last night I dreamed I was trying to cross a deep, fast river by climbing along the underside of *this bridge that began to sway & give as the moving water began to rise. I looked back & Ramasami & Singh were trying to follow me, & then I had Lim & Yap right there with me—the 3 of us barely hanging on. Must have been the brandy I got into out there at the burnings. They're so fucking pretty I just keep going back.*

* * *

Truman measured one day after the next in his final week of work. Chores were easy with immediate results. With schooling, he reached deep for purpose, not scolding anyone for anything. There was reading and writing, life skills math, life-skill commands, and made-up wishes to be understood, then expressed by the slower ones.

The walks and hikes were equally tough. Truman wiped away fast tears as his kids played about their daily strolls, unaware of the pain that had also surfaced in Fatimah and Zurina, spreading to Normah, Raj and Kamala. He stayed in three nights, relaxing and playing with the kids, while talking with Zurina and Fatimah, before reporting to headquarters on Wednesday for three days of processing out. He left for Kuala Lumpur after bathing Raj, a recent, painful business in an effort to check his out-of-control scabies.

Truman rode his cycle, intending to sell it upon his return to Kuala Harap, promising everyone a workless, unofficial week. That morning he also mailed off his final box of belongings, keeping the clothes he wore, two fresh changes of pants and three shirts amongst underwear and socks and manageable toiletries as carry-on luggage. His work boots could stay on his feet.

On his way out of Kuala Harap's little post office, a heaviness swelled in his chest. All three letters remained, missing pieces to an angry man's puzzle.

* * *

By midafternoon, Truman checked into the Southeast Asia Hotel. A note from Ben left at the desk gave him a comfortable roommate. That night he wrote in his journal of his preliminary closing-out itinerary. Other thoughts read:

Drank & ate burgers—saw Rocky III (not bad—Clubber???)

Drank until 3:00 a.m. with many others, some not in our group, here for the partying, I guess.

Thought of the kids & K.H. & of my lost friend, wrong time to be sad.

Lights of the city very pretty out big window (9th floor).

The next day the battery of details rolled in busier. Truman grew quiet as members of his original group found one another between rounds of termination concerns. As these others happily gabbed, Truman thought of the distant burnings and of the slide of the silent Pahang. That night he didn't write in his journal, and he found the partying vague two days hence when he tried to. There was quarreling over something between Americans and three Belgian engineers. Two more Indonesian volunteers were there for some reason.

On their final day, Ben and Truman accompanied two of the women teachers, making arrangements at a Peace Corps' travel agent of choice after their Bahasa tests measuring fluency, before their final payment for passage home.

Money, in crisp new stacks, changed hands for quickly-tucked-away tickets. Truman's own, MAS Airlines, booked him with a stopover in Penang, another in Bangkok, then on to Hong Kong. From there he figured he'd find the cheapest way home. He didn't care for the much-discussed plans of the others as he returned his cash, nearly all in U.S. currency, to a safety deposit box in the Southeast Asia Hotel. He'd pick it up in a week, enroute from Kuala Harap to Subang International.

Then came their last night as a surviving group, at last terminated. The spreading word had the celebrants meeting at the seedier, nearby Sentosa.

The drinking started early, with laughter, swearing and dancing in the dimly lit coffee house of the hotel's first floor. Their evening struggled briefly for that composite fraternity of two years before, but fueled with alcohol and poisoned with a handful of others, it swirled precipitously into singing and dancing amongst happy necking and small spats over things said and others imagined.

Truman's journal, reflecting the get-together, was a dateless several lines. Someone pulled Melinda's long hair, as she tried again at a Joan Baez ballad. Two guys fought briefly in the men's room, in the stench of urine, over one's never having liked the other and mentioning it.

A volunteer from Indonesia, touring Malaysia for fun, passed out, alone at his table, next to Truman and Danny's. Truman wouldn't write of him. He also wouldn't write of big Dave Hayden's entrance, bound for Iowa, already drunk, processed out a week before, after two years of indiscriminate roaming passed as service. But Truman would write of a conversation with this burly owner of an agricultural degree.

Making his rounds, kicking the drunken Indonesian volunteer into life, big Dave Hayden first glanced, then laughed, then moved for Truman and Danny's table.

"You, my farmer buddy!" he proclaimed too loudly. "I've been looking for you!"

Truman held to his beer, nodding a smile, then smiled again for the two women accompanying big Dave: the taller Laura Wurtzel, he'd learn later, and Doris Gorman, who he knew, pulling up chairs beside big Dave as he sat.

Aiming a thick finger, bent with drink, Hayden boomed, "You, Truman, buddy-boy! You must have a big fucking cock!" Big Dave laughed his laugh, taking another slug from his beer. Laura and Doris laughed for one another. Danny said nothing.

Hayden smeared beer from his whiskered chin with his thick wrist. He smiled broadly. "I couldn't believe it, Kramer. I was giving my best to this whore up in Ipoh a while back. And then, when we're done, she fuckin' asks me, all shy as shit, as she's gettin' dressed, if I know a Mr. Truman Kramer!"

Truman recoiled in his seat.

"You must be packin' some good pipe." Hayden smiled.

"Oh, David, no," chipped in taller Laura, pulling back her hair.

"Why must you guys even go to those places?" asked Doris, directing her question to all three, before pulling back her own hair, shaking her head. "Just adding to the exploitation."

Truman held to his beer. "Probably another Truman or something. I've been to Ipoh, but just passing through."

"Come on!" ribbed big Dave. "These workin' gals, they move around, and besides, how many fuckin' Truman Kramers are there in this goddamned country, or anywhere?" He laughed.

Truman, a little braver, asked, "What was her name, Dave?"

"Oh Christ, who knows? I was drunk as shit. Skinny woman with a fucked-up jaw, like it was broke and never set right."

"I believe that," offered taller Laura, done with pulling her hair. "Probably a Malay doctor."

Hayden drank again, then looked away toward shouting across the room. He leaned back in his chair. "Let's see," he said. "A western name, like they all use."

"Linda, Lori, Susan?" guessed Danny, smiling for Doris and Laura.

Truman watched big Dave Hayden.

"Bones, boy." Hayden smiled. "And a fucked-up tit. Sorry, girls." He laughed for his companions. "But, oh Jesus, a nasty scar." He shook his shoulders as though shivering.

Danny and taller Laura stole glances to Truman, owner of a cruel one himself.

But Truman, his smile gone, stayed fixed to Dave Hayden. "Well?" asked Truman, righting the drunken man to stay his course.

"Oh, let's see. I was pretty lit, you know."

Then another grin shaped his unshaven face. "That's right. It sounded like a tree. A goddamned tree. Honest to God, Kramer, oak or hemlock or elm or some such damned thing."

The large man smiled wide, then drank long, emptying his bottle, smacking it hard upon their wet tabletop, startling Danny and shorter Doris.

"I fuckin' got it! Goddamnit, I got it! The bar was the Paradise." He laughed. "And her name was Maple! She fuckin' told me, Kramer, that her goddamned name was Maple!"

CHAPTER 28

The next crummy day (Sept. something)

Couldn't sleep—even though drunk.

Well, I did it again. Dale Rowland only marked me up & I wrecked him. She did nothing but love me & I went & ruined her. I'll go to Hell for this one for sure.

God, I'm so sorry & I'm so sad about it.

* * *

An hour later, Truman motorcycled out of early-morning Kuala Lumpur, east, for the westward mountains.

Through the military checkpoint, toward the red ball of peaking sun, his head hurt with guilt, a hangover and the staying thought of only six days left. He was unemployed, attached to no one. He should have felt freedom, young and pure, tearing through the morning air. Instead, he felt the grim weight of responsibility, cycling up into the cool mist of the jungled mountains.

In Kuala Harap, Truman returned in silence, again poking around, making his catcalls and growls. Kamala and Yap sounded out first, then all who could, running, hobbling and wheeling forth to his return. Raj was happy to display his scabied hands and toes. He'd been washing himself with his medicated soap. Singh, his happy, shuffling-about self. Ramasami had great crimes to report. Lim had stolen something, and AhSoh smelled of excrement. Normah contorted and howled to Truman's feigned great interest.

And Truman tried to listen, as his final days, unmapped, blurred, a sad stringing of farewells waiting the following Sunday morning, his racing-in end. Sketchy notes in his journal gave chronology, starting with a visit to Fatimah's family in that prettiest of riverside kumpangs. In her older brother's home, a hundred yards off, he discovered a faded picture of Fatimah at nine or so, scowling alongside another little girl. A goat watched on in the background. A lump formed in Truman's throat.

Then he drank hard with Singam, taking pictures of one another down at the Kedua, then more at the wobbly tables of the all-night truck stop. The one swing beneath the Go Dog Go tree broke. Truman fixed it with hardware bought at Tan's. Her prepared little room upstairs seared his mind on his second of six days left.

He visited Zurina's home the next day, writing: "So poor, her father so old. Bland food sweetened with Zurina's shy effort as she prepared it."

Zurina remained kind from then on in. Truman didn't write of her younger sister, shuffling quietly about their shell of a home as Truman thought hard things of himself. That night he ducked Singam to return to the southern burnings. Sitting on his turned-off cycle in the darkness, he found the medicine no longer there. Across the starry distance a single fire burned, dancing skyward, licking the blackness. Truman watched, then kicked his cycle into life, never to return.

That night he went to the fort, wrapped in a blanket, just to think, then slept through the night.

The next night he drank with Singam, to be joined by Kumari's greasy father. The larger, older barber humbled himself to much-younger Singam. An Indian thing, figured Truman. This was after a fun morning hike with the kids, and a sad, for Truman, afternoon swim. As the kids hobbled and splashed about, Truman couldn't finish Kamala's castle in the sand, for above the opposite bank of the river Kuala Harap's red clay roofs topped the green of the riverbank trees. Tan's hardware was the fifth from the left. Beneath it, just downstream, beneath the bulbous rising of the Go Dog Go tree, were the tiles of his own riverbank Home. Truman's chest heaved. He hid it from the kids.

* * *

The next morning Truman drove east, bound for Kuantan, then south for Pekan, John Singer's old home. He never made it, grabbing breakfast and a *New Straits Times* midway. Over eggs and roti he read an article titled: "Some Kind Remarks Regarding U.S. Youths." "Despite what many think, many young Americans," the article read, "don't drink or smoke or wear flashy clothes. In fact, many have strong spirits to support themselves. But there are still many problems of drug abuse, homosexuality, murder and the mess in sexual relations. Even high school students are allowed to fall in love."

Truman threw the paper away. That night he finished *David Copperfield* on the swing overlooking the river. David's landing of lovely Agnes was painful solace, the peace of a true love realized, against his own leaving a woman who tried as hard.

At midweek, events and people stopped and started as dateless dashes and fast jottings in his journal.

There was more drinking with Singam. Truman drank too much, misting over for her in her pretty swimming suit. So skinny and fragile, and funny-looking and pretty.

He slept again out in the fort, and would for the next two nights, his last. The kids happily joined him, dragging out blankets and pillows as Truman carried mattresses. Raj's medicated bathing kept up, but Truman knew it was too little too late. The girls would never keep after it. His scabies bound to spread fast amongst the others. The thought tightened his throat and thickened his eyes.

* * *

Singh's mother hosted a farewell dinner out at her goofy son's home on her leased parcel of rubber plantation twenty miles east of Mentacab. Truman brought the retarded boy with him, and was taken with the serene beauty of Singh's sister at seventeen. He ate and sweated in the heat, relieved he hadn't met her until then.

Singh stayed with his family. Truman's mind, on his cycle ride home, took him to Ling's straight hair, the hard rises of her bones. He thought of her letters, of her efforts beneath him, efforts bared and opened to the likes of a drunken Dave Hayden. The hot wind streaked his tears.

Then final days came, bathed in sorrow, almost timeless. In the fort, Truman dreamed of vomiting a thick brown substance. The next day he tried to play with the kids, experiencing flashes of Mabel's face and voice, her home, the farm and the track bed. Haunting, jagged visions, interrupted with a heartbroken Ling, naked, serving herself to strange men from nowhere in the night.

* * *

Late Sunday morning Truman wrote sloppily in his journal, upon his lap, in a cab bound for Kuala Lumpur. Already gone.

Oct. 3, 1982—the end, I guess

I sold my cycle this morning to the cycle shop for 400 ringgits (not free, but close). I was in no mood to haggle. I'm sure they thought they were fucking me because they all started hacking away in Chinese, laughing & all. Fuck 'em. They'll still be talking about it tonight, with rice falling from their fucking faces in whatever shithole house they live in.

Last night I had supper at Mr. Martin's house (after visiting Kumari's house—2 of his barbershop pals were there—again saw pretty picture of his wife when much younger—she hasn't changed much). Mr. Martin's family was very nice. I think they could tell I was crying before coming. Mr. Martin spoke very softly over eating. His usually jabbering 2 kids didn't speak at all. He gave me a new wallet (a very nice one) & a very kind, "God Bless you, Mr. Truman."

Got back to the Home after sundown. Things were worse. I cried with Normah on my lap. Kamala cried, too, with Zurina & Fatimah. (Kumari's dad showed up all drunk & I had to run him off—lied to him about meeting him later that night.) Anyway, it was sad. Slept again in the fort & fell asleep fast—even before the kids & I woke up in the dark about 4:00 (before the call to prayer).

I felt so sad out there in the dark & I really wanted Fatimah or Zurina to come out & just love me—a really strong feeling—not creepy like I've been.

Everyone started waking up around 7:00. Azman was up & rocking & spinning away. I zipped around town after breakfast & said about 10 good-byes & then dropped off my cycle & walked back to the Home, feeling kind of good for a change (until back at the Home).

Found old Zurina out back by the clothesline, crying, & brought her in & then we all started. The first kids to cry were Kamala & Normah & then half the others—I think the slower ones were just scared seeing the grownups & the smarter ones crying. Then my cab came up the driveway & Zurina & Normah & Fatimah (& me, too) really went to town (makes me almost cry again, just writing it). The girls wailed away, "Minta ma'af. Minta ma'af!" between sobs (which means "forgive me" in case I forget). I would have fucking forgiven anyone for anything—then & now. I've never been so sad all at one time—except for Mom—I can still remember that lone light bulb in the kitchen as Barlow came out.

Then I said good-bye to the kids, one by one. Here's most of them:
Normah—cried heavily—let me kiss her wet cheek for a 1st
Raj—just cried away
Kamala—cried some (sitting in her nice new blue wheelchair)
Ramasami—1st child of my life—a "son"—smiled and rambled on about what he planned to do that day (I cried instead.)
Yap & Salleh—just walked around seeming very afraid
Kordi—smiled & kept repeating "bye bye"
Azman—shook my hand & pulled my fingers, spun like a champ & slapped the top of his head (better than when I found him)
Singh—still at home
Kumari—cried all morning—not about me—maybe a fight with Yap or Lim
Lim—cried from fear—kept trying to ask why everyone was crying in her chubby gestures

Oh yes, Singam showed up & hugged me & cried as he chained-smoked like a madman standing around out front.

I felt like it was finally happening, & like I was in extreme danger or something. Still feels that way. It comes & goes.
I'm half way to K.L. right now.

* * *

Truman, wearing his favorite jeans, a white shirt and his well-worn work boots, closed his journal and sat quietly in the back of his cab. His backpack of clean clothes rested beside him.

He rubbed often at his arms and thighs, when his chest tightened or heaved. His driver, speaking little, played the same cassette over and over as he raced west into mountains. One song would stay in Truman's head all day.

At the Southeast Asia Hotel, Truman withdrew his cash from his safe deposit box, choking up as he took another cab to Subang International Airport, another half hour from the sweltering city.

At the airport he tried to eat but couldn't. Instead, he took pictures of his gate, then two more of beggars. He looked up to the open-air balcony. His chest tightened. He had trouble breathing. He sat.

An hour and a half later, his eyes thickened and his vision blurred as he walked through Gate 13. He thought of John Singer as he turned, looking back, as Singer had a year before.

His chest seized. Only strangers moved about behind him.

The MAS Boeing 727 roared down the wavering heat of the runway, lifting off, nose up, its belly white to the horizon, climbing into a wide turning, north for Penang International, the single stop before Bangkok, enroute to Hong Kong.

Truman sat alone in the tail section, rereading his emergency instructions, silently eyeing the referred-to nearest emergency exit. He rustled in his bag, extracting his tattered, blue spiral notebook. He didn't open it, keeping it upon his lap, listening to the soft external whine of the jet's engines, fearing looking back into its pages more than the flying.

Landing at Penang International, Truman put his notebook away, sitting still, not talking to anyone. Then abruptly he rose, departing with his carry-on bag in his grasp.

He never thought of recovering the balance of his ticket for Hong Kong because he didn't care, throwing his boarding pass away in Penang's terminal.

In this town where he once listened to Bruce Statton ruminate presidential politics and heavyweight boxing, Truman entered a Bank Bumi Putra and exchanged $1,000 in U.S. currency for nearly 2,500 in ringgits. Ten blocks away he bought a used motorcycle and two helmets. His MAS flight was well on its way to Bangkok by the time he crossed the watery strait for the mainland on a crowded ferry, bound for Butterworth.

In Butterworth, he refueled his used motorcycle, a Honda, then wound his way out of the dusty city in the heat of the late afternoon, his carry-on bag and extra helmet strapped fast to his gas tank.

At a sign pointing south, he veered hard left, for Ipoh.

CHAPTER 29

Truman raced south beneath the late-day sun, bound for Dave Hayden's sighting, through Malaysia's northern tin mining region that seemed another foreign land, not Malaysia at all.

Amongst racing cars and bullish lumbering trucks, his eyes watered with images of the kids wandering the Home without him. No schooling, no hikes, no swimming, his shed out back empty. He tried to think ahead, curbed by his latest visa expiring in four weeks. He couldn't think into New Egypt, the farm and Aunt Mabel. How to explain?

He geared down for a turn, his chest heaving, thirty miles north of Ipoh.

* * *

Truman rolled into Ipoh as a warm darkness was falling. Weaving through the streets, he felt his way downtown, finding a cheap hotel. He checked in with his single bag, leaving the spare helmet locked to the motorcycle's frame.

In his room he washed the grime of his ride from his face and arms, then decided to mandi proper, stripping, bucketing water over himself in a tiled corner of the room. Drying his face before his room's small mirror, he thought he looked lonesome and frightened. He hid his cash above the hum of the fluorescent light, keeping 400 ringgits in his pocket. Then he lay on the bed, to rest and to think.

An hour and a half later he awakened with a jolt from a dream. It was another bridge, slippery with moss above roaring water. He sat up, amazed with Kumari's balance as chubby Lim crept along the ironwork, before slipping and falling to rocks below, bloodlessly splitting her head open. Then big Kumari, hand in her blouse and smiling, fell away, too.

On the edge of the bed, Truman shook his head hard, went for his watch and the time, then rose. He patted the cash in his

pocket, and left his room. As he locked his door from the outside, the rockish-song "Yellow River" blared from within the
adjacent room. He kind of liked it.

It was just after 10:00 p.m. when he kicked his used cycle
into life. He figured himself in good shape with the bars hopping until 3:00 or so.

Ipoh, smaller than Trenton, bustled with Chinese culture and
business. As Truman cruised for the seedier corners of town he
oddly felt at home, cycling into turns, looking for the bars. He
thought of his journal in his bag in his room. How he feared
looking back into earlier pages. Then twinkling lights appeared
ahead, flickering from strung-up lines. His first bar of the night.

It was called The Sunset Bar, and it was kind of nice. Inside it
was dark, nearly empty. Two girls approached. Both smiled. One
spoke in English, "Hello, John. Would you wish to join us?"

Truman went to his point. "I'm looking for a tall woman.
Chinese. Ling, or possibly Mabel, a name she likes to call herself."

Neither girl knew her, or admitted it. The friendlier one who
spoke in English said, "Perhaps at another bar. One not so nice
as ours." She smiled.

"Where?" Truman asked.

Her kindness left her. "On another roadway. Jalan Ikan Besar.
Not far away. Perhaps you shall return?"

She drew directions in the air as her friend watched. Truman
thanked her and was gone, out into the night.

He cycled around, getting lost, then stumbled upon several
bars amongst a sprawling of darkened and chained closed-up
shops, spaced between several open-air kedais. The sparkling lights
of The Paradise caught his eye. His senses jumped. Jesus Christ,
right where Hayden found her.

He parked and locked his cycle a hundred yards away, the
spare helmet locked to its frame. He approached the Christmasy
lighting, fussing at his hair, retucking his shirt.

This place was busier, with laughter and companionship in
half-booths. He strolled, looking about, not sitting in the candle-
lit darkness.

"Hello, John! From where?" a man called, inciting Chinese laughter in the dark. Truman smiled, then sat at an empty table, imagining her upstairs, working, unaware of his being there after their four months of not having one another.

A girl joined him. She was an Indian, slightly heavy. "Do you wish to have a date?" she asked.

"Sure. May I have an Anchor, too?"

The girl smiled, lit their candle, then hurried off, returning with his beer and a drink for herself. She snuggled in close. "Tell to me, what is your name?"

"Truman. Listen. Do you speak good English, *atau saya bercakap Baghasa Malayu?*"

"My English very clever." She beamed in the candlelight.

"Good. I'm looking for a friend of mine. She works here. If you help me find her, I'll tip you very good."

"You do not like me?" She pouted, reaching for the inside of his thigh.

"You're wonderful, and very pretty, but do you know a lady, a thin Chinese lady named Ling, or maybe Mabel, or Maple?"

"No. No lady here like that. My name is Wendy."

Truman paused, then said, "You don't get it. I'm looking for my friend. Only her."

He took a long swallow of his beer as a drunken woman tacked their way, maybe a Malay. She caught herself against the height of their booth.

Wendy turned in closer. "Where you from, my date?"

"Kuala Harap," Truman answered, watching the drunken woman, before rising and inviting her to join them. *"Sila dudoh. Dudoh."*

"No, no," whispered Wendy. *"Pundan, pundan,"* she sped up. "How you say? Transvestite? You no want her."

Truman's only shock was that he didn't care, and would have weeks ago.

This Malay, indeed a man, and less convincing up close, plumped down opposite Truman and the Indian girl. *"Boleh bercakap Bahasa Ingeris?"* Truman asked him.

"*Tak boleh*," the man answered, his lipstick smeared.

So Truman asked in Malay, and to his surprise, the man knew Ling, but only as Mabel, and that she had left The Paradise a few weeks before. Truman reached into his shirt pocket and slipped the man twenty ringgits, asking of her whereabouts now.

"This night. *Malam ini?*" asked Truman.

The Indian girl pressed closer, her warm breath catching Truman's cheek. "The Seaview. Two blocks from here," she said, raising her opposite palm for a tip of her own.

Truman dug into his pocket, hating having to do it, but wanting no problems.

* * *

Outside, in the lesser heat of the late night, Truman walked, renewed with hope. In minutes he was there, and suddenly aware of his need to use a bathroom.

He entered The Seaview and found the bathroom first, where he also tried to handsome himself without benefit of a mirror, before purposely seeking an older Chinese woman in a booth close to the bar. She looked him over closely, then became attentive to his vague story.

"I know this woman," she politely spoke, "as Ling, and two other names. A kind woman. I am pleased you have find her friendship welcome," she strained in English.

"Is she here tonight?" Truman asked, trying to hide his excitement.

"No, no. I am sorry to say, this night her night off. I shall be pleased to tell to her of your visit."

"Where can I find her?" Truman fumbled, wishing he hadn't. "She knows me. She'll be happy to see me."

The older woman looked hard again at Truman in the partial darkness. She leaned to his scarred side. She answered, "Perhaps she may be pleased. She is at The Blue Fox this night. Massage parlor on the road to Hospital Bahagia. Outside of city. I can tell you no more."

Then she rose from their booth, not looking back.

* * *

Truman refueled his cycle at a late-night gas station, getting directions for Hospital Bahagia. The ride was cooling. He hadn't realized his own sweating. The wind of the ride also brought beaches to mind, her swimsuit and sunblock.

Rounding a curve beneath tall dark trees, he thought massage parlor, no cuddling in booths, haggling prices, a simple menu of contact by candlelight. They had their straight girls, of course, but it was big Dave Hayden who brought him here. Then lights up ahead, two all-night kedais, and a third, a soft glow. He geared down. The Blue Fox read the sign. No Christmasy lights. Only two blue bulbs, 60 watts or so. His heart raced.

Truman slowed. Parked cars and several cycles lined both sides of the street. They could have belonged to residents as easily as to late-night patrons along the line of chained-up first floor shops. Truman killed his engine, gliding left, into an alley, one shop beyond The Blue Fox.

It was dark behind this shuttered business. Truman figured it family owned. Furniture. Uneven lengths of light planking and rotan, curved and straight, made up heaped piles beside and behind the building.

Truman rocked his cycle back up onto its kickstand, just out of a single slicing of street light angling in from somewhere. He took off his helmet. Cats fought somewhere not far off. Chinese music leaked from within The Blue Fox. Truman, frightened, became aware of his own heartbeat.

He unlocked his spare helmet, placing it beside his own, upon a smaller piling of scrap wood. He paused, picking up a length of wood. Too cumbersome. Then another, of rotan. Too long. He laid it back down, eyeing a third. Thick rotan. The length of a ball bat, light as a broomstick. He laid it between the two helmets, then stepped up into the alley, toward the street.

* * *

Truman entered The Blue Fox, jingling a bell attached to the top of the door. His shirt clung to the small of his sweating back.

There was a counter, and an open stairway to the side of two coffee tables surrounded with bamboo sofas and matching chairs. Three men, two Indians and a Malay, occupied the one sitting area, discussing something funny. A bearded white man, with long sandy hair worked behind the counter. He was larger than Truman, possibly in his thirties. He nodded a vacant hello as a shorter, well-dressed Chinese man emerged from the back through hanging beads.

"Good evening, sir," the Chinese man spoke politely to Truman through the music.

Truman choked, momentarily. "Ah, hello. I'm here for a massage."

The man waited for more, but just a moment. "Very good," he returned. "Have you a preference for our girls?" Truman supposed he meant race. "They are all quite suitable."

Suddenly a girl emerged through the beads. Truman startled. But she was Malay. One of the men behind him rose from their conversation to follow her up the stairway.

"Ah, yes. Yes, I do, sir. A lady named Mabel, or well, I'm pretty sure that's her name."

The white man's attention shifted to him. Truman pushed on. "Anyway, she's very nice. I'd like to see her if she's in, sir."

"I see." The Chinese man smiled, as the white man's eyes stayed to him. "At present she is occupied. But another Chinese girl can attend you, a nice thin one if that is your wish?"

"No, thank you," Truman steadied. "I'll wait if you don't mind. Over here?" He motioned toward the empty sofa arrangement.

"As you wish." The neatly-dressed man smiled. "Perhaps another twenty minutes. Would you care for a drink?"

* * *

Truman sat alone with his tea, trying to appear manly in this place a step up from the bars.

A man, Chinese, descended the steps. Minutes later a young woman emerged through the beads to accompany another of the trio upstairs. Truman recognized the system. Go up with your masseuse, come down alone. There was a back way for the women.

Two more patrons entered, jingling the bells, expertly convening with the smartly-dressed Chinese man as the bearded white man attended to something behind the beads.

Then another man descended the stairs, paid his bill and asked for another drink. Truman recognized him from the former trio, whose own masseuse appeared from the beads, leaving Truman next.

But it didn't. A heavy woman, an Indian, emerged for one of the men who had just come in. Truman wished his heart would slow. His back was wet again. Then the bearded white man emerged from the beads, with Ling behind him.

Truman rose fast. Too fast, kicking the rotan tea table. Her hair was longer, separating at her shoulders. She wore a pink T-shirt advertising something in Chinese.

She stopped and straightened wide-eyed, looking to Truman, prompting her Chinese boss to speak to her in Chinese.

She swallowed, then whispered to her Chinese proprietor. He turned to Truman, nodding, smiling above his pressed shirt and tie.

Ling led Truman up the steps, never looking at him, her feet sandaled beneath a knee-length dark blue skirt. Her pink T-shirt was tucked in. Truman's heart raced, near to her again.

The plywooded rooms had doors, instead of curtains. Truman was relieved, following her through the blue glow of the narrow hallway. That "Yellow River" song spun again from downstairs. Ling opened the fourth door and walked in, reaching for kept matches. Truman closed the door behind them.

"Ling," he hushed. "What happened to us?"

She turned, with her opened book of matches in her hand. Lines of fresh tears streaked her cheeks. Truman noticed the unevenness of her jaw.

"I am so sorry," she whispered. "I am so ashamed. You must pay me this time. It is the men's downstairs."

Truman grabbed her shoulders. "I'm not proud of myself either! I'm not here for that. I'm here for you! I can't believe I found you."

"Oh, I wish you did not search for me." She choked, dropping her matches.

She reached for them, fumbling.

Truman, faster, bent for them, snatching them away, flinging them across the tiny room.

"No candles. No rubdown. No sex. Just you!" he hushed. "I love you, Ling."

"You do not understand. You must pay me this time." She oddly shook. "There will be much trouble. Please understand me, Truman."

"Of course I'll pay 'em. Aren't you happy to see me? Didn't you ever think of me, or wonder about me, Ling?" he said, as he pulled her close, leading her to kneeling upon the mattress, with nowhere to sit.

"Oh, Truman," she cried, covering her face. "My life. I am so sorry to you. Oh, please. Why did you come to this place?"

"To find you, Ling! Come with me to America." He straightened her face to his. "If you're divorced, marry me. If not, run away with me!"

He grasped her harder, kissing her wet eyes, then the bridge of her nose.

"We're both all alone. It doesn't have to be," he told her. "We can have each other. We can take care of each other."

"I have no one," she wept. "You have your aunt—"

"Not any more. I'm too old. I don't want her anyway. I want you."

She breathed in hard jerks. "I am uglier now than when we have our meets. I have had terrible hurt, here on my face and—"

"Yes or no?" Truman demanded.

Her face stayed down. "We may never do it."

"I have the money. That's all we need, and each other. Yes or no?"

"Oh yes, but how? It will never work."

"Tonight! Now. We'll leave for K.L." He shook her with new joy.

She looked to him, silent. "Tomorrow shall be better. I am working now. My employers are downstairs and—"

"No more, Ling! None!" Truman shook her harder. "You're not theirs. You're mine! We can be ours. Fuck 'em down there. What do you have with you, right now that you'll need?"

"But the captain, and Mr. Steven down there," she whispered. "Mr. Steven is from Australia, and of such poor temper." She reached for Truman's sleeve with one hand. Her other touched at his scar.

"Sshh. What do you have with you, right now, that you will need?"

"How do you mean?"

"You know, papers and stuff. Money, clothes, your national ID? We have to kill some time. Let's make our plan."

"A plan? Oh no." She trembled.

Truman was earnest. "Turn on a light, or light that fuckin' candle."

She retrieved the matches Truman had tossed earlier and lit the candle, then knelt again on the mattress, in her tight skirt and tucked-in T-shirt.

She stayed with three other women in a room above The Seaview, where her clothes were, with a hidden 350 ringgits and sundries to be abandoned. In her purse downstairs, in the back room, was her government ID, tissues, nearly 200 ringgits, makeup, a brush, a comb, contraceptive gel, a second diaphram and a bank book—her savings account at an Ipoh branch of The Bank Of Hong Kong. She had no idea if her husband had divorced her or not. And she had never had a passport.

Truman assured her, "We'll deal with those things in Kuala Lumpur, after getting out of here. Together."

He'd go first, after paying his bill, as she'd circle around back, slipping out with her purse and its contents, to his motorcycle and extra helmet.

* * *

Downstairs, Truman strode as though satisfied, approaching the counter to settle his bill. In the sitting area behind him, two more men, an Indian and a Chinese man, looked to him.

"Did you find everything suitable?" the smiling captain asked, sliding Truman's bill across the polished wooden counter.

"Yes. Very nice," Truman answered, extracting his wad of Malaysian currency, thumbing the exact amount.

"Very well then." The little man smiled. "Good night to you."

Truman smiled. "Good night to you, sir." Mr. Steven, smoking, glanced up from his magazine.

Truman exited, beneath the jingling bell, into the warm quiet of the night, all too easy. He turned left into the alley beside the locked-up furniture shop.

Another alley, it dawned on him. The last, stinking, beautiful Malaysian alley, before slipping around back, into that darkness pierced with an angling of light from somewhere.

"Is that you?" Ling startled him, having moved faster than he thought.

"Sshh. Yes," Truman answered, kicking wood as he fumbled for the helmets.

"Here. Put this on," he said, out of the streaking of light.

Then it started. Coming from the darkness behind them.

"I say, what have we here, mate?"

Mr. Steven had followed her.

"Oh no," Ling uttered.

"Get on the cycle, Ling. Just get on the cycle," Truman's voice shook as he reached down for the length of cane he had placed between the helmets.

"We're just leavin,' and mindin' our own business is all," Truman stammered, grasping tight to his length of cane, keeping it to his thigh, out of sight.

"You must be something of a bloody asshole, mate," Mr. Steven spoke.

Then another voice rose from the darkness, Chinese and fast and sharp. Truman turned as Ling's voice answered the captain's, in Chinese, demure and subordinate.

She was backing off from the cycle, into the slicing of light. Her words were begging, and Truman knew it.

"She fucking quit!" Truman spoke hard. "Don't you guys understand?"

But the little man grabbed at her, his Chinese sharp and mean as he began slapping her. She was pitiful in the partial light, a helmeted skinny bug, jerked about and swatted at.

Steven laughed.

Truman gripped tighter to the hard rod at his side.

Then he stepped into a twisting fast swing toward the Australian.

The quiet darkness ripped oddly of cut wind and sudden smack, cane meeting boned flesh.

The bearded man backed into the ray of light, his face opened across his forehead and nose. He stood for a long second, then stumbled forward, reaching for Truman, seeking balance.

Truman pushed him off. He didn't fall. Mr. Steven's face was oddly contorted. Dark lines of blood appeared. Truman swung again for Mr. Steven's face. Then twice more, working at toppling him, cutting him down like a tree from the wrong end.

Truman turned fast.

"No, John," the captain responded.

"Get back, ya' fuckin' asshole!" Truman shouted. "Let her go!"

"Get on the cycle, Ling," he said, as Mr. Steven struggled into rising from the gravelled alley. Truman turned, caned him again, dropping him to the same spot.

Then he turned to the stout captain. "Ya' want some?"

"No. Please. Take her away."

Holding his length of cane, Truman mounted his motorcycle. Ling climbed on behind him. He rocked it off its stand and kicked it into firing. Turning slowly, he angled for the side alley, where he snapped on the headlight, dropping his length of cane.

In moments they turned right, out front. The soft glow of The Blue Fox faded behind them. The cool rush of night air. Ling's clinging to the refrain of that same song, "Yellow River."

* * *

Oct.—late 1st week—Thursday—not sure of date

We're more settled here at the S.E.A. hotel in K.L.—hot water, firm beds & tub & all.

A lot has happened since I last wrote in K.H. & thought about it on the plane. Ling is with me, listening to tapes (bought a new player) & flipping through a magazine. Of course, there was that business in Ipoh 4 or 5 days ago, which I'll never forget. I only want to mention our getting back to my hotel to get my bag & $. I noticed under the passing street lights of Ipoh that Mr. Steve's blood was all over me, so Ling & I switched shirts in this closed-up marketplace a couple of blocks away. She looked so pretty & skinny & so scared doing it all so fast. I could barely fit into her T-shirt (she is pretty skinny). Anyway, we took off for K.L. that night & made it here an hour after dawn.

She's been afraid of the cops ever since. I didn't want to insult her, but I tried to explain that it was just a fight behind a whore-house, for god's sake, & the only one hurt was a white guy (and hardly a diplomat at that). Anyway, we're safe & sound.

But holed up here, a whole lot more has happened. I hit the U.S. embassy to find out how to go about everything & they were all very kind. (They called P.C. headquarters to verify stuff, & I felt a little funny about that.) They (the embassy) pointed us in a couple of directions. It turns out Ling IS divorced (from some Ministry of something—claims she ran off a year ago—sort of true, I guess). To cut to the chase we're to be "registered" tomorrow so we bought new clothes. That was fun, too. (I even helped her pick out a dress.)

To another thing, it's strange being 2 hours from the kids & the Home—I feel real bad about not doing one last "farewell." (They all think I'm long gone by now.) Maybe it's best. I've dreamed of them since being here in K.L.—or nightmared. In one I feared for their safety, thinking they'd all drown & get hit by cars & things without me. In another I had a stick in my hand, & it rotted away in seconds as I looked down at it, then I couldn't find Ling again, who showed up out of nowhere.

Back to Ling. Her one side is pretty scarred up. At least mine doesn't bother me. Hers is sensitive. Maybe in America we can get her fixed. Her jaw is different, too, but it doesn't bother her (hurt her anyway).

Finally—I called Mabel (the real one) & asked her to wire me $ in care of Bank of America ($1,000 U.S.) to get Ling & I back. She was surprised, of course, & sounded doubtful, & she tried to fake excitement. She'll like Ling. I know I do. The $ should be here in 2 days. Mine's holding out though & Ling got what's left of hers from the Hong Kong branch downtown.

We've been seeing movies in the meantime & having a lot of fun (hold hands openly now & get silly over it). We won't swim again though—mailed her swimsuit home weeks ago—to remember her by—got a lot more than that now. I bought a new shirt I like. Ling asked me if I needed new work boots. (Being silly, I told her I'm buying a pair for her—1st thing at Burlington Center.)

Oh—another dream comes to mind—of trying to rebuild a section of Chet's one outbuilding & finding my Dart in it & then John Singer showed up & I told him about Ling & I & some guy listened in & laughed about us & I hit him & then John had a wife of his own & then I was on my old monkey bike at the ball field across from the grade school in New Egypt (but I was grown up) & watched some kid shag after a high flyball.

Well, I should leave off now. I want to take a hot bath before we go out for errands. Still have a lot to do today, at the embassy & two more Gov. Ministry buildings. There'll be long lines but we'll have fun.

* * *

And across two days there were many lines.

Truman and Ling were married, unceremoniously. Then they ate at McDonald's before returning to the Southeast Asia Hotel, where they showered, getting into each other's way, finding it wonderful. Truman thought her pretty as she apologized for her recent poor complexion. She sat, wrapped in towels at tubside as he shaved. She wished him clean-shaven.

At the U.S. Embassy their union was quite believable.

Truman was frank with a truthful accounting of their to-getherness. His testimony shied silent Ling. Their embassy attaché, Rick Rivera, a slender Hispanic man from New Jersey, and easy to talk to, listened thoughtfully, then wished the two well, seeing to Ling's alien status with temporary documents, along with instructions for follow-up once the couple was stateside. He suggested the Federal Building in Philadelphia. Truman, attentive, thought of The Children's Home, vanloads of unruly juveniles crossing the big bridges of the Delaware.

Then came the business of a passport. Being in the nation's capital, and willing to endure long lines, the process lasted all of two days. The two shouldn't have been concerned with the ruling Malay disposition more than happy to pack off a female Chinese national, ovaries and all.

From loving Mabel, Truman's money arrived for the boy she found long ago, to lose so recently to a woman from the side of the world that had taken her Fritz. She wept over a pot of coffee at her kitchen table. Nice Ken Herndon listened long, then stayed the night.

Ling worried over Mabel's accepting her. Few women had.

Truman's own thoughts ventured to the few men of his life. Old man Barlow Archer would have liked her. He liked everybody. Certainly, Juan will, perhaps to a fault. Chet Van Heflin, though, mattered most, with his gentle way with the boy from the Pines. Truman hoped Chet's first meeting with Ling to be with the three of them, very much alone, out in the broad yard Truman mowed as a boy.

Then their final morning came. Ling wept in the cab to Subang International. Truman thought of the children out in Kuala Harap. He tried reading that morning's *New Straits Times* to fend off the images.

Holding hands, they boarded their flight, a wondrous first for well-dressed Ling. She picked another dark blue thing, a dress with a big white collar with equally large white buttons down the front. Truman liked watching her putting it on in their room as she worked at the half-dollar-sized buttons, thinking of her womanliness beneath, wondering if that made him still a boy.

She laundered the same dress a day and a half later in a hotel in Tokyo, to wear it again, to America, for him.

Seven hours later, out of Tokyo and over the Pacific, Truman started an entry in his journal, an entry dated: "October—not sure when. It's again that dateline thing beneath us somewhere."

But his pen rested in his stilled hand. He had fallen asleep, his thoughts swept away, waltzing within sleep's sweet lure. There was the skin of the thin woman beside him, then Kuala Harap, the echo of scampering brown children. Then silos and cows floated through, followed by a heavily-weeded, grown-over track bed. Then the woman again, the shopkeeper's wife, her voice, her dark eyes and hair giving way to a grassy ball field, groomed and sandy. Kids moved and hollered, evaporating away. Their shouts and laughter remained as a Pineland forest materialized, opening into a sandy graveyard.

One stone rose from the grass of the others, turning slowly. Truman saw its sad name: April Kramer. Then it faded away, melting into the realness of a hand.

A thin hand taking his own. Raising it to her mouth, believing it asleep.

Kissing it.

Praying grace at her table of want.

Did you enjoy this book?
Visit ForemostPress.com to share
your comments or a review.